THE SANDYCOVE SUPPER CLUB

BY SIÂN O'GORMAN

B

Boldwood

First published in Great Britain in 2022 by Boldwood Books Ltd.

Copyright © Siân O'Gorman, 2022

Cover Design by Head Design Ltd

Cover photography: Shutterstock

The moral right of Siân O'Gorman to be identified as the author of this work has been asserted in accordance with the Copyright, Designs and Patents Act 1988.

A CIP catalogue record for this book is available from the British Library.

Paperback ISBN 978-1-80048-387-3

Hardback ISBN 978-1-80426-798-1

Large Print ISBN 978-1-80048-386-6

Ebook ISBN 978-1-80048-389-7

Kindle ISBN 978-1-80048-388-0

Audio CD ISBN 978-1-80048-381-1

MP3 CD ISBN 978-1-80048-382-8

Digital audio download ISBN 978-1-80048-384-2

Boldwood Books Ltd
23 Bowerdean Street
London SW6 3TN
www.boldwoodbooks.com

Believe that a further shore... is reachable from here

— SEAMUS HEANEY

For Merlo and Steve

PROLOGUE
ONE YEAR EARLIER

The man in the black T-shirt and skinny jeans looked out of place in the party which was full of Richard's accountant colleagues. The man had the kind of beetle-black eyebrows (for which I had a particular penchant) and a Heathcliff glower (again, swoon) as though he was taking mental notes about everyone at the party, judging their city suits and short back and sides.

'I know we are only here for gender balance, Roisín,' said Jools. 'But if I talk to one more man about how I know Richard and where I went on holiday, I am going to scream.' She took a swig of champagne. 'Or, at least poke out an eye with one of those cocktail sticks. With the sausage still attached.'

It was the Friday before Christmas and Jools and I were standing beside Richard's white plastic tree – Richard's only nod to kitsch – dressed in our festive finery. A pair of glittery reindeer antlers boinged on Jools's head and my flashing star earrings which earlier had looked fun and seasonally appropriate felt suddenly ridiculous when the man's glower turned in our direction.

'Who is he?' Jools whispered from behind her glass of champagne. 'He's either an escaped convict or someone who's lost their way to the nearest hipster coffee bar.'

'He's not an accountant, that's for sure,' I whispered back, trying not to stare, but it had been four years since I had even the slightest brush with anything approximating romance and sometimes I wondered if I would die, old and alone, my body cobwebbed and withered. 'Nor do accountants have copies of Kerouac in their jeans pockets.'

Richard had insisted Jools and I come to the party to celebrate his elevation to chief operations officer of one of Dublin's biggest financial firms. 'I need you both,' he'd told us, 'to dilute the highly charged febrile financial atmosphere when accountants get together. Honestly, sometimes these parties can get out of control with all the talk of spreadsheets and tax. And anyway, it's a chance to meet some nice accountant, someone who will whisk you off your feet. Although whisking off feet isn't very accountant-y, but perhaps dazzle you with his ability to balance books and calculate long sums in his head.'

Richard was now a high-flyer in the world of high finance, Jools was now a personal trainer at an exclusive gym where her clients ranged from minor television presenters to the overpaid members of the corporate elite, and I was an admin assistant in Sandycove County Council planning department.

Jools and I were old school friends and were from Sandycove, a small village just south of Dublin. When we'd both ended up at University College Dublin – she studying sports science and me doing a general arts degree – we met Richard in the first month. He'd arrived straight off the bus from Dingle, Co. Kerry, his eyes firmly fixed on success in the world of high finance. Jools and I soon noticed the boy who stirred boiling water into a packet of curry noodles in the halls-of-residence kitchen every night.

'We can't let you eat only Super Noodles,' I called over.

'You'll become anaemic and die,' said Jools.

Young Richard turned and looked at us. His fringe looked as though it had been cut with nail scissors; his polyester suit crackled as he walked. 'They are thirty-five pence per packet, take three minutes to make and four minutes to eat,' he said. 'I have an essay to write.'

'We'll give you dinner for free,' I offered.

'And it's good for you,' said Jools.

The young Richard hesitated. Later on, he told us that he hadn't planned on making friends at university in case they derailed his studies and ambitions but within a month he was singing along as passionately as us to 'Like A Prayer' in the college karaoke bar.

And now, at Richard's Christmas party, Jools swigged back her champagne, dislodging her reindeer headband. 'I'm only having one glass but if you are only going to have one make it a good one.'

'That didn't used to be your philosophy,' I said, tearing my eyes away from the brooding man. 'You used to be cheap and plentiful.'

'I have to be sober for when I go home to Darren,' she said. 'He hates me drinking anything apart from coconut water.'

Jools's boyfriend, Darren, ran a bodybuilding and boxing gym and had an ego the size of the barrels of protein powder he consumed and couldn't pass a shop window without having a not-so-sneaky peek at himself. Richard once described him to me as having a brain the size of his testicles – 'both probably invisible to the naked eye'.

'Darren says that food is overrated and it is far easier to just replace everything with a protein shake,' said Jools. 'I can't remember the last time I ate something without having to work out the macros in advance. I'm exhausted. You know what I want? Carbs. Lots of them. Double, triple, quadruple carbs, but Darren would undergo a lobotomy rather than let bread or pasta over our threshold.'

I managed not to say that I thought Darren had had that lobotomy years ago but then I realised the man with the eyebrows was standing in front of us holding up a bottle of champagne.

'I've just stolen this from the fridge.' His eyes lingered on mine. 'I thought you two might like a glass?' No one had looked at me like that since Paddy.

'I can't,' said Jools. 'I'm just having the one. I'm driving... But...' She smiled at me. 'Roisín would, wouldn't you, Ro?'

I found myself nodding and handing over my glass. 'I suppose I could be persuaded.'

'It is Christmas,' the man went on, handing back my glass. 'Although, obviously, I'm not a fan.'

'Of Christmas?' I sipped from my glass, intrigued. Who didn't like Christmas?

'I was traumatised as a child,' he said. 'Something to do with not getting the typewriter I was desperate for and getting the BMX which my mother thought I should have asked for.'

I laughed, thinking he was joking, but he looked totally serious. Maybe he had been actually traumatised? I rearranged my face to one of concern. Maybe it was the injustice of the situation, maybe it was the fact that I had not had a whiff of anything romantic for years, that made me want to carry on talking to him.

'I once got a BMX for Christmas,' said Jools. 'But it was my brother Paddy's old one.'

Jools had been oblivious that I, her best friend, and her brother had had a fling four years ago and had spent most weekends together, secretly stealing away from parties, staying in bed for days at a time or cycling up to the mountains in Wicklow, lying in the heather and watching the clouds scudding across the sky, his hand in mine. We never got past the stage of just friends with benefits, and also, it was too weird to be romantically involved with Paddy, someone I had known since I was thirteen, and I never wanted to come between Jools and Paddy. Their mother had died when they were really young, and then, when Jools was sixteen, their father died of cancer.

When Paddy had first left for Copenhagen, I'd walked around in a daze, writing emails which I immediately deleted, desperately wanting him to come home or wishing I'd asked him not to go. But he wouldn't have gone if he'd had real feelings for me and now, listening to the man with the eyebrows, I felt I was finally ready to move on. Spring had sprung after a long winter.

The man held out his hand. 'Brody Brady,' he said.

His hand felt soft and light, his name familiar.

'Roisín Kelly,' I said. 'Aren't you the columnist for the *Irish Times*?'

'Well... unless there's another Brody Brady,' he said, smiling.

'He writes that column,' I told Jools. '"Man Overboard", about modern life...'

'And much, much more,' said Brody. 'I like to think that I cover the gamut of the experience of the Irish male.' He smiled at me again. 'Everything from why the pint is an inalienable right to why the shirt and tie is like a noose around the neck of the Irish man.'

'I read your column last week,' I said, 'you were talking about how we as a society have lost touch with our rural past...'

Brody nodded. 'I've actually been commissioned to write a novel,' he said, 'exactly about that. I'm excited to get what's up here...' – he tapped his forehead – 'on to the page.'

A writer. He was the exact opposite to Paddy who was into bikes and fixing things. I was so ready for different.

'I'm going to have to go,' Jools said, looking at her phone. 'Darren's texted, he's on his way home. Roisín? Are you staying?'

I quickly glanced at Brody. 'I think so,' I said. Gratifyingly, he looked pleased too.

'So, you know I'm a writer,' he said, when it was just the two of us. 'What do you do?'

'I'm just in the planning department at Sandycove Council.'

'Never say "just" when it comes to honest toil,' he said. 'Where would we be without planners? How would buildings be built or cities evolve?'

'I haven't thought of it like that...' It felt quite hot under the steady gaze of Brody, as though in conversation with an anglepoise lamp. 'Actually, we're going through a bit of restructuring. One of our planners had to be sacked because he was taking bribes from developers. There was a huge case about it...'

'Ah! The Sandycove Brown Enveloper?' Brody looked delighted. 'I read about him. Didn't he have to be extradited from Spain?'

I nodded. 'He was living in a mansion in Marbella and existing on crisps and caviar, apparently. My poor boss was interrogated about why none of us knew that he was taking backhanders. And Dermot, one of our other planners, said he had opened so many envelopes stuffed with cash he probably had repetitive strain injury. It's left us all a little shaken.' I looked back at Brody. 'It's all been somewhat fraught.'

'No, please go on,' he said. 'I love hearing these kinds of stories about office life. It's like a zoo to someone like me who works on my own all day. You never know.' He winked, refilling our glasses with the air of a man about town, as though he had bought the champagne, not pilfered it from Richard's fridge. 'It might make its way into one of my novels.'

'So, how's the novel going?' I asked.

'It's my second book, actually,' he said. 'My first was a collection of my columns. My mother bought ten copies but as she and my dad are more *Daily Mirror* readers, it remains unread.' He shrugged. 'But it's fine. I don't expect them to understand what I do. I was always a cuckoo in the nest. Once you realise you are an outsider in your own family, it makes it easier. My brother, Roger, fitted in very well. Thankfully, he's in Australia now, working on a sheep farm or something. But I'm looking for somewhere to write. I'm flat-sitting upstairs while my agent's aged aunt is on holiday. She needs someone to water the plants and feed the dogs, and vice versa. I bumped into the man with the bow tie over there...' – he nodded towards Richard – 'while I was wrestling with the rubbish chute and he invited me along. But he didn't tell me it was a party of accountants. Being a word-smith, I feel like a fish out of water. Anyway, once Aged Auntie is back from Morocco next week, I need to find somewhere else to live and a room of my own to write.' He stopped, staring at me, blinking. 'You know,' he said, 'you have the most beautiful eyes. The kind of eyes I would like to get lost in.'

For a moment, I didn't know what to say, but cleared my throat. 'I have a room,' I said, quickly.

'Really?'

'Would you like to see it?' I said.

'I would! I would indeed.'

'It's in Sandycove...'

Brody thought for a moment. 'It's a bit far out of town but maybe it's time I gave the suburbs a chance.' He smiled at me.

Within a week he had moved his laptop into the spare room, along with his osteopathic chair and, weirdly, an old broken television, and had professed his undying love, which I gratefully accepted.

Our lives were suddenly only about each other. Every evening I would cook and he would tell me what he'd been writing, on weekends we went on literary tours of Dublin or long windswept walks along the seafront in Sandycove. He would write notes and leave them for me to find declaring he was so in love with me and that he had never believed he would find something like this, *so pure*, he wrote, *something so beautiful*. Sometimes his voice broke a little as he expressed his feelings. 'I am in awe,' he said, 'of love, that we humans are allowed to experience this emotion. When you find your person, it is truly humbling.'

It felt as if we were in a magical bubble of love which would never burst. The love bombing was on another scale, it was an intoxicating blitzkrieg of bliss.

Six months later, we were standing on the top of the Martello Tower in Sandycove, close to the crashing waves of the Irish Sea and where James Joyce, Brody's literary hero, had lived, when he dropped to one knee. 'It feels appropriate on this hallowed ground,' he said, 'to ask you to marry me.'

'Yes!' I squeaked. A week later we were married.

The End. Curtain up. Rousing music... cut to me settling in for my happy ending.

... if only.

* * *

Wedding menu
West Cork smoked salmon on fresh brown soda bread
Irish cured meat platter with pickles
Courgette and whipped feta on toast
Parmesan, crushed pea & garlic bruschetta
Wicklow tomato & basil salad
Chocolate celebration cake
Champagne

The morning after the proposal I cycled from my house to Mum's with my big news. I'd already booked the registry office for two weeks' time – 1 June – and asked Jools if she would help me with all the preparing and cooking. My true passion was cooking and with Jools as my sous chef it would be like the dinner parties we used to have, only a bit bigger. And if Jools thought I was getting married in haste, she didn't let on, but from Mum there was a moment's silence and then she asked if I was sure.

'Yes,' I said firmly. 'Totally.'

'But are you sure sure?'

'I've never been happier,' I said, reaching over and taking one of her biscuits. 'He loves me and I love him. It's the real thing. When you know, you know.' I shrugged nonchalantly. 'How long did it take for you to say yes to Dad?'

Mum hesitated because Dad had proposed after one week and they were married within a year. And okay, so she and Dad divorced when I was ten and Shona was eleven. Dad had then moved to the south of France with our stepmother, Maxine, who was as warm and emotional as a wooden spoon.

'I love him,' I said. 'And I want to marry him.'

Mum opened her mouth and then closed it again. 'You can have the wedding party here,' she said, relenting for my sake. 'The kitchen is big enough and we can spill out into the garden, if the rain holds off. We could fit at least eighty people in the garden and maybe have a band... the ukulele orchestra would definitely play... and what about dancing... we could use the summer house as the bar... I'm thinking a champagne reception first of all and...'

Mum's garden was beautiful, a wild, unkempt square, with tall granite walls on three sides, the old lean-to summer house on one side and a small collection of gnarly apple trees on the other.

My sister, Shona, was slightly more forthcoming. That evening, at the hastily convened engagement party in The Island, our local pub in Sandycove, she cornered me at the bar.

'Are you out of your mind?' she hissed.

'No,' I said. 'I am perfectly in my mind. I am in love! I am floating on a magic carpet of love.'

Shona looked bewildered. 'Why are you being so impetuous?' she said. 'You can't rush into something like this! You must cease and desist immediately.' As a stay-at-home mother to my gorgeous nieces, twins Daisy and Kitty, Shona liked to remind people she was still the scary lawyer she'd once trained as. Beside her appeared Richard, bathed in a light sweat and wearing a determined expression.

'I've just flown in from Brussels, I managed to get an earlier flight... I can't believe it.'

'You see!' said Shona. 'It's not just me.'

'I want to get married, I'm in love. Is that a crime?'

'No, of course it isn't,' Richard said. 'But marrying anyone after a couple of months should be a crime.'

'I am sure there is some impediment,' Shona was thinking. 'Some precedent...'

'It's been six months, actually,' I said to Richard. 'And it's all your fault. I met him at your party.'

'I wanted you to meet a nice, safe accountant, not some irrational writer! An accountant wouldn't propose after a mere few months!'

'Six!' I shouted.

'She has abandonment issues,' Shona told Richard. 'She's never got over Dad leaving.'

'Thank you, Sigmund,' I said, folding my arms and wishing the people I loved could be pleased for me. 'I love Brody,' I said. 'And Brody loves me. It's nice... we're happ—'

'But life's not all about love,' interrupted Richard. 'It's about making the right choices.'

Shona nodded vigorously in agreement.

'Look at me,' he went on. 'I don't have time for love, because I am too busy doing the right thing. My career, paying my mortgage, being sensible. Why not concentrate on getting a new job? One that you actually want to do... like cooking...'

'Look,' I said. 'I'm only getting married. It's hardly anything drastic.'

He was silent for a moment. 'Roisín...' Richard narrowed his eyes. 'Don't marry him.'

'Why not?'

'Because...' He searched around for a reason. 'He's a writer. And writers don't make good partners. They are self-obsessed. It's all about them.'

'Richard, please,' I said. 'Brody needs someone to help him achieve his dreams and I want to help him. They are my dreams too, now.'

'And what about your dreams?' said Richard.

'Exactly!' agreed Shona.

'I don't have any.' I tried to think. 'Once you get to know Brody you will love him. I promise, I'm doing the right thing.'

'Promise us?' said Richard.

'Promise,' I said.

Richard gazed at me for a moment, contemplating, and when Shona shrugged I knew I'd won. Now, all I had to do was get married and stay married. Simple.

* * *

A week later, we all gathered at the registry office – me in a strapless black dress with a gold headband that Jools insisted didn't look ridiculous, Brody in a jacket and jeans and a black T-shirt with *Mr and Mrs (Word) Smith* on the front. He brought me over to meet his parents.

'Roisín, my ma and pa,' he said. 'Ma and Pa, Roisín, my wife-to-be.'

His mother was a tiny bird of a woman, dressed in a peach outfit and matching hat, like the Queen Mother.

'There was a time,' said his dad, wearing a tweed suit, three sizes too big, 'when we were Mam and Dad. Seems like a long time ago now. That was before he swallowed a thesaurus.' He gripped my hand. 'Are you sure you can take him on?'

I laughed. 'Of course! I can't wait!'

HIs mother took my hand. 'I'm Sandra and this is Jim.' She smiled up at me. 'We're delighted to finally meet Brian's fiancée.'

Brody glared at her. 'My name's Brody.' He seemed like a sulky teenager around his parents.

'I mean Brody,' she said. 'We're trying to get used to the new name but it's not easy. He never liked Brian. Tried lots of different names, didn't he, Jim?'

Jim agreed. 'He tried out a few mouthfuls. Isambard was one. That was never going to work. Not in Finglas. Wolfgang, that was another.' He shook his head. 'Brody seems normal in comparison.'

'So, what do you think of my beautiful bride?' Brody asked, changing the conversation. 'My muse, my inspiration, my afflatus...'

Jim laughed. 'I thought that's what you get when you eat too many beans!' The smile on his face died slowly as he looked back at Brody. 'Sorry, son,' he said. 'I forgot where I was.'

'We're very proud of Brody,' Sandra told me. 'A novel! I was telling the girls at work. Bernie wants to know when it will be in the shops. Says she will definitely buy it,' she said to Brody. 'Boost your sales.'

'Put me down for ten copies,' said Jim. 'I'll hand them out to the boys at the bus garage.'

'I doubt Bernie can even read,' said Brody. 'And as for the bus drivers, I think the only thing they read is the sports pages in the tabloids.'

'The book has to be ready in a year's time,' I said, brightly. 'My job is just to make sure that Brody doesn't have to worry about anything. Just writing.'

'Are you nervous?' Sandra asked him. 'I would be. A book! I don't understand how you get from an empty page to a whole book!'

Brody shook his head. 'Never be nervous for nerves are nothing.'

'Who said that?' Jim asked. 'Shakespeare?'

'I did,' replied Brody loftily. 'And anyway, why would I be nervous? Ma, you should be delighted that I have a room of my own and a wife who is an amazing cook. The steak you did,' he said, turning to me, 'the other night was the best I've ever had. The meatballs with that tomato sauce. The roast lamb...' His stomach was definitely paunchier than it had been a few months earlier because I was holding up my end of the bargain and keeping him well fed and watered. 'Roisín's job,' he told Jim, 'is to keep cooking, mine to keep writing. It's a match made in heaven.'

* * *

Everyone cheered when we said *We do* and had our first kiss as a married couple. Even Shona, who was standing with Ross and their twins, Kitty and Daisy, looked quite moved. She dabbed at her eye from time to time, her arm in her husband Ross's, the twins dressed in identical outfits. Mum was on the other side, smiling encouragingly. In the row behind was Dad, back from France for the weekend, and looking his normally distracted self while my stepmother, Maxine, looked utterly bored.

Back at Mum's house, everything had been prepared. The food was all done, it was just a case of handing out the plates of finger food, making sure people had enough salad and that their glasses were topped up. Richard and Jools insisted on being the waiters, the champagne flowed and for the first time since we announced the engagement, I began to relax.

Mum and Dad, not having spoken for at least a decade, had been chatting nicely to each other while Maxine was in the bathroom. Shona and Ross and the girls were dancing in a circle together. Mum had a glass of champagne in one hand and was chatting to Jools. Richard had now broken out his trademark breakdancing moves – something he reserved for when he was seriously drunk – and Brody's mum and dad were jiving together. It was a warm summer's evening and Dad whirled me around to 'Celebration' by Kool & the Gang – which was part of Richard's playlist.

'I didn't know you could dance,' I shouted in Dad's ear.

'It was the only thing I enjoyed in school,' he shouted back. 'The boys had to dance with each other back then and because I was tall, I always got to lead.' He twirled me around again. 'I hope you and Bridie are very happy together,' he said.

'Brody,' I corrected him for the tenth time that day.

Sitting under the apple trees on one of the chairs which had been borrowed from our neighbours, Brody was writing in his little notebook which he brought everywhere with him.

'What's he writing?' asked Dad, following my gaze, as the song came to an end and we all took a breather.

'Ideas,' I replied. 'You never know when you might get a good one, according to Brody.'

Dad opened his mouth, ready to speak, and then closed it again.

'I had better go and find Maxine,' he said. 'Don't want to be accused of abandoning her.' The twirling stopped and the music ended and he walked way. But if I felt abandoned myself, this time it didn't matter. Finally, I had someone just for me, especially as we were off to London for five days' honeymoon. I couldn't wait.

I walked over to Brody and put my arm around him.

'I love you,' I said.

'I love you too.' He slipped his little notebook into his jacket inside pocket.

'Having a good day?'

Brody pulled me onto his knee and whispered into my ear, 'I'm a lucky, lucky man. To have met a mermaid with eyes like rock pools, hair like seaweed, 'tis fortune indeed.'

We were going to be happy, I thought, despite people's initial misgivings, everything was going to be all right.

1

ONE YEAR LATER

'Right! Listen up, people!'

JP, our head of planning in Sandycove Council, was standing beside the plant which was tinged with brown and on which still dangled a couple of Christmas baubles, despite it being 1 June. 'I have had a few ideas...' he said. 'I know it's a Friday...'

We were all still in recovery from when it was discovered that one of our planners was a recipient of favours and backhanders. Since he was uncovered – and was now behind bars – planning decisions had become very tentative. Frank would ask Dermot and Dermot would ask Frank to oversee each other's work and although I wasn't a planner, just an office assistant along with Saoirse, both of us reporting to Belinda, our office manager, we still double-checked everything, trusted no one.

It was my first wedding anniversary and I was planning the celebratory dinner I was going to make for me and Brody that evening. He'd been asleep when I'd left for work that morning but I was feeling optimistic that married life might improve now we'd got year one out of the way and we were so close to Brody's deadline which meant that the novel had to be done in a matter of weeks. Once the book was done, I hoped, we might get into a better routine, one which didn't only revolve around the book. I wanted the Brody I married back, the loving, romantic man who adored me, not the man who was shut away in his study all day and all evening, only appearing for food at dusk, like a literary hedgehog.

JP was now sitting on the edge of Belinda's desk, dislodging her mug full of pens and a mini figurine of a flamenco dancer. 'Come hither.' He beckoned with his finger. 'For I have been on a course…'

There was a collective gasp.

'Never go on a course,' said Dermot. 'They are hotbeds of brainwashing. Very dangerous.'

'So that's where you disappeared to on Monday,' said Belinda. 'I was wondering… I said to the others…'

JP ignored them. 'Impromptu meeting, I need to parlay the findings, or whatever the particular business phrase is.'

'Cascade,' said Frank. 'I have heard the word cascade being bandied about by the type of person who frequents meetings. Cascade information.'

'Will there be biscuits in this impromptu "meeting"?' Dermot made little inverted commas with his fingers. 'As you all know, I don't get out of bed for anything less than a chocolate digestive.'

'Biscuits are available in most shops, Dermot,' said JP. 'Buy your own.'

'There's some digestives in the kitchen,' said Belinda to Dermot. 'Nice fresh packet of Jacob's.'

'I may have started on those.' Frank was entangled in his phone cord. 'A packet of digestives is a red rag to me. I charge towards them.'

'Let me get this straight,' said Dermot. 'You're the bull. The biscuits are the red rag. Are you suggesting Belinda is the matador?'

'It was a metaphor, Dermot,' said Frank flatly.

'I thought you said matador,' said Dermot.

'Ignore him, Belinda,' said Frank, the phone cord finally free. 'Thank you for bringing in the biscuits.'

'You're very welcome, Frank.' Belinda gave him a smile. 'My Johnny, when he was alive, was partial to a digestive. Would have put a packet in the coffin if the priest had let me, but he was one of those priests, the ones who don't let you do anything, and just want to do everything by the book.' Her beaded necklace rattled as she shook her head in disgust.

'The Bible,' said Dermot, now seated in front of JP. 'That's the book by which they do everything. It's time they got a new one.'

'Well, we'll have to ask Roisín's husband to write something, won't we?' Belinda smiled at me. 'It must be so inspiring to live with a writer!' She sighed. 'Once, years ago, Johnny and I went to a talk by Sir Jeffrey Archer. He was in town for a book signing and when Sir Jeffrey walked past us, Johnny had a funny turn. He said it was like coming face to face with God,' she went on. 'All those marvellous thoughts and ideas, all tied up in one person's brain. Your husband must be coming out with clever things all the time.'

'It's not quite like that,' I admitted.

In fact, the last year had been lonely and the gleam of living with a writer was somewhat tarnished. Brody was so consumed by the book that he stayed up past midnight and would fall straight into a snoring sleep. He rarely even kissed me these days, never mind anything more. But I was being selfish. It was Brody who had all the pressure and stress and you could even see the toll it had taken on his body; he'd grown larger, hairier and the frequency of showers had decreased, as though he really was living in the wild, just him and his laptop against the world.

Dermot was scooting himself across on his chair; Belinda had left her desk which was still commandeered by JP's behind and was perched on mine. 'Meetings are unnecessary these days,' Dermot said into JP's ear as he went past. 'I thought we all knew that. The efficacy and usefulness of meetings were debunked. Everyone gets on with their jobs. Communicate anything anyone should know in a short email. And that's it.'

'But this meeting might change your life, Dermot,' said JP. 'I mean, it most definitely won't... but you don't know that. Give this meeting a chance.'

'I'm not a great fan of taking chances,' said Frank. 'I prefer the status quo.'

'They were a terrible band,' said Dermot. 'I would keep that side of your life quiet, if I was you.'

'Frank,' said Belinda, 'you should give things a chance. After Johnny passed away, I could have stayed in every night, but if I hadn't been walking past the parish hall that evening, I would never have come across the salsa group, and I would never have met all my friends, and gone on that trip to Málaga.' She smiled across at Frank. 'Take a risk, Frank.'

JP was already standing up. 'Okay... I get it. None of you like impromptu meetings. Why don't I schedule one for three minutes' time in my office. Is that better?' He looked around, catching Saoirse's eye. 'Saoirse, you too... See you in my office in three minutes.' He turned and left us and, reluctantly, with a huge sigh, Saoirse looked up from her phone.

'What's going on?' she said. 'Is JP dying or something? Or...' She looked over at me. 'Breaking news... Roisín's made a new cake? Or she's experimenting with vanilla... or some new ingredient that no one likes.'

The embarrassing thing was, I had made a cake. The night before, after Brody had gone back to his study, I had gone back into the kitchen and started baking, just to soothe my soul and try and keep me focused on the last few weeks until the deadline. I had begun to think that this marriage wasn't the great success I had promised everyone it would be. But hopefully, there was still time to turn this marital Titanic around. And baking and cooking was the most soothing thing I did, that wonderful alchemy of ingredients, molecules magically metamorphosing, a cake rising, egg whites transforming into a snowscape, a potato changing from inedible into myriad utterly delectable meals. And because Brody didn't like cakes and had once explained 'women like cakes and men like meat...', when I did bake, I brought the results into work.

'Actually,' I admitted, 'I do have one. Lemon drizzle. I made it last night.'

A frisson of excitement rippled through the office, even Frank was up and searching for the large cake slicer. Except for Saoirse. 'Of course you have,' she said. 'The office feeder. Predictable as a weathervane.'

2

We reconvened in JP's office.

'Thank you for coming...' he began.

'Our pleasure, JP,' said Belinda, a plate and fork with a slice of the cake perched on her lap.

'Wouldn't miss this unnecessary meeting for the world,' said Dermot, his slice balanced on his knee. Frank had his on a paper napkin, and JP's slice was on the teetering pile of files which never decreased in height.

'I will talk as fast as I can and will get to the point...' sighed JP, defeated.

'Didn't you know sugar was as bad as smoking twenty cigarettes a day?' piped up Saoirse. 'And if we didn't have a feeder among us, then some of us...' – she looked pointedly at Frank – 'wouldn't be straining out of our clothes and putting pressure on the suspension systems of our office chairs. It's just that I was reading this article,' she went on, 'about how it is really passive-aggressive to bring cake into an office environment, when no one has asked for it. I mean, if it was a birthday party and someone had specifically asked for a cake, then fine. But in a work environment, where no one needs or particularly wants cake, then it's a passive-aggressive act of war. It's a power move, that's what it is.'

Saoirse was the kind of person who needed someone to feel superior to, and as we were at the same level in the department, that person had to be me. Over the years, I had learned to shut out most of her noise but sometimes her negativity penetrated.

'I love Roisín's cakes,' said Frank.

'You can take those cakes from my dead, cold hand,' said Dermot. 'If that's being passive-aggressive, then bring it on.'

Belinda winked at me. 'Good enough to forget the diet.'

JP held up his hand. 'People, please. Now, I am going to exhibit my own power move and call this meeting to order. First of all, thank you for coming...' He paused. 'Apparently, that's what you are meant to say at the beginning of a meeting, tell people that their time is precious and that you acknowledge it. Whether...' – he raised an eyebrow, his face straight – 'you believe their time to be precious or not.'

'Mine is,' said Dermot. 'It's so precious, it's kept in the Tower of London, guarded by ravens.'

'Mine definitely isn't,' said Frank. 'Anyone can waste my time if they like. I've nothing better to be doing.'

JP held up his hands. 'Come on, let's get this over and done with. It was a leadership course. Instilling job satisfaction and passion in your team.'

'Good God.' Frank was visibly shaken.

'Passion, JP?' said Dermot. 'Have you lost your tiny mind?'

'We are still on probation as a department,' said JP. 'I have to be seen to be very involved in my team. A hands-on role rather than hands-off...'

'I like to save passion and satisfaction for other areas of my life,' said Dermot. 'As I am sure do my other esteemed colleagues.'

'You should live your whole life passionately,' said Belinda to Dermot. 'My Johnny, before he was ill, God rest his soul, used to say that if you wake up happy and go to sleep with a smile then you have everything you need in life. Work should make you feel like getting up in the morning.'

'Raise your hands now,' said JP, 'if you have a high level of job satisfaction.'

Belinda raised her hand.

'Okay... that's not good,' said JP. 'Right, raise your hand if you have a moderate level of job satisfaction.'

No hands were raised. Saoirse was busy scrolling through her phone.

'Okay, let's try again, raise your hand if you have zero job satisfaction and you are only here because the thought of trying to find anything else in this job market is even worse.'

Dermot raised his hand. 'Me,' he said. 'Definitely me.'

JP looked at me. 'Roisín, where do you fit in?'

'Oh, don't ask her,' said Saoirse, rolling her eyes. 'She's always happy. It's all that sugar...'

'And she's just recently married,' said Belinda. 'Don't they say that the first year of marriage is the best? It must be your anniversary soon?'

'It's today actually,' I said.

Belinda clutched my hand excitedly but Saoirse closed her eyes in pain. 'Oh Christ,' she said. 'So that's what the cake is for...'

'Happy anniversary etcetera, Roisín,' said JP, 'and thank you for the cake, but tell me this and tell me no more, where upon my megatron spectrum of job satisfaction do you fall?'

'Somewhere in the middle?' I said.

'Okay. Not bad. So room for improvement. Saoirse, what about you?'

She looked up. 'Sorry, JP, what did you say?'

'Are you satisfied with your job?'

'No, obviously not. Still waiting for my promotion. But the work is easy, and I only live five minutes away so my commute is negligible. The quality of colleagues could be improved but... on the whole, not too bad.'

'Is there anything...' – JP had a rictus smile on his face – 'that we can do to increase your level of satisfaction?'

'Stop asking questions?' Saoirse said. 'Not wanting to be rude, JP, or anything. But I just have a low tolerance for people. No offence. So, yeah, job satisfaction is fine. If, that is, you stop your blather.'

There was gasp from Frank and Belinda, which often happened when Saoirse tipped over from her normal truculence to downright rude. JP remained stony-faced. 'Thank you, Saoirse, for your contribution. Now, Frank,' he went on, 'what about you? You are the longest-serving team member, you've been a planner since... I don't know...'

'The Dark Ages,' said Dermot.

'... a long time,' agreed Frank, his face reddening. 'I would say I would be somewhere in the middle on your megatron of job satisfaction. Could say the same about my whole life. Middling.'

Belinda gave him a concerned look as JP pushed on. 'Okay, now we're getting somewhere,' he said. 'Belinda and Saoirse are happy – albeit with caveats – with their work, is that right?'

Saoirse was staring at her screen again as Belinda nodded. 'Very much so, JP,' she said.

'So, Dermot, Frank and Roisín need assistance to increase their passion and satisfaction at work, is that right? Do any of you have any thoughts about how I can help with that? Dermot?'

'I think I'm a lost cause,' Dermot said. 'I wish I could offer my services to you as a guinea pig in your leadership endeavours, but I would prefer to be left alone with my despair. And cake.'

JP turned to Frank. 'What about you, Frank, anything I can do to help?'

Frank was still red. 'I think I have a lot of work to do on all areas of my life,' he said, shyly. 'I am working through a list. I am a member of a Men's Shed and, well, we have a few chats about this and that, and they came up with a few ideas for me. So, I'm kind of already on that path, so to speak.'

JP turned to me. 'Roisín, what about you? What can we do to increase your job satisfaction?'

'I don't know,' I said. 'I mean, I'm fine…'

'What about more responsibility?' JP asked. 'Perhaps we could sponsor you to take a diploma in planning? And work to a degree. All taken at night, of course, and paid for by the department but it would be a step forward?'

I really wanted to tell him that being a planner wasn't part of my life plan. My only plan was to get to Brody's book's deadline and then make my marriage work. I didn't have the energy for anything else. 'Maybe,' I said, half-heartedly.

'Saoirse, would you like to do a diploma in planning?'

She glanced up. 'Would I get time off work?'

JP shook his head. 'It would be done in your own time. Sorry. It starts in September, so in three months' time, but until then, you could take on a planning application?'

'So more work, same pay?' she asked.

'Well...'

'Anyway, I have a life,' she said. 'Like, when I leave here, I leave here physically, mentally and emotionally... God, anyone would think I didn't do very much all day.' I was aware of Dermot and Frank's eyes flicking over to each other but JP looked so defeated I felt bad we'd all dismissed him so easily.

'I'll do it,' I said. 'If you think it's a good idea...'

He nodded, looking brighter. 'Thank you, Roisín,' he said. 'At least someone in this organisation is actually committed to the department. Belinda is also the exception. And now,' he said, 'I am going to have some cake.' He smiled briskly at us. 'Thank you for your time, etcetera, it's very precious to me, etcetera, etcetera. You can make your way out.'

3

There was no answer from Mum when I rang on her doorbell. Faint strains of music flowed from the kitchen and so I would have to go around the back, through the garden. I locked my bike to the railings and walked down the small, grassy lane to the side of our house, past the high granite walls covered in escaping Virginia creeper, to our curlicued wrought-iron back gate and into our garden.

Stepping into this world of green, I was, as always, immediately lashed in the face by long tendrils of jasmine, before being filled with the scent of the honeysuckle which trailed through the lilac tree, the wild hollyhocks and harebells, and the sound of the blackbirds who had their nest in the gutter of the old summer house. It was like a secret garden, an oasis from the busy road outside, a little Eden. And from the kitchen, as I walked along the curving path past the apple trees, across from the raised vegetable beds and along by the clover lawn, I could hear Édith Piaf's voice singing loudly from the kitchen. I knocked on the door. 'Hello? Mum?' Inside, she was leaning against the Aga, singing just as lustily as Édith. 'Bonjour!'

'Ah! Roisín!' Mum turned down her old tape machine. 'How lovely to see you, and it's your anniversary today!' She hugged me. 'A whole year!'

Since her initial misgiving, Mum had been utterly positive about Brody even though he hadn't managed to make many appearances at family occasions over the last year. 'I'm in the zone,' he'd say, like a man trudging through life, and so I made yet another excuse for his absence. 'Writing a novel is like having to solve a vast puzzle, and once you are in the puzzle-solving zone, you can't leave.' He made it sound like he was living in a Dan Brown story.

'So, what are you doing to celebrate?' Mum asked, filling the kettle at the sink while I sat on one of the chairs beside the Aga. 'I do hope Brody is taking a night off from writing?'

'I'm making clams and spaghetti... and my melting chocolate pudding things.' As I spoke, I realised I didn't know if Brody actually liked clams or not. There was a lot I didn't know about him, such as what party he voted for at the last election or what the first record he ever bought was or whether he was a dog or a cat person (dog, I hoped). I didn't even know his favourite flavour of crisps.

'By the way,' she went on, 'I meant to say, your dad is coming to stay and I thought that you and Brody would like to come round to dinner?'

My mug nearly dropped from my hand in shock. 'Dad is coming to stay with you? You mean Dad, as in my father, the man who ran off to marry Maxine all those years ago?'

'The very one,' she said, smiling calmly. 'I thought he might have contacted you?'

There had been a missed call last week from him and another yesterday but I hadn't had a chance to call him back. Mum and Dad had kept their communications very much on the down-low over the years, politely acknowledging each other at various events, but with Dad in Cannes with Maxine, there were few times when their paths actually did cross. 'He's not dying, is he?'

'No, definitely not dying and his usual fit-as-a-fiddle self but he has to come to Dublin to sort your Uncle Philip's will... plus, reading between the lines, I think Maxine has ended things.'

'Really? Poor Dad.' I couldn't imagine Dad anything but his ebullient self. He swept through life on a wave of endless confidence and optimism. Even when he left Mum – and us – all those years ago, he didn't seem too upset. Over the years, Shona and I had spent holidays with him and

Maxine and there was always that small, niggling feeling, however much we loved him, that he'd had an easy life. He hadn't ever had the stuffing knocked out of him, not like it was knocked out of Mum when he left.

'But why are you letting him stay?' I loved Dad, obviously, but there was something in the way that he prioritised his happiness over the family, and how easily he and Maxine began again in Cannes that had made my feelings complicated. Dad used to ring Shona and me every week and ask cursory questions about school and friends and would then tell us about their life in the south of France – his yacht-designing business, or what Maxine had done with the apartment or what new wine he had discovered. After a few years, Shona refused to take any of his calls and left it all to me.

'He hinted – very heavily – that he wasn't much keen on staying in a hotel for the next three weeks,' said Mum. 'Or setting up camp in his dead brother's flat – full of ghosts, he said. So he's staying in our box room, on the single, rickety bed. He seems delighted with the arrangement.' She smiled at me. 'And he's looking forward to seeing you, Shona and the twins.'

After Dad left, I remember trying to be the best daughter ever to Mum and would enact secret acts of kindness every day, just to make her life better. I would move her slippers to warm on the Aga, find her keys and put them beside the front door for the morning, make sure the kitchen was tidy and that her special chair and cushion was dog-hair free. Snuff, our permanently ancient Jack Russell, somehow always found the energy to jump up onto chairs to be close to Mum.

'But it doesn't mean you have to be kind to him,' I said.

She shrugged. 'Why not? Now, I realise that none of it mattered. I still had a happy life without him, living here with you both. I cut off all contact because I just couldn't face him and now... well, looking back, I wish I had let him go with love and kindness. My life carried on, I had you two, the house, the garden... It wasn't his fault that he met Maxine and fell in love with her.'

She stood up and went over to the dresser, which slumped under the weight of everything that was piled on top, from her handbag to chipped cups, cracked plates, newspapers and books, and plucked a letter from behind a photograph of the twins. 'Here's the one that arrived this morn-ing.' Mum took out her glasses from her pocket. 'He seems very well, actu-ally,' she said, peering at his scrawly handwriting. 'Wonders how I am. Asks after you two, the twins... a bit of memory lane.' She squinted at the letter and read from it. 'I was channel-hopping...' She looked up. 'He means watching television, not hopping over the channel.'

'I know.'

'I was channel-hopping and caught *Raging Bull* the other day. Do you remember us going to see it on our first date?'

'That was your first date? An exceptionally violent film? No wonder things worked out the way they did.'

Mum laughed. 'I was studying French and politics in Trinity and the only films I had seen for a while were all these French New Wave films... this was something a bit different.' She paused. 'As was your father.'

'I would never have put you two together,' I said. 'You would never have coped with the south of France.'

'The heat isn't me,' she agreed. 'I like the rain of Ireland.' She read on. 'I am writing from a table in the town square. Sitting over a glass of very good red wine. And I thought of you and what you might be up to.'

'Nice of him to think of you...'

'He's indulging in nostalgia,' she said. 'He asks if I remembered the trip we made to Paris and we went out and ordered the menu of the day, and both ate what we thought was steak. Delicious, we thought. But then, after-wards, we realised it was horse.' She was smiling to herself. 'We had such a nice time.'

'When is he coming?'

'He arrives next Friday.'

'Is he going to pay you for board and lodgings?'

She laughed. 'I wouldn't charge an old friend.'

'An old friend? An old friend? It's the man you married who ran off with a younger woman, remember? Left you with two small daughters. You were heartbroken, if I remember correctly.'

'Disappointed,' she said. 'Hurt. And, yes, a little bit heartbroken. But that's in the past. You get over heartbreak eventually.'

I thought of the only time I had experienced something similar. Of course, it was nothing compared to what Mum went through. Paddy and I were never a couple as such, and yet... for months I felt like a part of me was missing. I wished I could have told someone about it, but Jools – my usual confidante and his younger sister – was obviously not available. Life moves on and you eventually realise that you have to catch up with it.

I looked at the old clock on the wall and realised that it was time to go home and start on the anniversary dinner.

'I'd better go,' I said to Mum, standing up.

'You give Brody a big hug from me. Do you think he will come to Daisy and Kitty's birthday party tomorrow?'

'I'll ask him,' I said, both of us knowing that Brody wouldn't be there.

* * *

On my cycle home, I took the sea road, where the coast tips into the sea, past the small, sandy cove which gives our village its name and where Irish-Sea-hardened elderly women braved the waters, the evening sun beginning to suggest it might not hang around for much longer. The sea shimmered in the pink light and the members of the yacht club were on their Friday-night wind-powered skit across the bay.

I thought of *Shining Light*, Dad's little boat, and how he, Shona and I, all in orange life jackets, would pull on the sodden ropes, sea water crystallising on our faces so when you licked your lips you'd be tasting salt for days, and battle the waves. From Sandycove yacht club, we'd roll over the waves, keeping land in sight, Dad shouting orders to pull on the ropes, the sails filling up with wind and we'd shoot off, straight out to sea towards the headland of Howth, the three of us against the world. It was magical.

Afterwards, back on shore, the sun beginning to set, Dad would hold our hands as we walked into the yacht club where Shona and I were given a bottle of Club Orange and a packet of Tayto crisps. One day, Shona didn't feel well and when we arrived home Dad lifted her into the house, her ten-year-old body like an injured princess's. I remember being jealous of her, wishing I could be carried indoors. But that night, when a much-improved Shona and I were tucked up in bed, Dad poked his head around our bedroom door.

'Feeling better?'

There was something strange about the way he didn't quite look at us. And he had his coat on.

'Daddy?' Shona said.

'Yes, sweetheart?'

'Are you going out?'

He paused for a moment. 'Yes.' He stepped into the room and sat on the end of her bed. 'Come here, Roisín,' he said to me, holding out his hand. 'Come over here for a moment.' The floorboards were cold under my feet but I didn't take his hand. Instead, I slipped into bed with Shona – something she would never have normally let me do but there was strange energy in the air, as though we both knew what was coming.

'I am not going to be living here any more,' Dad said. 'Remember Maxine? We met her at the yacht club a few weeks ago?'

We both nodded. He was leaving. Us, the house, Mum... *Shining Light*. There were words about how much he loved us, how nothing would come between us and that things wouldn't change, not really.

'I'm going to live with Maxine,' he said. 'Your mum and I both think this is the best idea for all of us. And you can come and stay whenever you want.' He looked from me to Shona. 'You'll have two homes... and a...' He stopped for a moment as though he wasn't sure quite what word to use.

'Stepmother?' suggested Shona, her hand under the blanket reaching for mine.

Dad nodded slowly, as though the idea of Maxine playing some kind of role in our lives hadn't occurred to him before. 'Perhaps,' he said. 'But I shall keep you both fully informed. Now you will have two houses, two bedrooms... two...' He stopped again. Was he really going to say, 'two mothers'?

Shona wriggled further into the bed and closed her eyes as though she wanted to go to sleep. I copied her, wriggling down as well, closing my eyes.

'Well, so...' Dad stood up. 'I'll go now but I'll call you tomorrow. And we'll go out on *Shining Light* soon. Yes? The Three Musketeers?'

I peeked at Shona but her eyes were still shut and Dad was already at the door. 'See you, girls,' he whispered. 'Love you.'

We heard Mum and Dad's whispered voices and then the front door closing and, finally, the sound of the car driving away.

Shona opened her eyes. 'I knew he'd do something like this,' she said. 'Mary's dad did the same thing. And Amanda's. Amanda's mum says all men are horrible.' Her lip wobbled for a moment. 'At least we know Dad is like all the rest of them.'

Mum knocked on the door. 'Girls?'

'Yes?' Shona's voice was tinier than I'd ever heard it. Mum stepped inside and sat at the edge of the bed, her face illuminated from the light on the landing.

'We're going to be absolutely fine,' she said. 'Nothing much is going to change. Everything's going to be okay, I promise.'

'Do you want to get in as well?' Shona's tiny voice was muffled by the blankets as she edged in further to the wall and I made space for Mum, who lay down on the outside of the bed, her arm around the two of us. Her face glistened as though she'd been out on *Shining Light*. I shut my eyes again and we lay in silence. Eventually, Mum got up and kissed us both. 'I love you,' she said. 'And Daddy loves you and Snuff loves you and everything is going to be all right.'

Neither Shona or I spoke in that dark and silent world. I kept waiting for Shona to push me out or to make me go back to my own bed but she let me stay all night, the two of us in her single bed, the night Dad left us for another woman.

4

__Brody & Roisín's first anniversary celebratory meal__
Spaghetti vongole made with Kilkee clams, chilli, parsley and garlic
Sourdough bread
Chocolate fondants
Champagne

'Hello, Brody! I'm home!'

Brody rarely answered as his noise-cancelling headphones drowned out what he called 'extraneous ambient annoyances', meaning the kids on the street playing football but also, obviously, me. But I had half-hoped he might make an exception for tonight, perhaps there might have been an anniversary card on the mantlepiece. The card and present I'd left him on the kitchen table were untouched. He mustn't have seen them, I thought, and it was silly, really, buying presents for anniversaries, especially as Brody had his mind on bigger and loftier things. But sometimes all I wanted, even more than him finishing the book, was to come home and for us to feel more like a normal couple, to kiss and share stories of their day. These days, a pat on the head like a dog would have been something.

Over the last year, Brody had taken on the demeanour of a bear who had woken up from winter hibernation, slightly grizzly, and often grumpy, his beard increasingly like something you might find down a drain. Soon, I thought, he would wash again. Soon, he would start wearing deodorant again.

In the kitchen, I started on dinner and with the pasta water on a boiling swirl, the parsley and garlic chopped, the clams steaming, I laid the table, using the Irish linen napkins Richard bought us as a wedding present and digging out my antique champagne flutes. I called up the stairs.

'Dinner!'

It always struck me as convenient that the noise-cancelling head-phones never obscured the call for dinner, as I heard the study door open, and Brody's feet on the stairs. I stirred the clams into the oil, chilli and garlic, and tipped everything into my large serving bowl. Brody stood in the kitchen doorway, confused by the sight of the candle, the glasses, the bottle of champagne.

'It's our anniversary,' I said.

'Ah...' He walked slowly to the table. 'Yes, of course... our anniversary.' He smiled at me. 'Roisín, you will have to forgive me. My head is in the clouds...' He kissed me on the lips, like a woodpecker.

'Too busy thinking about plots and characters to worry about the prosaic.' I abandoned hope that this evening would be any different to all the others. Over the last year, I had discovered how much the book had taken over everything. Of course he wasn't going to remember our anniversary. 'It doesn't matter...'

'You're not sulking?' he said. 'You know I don't do sulking. I am, as you know, a words man. Silence is for those who can't string a sentence together.'

'It's just that...' I began.

'Look, maybe I should have been clearer. I don't do anniversaries. Or birthdays. I detest festivities of all hues and persuasions for their utter pointlessness and ridiculousness.' He picked up a discarded paper clip and began to twist it.

He was right. Over the last year he could not have been clearer. My last birthday was spent with Jools and Richard because Brody was too busy writing. At Christmas we'd had a speedy dinner at his parent's house although they couldn't have been more welcoming. 'The usual packet stuffing and frozen turkey and disappointing crackers,' he'd said, before slipping upstairs again. Apart from our wedding, he didn't do celebrations so why did I think he might want to acknowledge our anniversary?

'It doesn't matter,' I said. 'I'm sorry. Let's just have a nice dinner.' The champagne could wait, I thought. We would open it in a few weeks on deadline day.

'I'm sorry too,' he said. 'It's just the way I am.' He gave me a small smile and I had a flash of the Brody of a year ago.

I slid the present towards him. 'I bought you something.'

'But I don't have anything for you...'

'It's okay,' I said. 'I don't need anything. Anyway, it's only small.'

He unwrapped the paper and picked up the long, slim box inside. 'Is it...?' He examined the outside, happier than I had seen him for months. 'My own Montblanc pen?'

I nodded. 'It's special edition. Titanium or something. The ink doesn't dry out and you can use it on the moon.'

He laughed. 'Well then, that is exactly what I will do. I will write on the moon, a love poem just for you.' He came over and stood beside me, his hand on my shoulder, his face in my ear. 'Thank you, Roisín... moon, June, spoon... you see, my poem is writing itself.' Brody held up the paper clip. It was in the shape of a ring. 'A present for my wife?'

I considered taking it and squashing it under my shoe but I didn't want to be accused of sulking again so I took it. 'Thank you.'

'Try it on,' he said. 'See if it fits.'

I jammed it on my finger, one end poking into my skin. 'Thank you,' I said, turning to kiss him, but he was already moving away.

'Now, let's eat. I'm starvatious. What is it?'

'Clams,' I said.

'Lamb? Great!'

'Clams. Seafood. Like mussels but nicer.'

'Seafood?' He looked aghast.

'And spaghetti,' I explained. 'Mixed together.'

'Bolognaise and seafood?' Even behind his beard, disgust curled on his lips.

I laughed. 'No! Look...' I lifted off the lid of the dish and began to serve him a portion. 'You'll love it.'

Brody stared at it. 'It's like that television programme where people are forced to eat witchetty grubs...' He poked at it with his fork. 'Ma and Pa used to watch it. But these look like the ovum of some unhatched exotic insect. Is it even food? It looks like something that fell out of my nose when I had that cold that didn't stop, the snot was something else...'

Suddenly, I knew I would never eat clams again.

'This is bait, not food,' he carried on. 'What am I? A salmon?' He roughly forked at the pasta as though searching for a sock in a laundry basket. He scooped some up and carefully brought it to his mouth, his tongue darting out like a frog's. He then nibbled and began to chew. 'I've had worse,' he said, eating a bit more. I watched as he finished the plate. 'What's wrong with you? You haven't eaten anything.'

In exactly a month, the book would be finished. There was still hope to recover the Brody of the past, the one who said that I was the best thing to happen to him, the one who thought everything I did was amazing. A year ago, he was an attractive writer and now he was more slob, often with the remains of a black cherry yogurt in his beard, and the pong from his T-shirt which he wore on a loop was something of a turn-off.

Brody flung his knife and fork on the plate and pushed everything away from him. 'I was so hungry,' he said, 'that I even ate those horrible maggotty things.' He stood up, thrusting his brand-new Montblanc pen in the air like Henry V going into battle. He tousled my hair like the mane of his loyal steed. 'Once more!' he shouted. 'Unto the breach!'

* * *

Later, after I had cleaned the kitchen, the doorbell rang. Mr Daly, my elderly next-door neighbour, was standing there holding a tin of baked beans and the can opener. Dressed, as always, in a brown suit, hair neatly combed – a vision of sartorial perfection compared to Brody, but there was something about the look on his face which made me think that maybe he wasn't coping.

'I'm so sorry to bother you, Roisín,' he said, 'but I'm having trouble opening these beans for my tea... it's these openers, so stiff, and my fingers can't quite get them to turn. I was just about to get the hammer out but I thought it might be easier to ask you... if you don't mind.'

His wife had died last year and the whole street had gone to her funeral. I tried to remember if there was anyone with him that day, a son or a daughter, but I couldn't remember anyone else, just him, standing with the priest, shaking everyone's hands. When it was my turn, he took my hand in both of his. 'You're freezing,' he had said. 'But you know what they say, cold hands, warm heart.' He didn't even give me a chance to say how sorry I was for his loss. Maybe Mr Daly was as lonely as me on a Friday night.

'Of course not.' I took the rusty tin opener from him and twisted the butterfly opener, the tin slowly revolving. I handed it back, and then hesitated. 'Is this all you're having for tea?'

'I tend to have beans most nights,' he went on, 'but it's either my arthritis or the tin opener that is making it increasingly difficult.' He gave me a grin. 'I tell you what, if I brought around some tins, enough for a week, would you open them for me, and I could keep them in the fridge.'

'You'd eat baked beans every night?'

'They are very nutritious,' he said. 'And quick to prepare and to eat. It means I don't have to think about dinner, beans keep me going and that's all I need these days.'

'Would you like some dinner here?' I said. 'I have made clams and spaghetti... there's loads left.'

'Clams?' His whole face brightened for a moment. 'But I couldn't possibly,' he said.

'You'd be doing me a favour,' I said. 'It's going to go in the bin otherwise...'

'Well, if it meant I would save them from an untimely rendezvous with the kitchen bin.'

'Come on in,' I said. 'I'll get you a bowl.'

He sat at the table, with one of my linen napkins tied around his neck, and tucked into a bowl of clams and spaghetti, spooning the gleaming juices into his mouth, his eyes closed. And then, finally, he finished, his knife and fork clattered to a halt on the side of his bowl.

'Now that, Roisín,' he said, 'is what I call great cooking.'

'Really?'

He nodded. 'I haven't tasted the like in years. I used to cook for my Nora every night but after she passed on, it just left me... do you know what I mean?' He peered at me from across the table. 'It left me thinking that having no one to cook for meant that there was no point cooking. I've lost the habit. I was a cook in the Merchant Navy and then I met Nora, and it went from there... cooking for myself isn't quite the same.'

'You can eat here anytime,' I said. 'I'd love to have you.'

'I couldn't possibly impose,' he said. 'And thank you for this evening. You have enlivened my taste buds, made them dance a jig, and soothed my soul.' He stood to go. 'Not bad for seventy-two in a few months,' he said. 'I'm not ready to join Nora yet... I have this feeling that life still has something in store for me.'

I walked him to the door, where he clasped my hands in his. 'The most delicious meal by a country mile,' he said. 'Thank you.' He picked up his beans, slipped the tin opener in his jacket pocket and waved to me on the doorstep. 'I would return the favour but I don't think beans is quite up to your standards. But tea and biscuits are available anytime you need it.'

'Bye Mr Daly,' I said. 'Thanks for coming.'

'Thank you for having me! I will remember that for a long time to come.'

Mr Daly, I thought, had just saved my wedding anniversary.

5

The following morning I was up early to make a start on my nieces' ninth-birthday cake. My sister, Shona, called at 8 a.m.

'You're not going to be late, are you?' She sounded tense.

'Mum and I are going to be on time,' I said, 'like you told us to. Why, what's wrong?'

'Nothing. It's just that... nothing...'

'Shona?'

'It's just that Ross is going to be late... very late, too late really, so it would be nice if my own family were on time.' Ross and Shona had been together since Shona's first year in law school, marrying just after graduation when she was pregnant with the twins. 'It's just you and Mum, and Hugh and Fionnuala, and I don't want to have to talk to my parents-in-law on my own.'

'Shona, are you okay?'

'Of course I am!' She sounded on edge. 'I need everyone in and out quickly,' she said. 'Starts at two, over at three thirty.'

'What is this?' I said. 'A North Korean military parade?'

'Well, I'm sorry that it has to be like this, okay?' she snapped. 'I've got things to do, that's all...'

'What things?'

'Things. But you're going to have to do all the talking to Ross's parents. I don't think I can stand another second with them with all their questions... she doesn't stop asking about every single detail of our lives...'

'Why is Ross going to be late?'

'Oh my God, you're as bad as Fionnuala!'

'But why?'

'He's working.'

'On a Saturday?'

'Of course on a Saturday! What is wrong with everyone? People work on Saturdays. Just because you don't doesn't mean that other people don't either. Anyway, don't be late...'

'We won't...'

'And talk to Fionnuala and Jack...'

'We will...'

'And it's only until three thirty. It can't go any longer...'

'Got it. By the way, Shona...' I was about to ask her what she thought about Dad coming to stay with Mum but she had put the phone down and was gone as though there was something seriously wrong.

* * *

'Shona told us not to be late,' I said later, getting into Mum's car, carefully holding the chocolate buttercream cake specifically requested by Daisy and Kitty.

'She told me the same,' said Mum. 'Anyway, I can't believe the twins are nine,' she said, indicating and pulling out on to the road. 'Seems only yesterday that Ross phoned me from the hospital. He was at a payphone and didn't have enough change. And so the money ran out and it wasn't until I went in myself did I realise there were two of them!' She turned to me, smiling. 'And there was Shona looking so lovely... and tired... I can't remember ever seeing her so happy. And such beautiful babies.'

'They were beautiful,' I agreed. 'Still are.'

'What have you bought the girls?' Mum said.

'Everything identical, obviously. Books, cool tie-dye hoodies, sweets, novelty socks.'

'And how was the anniversary meal?' said Mum. 'I bet Brody was mad for the clams...'

'Oh, he loved it,' I lied smoothly. 'Was practically licking his plate.'

We parked on the gravel drive, alongside Shona's black tank of a car, and across from Hugh and Fionnuala's metallic-beige Mercedes. 'Does a driveway have to be this big?' I said. 'I'll get my ten thousand steps in just walking from the car to the house.'

Mum laughed, but not too loudly as there was always a slight feeling of nervousness going to Shona's, a sense we didn't want to let her down. It was all so different to our normal lives – bigger, richer, glossier – and there was the feeling that it was slightly too much for Shona as well.

'Do I look all right?' Mum asked, as we stood on the doorstep.

'You look great,' I reassured her. 'How do I look?'

'Gorgeous,' said Mum, giving me a quick smile as we could hear footsteps on the sleek tiles and we bristled to attention. Shona answered the door. 'Where did you two get to?' she said.

Mum hugged her. 'Hello, darling, how are you?'

'Fine, fine...' Shona escaped from Mum's arms and took the cake from me. 'Chocolate?'

'Of course. Names spelled properly and everything. Dozy and Katty.'

Shona rolled her eyes. 'You go into the living room and I'll put this in the kitchen.' She paused. 'Thank you for making the cake,' she said in a quieter voice. 'You make the very best ones. I really appreciate it. And thank you for coming, both of you.'

'My pleasure,' I said.

'We wouldn't miss it for the world,' said Mum.

Shona pushed her towards the living room. 'Go in and say hello!'

I hovered for a moment and pulled on Shona's sleeve. 'Everything all right?' I asked.

'Fabulous!' she said. 'Everything is simply wonderful. I am living the perfect life, don't you know?' She shook me off and went into the kitchen. 'Now go in there and be nice to them!'

Inside, the whole house was a like a show home, all hard corners and with few soft edges and, in the living room, the sofa had no rugs to pull over you and the heating was always on too low.

'Ah! Fionnuala, Hugh,' Mum was saying as she walked in. 'How lovely to see you both again. And where are the birthday girls?'

Daisy and Kitty were hidden behind a huge pile of presents, watched over by Ross's parents sitting on the two armchairs on either side. The girls stopped the ripping of paper for one moment to put their arms around Mum's waist for a second and then squeeze me. 'Hello, Auntie Roisín,' said Daisy, as I kissed her head.

'Hello, Daisy-chain,' I said. 'Hello Kitty-kat. How are my joint-favourite nieces?'

'We're your only nieces!' they both chimed as part of our finely honed routine before returning to destroy wrapping paper, shrieking as they uncovered something else new and shiny.

'Ah! Roisín!' Hugh stood up, dressed in scarlet trousers and a navy golf-club jumper, and shook my hand. 'You're here to share the annual mayhem!'

Fionnuala, dressed as always in a bright jacket with large shoulder pads, gave me a regal wave, her gold bracelets rattling and her diamond rings sparkling in the light. 'We were wondering when you'd be here,' Fionnuala said, grasping Mum's hand in her slightly strange two-hand shake. 'Ross, as you know, couldn't make it,' she went on. 'He's working so hard these days.'

'I know,' said Mum, 'it's such a shame that he will miss—'

'The poor boy is working on a Saturday,' interrupted Fionnuala. 'What a work ethic. My father was the same. Worked every hour God sent. Died the day after he retired. Ross has definitely inherited his genes. But his father...' – she looked across at Hugh – 'couldn't wait to be out of the office every day, could you, Hugh?'

'Hated work,' said Hugh, agreeably. 'Don't much like being retired either but at least I can play a round of golf when I like.'

'Under my feet, more like it,' said Fionnuala. 'Your Shona is so lucky with Ross. So blessed to have a worker.'

Shona had placed herself on one of the hard, dining chairs, her hands neatly folded in her lap, legs tucked in, eyes on the twins as they ripped open the presents from Mum.

'Wow! Bubble wands!' they yelled.

'Darlings,' said Shona, 'don't start blowing them in here. They'll get on the oak floor and make marks that no amount of scrubbing will remove. You can do it in the garden. Or when you go to Granny's house.' She gave Mum a hard stare. 'She doesn't mind marks on the furniture.'

'Such a pity Ross has had to work,' said Fionnuala again. 'It's such an all-consuming role, the law. He was always like that. Never sat still. Not the kind of person who could ever have an idle moment. He gets that from my side of the family.'

A lifetime of not speaking up had killed Hugh's spirit entirely. Instead, he nodded gamely. 'Yes, we're all idlers. Thank God Fionnuala injected some active genes into Ross and Ronan.'

'And brains,' Fionnuala reminded him. 'Neither are your family renowned for their brainpower.'

Mum and I smiled politely and, when I glanced over at Shona, she rolled her eyes.

The twins had now ripped open a bat-and-ball set. 'Yay!' Kitty shouted, serving the ball towards the curtains.

'Kitty!' shouted Shona. 'How many times? Do things like that in the garden! Put it away!' Kitty and Daisy put the bats to one side and started on another present.

'So, Roisín, how is the world of work?' asked Hugh, vaguely.

'What is it you do again?' Fionnuala asked.

'I work in the council,' I said. 'In planning, just admin. Not very interesting or important...'

'The council?' said Fionnuala. 'Ah, yes, I forgot. Because I need to have a word with you about dog fouling. It's out of control. I power-walk Sandycove pier every Tuesday and Thursday and those dogs are allowed to do what they want, where they want...'

'That's not my department,' I said. 'That would be Environment.'

'Would you be able to talk to them about it, though?' she went on. 'Tell them it is ruining our walks. The other day I saw a man with a large dog.

And it then deposited an amount the size of itself. We were appalled. Catherine said she felt quite faint—'

'Why don't we go and have the cake now?' interjected Shona, standing up. 'We'll go into the kitchen. Come on, Kitty, Daisy. Put down those hideous things...'

'But Granny has given them to us. They're lightsabres...'

Shona glared at Mum. 'Plastic?'

'They like *Star Wars*,' said Mum, guiltily. 'They're just a bit of fun... and it's physical play, they can have fights with them...'

Shona looked heavenward for a moment as though gathering spiritual strength. 'Come on, then,' she said, teeth gritted. 'Into the kitchen.'

The six of us trooped in, the twins both with their arms around Mum. 'Thank you, Granny,' whispered Kitty. 'The best presents ever.' Daisy was nodding with her.

The kitchen was huge, with glass doors leading to the garden and on one wall a vast bank of units, appliances and doors and drawers. The work surfaces were totally bare, except for a kettle. Everything was neatly in its place in a drawer or a cupboard, not a crumb or cup out of place.

'Come and sit down at the island,' said Shona, hurrying us along. 'Quick, quick... Mum, you sit there, Roisín, grab the plates from the cupboard...'

'We'll have to make sure to save a big slice of cake for your dad,' Mum said to the twins who were now both wearing the hoodies I had brought over their party dresses. Shona was lighting the candles. 'Happy birthday...' Shona started singing, so we all joined in. '...dear Kitty and Daisy!'

'Again,' said Daisy, 'but this time dear Daisy and Kitty.'

We sang it again just for her before Shona sliced the cake and handed it out. For a moment there was silence. 'Heaven,' said Fionnuala, closing her eyes. 'So light...'

'Delicious,' Mum said, smiling over at me. 'Your usual standard.'

'It's a step up from a packet cake,' said Hugh. 'Although I do like a Mr Kipling. When Fionnuala is at her book club, I have been known...'

Fionnuala interrupted him. 'What is it exactly?' she asked. 'Chocolate sponge?'

'It's a mousse base,' I explained, 'and an Italian buttercream...'

But Fionnuala's brain had already moved on. 'Beautiful flowers, Shona,' she said, nodding at a vast bunch of lilies on the counter. 'Are they from Ross? I used to say to him, always send flowers to the woman in your life. Hugh here never got the memo but I thought if I have some influence in the world, then I was going to make sure my boys knew to send flowers.' She put the last of the cake into her mouth.

'I bought them, actually,' said Shona. 'When I was in Dunnes doing the shop yesterday.' The twins were in some kind of cake-eating competition, both eating slower than the other to make their slice last longer. Shona looked over at them. 'Can't you just eat normally?' she snapped. 'Come on, eat up.'

'You? Oh Shona, no! Women should not buy themselves flowers. I once heard of a woman who bought a diamond ring for herself. She was divorced though, which says a lot. That kind of carry-on suggests you should not be treated specially.' She wagged a finger in Shona's face. 'Be warned!'

The twins were now trying to act as though they were eating normally but were staring at each other. Daisy's mouth was chewing away but there was nothing in it.

Fionnuala and Hugh exchanged glances and got to their feet. 'Well, Shona, thank you,' said Fionnuala, formally. 'Yet again, another lovely occasion. And Roisín, the cake was divine. Wasn't the cake divine, Hugh?'

He nodded. 'Divine,' he repeated dutifully, as they went into the hall to find their coats in the cloakroom.

Mum looked at me and then Shona. 'Would you like us to stay and help clear up?'

'Yes, we can stay longer,' I said, hoping that perhaps Shona might relax and not be in such a hurry to get rid of us.

'Would you mind if you didn't?' Shona asked. 'Only that I'm...' She stopped.

Mum and I waited for her to finish.

'I'm a little... tired, that's all.' Her smile was forced. 'And we've got Daisy and Kitty's cousin's communion tomorrow.'

'And it's ours next Saturday, remember, Auntie Roisín?' said Daisy.

'And you're going to make another cake?'

I nodded. 'And the buffet...'

'What's a buffet?' they said in unison.

'It's a table of food and you help yourself.'

'Cool. Like a breakfast in a hotel and everyone balances as much as they can on a tiny plate.'

'Exactly.'

'Auntie Roisín's going to make more cake for ours,' said Daisy.

'And meringues,' said Kitty. 'Are you, Auntie Roisín?'

'I am.' I smiled at them. Shona had asked me months ago to cater for the party. It wasn't too hard, just a buffet for thirty people. I'd been looking forward to it ever since. A whole day cooking and preparing, making food for an appreciative audience was a pleasure.

I went over to the twins and kissed them on their heads. 'I love you, Daisy-chain and Kitty-kat. See you next Saturday. And what about I bring you to the cinema some time, okay?'

'As long as it's our choice, Auntie Roisín,' said Daisy. 'We don't trust yours.'

Kitty nodded. '*The Cat From Outer Space* was an insult to our intelligence,' she said. 'We are now nine and need more challenging films.'

I laughed. 'Okay, it will be a mutual decision. Something that we all want.'

'And sweets?' Daisy gave me her most winning of smiles. 'Just a few little sweets.'

'Just a few,' I promised. 'Now go and give your grandparents a hug goodbye, okay?'

They nodded, slipped off their stools and went into the hall where they wrapped their arms around Fionnuala and Mum, and then Hugh.

'Tell Ross to call me,' Fionnuala commanded Shona. 'He was too busy to return any of my calls. But I suppose we will see him at Ronan's tomorrow for their Joshua's communion. And, of course, we have the twins' communion the following Saturday.'

'Say thank you to Roisín,' said Shona.

'Thanks for the cake, Auntie Roisín,' said Daisy.

'Yes, thank you, Auntie Roisín,' said Kitty, who still had buttercream around her mouth.

'You're welcome, sweethearts.' I gave them one last kiss and a hug each and then hugged Shona. 'What's going on with you?' I whispered in her ear.

'Nothing, just leave it, okay?' she said under her breath and then turned to hug Mum. 'Thanks for coming,' she said, all smiles. 'I'll be in to see you this week. When Dad arrives. And I know I asked before, but why can't he stay in a hotel like a normal divorced person?'

'I asked the same thing,' I said.

'Ah, well... maybe we're not normal,' said Mum, hugging her tightly. 'I love you, Shona.'

'I love you, too,' said Shona. 'I'm sorry,' I heard her say quietly to Mum. 'Just things are getting on top of me.'

Mum gave her another hug. 'It's okay,' she said. 'See you next week.'

Hugh and Fionnuala tooted their horn as their car pulled out of the driveway ahead of Mum and me and then we turned back to give one last wave to Shona and the twins, but the door was closed.

'Do you think she's all right?' asked Mum.

'Hope so. Maybe she was just annoyed that Ross was working.'

Mum nodded. 'And do you think Brody will come to the communion? It's been ages since we last saw him.'

'He's—'

'I know,' she cut me off. 'He's writing.' She seemed suddenly charged, as though she really wanted to say something and really wanted me to hear it. 'All I want for you and Shona,' she said, turning to me, 'is for you both to be happy. And you have to know you deserve it. You have to believe in yourselves.'

I was silent for a moment. 'I do believe in myself,' I said, but I knew it wasn't true. I had nothing to believe in, no special talent, no book to write, no business to run. I just existed in the shadow of everyone else. Not everyone could be a star. The world needed those of us in supporting roles.

'I would like to see you take a few more risks...' said Mum.

'Like skydiving or eating that yogurt that's been in my fridge for three months?'

Mum laughed.

'I did marry someone after a year,' I reminded her. 'That was risky.'

I was hoping she'd laugh again, but instead she just shrugged.

'I just meant putting yourself out there,' she said. 'Doing something you are passionate about, that makes you happy – like food and baking. I think you are wonderful. I just want you to know it too.'

6

The lovely summer's day melted into a lovely summer's evening with warm air, the sounds of people in their gardens drinking wine, the smell of sausages on the barbecue and the feeling that you get on summer evenings in Ireland, those scant few weeks where good weather becomes almost normal, that the whole world is having fun.

Except for us. Brody was working upstairs and I was flicking through the channels fruitlessly hunting for something to watch. None of my friends were available as Jools was at the gym with a client and Richard was working abroad. The invitations for Saturday nights out with friends had dwindled once I was married, everyone assumed Brody and I were content in our love nest of the newishly married.

I knocked on the door of the study.

'Fancy watching something?' I called, my voice flattened against the wood. I could hear the sound of his headphones being removed.

'What?' Brody sounded irritated.

'TV... you know...'

'TV?' It was as though it was a new concept that he'd never heard of before.

'Yes, TV... it's Saturday night... we could just watch something.'

'Like what?'

'I don't know...' He still hadn't asked me to come in.

'Can I come in?'

A huge sigh. 'One moment...' I waited and then the door opened a crack. Through the mass of Brody beard, he looked crumpled, his face squashed, his eyes half asleep. 'Roisín, I'm working...'

'I know, but just a couple of hours... an hour?'

'And watch some banal Saturday night TV where everyone is wearing sequins and grinning their heads off?'

I nodded. 'We used to...'

'I am a writer,' he said. 'I write. You go and waste your time if you like. Or better still, read a decent book. One which doesn't have pictures in, or feature anyone kissing...' I could make out a sneer under the facial hair. Where was that handsome man I fell for that night at Richard's party? Sometimes it felt like he was a misremembered memory. Had I imagined it?

'Brody...'

'Sorry, Roisín...' He remembered to smile this time, his tone softened. 'It's just my opinion. Some books will change your life but many are a waste of time. I am trying to write the former, but I won't be able to if you keep nagging me to watch crap television...'

Nagging. The word hung in the air, as though we had crossed a line.

'I love you,' he went on, 'but I really need to get on. I'm in the middle of a scene. Seamus is trying to buy a part for his tractor, a 1976 Massey Ferguson. It's a big moment.'

'Why is it a big moment?'

He sighed heavily. 'The tractor represents the strength of Seamus Senior, his father. He died in a hay-baling accident... when Seamus Junior was ten. It's just something that has stayed with him...'

Hopefully, I thought, Seamus would have a happy ending after everything he'd been through. But I wanted our happy ending too. Brody pecked me on the cheek with an air of great gravity.

'Wish me luck.'

'Good luck.' I felt I was waving him off to war.

'Thank you.' He gave me a nod. Please don't salute, I thought. He saluted.

Downstairs, I opened a large bag of crisps and ate them standing up in the kitchen and then contemplated opening a bottle of wine, while I wondered what on earth to do with my evening. It was only 8 p.m. so too early to go to bed and I couldn't phone anyone as it would be proof my husband didn't want to spend the best night of the week with me. And then I remembered the bins which I still hadn't brought in from the day before. Finally, something to do.

Outside, I found my bin in a cluster with other bins, and just as I was pulling it back to my house, I saw Mr Daly coming towards me.

'I think mine might be one of those,' he said.

'I'll bring it over for you,' I said. We each had a small front garden and in mine were a few pots, a bench and a place for my bike, and two bins. 'It's no problem. You go back inside and I'll put it in the front garden for you.'

I tugged his bin across the pavement, following him to his front garden where he had sat down on the windowsill. I manoeuvred his bin into place and then I heard a voice behind us.

'What's this, then?' It was Anna who lived down the road. 'Neighbourhood bin night?'

'Something like that,' I said.

I had always felt a little bit sorry for Anna because her last boyfriend was extremely shouty and his voice would carry through the walls and on to the street. When I saw him leaving with a box of things, I gave a silent cheer.

'See you, Roisín,' she said. 'Bye, Mr Daly. Say hello to Brody for me.'

I didn't even know she knew Brody.

I turned back to Mr Daly. 'How are you?' I wondered if I should offer him some more food. 'Have you eaten?'

He nodded. 'I had a carton of soup,' he said. 'Much easier to open than the tins. And I've been doing a little clearing out.'

'Decluttering?' I said.

He nodded. 'Nora used to call it "sweeping the decks" and me being in the Merchant Navy knew what that meant. She used to say that if she didn't keep a close eye on me, I would have the house full of bric-a-brac. Wouldn't let me bring things home, was always recycling and throwing things out... but since she died, I don't know... it's got the better of me. It's the charity shops, you see. Full of useful things.' He smiled. 'I bet she's looking down at me, wondering when I am going to start throwing things out. She made me promise, you know.'

'Did she?' I went and stood beside him.

'Well, in the end, when she was confined to the bed, she knew I wasn't good at the getting rid, just good at the bringing in. She managed to get up one day and was really upset with me, broke my heart to see her like that. This morning, I woke up and thought "Today's the day. I'll do it for Nora!"'

I sat on the window ledge beside him. 'How tidy did you need to be in the Merchant Navy?'

'Immaculately so,' he said. 'It was easier because we were at sea most of the time, and I didn't get a chance to rifle in any of the bazaars or the markets. I was too busy trying to buy food for the lads.'

'Maybe I could open those other cans for you now?' I wished I'd remembered to get him an electric can opener.

'Would you mind?'

'Not at all,' I said.

Inside, his house was a mirror image of mine but his was fifty shades of brown. The geometrically patterned wallpaper was brown and gold, the carpet brown and swirly, the central lamp shade was a heavy brown and cream, and thick with dust. In fact, dust particles clung to the air, you could feel them as you breathed in. There was a mahogany mirror on the wall of the hall, with Mrs Daly's Mass card tucked inside the frame.

'Just in here,' he was saying, pushing open the door to the front room. 'I'm feeling very proud of myself and I thought I just needed to show someone. My Nora would have been very pleased.'

For a moment, I couldn't find the words. It was as though a truck had unloaded itself in his house. There were cardboard boxes everywhere, piles of newspapers spilling on to the floor, there were odd bits of metal, an old video player which didn't have a plug, one box was full of radios, there was even a wheelbarrow lying beside the old sideboard. There wasn't anywhere to sit down as the sofa and the two armchairs were piled high with more boxes. Piles of old coats were on one of the chairs, there was another box of old metal toys and in front of the electric fire a space had been cleared where an old army camping stool was set up in front an open scrapbook on the coffee table.

Every time I breathed in, I felt the dust settling on my lungs, making me feel almost claustrophobic.

'I am doing newspapers first,' Mr Daly was saying. 'I thought if I focused on one group at a time. This week, newspapers, next week, books. Do you think that's a good idea?'

I nodded. 'Definitely.'

'I know things have got out of control. Nora warned me this would happen, and she was right. I just couldn't help it, for some reason. She knew I was the kind of person who liked to keep things, and when she became ill, she wasn't able to keep on top of it. I have a habit of having to keep things for a rainy day.' He held up an umbrella which I could tell was broken. 'You see?' He smiled again. 'Do you have time for a cup of tea? Just a bag in a mug? Now, I must warn you, it's just as bad in the kitchen.'

He was right. It was like an old and forgotten junk shop; the table was piled with more boxes, papers, cans of food. The stove was a rusty, white, wobbly construction with an overhead grill. Even it was covered with a stack of saucepans and frying pans, none of which were clean, and the sink and draining board were crammed with tin cans, boxes of dried peas, the kind of food that the supermarkets just didn't sell any more. I stood for a moment taking it in while Mr Daly turned on the kettle and found two cups on the draining board.

'I know it's a bit of a mess,' he was saying. 'Nora wouldn't be pleased, I have to say. There's a point, I now realise, when it tips over from being busy to being impossible to live in. It takes over.'

'If you would like some help,' I said, 'I could come round. I know it's hard to throw things out, but it might be nice to be able to sit at your table. Or cook a meal?'

'Cooking is impossible these days,' he said, sitting down at the kitchen table. 'It takes too long to clear a space and then where do you put everything? And anyway, my serious cooking days are gone. Tins are much easier. And anyway, it's not the same cooking for one. I like to cook for people. Nora always enjoyed everything and the lads in the Merchant Navy were always so hungry. And you had to be inventive. You'd have your rations which had to last and no one wanted to eat just slop so I began to bring along my own dried chilli or buy lemons when we docked somewhere or whatever else I could find. We tried chickpeas for the first time in Tangiers and there was squid in Marseille... and olives.' His eyes brightened.

'How did you meet Nora?' I lifted a box off another chair and sat opposite him.

'In a bookshop on Dawson Street, in Dublin's city centre, just beside Trinity College,' Mr Daly went on. 'Being a clever sort, she'd just graduated and had got herself a summer job on the very top floor of the shop, with this wonderful view of the city. You could see all the way down to the River Liffey. And anyway, there was me, straight off the boat, legs still wobbly – they always took a few weeks to settle down – and I climbed all the way up to the top floor where they had all their cooking books. There was one I was looking for which I'd read about in the *Irish Press*. There I was, looking out of the window, wondering if you could see down to the docks and if our ship would be visible, when this very pretty girl asked me if I needed any help.' He smiled at me. 'And do you know what I said?'

I shook my head.

'I said, "Only from you." And I don't know what made me so bold, but it just came out. I'd fallen in love, you see, and that makes you courageous. "I'm Harry," I said. "Harry Daly." And she said that she was Nora Walsh. I told her that I was looking for a particular book. Normally, I was a very shy fella, going bright red whenever I talked to a lady. But there was nothing like that with Nora. We were best friends from the moment we set eyes on each other. Luckily, it was a very quiet department. Not many men in the cooking-book section. And then I asked her to come to mine for dinner. And she said yes, much to my delight.'

'What did you make her?'

'The recipe I'd seen in the *Press*. Chicken with preserved lemons, and I served it with rice, green olives and pistachios.' He smiled. 'She was very impressed. And so was I. Back then, it was all plain food, bacon and cabbage, that kind of thing. Not that there's anything wrong with it, mind you. But sometimes you need to take your taste buds on an adventure.' He smiled again.

'He was working late,' I whispered. Jools nodded understandingly and didn't say another word.

As we walked into the village, we could talk in normal tones again and I told her about Dad.

'It's as though Mum has forgiven him,' I said.

'But why shouldn't she?'

'Because...' I tried to think why she shouldn't. 'Because he doesn't deserve it. I mean, I am not saying she should hate him, but not make it easy for him.'

'Maybe she feels differently,' said Jools. 'You're protective of her, understandably, but maybe she's just moved on? Maybe she's just ready to get on with things?'

'Maybe...' All I knew was that I wasn't ready to forgive him, even if it was more than two decades ago. He'd hurt Mum, and I wasn't sure if we'd ever have anything but a simple father-daughter relationship. I changed the subject by telling her about Mr Daly.

'He's a hoarder,' I said. 'I'm going to help him tidy up a bit. And he only eats beans...'

'They're good for you,' she said. 'Lots of my clients eat beans. I eat beans. More protein in them than a horrible shake.'

'But Mr Daly used to be a chef,' I said. 'He cooked in the navy and then for his wife and now he only eats beans or cartons of soup.' I reminded myself to pick up an electric can opener. If he was going to exist on beans, then, at least, we could make it easy for him. We were now walking along the main street in Sandycove, past the butchers and the boutiques, the bank, The Island pub and James's deli on the corner.

'Do you think it would be patronising if I brought him food?' I asked. 'Just every now and then?'

'He can always say no,' she said. 'I wouldn't complain if you brought me food. Last night, I had a bowl of cereal for dinner. Mind you, it was nearly midnight and I was exhausted. This new client can only come after all his meetings. He's quite terrifying, turns up with excess adrenaline and testosterone from shouting at people all day and then shows me a picture of Chris Hemsworth and says he wants to look like that. He pays well but it's almost worse when they pay well because you then have to do exactly what they want. Who works out at ten on a Saturday night? Who?'

'A sociopath?'

'A psychopath.'

In Alison's café, we found our usual table at the back. Jools took a spare chair and put her foot up. 'I've damaged my cruciate ligament,' she explained. 'It needs to be elevated. The physio said to put only the lightest pressure on it.' She pulled up her leggings for a moment to show me her strapped knee. 'I won't be able to run the marathon this year...'

Jools had been running the Dublin Marathon since college, raising thousands of euros every year for cancer in memory of her parents. I was always somewhere along the route cheering her on, water in one hand and Jelly Babies in the other.

'I'm just so disappointed about the charity,' she was saying, her leggings pulled back down again. 'I've always managed to raise at least ten thousand euros... I'll just have to double my efforts next year.'

'I'll run it,' I offered rashly. 'Or I could do a cake sale? Is it possible to sell ten thousand euros' worth of cakes?'

'Richard's offered to swim from Sandycove to Howth,' she said.

Howth was the strip of land right across the bay that looked like a long-lost faraway shore.

'He'll die,' I said, 'or he'll be eaten by an angry seal, or stung to death by a jellyfish.'

'Or the cold,' said Jools. 'You know what he's like in the cold. Remember that time he strapped a hot-water bottle to his body using a dressing gown belt and it burst and his scream was heard all the way to Wales.'

'We really don't want him succumbing to hypothermia, my conscience couldn't take it.'

She nodded. 'Richard did have another idea... a supper club...' She looked at me.

'A supper club?'

'We put on dinners for people, charge them and the money goes to charity. But you'd have to be totally on board,' she said. 'You're the cook out of the three of us.'

I wished I could help but the thought of cooking for strangers, putting myself out there, charging money for my food, was frankly terrifying. 'I'll try and think of something else,' I said, picking up a menu.

'So, how was your anniversary?' said Jools. 'What did you do? Did you go to a nice restaurant?'

I shook my head. 'We just stayed in... you know...'

She nodded. 'The book.'

'Yes, the book.'

I hadn't told Jools how difficult I was finding it being married to a writer. As the deadline grew closer, Brody seemed increasingly on edge, almost to the point of mania. I couldn't remember when we'd last had anything approximating a normal conversation.

'It's nearly finished though,' I went on. 'In a month's time he has to deliver it to his publishers.'

'You can go out to celebrate then.'

'Definitely.' I sounded confident but would Brody and I just find our groove as soon as the book was done? Would he start showering and shaving again? Would he emerge blinking into the sunlight and be able to talk about things other than the non-adventures of Seamus?

Jools glanced out of the window but her face suddenly fell. 'Don't look now, but it's Darren.' She hid her face behind the menu.

Darren was standing talking to someone on the street, all broad shoulders and mean mouth, hair gelled into submission and a pair of ludicrously youthful trainers on his feet.

'It's just so infuriating that he's doing so well,' said Jools. 'He's opened another gym, his girlfriend is Ms Rippling Body for UK and Ireland... and...' She stopped.

'And?'

'I'm stuck here, working my arse off for clients who think I am available twenty-four-seven and with a banjaxed knee.'

'Personally, Jools, I wouldn't want to be Ms Rippling Body UK and Ireland,' I said. 'Nor would I want to be with Darren. Now you've seen the light, would you? Be honest. Come on. He's a cheating, self-obsessed fool. Those trainers look as though he bought them in Start-Rite.'

She giggled. 'He was really boring,' she admitted, as Darren moved away from the window, walking with a swagger, swinging his giant arms. 'All that protein powder went to his brain,' Jools went on. 'And you know he didn't have a single hair anywhere on his body?'

'Anywhere?'

'Anywhere.' She shuddered. 'It was quite a sight.'

'Like one of those horrible Chinese cats?'

'Exactly.' Jools laughed again. 'I'm ready to meet someone else but the thought of dating apps fills me with horror so I have decided to psychologically prepare myself for being alone for the rest of my life. Just me, eating toast in front of the TV. Maybe get a dog...'

For a moment, I became lost in her reverie as well. It sounded like an impossible dream – a single, toast-eating, dog-owning utopia – and no writer upstairs.

'At least you have someone,' she said. 'You never have to go back out there ever again.' Her face brightened suddenly. 'Paddy's come home! Did I tell you? There was a lease going on the old launderette and he signed it last week. He's opening up a bike shop. He's always wanted his own bike shop... remember?'

I nodded, trying to take it all in, keeping my face impassive. I hadn't seen him since the morning he left for Copenhagen. I felt a tug, the kind you have when you hear something which still has the power to trigger a memory of something significant. I had thought by falling in love with Brody and getting married that Paddy was now just an insignificant fragment of my past. But he was here, back in Sandycove, and I discovered feelings which I had thought were long dead, had only been in a shallow grave.

'He says he missed Ireland too much,' Jools was saying. 'We'll all have to meet up sometime.'

'Yes, maybe,' I said, signalling to Alison that we were ready to order. I wouldn't think about Paddy, I told myself. I would just focus on getting Brody to the finishing line. Paddy was just an old friend, long gone and didn't mean anything to me any more. 'Goat's cheese salad?' I said to Jools.

She nodded. 'Of course. Do we ever eat anything else?'

8

'I have an idea...' Richard was on the phone.

'Careful,' I said.

'Has Jools told you about her cruciate ligament?'

'She told me at lunch yesterday.'

'You two had lunch yesterday?'

'We go for lunch most Sundays.'

'Most Sundays?' He sounded affronted. 'What about me?'

'We used to invite you,' I said, 'but you were always away.'

'Yes, but I still want to be invited. I have an acute case of FOMO.'

'Where are you phoning from now?'

'Monaco,' he said.

'You see?'

'But it's a horrible place,' he said. 'I haven't seen the sky for three days or seen beyond these four walls, never mind the casino or the beach. The hotel is an airless, culture-less hole and I'm working eighteen-hour days and eating the worst and most expensive sandwiches known to mankind.'

'That sounds awful.'

'It is, it really is. It's just... well, I've been doing a bit of thinking.' He paused. 'I want to change my life... and I am not quite sure how... but I know I don't want to be stuck in an office with no daylight and no... meaning. Do you know what I'm getting at?'

'Yes, of course...'

'There's a million thoughts in my head, other than work, and for the first time in my life, I want to go off-plan, go wild, off-grid, have an adventure.'

'Me too,' I said. 'But I don't even have a plan to go off from. Apart from waiting for Brody to be finished with the book. Then, I'm going to have a plan.'

Richard was silent for a moment and then asked, 'And how is Our Great Writer?'

'Still writing,' I said.

'Well, I hope he is being nice to you,' said Richard. 'I feel entirely responsible for you two meeting. If I hadn't been so profligate with my invitations the night of my festive shindig, then you two would never have met.'

I really wanted to tell Richard that living with a writer on a deadline wasn't a bowl of cherries but that would mean telling him he'd been right. But there was still time to fix everything. Just get the book done and then we'd be back to where we'd been.

'So what are you going to do about work?' I changed the subject.

'I'm going to ask to step down a rung. I should never have taken that promotion, it just made me a slave to the machine. No more travel. I want to see more of my flat, my city, and my friends... And...' He was about to say something and then stopped.

'And what?'

'Nothing.'

'Go on.'

He dropped his voice. 'I can't speak now, but I'll talk to you about it sometime. It's about me.'

'Okay...' I said, wishing he would just tell me now.

'Look, I'll hear back from head office when New York wakes up and I'll let you know. And I have a plan for us... It came to me in a fever dream as I sweated my way through another Monégasque night.'

Was this the supper club idea that Jools had mentioned? I would have to come up with a better idea before this one took off.

'Look,' he said, 'I'll be back this afternoon and I'll tell you all about it in person. Let's meet in The Island, Thursday evening. Love you, Roisín,' he said. 'I've missed you and Jools. And now you have to invite me to your Sunday lunches.' And he was gone.

* * *

Over dinner, Brody was filling me in on the latest adventures of Seamus. Apparently, he was planning a trip to the post office to send a letter to an aunt who lived in Birmingham. 'He decides to wear his brown tweed jacket,' said Brody.

'To the post office?' I was trying to look interested but as it was the kind of book in which nothing much happens and lingers on the metaphysical – shafts of light, breaths of wind and all that – it was difficult.

'And his best tweed cap,' went on Brody. 'Going into the village is a big deal. And so he takes the jacket and he remembers his father wearing it...'

'Seamus Senior.'

'Yes, Seamus Senior was wearing it the day when some American arrived to try and buy some of their land...'

'Oh yes?'

'Not long after the American arrived, his dad died in the—'

'Hay baler, I remember.' I perked up. 'Are you suggesting the American killed him? And maybe Seamus Junior can solve the mystery?'

Brody pulled a face. 'It's not The Famous Fecking Five,' he said. 'This is a serious novel. An existential novel.'

'Of course.' At this point my interest waned significantly, but at least he was writing, I thought. We were nearly there. 'So, does he send the letter?' I queried.

'What letter?'

'The letter to his aunt in Birmingham?'

'He decides not to go.'

'He doesn't go?' Plot twist, I thought.

Brody shook his head. 'He wanted to go but going to the village was too much for him. Which reminds me, I need to read up on grass.'

'Grass?'

'All types. Seamus knows his grass. Everything from rye to white clover. Seamus thinks about grass a lot. He can look at a field and name a hundred species.'

'Grass?' I said again.

'Yes, of grass! Stop saying grass!'

'You brought it up!'

'It's just that you don't get it,' he said. 'It's art and you seem to try and make everything sound as though it isn't important.'

'I don't.' I hated arguing and avoided it whenever I could. 'Sorry, Brody, I shouldn't have asked all those stupid questions.'

'I'm just tired,' he said. 'Exhausted.'

My initial thought was that all he'd done was sit on an ergonomic chair at my old oak desk. He had free and easy access to a fully working kitchen, complete with an expensive and complicated coffee machine. But then, of course, I had no idea of the mental energy it took to write a book and the general brain strain.

'It sounds really hard,' I said. 'Being a writer.'

Brody managed to nod. 'It is,' he said, his face forlorn. 'It is hard... it's not easy at all.' He was tearing up a little, his voice on the edge of wobble. He stood up suddenly and came over to me, his hands on my shoulders. 'I love you, Roisín,' he said in a gentle voice. 'I know I can't be much fun with me working so hard and still going every evening. You must be lonely.' He knelt down beside me.

'I love you, too,' I said. 'I just want us to be happy. And when you have finished the book...'

He pulled away from me, his body stiffening.

'But look,' I pressed on, 'when it's finished, I thought we'd have a big party. Invite everyone we know... and then go away, just the two of us and perhaps, I was thinking...' A baby, I thought. I would love a baby. But Brody seemed to read my mind.

'We need something else... some small being that will stop the loneliness, something to focus on...' He took my hand.

'Brody, you're not suggesting...?' I felt excited, something which I hadn't felt for some time. He was serious about us, we'd have a child, this was our next step together.

He nodded. 'I think it's exactly what we need. Something to love, something to love us back... the sound of tiny little feet, the cute little face... the tiny little teeth...'

'Teeth?'

He nodded. 'I love their little teeth, the way they eat sunflower seeds and chew things...'

'But Brody... it would choke...?'

'Hamsters love sunflower seeds,' he said, sliding back into his chair. 'I really feel this house is missing a pet hamster. They bring another dimension to a home, they are the most amazing creatures. So small, but so clever. Their little faces... their huge cheeks... I had so many when I was a child and my hamsters were always there for me. Hammy, obviously. He was my first, but then there was Harry, Harriet, Shaggy, Scooby...'

I looked at him, reality dawning. 'For a moment there,' I said, 'I thought you meant a baby. A human baby.'

'Babies!' he laughed. 'Oh, I hate babies. Give me a hamster over a human baby any time. The hamsters can be our babies... we could breed them...'

He's gone mad, I thought. The book has driven him mad.

'I don't like hamsters though,' I said. 'I don't think animals should be in cages.'

'Yes, well, we are all in a cage,' he said. 'Sometimes literal, sometimes metaphorical. Society is a cage. That's why we need a hamster, to remind us of the perilous state we are all in.' He stood up. 'Now, I am going back upstairs... this book isn't going to write itself.' And he smiled to himself as though he'd said something that amused him.

* * *

Through the living room window, I saw Harry walking past, a newspaper under his arm.

'Harry!' I called after him, from the front step. 'I've bought you the tin opener.' I ran outside and handed him the bag. 'It's electric, you just plug it in and away it goes.'

'Does it now?'

'No effort required,' I said.

'My kind of tin opener,' he said, reaching into his inside pocket. 'Now, how much do I owe you?'

'Nothing,' I said. 'Please. It hardly cost anything. Seriously.'

He still had his hand on his wallet. 'Please, Harry. Just a neighbour thing, and they were half-price in the shop and they are so cheap.'

He reluctantly put his wallet away.

'How are you getting on? How's the tidying going?'

'Grand, thank you,' he said. 'Just grand.' But he didn't look his normal, smiley self.

'You sure?'

'Well, it's Nora's anniversary today so it hasn't been a great day, not really. But I'm getting through it. I was just down in the church lighting a candle and saying a prayer. Not that I go in for all that, mind. But Nora would like it. And I said a few words, that I was missing her and hoped she was all right up there, or wherever she is.'

'Would you like a cup of tea?' I asked.

'I'll be grand, I will,' he said. 'Last anniversary was the worst, being the first, this is the second and although you always miss the person you love, I have found you have to stay quiet enough so you can hear them.'

I nodded, thinking I understood. 'Maybe I could call around later this week and we could start on the front room?'

'You're very good,' he said. 'I would love an extra pair of hands. I've also roped in Cyril at number seventeen to give me a hand clearing things out. He's a stickler for getting things neat. Says he hasn't been challenged as much since he retired from the university. He's also getting first dibs at some of the things. He went home earlier with two radios and a toaster. He's good at fixing things, so he says he's going to try and sell them on. He was professor of engineering, you know.'

Thank God for Cyril from number seventeen, I thought. There was now two of us trying to mind Harry. And I liked minding him, as though there was more to my life than just keeping house for Brody.

9

On Thursday, JP placed a file on my desk. 'Ms Kelly,' he said, 'get your teeth into that.'

Printed on the front were the words:

Lady Immaculate Hall, Seafront Redevelopment, Sandycove

This particular planning application had been lingering in the department for the last eight years. Even though it had changed developers and architects several times, we could never get over the line. The building had been once owned by an order of nuns who bequeathed it to the council who had then put it out to tender for a developer. It was the area around the Hall that people were interested in, not in having to put in millions of euros to bring a decrepit and unloved building up to modern standards. We knew that there was a community group who used it to make lunches every day but, beyond that, the hall was slowly being left to rot. When I was a child, it was full of groups, everything from Irish dancing and ballet to scout groups and ballroom dancing. Now, everyone apart from the community lunches, had moved on to the brand new Mounttown Centre.

'You said you wanted to make your job more interesting, didn't you?' JP went on. 'It's a tricky one, granted. But I thought you might be able to attack it from a fresh perspective, not the jaded ones of Frank and Dermot. Panic not, I don't expect you to get anywhere with it. Just have a look at it, from a planner's perspective, and see if you uncover some chink, some light that may change its fortunes. A fresh and unsullied mind might be what it needs. You never know.'

'You're lucky,' called Dermot over from his desk. 'My mind is like rotting vegetables that have been left at the bottom of a wheelie bin.' He grinned. 'Hasn't stopped me reaching the pinnacle of my career. Frank's mind, however, is about as fresh as his sullied underpants.'

JP ignored him. 'It's called professional development, Roisín,' he said. 'I have to mentor at least one of my team.' He looked around the office. 'No one else seems to want the benefit of my new-found skills.'

'You can mentor me, JP,' said Dermot. 'Teach me a few of your tricks. How to tuck your trousers into your socks when you cycle or how to write illegibly.'

'Thank you, Dermot,' said JP. 'Insightful as ever.' He turned back to me. 'Just because we went to college together, he thinks he can say anything.'

'Respect goes both ways,' said Dermot, gaily. 'And I know where your skeletons are buried. Along with that packet of skunk seeds you smuggled in from Amsterdam.'

JP rolled his eyes.

Saoirse was looking at us from her desk like a meerkat. 'What's going on?' she asked.

'I am giving Roisín extra responsibilities,' he said. 'Have you changed your mind?'

'No thank you, JP,' she said, returning to swiping through her phone. 'I am swamped as it is. Roisín mustn't have been busy in the first place.'

'Now, I don't care if you approve or turn down the planning,' said JP to me, 'just make a bloody decision, which is more than can be said for what the two people who are paid to be planners in this department have done.'

'JP, would you mind leaving me out of this?' said Frank. 'I object to being ridiculed and demeaned.'

'Apologies, Frank.' JP turned back to face me. 'Give it a go, what have you got to lose? I think having someone incorruptible like Roisín would be a good thing, because we need to be whiter than white, purer than the driven snow, transparent to the point of nakedness...'

'JP, leave your fantasies at home where they belong,' said Dermot.

JP rolled his eyes. 'God, grant me the serenity to accept the things I cannot change,' he said, walking away. 'The courage to change the things I can, and the wisdom to know that when I retire – which cannot come too soon – I never have to work with Dermot O'Grady ever again.' He disappeared into his office.

'Good luck with that one,' Dermot said to me, exchanging a look with Frank.

'Lady Immaculate Hall is a tough nut to crack,' agreed Frank.

'An impossible nut to crack,' said Dermot. 'It's the Berlin Wall of planning. You're so desperate to get over it, but whatever you try, you get shot down.'

Belinda looked up. 'Dermot, please. Inappropriate jokes were banned in the office after your last one.'

'Moi?' Dermot feigned child-like innocence. 'Never.'

I jogged after JP, clutching the file to my chest, and knocked on his open door. 'JP,' I said, going in, 'I should have been clearer. I don't think I want to take on more responsibility. I mean, it's just that I am busy and there's all my other work. And maybe I should have said that I was very satisfied in my work. I don't need mentoring or anything like that.'

'It's an opportunity, Roisín,' he said, leaning back in his chair. 'We need a new planner in the department. Frank and Dermot are snowed under since He Who Shall Not Be Named was banged up... I need someone I can trust implicitly. And I have worked with you for... how long?'

'Ten years.' I never meant to end up as an administrator in planning but I had temped in the office for a few months and JP had asked if I wanted to stay on.

'That long? That's longer than my marriage lasted,' he said, motioning me to sit down. 'Not as long as I've been a Bruce Springsteen fan, however, or I have battled with my receding hairline. All I am asking you to do is take a look at the planning, make a decision whether yes or no.'

'So a yes to the planning means that the Hall is knocked down. And a no means that we are back where we started?'

'Exactly. The development of the old amusement arcade is simple. What's not simple is Lady Immaculate Hall. It's in the care of the council but the council is reluctant to spend the amount of money needed to do it up. The developers just want it gone and the community – as they invariably do – are protesting. And if you decide no, then we do what we always do and the building is left to what we call benign neglect, which then moves to benign decay, which then moves to not-so-benign demolition. And we start again – this time without a potentially architecturally sensitive building at the heart of it and planning is far more likely to go through. The problem is benign neglect, decay and demolition can take a long time. Do you know the Hall?'

'I used to go to Irish dancing classes there. And my mother used to bring us to the garden fair there every year...'

'I knew you'd know it, being a local and all. So, it's currently a community centre. It doesn't have an owner as such as it was bequeathed to the community. The council, in some loose agreement the details of which are lost in the mists of time, took over the running of it.' He leaned back in his chair. 'Look, it's a poisoned chalice but I need something to give you so you start gaining planning experience. You said you wanted more responsibility, didn't you?'

'Not rea—' I began.

'Look, all we need is a resolution one way or the other. It needs to be gone from our department. Why do you think Frank and Dermot are the way they are? They've been driven to it by this very application. All I need is for a definite yes or no just so we can say that we have given it every possible chance. I'll be away for a couple of weeks from tomorrow...'

'Holiday? But you hate holidays.'

'It is more a period of self-reflection,' he said. 'I am currently in the excruciating position of having to face a few hard facts about myself and my terrible habits which were mainly watching too much sport and not spending enough time with my wife. Obviously, now my ex-wife. Emotional unavailability, if you will. Or that's what my therapist calls it. Making yourself emotionally distant so you don't have to do the hard work of living with and loving someone.' He pulled a face. 'Well, I'm learning the hard way now. I'm living in a pretty grim one-bedroom flat over on York Road, on the less salubrious side of Sandycove. Going on "holiday"' – he made quote marks in the air – 'is all part of my therapy. My aversion to "holidays" is another reason why my ex-wife found me so intolerable. She had to go on walking holidays in a group because I refused to go with her. She did the Camino de Santiago, went to Machu Picchu... even Everest Base Camp. It was there that she met Gruffydd.' He paused. 'Six foot seven, built for coal-mining and recites Dylan Thomas with minimal encouragement.'

'Oh dear.'

JP picked up a framed photograph of a smiling JP and an older version of himself, both carrying rods. 'I'm going to be fly fishing with my old dad for a couple of weeks, reignite my old passion for landing a trout. It's in Connemara, just by Lough Corrib, the most beautiful lake in the world. There was this island we used to swim out to when we were young, and we'd spend all day there. My God, the taste of fresh trout, fried up over a fire you've made yourself. And you'd look straight across the lake, down into the Maam Valley, and you'd almost believe in God.' He paused. 'Almost.' He sighed. 'We've all got to focus on things that make us happy, something we are passionate about.'

'But—'

'Let me be your cautionary tale, Roisín,' he went on. 'Look, being a planner would mean more money and not more hours. I am not asking you to be a manager because that way madness lies. See this as a little enhancement of your daily life.'

'I'll try,' I conceded.

'Great...' JP picked up a form and made a large tick. 'Another satisfied employee,' he said. 'This time on Saturday, it will just be me and the old man, dressed identically and comically in our over-pocketed gilets, flat caps and gigantic waders, and just the sound of the ripple of lake water as the dragonflies dart along the surface. And then in the evening, we'll have a whiskey in the bar of Pat MacDonogh's pub, talking hurling and the fine art of fly fishing.'

'Sounds perfect.'

'Thanks for giving it a go, Roisín,' he said. 'And remember, no backhanders!' He grinned. 'I don't want to see you driving around in a Mercedes and smoking Havana cigars.'

'Marbella, here I come!' I tried to laugh but I was full of dread. Who wanted to take on the poisoned chalice of planning?

10

The Island, my local pub in Sandycove, was a small, cosy bar with fishing nets, old glass buoys and photographs of the harbour on the walls. Richard, Jools and I sat in the small courtyard at the back of the pub, at our usual table, in the warmth of a June evening.

'So,' said Richard, 'something sparkling? My life needs an injection of fizz. Prosecco, okay?' He signalled to Mike behind the bar and then turned back to us. 'So, how are you both?'

'Well, apart from my knee,' said Jools, 'I'm fine. Still holding classes but not really jumping about as much. And I bumped into Darren yesterday. Again. But this time we had to converse. He's engaged. As in to be married.' She looked over at me and pulled a face.

'Not to Ms Rippling Body UK and Ireland?' I asked. 'The poor woman.'

'Exactly,' said Richard. 'Does she have a brain, self-esteem, eyesight?'

'She looks like one of those bog bodies which are thousands of years old,' I told him, 'and were preserved in farmers' fields and are now in the National Museum.'

Jools picked up her glass of Prosecco that Mike had just placed on our table. 'I know I am well rid,' she said. 'And he has a weird greenish tint to his skin, and he's overdone the teeth bleaching. They are now practically translucent. Remember the time he thought Snowdonia was a place in *The Lion, The Witch and The Wardrobe*?'

'You deserve someone so much better,' said Richard. 'Like a Greek god or someone mythically fabulous.'

'In Dublin?' said Jools. 'I don't think so. And I'm getting old...'

'You're thirty-two!' I exclaimed.

'Exactly,' she said.

'Well,' began Richard, 'I feel like I have aged about twenty years in the last year and a half, ever since I took on the job.' He grabbed at his face and thrust it towards us. 'I'm ancient, like a haggard old man. I looked in the mirror in that awful hotel and guess who I saw?'

'A ghost?' I suggested.

'My father,' replied Richard. 'My father. John-Joe himself. If you'd put a tweed cap on my head and knocked out a tooth, I would have looked exactly the same. I almost had a heart attack.'

Richard was uncharacteristically animated. 'I want to live now, in this moment. I am going to sip my Prosecco and wallow in this exact minute, here, back in lovely Dublin, with my two best friends. I never, ever want to be in an airless room ever again, staring at numbers and trying to find clever ways of ensuring my client does not pay tax. It's no way to live, my soul is dying... what have I been doing it for?'

'Your massive salary?' Jools responded.

'Your bonuses,' I said. 'That gorgeous flat you own. That expensive suit.'

'But my dad didn't care about suits and flats and being able to fly first class,' he said. 'He didn't bring me up to value these things.' He topped up our glasses from the bottle of Prosecco. 'I just want a simpler life. If you put me in a milking parlour and told me to get on with it, I wouldn't know what to do. And I wouldn't want to get my wellies muddy. Dad would be ashamed. What happened to me? Where did little Richie go?'

'He followed the money,' I said.

'He sold his soul to the devil.' Jools winked at me.

Richard nodded, sadly. 'I have, I really have. But!' He brightened. 'Good news, head office have agreed to my demotion. They said it was the first time in the company's history that someone had asked for less money and fewer hours.'

'You've done the right thing,' I assured him.

'And we'll get to see more of you,' said Jools.

'Life is slipping by,' Richard went on. 'Haven't you noticed?'

'I want it to,' said Jools. 'I want my cruciate ligament to be healed and then I can run again.'

'And I want Brody to finish his book,' I said. 'And I want to get this stupid planning application done. My boss wants me to become a planner.'

'A planner?' said Richard. 'I thought you wanted to be a chef...'

'That's never going to happen,' I said. 'And maybe this is good for me. I know enough about it from all my admin work and this is the next step.'

Richard looked at me sceptically. 'In all the years you've worked there, you've never mentioned being a planner.'

'Well, things happen...'

'But you love cooking,' said Jools.

'I know... but I am never going to make a living from that. This is a proper job.'

'Well,' said Richard, 'this brings us neatly to my big idea to raise money for Jools's charity and brings in our Roisín's very special and very specific talents...'

Not the supper club, I thought. 'I was thinking of a cake sale in work...'

Richard held up a hand as though chairing a work meeting. 'A fine and honourable idea. And yes, of course we could do such a thing. I too could do something similar, maybe a sponsored twenty-four-hour Irish dance, impress my fellow accountants with my long-latent skills.' His voice dropped conspiratorially. 'I was good, though. Mammy still regrets me not making a career out of it and can be heard telling people I could have been the next Michael Flatley. I was telling Sam earlier.'

'Sam?' Jools asked.

'My new assistant,' he replied. 'My right-hand man. Couldn't do without him...' Richard went slightly pink for a moment. Something was up. Richard had always been very private about his love life, though we had seen him fall for a few men over the years. There was that German baron von something with whom Richard became obsessed and lingered in the college library whenever the baron was studying there. And there was also our next-door neighbour, a carpenter called Thomas Duffy who Richard began commissioning presents from, just so he could have long conversations with him. But the way Richard was talking about changing his life and his misty eyes when he mentioned this Sam was somehow different.

'Anyway.' He focused back on us. 'Back to my idea. What do you think about a supper club?' Richard was looking straight at me. 'It's a genius idea,' he went on, 'even if I say so myself. Now, hear me out. We host a dinner party for thirty people – on three consecutive Saturdays – and we raise as much money as possible. Venue to be confirmed. Sam is going to look into any unused premises, organise the online booking and is already researching the rules and regs of a supper club. We're thinking of twenty-five euros a head? Most importantly, it will be fun! And...' He looked at us from over the rim of his glass. 'It might even help us all grow as people.'

'I don't want to grow any more.' Jools pouted. 'I've had enough of trying to be better, to be wiser. If I watch another TED Talk, I'm going to scream. But I do want to have more fun.'

'No way.' I was adamant. 'I can't. Not cooking for paying guests. It's fine cooking for friends or for small family events, but in public? Not a chance. I have Daisy and Kitty's communion on Saturday and that's fine. But—'

'Please. We need you,' Richard pleaded. 'We can't do it without you. Otherwise, it's just a club, minus the supper.'

'If Roisín doesn't want to—' started Jools.

'Hear me out,' Richard interjected, holding up his hand again. 'It's only a pop-up restaurant. It was Sam who came up with the idea because I told him that Roisín was a superb chef...'

'Hardly,' I began to protest, panic rising like floodwater.

'Jools will be sous chef and I will be maître d'... just like at the dinner parties we used to do.'

After graduation we used to have open-house Sunday lunch for some-times as many as twenty people. Me in the kitchen, Jools dashing about serving, Richard folding napkins and stressing about not having enough glasses. Paddy was always around and he made the long table from two old doors he'd found in a skip which we used in the garden in the summer and we had an old linen tablecloth we found in a house clear-out on Fitzwilliam Square. But that was for fun, no pressure, and definitely no money. I'd already been pushed into something at work, and now my friends were trying to push me into this.

'Richard, I can't,' I protested. 'I would prefer to do sponsored hula-hooping or anything rather than—'

'What exactly is the problem? You always said you wanted your own restaurant...'

'Yes, but that was years ago...' I tried to think what was wrong. 'But this is real.'

'So you don't want your own restaurant?'

'No, I do... but...' It was easy to dream but I never really thought of doing anything about it.

'Well then!' Richard folded his arms. 'We're doing it.'

'But I'm not trained,' I wailed.

'That doesn't matter,' said Richard.

'But health and safety. Doesn't everything need to be done in industrial kitchens?'

'Not supper clubs. Sam's in the middle of the research but there are special temporary licences you can get. He's going to check out legals, insurance, that kind of thing. All we need is a location. So, are we in? Jools?'

Jools shrugged. 'If Roisín is.' She looked at me.

'We'll be there as your support,' said Richard, 'every step of the way, won't we, Jools?'

She nodded. 'Completely. Every step of the way.' They both looked excited and Richard raised his glass. 'To our supper club! Roisín, are you in?'

I was going to have to say yes. When would I ever gain a backbone?

'Are you sure you don't mind if the food is basic?' I asked.

'Depends what you mean by basic,' he replied. 'We're not talking alphabetti spaghetti on toast. I do want you to challenge yourself...'

'No sauces or foams...' I insisted.

'Obviously not,' he agreed. 'They are so over.'

'Nothing that involves glazing, or sous vide or hours of brining. Nothing cheffy.'

'Of course. They are so tedious.'

'And you're happy for me to choose the menu.'

'Yes... but run it by me and we can discuss it? Relinquishing complete control is really not my thing.'

'And we're doing it for three weeks.'

'Yes, starting next Saturday. And don't worry about our guests, they are always nice when it's for charity. They won't mind if the food's terrible. Not that it will be, of course. It will be divinely delicious. All you have to do is cook.'

'And Paddy can help,' said Jools. 'I've already mentioned it to him. He says he can't wait to see everyone again.'

This was a nightmare, I thought. At least I would be stuck in the kitchen, no one need see me, especially Paddy. And I had Brody to think about. But I worked out the dates in my head. 'The final Saturday would be the day after Brody's deadline,' I pondered. 'It could be part of the celebrations.'

'Absolutely,' said Richard, smoothly. 'Who wouldn't want to celebrate such a momentous occasion?'

11

As I began cycling home, my head was full. Not just this idea of Richard's which meant that I would have to go public with my cooking and be critiqued but also Paddy. Of course I was still thinking about him, I told myself. At that moment, my husband was AWOL and I was bored and lonely. In a month's time, all would be well.

It was still only 9 p.m. and I turned left at the junction in the village and went to see Mum.

The sky was still light, the day stretching its limbs into the setting sun and, after I locked my bike to the railings, I walked down the lane to the side of Mum's house and pushed open the gate.

She was sitting in the old deckchair, a book on her lap, her small transistor radio on the grass beside her, the voices crackly and indistinct. She looked over and smiled.

'Hello!' I called. 'I thought I'd see how you are?'

'How lovely to see you,' she said. 'What are you doing here at this time?'

'I was on my way home and I... I just thought I'd pop in.' I didn't want to tell her I was reluctant to go back to Brody. 'The garden looks really beautiful,' I said, looking around. 'As always.' I sat on the chair beside her.

'Is everything all right?' Mum always seemed to know when I was worried about something.

'Jools has hurt her leg and can't run the marathon this year...'

'Oh, the poor thing... is she okay?'

'She will be but Richard wants us to do some kind of supper club for Jools's charity and he wants me to do the cooking.'

I scanned her face for any reaction that might back up my reticence. If she showed any concern for me – such as lack of talent or ability – then I would be completely justified in backing out.

But Mum looked thrilled. 'I like the sound of a supper club,' she said. 'What a wonderful idea.'

Richard and Mum had adored each other from the first moment I brought him home. He always called her his Dublin Mam. And he'd stay up late chatting to Mum about life and everything he had discovered about it. One year, when he was revising for exams, he stayed with us for Christmas and Mum taught him gin rummy and they had long late-night sessions, listening to Édith Piaf and drinking her home-made blackberry wine.

'Don't you think it's too... exposing?'

Mum looked at me for a moment. 'But you're doing food for the communion on Saturday, isn't that exactly the same?'

'That's just making a few sandwiches and a cake,' I said. 'It's not really putting myself out there.'

Mum gave me a look. 'A few sandwiches,' she said. 'Your idea of a few sandwiches is a perfect poached salmon, three different salads and some tiny canapés...'

'Well...'

'That's exactly what you're doing, isn't it?'

'Maybe,' I admitted, 'but this is different. The supper club is me pretending I have a restaurant. It just seems so full of myself, so arrogant. Everyone will think that I think I can do it.'

'But you can...'

'I can't.' I felt about five years old, embarrassed by my very existence. When had I become so pathetic? But faced with the thing I wanted most, it was hard to make that leap.

'Well, then,' said Mum, 'you really should do it. Listen to your gut, the thing you want most is often the hardest to reach for. All the more reason to go for it. Courage and confidence, Roisín,' she went on. 'There is no point being a talented cook if no one gets to know about it.' She took my hand. 'The amount of people I have met with little discernible talent but over-endowed with confidence is shocking. I think it's about time someone like you gets an opportunity. How many is it for?'

'About thirty people. And we don't have a location... so it probably won't happen.'

'What about here?' she said, immediately. 'In the garden, use the summer house if it rains and outside if the weather stays fine. It worked beautifully for your wedding. If Richard approves, of course.' Mum smiled at me in that maddening way that meant that the deal was sealed.

'Maybe...' I could see what Richard thought of Mum's idea about using the garden. I stood up, thinking that it was time to go home and see Brody.

'By the way, your dad is arriving tomorrow morning,' Mum went on. I sat down again. 'I've made up the spare room and I'm trying to remember what he likes for breakfast.' She took a letter from the book on her lap. 'Here's the latest missive. Still meandering down memory lane.' She read aloud, 'Do you remember the first flat we had? On Leeson Street? I was trying to recall the name of that old landlady. She used to smoke cigars and drink with Brendan Behan? And there was an infestation of woodlice which I wasn't quite manly enough to deal with but you did with a contraption fashioned from a shoebox. And we went into St Stephen's Green to release them.'

'Are you sure it is Dad writing and not some other person? It doesn't sound like him.'

'Let me remember the landlady's name,' said Mum. 'Yes, it was Mrs O'Faolain. We moved into the flat when we came back from our honeymoon.'

I couldn't place this Mum and Dad, who had lives before marriage, before children and before divorce.

'I'd better get home,' I said, standing up again, and wishing I could just stay here in this little Eden with Mum and not have to think about anything beyond the walls of the garden.

Proposed menu for the stupid supper club
Baked beans served on toast
Baked potatoes and cheese
Cheesy pasta
Magnum ice lollies
Tea and biscuits

Mum:
Would you like to pop in? Your dad's here. Will ask Shona + the twins. I've made some apple tart xxx

On Friday morning, I called Shona from my desk at work. 'Did you get a text from Mum?'

'Maybe,' she said. 'I haven't checked. The girls both had lost their lunch boxes and then Daisy wanted to bring that bubble wand to school even though they've been banned because one of the boys drank bubble mixture. And then Kitty told me – just as we were leaving the house – that she had forgotten to write a poem about making your holy communion. In the end I dictated something to her in the car on the way. Talking of which, do you have everything for tomorrow?'

'Of course,' I said. 'I've made my lists and the food is being delivered tonight. And I've ordered the salmon from the fishmonger's in the village.'

'Thank you,' she said, softening. 'Thank you... let me know how much to give you for the food...'

'I like doing it,' I said. 'I don't want anything.'

'You always say this! Just let me give you, at least, the money for the shop. We love having you cater for us... you're better than any of those ones who do the little blinis and vol-au-vents...'

'What's wrong with vol-au-vents?'

'Nothing,' she said, 'it's just whatever you do, it's always amazing. You're a professional. Otherwise, I'd have to do it myself and we'd only have ham sandwiches and crisps. So, please let me put some money in your account for the food shop, okay?'

'Okay...'

'And I've forgotten why you called.'

'Dad's here. He's arrived.'

'So!' said Shona. 'The rambler returns! So what are we meant to do about it? Fire the confetti cannons? And that means he'll be here for the stupid communion. The last thing I need on top of everything else...'

'Mum wants us to call in. She's made apple tart.'

'I'll have to see how my emotional and psychological state is by five,' said Shona. 'Might have dipped quite significantly by then.' She sighed. 'To be honest, Ro, I can't give this much more of my emotional energy. I've got my own stuff going on.'

'Like what?'

'Like my LIFE!' When Shona roared like that, I'd learned to back off. It usually meant that she was seriously stressed and I'd always been the one she could take things out on.

'Like all the things I've got to do to keep this whole fecking shebang on the road!'

* * *

Saoirse loomed over my desk like a blonde Godzilla and I quickly hid the menu I'd been planning for the supper club. Richard had said he wanted to hear my ideas as soon as possible.

'How's the planning application coming along?' she said.

'I haven't started yet,' I said. 'And it's impossible. It's at stalemate. He just wants a final decision and the building can be left to rot.'

'I bet I could have done it,' she said. 'If he'd only asked me.' Saoirse was the kind of person who wanted what you had just because you had it.

'But you said you were perfectly happy,' I explained. 'Remember? In the meeting?'

She looked at me blankly. 'I probably wasn't listening. Anyway, it's not fair. And now he's going on holiday which is annoying...' She rolled her eyes. 'I mean, why didn't he ask me directly? I can't spend my life doing admin for these useless morons...' She turned to glare at Dermot. 'Yes, Dermot, I mean you. And Frank.'

'Maybe JP thinks Roisín is more intelligent and more capable than you?' suggested Dermot, sweetly. 'Not that I think anyone could be more intelligent than you, Saoirse.' He threw a paper clip at Frank. 'Don't you agree, Frank?'

'I'm recusing myself from this conversation,' said Frank. 'I don't want to discuss who's the cleverest in this office.'

'Because it's me, that's why,' said Dermot. 'Sorry, folks.'

Saoirse glared at the two of them. 'You're plankton, that's what you two are. No wonder you both are perennially single. Isn't that right? Dermot, still desperately seeking someone? Frank, still going home to microwave meals for one? No one would have you, not even other plankton.'

There was a sharp gasp from Belinda.

'Joking!' said Saoirse. 'Can't anyone take a joke around here? What's up with you, Roisín? Why don't you make us all a nice cake and we can all be friends.' She laughed. 'Joking! It's called office banter. God, it's like working with Carmelite nuns. I should know, I was taught by them.'

13

Shona was reversing her huge car into a space, the twins waving from the back, just as I was locking my bike to the railings outside Mum's house. Shona inched forwards and backwards as though she was ironing the road with her car, eventually managing to get within sight of the kerb.

'Having difficulty?' I shouted through the glass.

'What?' Shona rolled down the window.

'Your car,' I said. 'It would be easier to park Air Force One.'

'What are you going on about?' she retorted witheringly. 'Just because you are a smug bicycle owner, it doesn't mean you can go around giving unsolicited comments.' She pressed the window up and inched forwards and backwards a few more times, before turning off the engine. Daisy and Kitty fell out of the car and hugged me.

'How was school today?' I put my arms around both of them.

'Boring.' Daisy pulled a face.

'Do you still do religion or has everyone moved on from that, even the teachers?'

'No, we still do it,' Kitty replied. 'Especially because we've got the communion tomorrow. But Daisy and I only need to do half the work of everything in school. She does one half and I do the other. And then we copy.'

'It's genius,' said Daisy. The two of them grinned at each other.

'I wish I had a twin,' I said. 'I would only need to do a half-day's work.'

They both nodded enthusiastically. 'Yeah, you'd only need to live half a life,' agreed Daisy. My laugh was as inauthentic as a tan on Christmas Day. I didn't need a twin to lead half a life, I thought. I was already doing it perfectly well on my own.

'Sorry for saying that about your parking.' I said to Shona, while the twins were trotting up the path to the front door. 'It can't be easy to park a tank in a suburban setting.'

She nearly smiled. 'And I'm sorry for being so awful and irritated. I'm just... I don't know...'

'So am I,' I said. 'I'm just, too.'

Shona looked immediately concerned, her whole face softening as it always did whenever I showed the slightest sign that my life wasn't perfect. But I couldn't complain, because I didn't have two children to worry about or all the stresses and strains of Shona's life.

'I'm fine,' I backtracked. 'Everything's fine. Let's go in and see Dad.'

* * *

Dad answered the door wearing a pair of navy cargo shorts and a loose blue shirt, as though still living on the Riviera, his arms outstretched. 'Well! Who do we have here? Is this Kitty and Daisy? Two little brainboxes, I hear. Nobel prize winners, UN peace envoys, captains of industry in the making! I haven't seen you since last summer.' He hugged his granddaughters and then stood up, smiling, his gleaming teeth set against his permanent tan, matching his full head of snow-white hair. He was still trim, still handsome. 'How are my two lovely big girls?'

He hugged Shona first, kissing the top of her head. 'My Shona,' he said. 'And my Roisín.' It was my turn to be squashed under his arm, that smell of Dad, clean cotton and Creed aftershave. For a moment, I stayed there. All the feelings I had for Dad, all the love and all the other, far more confusing emotions, hung over me. I wished I could just hug him back and love him simply but it wasn't that easy.

'Welcome...' I was about to say 'home' when I stopped. I meant to welcome him back to Ireland but not home. Shona gave me a look, as though she was feeling the same kind of slightly confused awkwardness.

'Thank you, darling,' Dad said, smoothly. 'It's wonderful to be back in this rain-benighted land again. How I have missed clouds and the constant threat of rain! It's good to be back for a long old stretch. Now, your mother's in the garden, talking to a friend of yours, Roisín, and some other fella about some supper something or other. Robert? Something like that.'

In the garden, Richard and Mum were sitting on the two chairs in deep conversation. Another man, handsome, immaculately dressed just like Richard, sat on the rug in front of them, making detailed notes. Daisy and Kitty ran ahead to play on the swing.

'Ah!' said Richard, looking up. 'Here is the woman herself. And the lovely Shona.' He stood and hugged Shona. 'How are you?' he said. 'Haven't seen you in years.' He turned to the man. 'Sam, this is Shona and Roisín, Shona and Roisín, this is Sam. And it's perfect, Roisín. We have it all sorted.'

'What's going on?' Shona asked.

'A charity supper club,' I told her. 'Richard's making me do it.'

'She's scared,' said Richard. 'But I say, feel the fear and cook it anyway. We need Roisín's not inconsiderable skills as a chef in order for it to happen but Roisín is trying to decide whether to do this or spend another Saturday evening at home waiting for her husband to finish his book. Which, by the way, has to be good after all this fuss.' He winked at Shona.

'I am expecting *War and Peace* at this rate,' Shona said, and she and Richard snickered for a moment. 'But,' she went on, 'the supper club idea sounds perfect.'

'Hopefully it will be.' He sounded confident. 'And this garden is perfect. It's so kind of you to offer it, Maggie, and there's the summer house where we can put the bar.'

'We'll all help out,' Mum offered. 'If you need us.'

'Or we can make ourselves scarce,' said Dad. 'Leave the young folks to their endeavours. We could go to the pictures, Maggie? Like the old days. What do you think?'

Mum nodded. 'We'll see.'

'We're going to put up a string of lights from here to... here.' Richard stood between two apple trees. 'I'm thinking drinks and nibbles here...'

'In the orchard,' suggested Sam.

'Orchard?' I queried. 'It's just a few apple trees.'

'Sam is a visionary,' Richard explained. 'And maybe you don't realise how beautiful the garden is. The houses in this part of Sandycove are stunning, but this one's the nicest because it's untouched. Wild, rustic. Not a topiary hedge or strimmed edge anywhere.'

'We will need the lawn mown.' Sam looked at his notes. 'And the summer house checked over by health and safety.'

Richard nodded. 'When will we hear on the application?'

'We should hear tomorrow,' Sam replied. 'Just need to get the temporary entertainment license.'

Mum, Dad, Shona and I stood while Richard and Sam discussed our garden as though it was now in public hands. The supper club was already happening, I realised, whether I liked it or not.

'Now, we need a name for the supper club,' Richard announced. 'Any ideas?'

'The Sandycove Supper Club...' suggested Mum.

'Maybe...' Richard wasn't convinced.

'The Summer Supper Club?' Shona asked.

I looked around at the garden. If it was going to be held here, then maybe we should call it after the garden, the way it opened up to you as you pushed in through the back gate, the smell of the jasmine, the honeysuckle scrambling over the arch.

'Perfect!' Richard smiled. Everyone was nodding enthusiastically.

'The Garden Supper Club?' I offered.

'Better,' he enthused.

'Or the Little Eden Supper Club?' I tried again.

'Bingo!' Richard looked delighted. 'The Little Eden Supper Club is born. Now, we'll go and leave you to your...' – he arched an eyebrow at me – '... reunion. We'll go and forage for some food. Thank you, Maggie.' He hugged Mum goodbye. 'We'll finish our chat another time, and yes, I do believe Liam Neeson is undervalued as a cultural export, and yes, let's think about that weekend in Barcelona in the autumn. It's exactly what we both need.' He turned to us all. 'Goodbye, Shona, Jack.' And then he hugged me. 'I'll call you later, can't wait to hear what the first menu will be.' I mumbled something in response. 'There's no point being talented,' he smiled infuriatingly, 'if you can't show it off. Let me know what you are planning.'

When he and Sam had left by the side gate, Mum turned to us. 'Now, who's for some apple tart?'

'Finally,' said Dad. 'I arrived five hours ago and I've been looking longingly at it ever since. Irish apple tart is a very different beast to French apple tart.'

'Which is better?' Shona asked as we walked inside, Daisy and Kitty holding Mum's hands.

'Irish, of course,' Dad replied. 'And your mother makes the best Irish apple tart which must make it the best apple tart in the world.' He grinned at us, and I realised that he'd already made himself totally at home.

We went inside and Mum made a pot of tea and we sat down at the kitchen table.

'Shona, Roisín, tea? Will you get the cream out of the fridge, Kitty? Daisy, the jug on the dresser? And girls, you can bring your granddad up to speed on your busy lives. How were the violin exams? Did you both get into the soccer club?'

Mum poured the tea while the twins answered her questions, Dad listening and nodding away.

'How is Ross?' Dad asked, when they had finished. 'I must meet him for a drink in the yacht club some evening.'

'Why don't you ask about Brody?' Shona replied, stiffly. 'I'm not the only one married here.'

Five pairs of eyes turned to me. 'And how is the man in question?' Dad asked.

'He's fine,' I answered. 'He's nearly finished his novel.'

'Don't you find writers go on about their books in a disproportionate sense?' Dad went on. 'I knew two writers in Cannes and you would think they were saving lives the way they went on about their works in progress, as they called them. One of them became afflicted with writer's block for three months and the only thing that shook him out of it was a very expensive course of hypnosis. Oh, thank you, Maggie.' He accepted a slice of apple tart from Mum. 'Ah, still got the Wedgwood Blue Pacific, I see. A wedding present, if I remember rightly?' He smiled at her. 'Where's that gravy boat you used for custard?'

Mum was about to speak when Shona interrupted.

'So, where's Maxine?' she asked. 'Does she know you're here, staying with Mum?'

'Well,' Dad began, a forkful of apple tart suspended in the air, 'I'm afraid Maxine and I are having a teeny-tiny holiday from each other. She's decided she wants to live alone. Forever. So, not so much holiday as a total break. And therefore, not being someone who likes to waste a second of this precious commodity called life, it is the perfect time to return to Dublin, sort out Philip's will once and for all, and...' – he glanced at Mum – '... rely on the kindness of friends.' She smiled back at him, sitting down with her own slice of apple tart. 'By the way, Maggie,' he smiled, 'this is superb.'

'Next time I'll make custard to go with it.' She looked up.

'In the gravy boat,' they said in unison, and laughed.

Shona and I looked at each other.

'So, are you and Maxine actually getting divorced?' I asked.

'Such an ugly word, that,' Dad replied, 'but yes, yes we are. And delightful as Maxine is, she has made it very clear that she is rather keen to never see me ever again. Her final words were, and let me just get this right, she never wanted to see my "stupid mug"...' He made inverted commas in the air. 'Or hear me "slurp my tea" or have to endure another of my "interminable stories" ever again.' He looked over at the twins. 'Sorry, girls, but not everyone finds your grandfather as charming as you do. Can you believe it?'

They both giggled and he smiled over at them.

'Apparently,' he went on, 'my voice has been grating upon Maxine's synapses for some time.' He looked at Mum, who was also smiling, as though she found him highly amusing, and he certainly seemed to want to entertain her. It was as though they were falling into a long-lost groove.

Shona glanced at me again and then turned back to Dad. 'How long are you staying for?'

'A couple of weeks?' Dad checked with Mum. 'Whatever Maggie wants. I may have overstayed my welcome already?' He looked at her, slightly coquettishly. 'Have I?'

'No, Jack,' she said. 'Not yet. I'll let you know when you have.'

'Why don't I bring the twins out into the garden and see if they want another push on that swing?' Dad suggested. 'Come on, kiddlywinks...'

We watched the three of them go into the garden and then, through the window, we saw Dad bring them over to the old wooden swing which had hung from the largest apple tree for as long as I could remember, the two girls scrambling on the seat together, just the way Shona and I used to.

'Was I too harsh?' Shona asked. 'I mean, I just want clarity... I think it's only fair.'

'Of course,' soothed Mum. 'And I understand where you're coming from...'

'You two haven't spoken for years,' went on Shona. 'Couldn't be in the same room. For my wedding, we had to sit you on opposite sides of the ballroom. Remember? Roisín spent the entire time running between the two of you making sure you were both happy.'

'It feels like a very long time ago,' said Mum. 'I can't even remember half of it all. Now, we are just very special friends, with history together, two daughters and two adorable granddaughters.'

'But he's just staying for a holiday, isn't he?' I tried to clarify. 'He's not moved back in?'

'Of course not!' She was about to say more when we heard Dad and the twins coming back in again and Shona stood up.

'We have to go, the girls haven't done their homework yet. And we've got a million things to do for the communion tomorrow.'

'So have I.' I stood up, too.

'Maybe I could collect the girls from school one day?' Dad asked as he walked back in. 'Bring them home here and make them a little snack?'

Shona looked momentarily flummoxed. 'You mean...? Collect them from school? Like a normal grandparent?'

Dad laughed. 'Well, now I'm back... it would be exceedingly pleasant to be employed in such a way. Whenever they came to France, they were too busy dive-bombing into the pool to talk to me.' He turned to Kitty and

Daisy. 'You'd like Granddad to collect you from school some time, wouldn't you? Do your homework with you? My specialist subjects are history and maths. What do you think, girls? Fancy being taught by your old granddad?'

Daisy and Kitty looked quite pleased. 'Except we don't do maths or history,' said Kitty.

'I mean, we are meant to do maths and history, but we have decided we don't need to,' added Daisy.

'Not if we are going to be fashion designers,' explained Kitty.

'Well, I am sure I can help you work on those skills.' Dad smiled. 'I was known in my callow youth to be quite the head-turner.' He turned to Mum. 'I was always quite the style maven, was I not? First man in Dublin to wear a neckerchief and a Breton striped top. I fancied myself as something out of a French film. Jean-Paul Belmondo, eat your heart out.'

I thought, disloyally, of Brody who only wore his old tracksuit bottoms, the ones which were wearing away at the knees, and his T-shirt, the one that he pulled off at night and picked up from the floor every morning and which had taken on its own life, as though all the bacteria which clung to it moved as one.

'You looked more like a gondolier.' Mum smiled.

'Ah, but a handsome gondolier, wouldn't you say?' He pulled what he thought was a sexy pout, making Mum laugh. Oh my God, he was flirting with her.

Shona looked disgusted, as though she'd just witnessed an unspeakable horror. 'I'm going,' she announced. 'Come on, girls.' She took one of the slices of apple tart Mum had placed in old Tupperware containers for Ross and Brody.

I said goodbye to Dad as he hugged Daisy and Kitty and then squeezed me and Shona in turn.

'It's good to be back,' he said, 'among my favourite people. Now, Daisy and Kitty, I'll pick you up on Monday and Granddad's school starts as soon as we come home.' He winked at them. 'I'll teach you everything I know, all my wisdom, my nuggets of genius, my incendiary insights.'

'Dad,' Shona pleaded, 'if you are going to collect them, just let them get on with their homework and please, whatever you do, don't pass on any of

your so-called wisdom. And we'll see you all tomorrow for the communion. Now, don't be late!'

* * *

Back at home, Brody came downstairs to meet me. 'Hello!' I smiled at him,
delighted. It was so nice to be greeted. I'd given up on the lingering kisses
he would bestow on me every time he returned from work.

'Just FYI and all that,' he said, 'I've bought a hamster.'

'A what?'

'A hamster.' He stood in the hall, arms folded.

'A real hamster?' I asked. 'Or a toy one?' Please let it be a toy one, I
prayed. Please, just a little stuffed toy.

'A real one, of course,' he replied. 'He's upstairs, having a nap.' Brody
scratched an armpit. 'He's got these incredibly intelligent eyes, like he
holds the wisdom of the world within his tiny, furry body. He's called
Fyodor, by the way. He's like the baby brother I always wanted and never
got. Nothing like my real brother, Roger.' Finally, he reached out for me
and drew me into some kind of hug where my face was pressed into his
chest, the smell of him wasn't just sweat, it was a something danker,
deeper, swampier. I determined to wash that T-shirt that evening whatever
happened. 'It's like we're now a little family.' He released me. Brody looked
happier than I had perhaps ever seen him. Even on our wedding day, his
eyes hadn't sparkled like they did when he talked about Fyodor.

'Brody, when you say he's upstairs,' I asked, 'where exactly upstairs?'

'The bedroom, of course. Where else would he be sleeping? It's quiet
up there and he'll be able to sleep soundly. Did you know hamsters are
nocturnal? Therefore, when he's awake he senses the presence of other
mammals. We will have to be really quiet around him.'

'But...' I began.

'We don't want Fyodor getting lonely, do we?'

'Fyodor? Brody, listen, that's not a good idea... not in the bedroom. The
carpet's nearly new.'

'But I hate carpet,' he said. 'Think how many germs are contained in
the fibres. They are hotbeds of bacteria and filth.'

I kept myself from looking pointedly at his foul T-shirt. 'But he's a rodent,' I said.

'Hamsters aren't rodents.' Brody looked shocked. 'They are small and very inquisitive mammals. Like dogs but better. More portable for one thing.'

'Portable? Hamsters aren't portable...' I began, wary of coming between Brody and his new-found enthusiasm. But perhaps if having a hamster helped him focus on finishing the book, then I should get behind it.

'Look, if it bothers you that much,' said Brody, 'I'll pull up the carpet. I need Fyodor as a stress releaser. Come and have a look at him.'

He's gone mad, I thought as I followed him upstairs. The book, the solitude and the pressure had driven him insane.

Brody pushed open the bedroom door and there, on the floor beside the window, was a large cage where sawdust had already been pushed out onto the carpet. There was a red wheel and a mound of fluff. Brody slipped his hand in and clutched at something and quickly brought both hands to his chest. 'He's very shy.' He lifted up his fingers on one hand and inside was Fyodor. 'Isn't he lovely?'

Two bright black eyes blinked back at me. He did look intelligent, I thought. Maybe he too would end up writing a novel and I would have to support his writing career as well. Except, he was still a rodent. In my bedroom. 'I suppose.' I tried to sound enthusiastic.

'You suppose?' Brody thrust Fyodor close to my face. 'A defenceless creature and you can't summon up some unconditional love?'

'He is very sweet, Brody,' I conceded. 'It's just that rodents...'

'He's not a rodent!'

I was pretty sure hamsters were rodents but decided not to stand my ground. 'Brody, be sensible. Just not the bedroom, okay?' I tried to think of somewhere he could go. Not the kitchen. Gross. The hall wasn't big enough. 'Could he go in the garden?'

Brody looked as though I had told him I was going to flush poor Fyodor down the toilet. 'I'm surprised at you.' He looked at me coldly, putting Fyodor back into the cage. 'I thought you were kinder than that.'

'I am,' I protested. 'I mean, I am a kind person.'

Brody didn't say anything, just fiddled with the ball of fluff which looked to be Fyodor's sleeping quarters.

'I am, Brody!' I could feel madness slipping into my voice now. Maybe novel-writing mania was catching? I tried again. 'I love Fyodor,' I said. 'He's gorgeous. It's just I can't sleep with him in the bedroom. Can't you put him in the spare room, I mean, your study, and he can be your talisman while you write? Help you with the final push as you finish the book? Only a few weeks to go!'

Brody's gaze was a second too long.

'Everything all right?' I asked.

'It's just that you keep going on about the book. How am I expected to write it if you keep banging on about it?'

'Come on,' I soothed. 'Let's put the cage in the... your study. And I promise never to mention the book again. I just want you to be happy.' I took his hand in mine. 'That's all I am concerned about.' I hoped my voice conveyed the requisite warmth, enough to see off any more sulks. And who knew, maybe I would actually learn to love little Fyodor as well? By the end of the month, he'd probably be sleeping with us in the marital bed like some kind of rodenty son. Brody sat almost meekly on the bed. 'I'll make you a cup of tea,' I whispered again. 'And a nice biscuit.' I realised this was some kind of game I had to play, as though I was on a reality game show and I had to work out how to pretend to be happily married.

14

Daisy and Kitty's first holy communion
Canapés
Poached Connemara wild salmon, home-made hollandaise
Asparagus and parmesan quiche
Potato salad, pasta salad, green bean salad
Mini meringues, whipped cream and Wexford strawberries
Celebration white chocolate buttercream cake

'Have you remembered the double cream?' Shona called just after 7 a.m. on the following morning. 'I was in the supermarket at ten last night and there was none to be had. It's like trying to score the last Furby on Christmas Eve. No cream, no Prosecco and no puff pastry anywhere. Communion season is crazy. One woman was practically crying because someone snatched the last Viennetta out of her hands.' She stopped. 'Sorry. It's early. I know I'm wired. Did I wake you up?'

I hadn't slept well after a fitful night listening to Fyodor on his wheel as though training for some hamster marathon. I'd also been trying to remember if I'd bought everything for the communion.

'No, I was awake,' I replied. 'Just making coffee. And I have the cream. And extra milk and I even remembered the sparklers for the mini pavlovas.' My day was planned meticulously – poach salmon, make meringues, boil potatoes for salad, prepare both quiches and the cake... everything else could be assembled in Shona's.

'Oh, thank God.' Shona sounded disproportionately relieved. 'I couldn't sleep,' she went on. 'Just trying to... anyway, it doesn't matter. You will be here by eleven, won't you? We're going to the church then and we'll leave you here.' She sounded anxious.

'Don't worry, Shona,' I soothed. 'Everything will be fine. You and Ross just have a nice morning, I'll get the food done and I'll see you later. Did you put the drinks in the fridge? Is there ice in the freezer?'

'Ice? Ice? Did I make the ice?' There was panic in her voice. 'Did I make the ice? I can't remember, Roisín... I can't remember if I made the ice!'

'Where's Ross... surely he can go and track some down?'

Shona was now in a kind of feverish state. 'My hairbrush... Daisy stole my hairbrush... and Kitty's painted her nails scarlet... and I can't find my nail polish remover...' There was a strangling sound as though she was choking on something. Shona, I realised, was hyperventilating.

'Shona... is everything all right?'

'It's Ross...' she whispered. 'He's disappeared.'

'What do you mean?'

'I mean, he's disappeared. A month ago.'

'A month? You mean kidnapped? Taken hostage?'

'No! Of course not! This is South County Dublin! We don't go in for hostage-taking here. Jesus! No, he's disappeared on his own bloody volition. He's kidnapped himself!'

'You mean he's left—?'

'Yes.' She was crying now. 'I've been holding it together, hoping he'd come home. But one day turned into another and then a week... and now this... his daughters' communion! I've been looking out of the window all week, thinking surely he'll come back now and I don't have to make excuses for him any longer and no one will be any the wiser...'

'What did he say? How did he explain...?'

'Just said he couldn't do it any more. Packed a bag and left. He's been going into the office, I know because I have done a bit of stalking. Me in my Land Rover with a pair of the girls' plastic binoculars. And there he was, walking around as though all was well with the world, and there's me sitting in the car crying, holding a pair of pink binoculars. One of his colleagues saw me and I had to wave back, praying my mascara had not run down my face and I did not look like some crazy woman. Which, of course, I totally am.'

'You've been driven to it,' I said, feeling furious Ross would leave her. And on what grounds? Shona had been devoted to him and the twins and to making their whole lives work.

'Anyway,' she went on, 'I went back the next day, with the pink binoculars again, and he was with that woman he works with, Victoria somebody, and he looked happy as though there was nothing going on, as though he wasn't having some big life crisis and he hadn't left his wife and children. But there he was smiling and happy and it got me thinking that Ross isn't the kind of person who smiles very much and doesn't actually have a sense of humour. Has he suddenly developed one?'

'I don't know...'

'So I was suddenly infused with this shot of craziness, like I had been electrocuted and I shouted at him on the street, like a banshee.' She groaned. 'Oh God. I am so mortified.'

'Go on...'

'He didn't stop walking, just sped up a little, and the two of them power-walked up South Anne Street, and then I lost them. God, I'd make a useless detective... I can't even do that properly.'

'You need a better pair of binoculars, for one,' I said, trying to lighten the tone.

'Please don't tell anyone.' She pulled herself together. 'If you do, I will kill you. Promise?'

'I promise...' When Shona turned all mafia like that, you had to agree.

'Because I swear to God—!'

'I promised, didn't I?' All these weeks, Shona had been pretending everything was all right but Ross had been gone. 'Why didn't you tell me?'

'I was hoping he would come back and then no one would know. I am just going to get through the day. Big smile, happy face, tra-la-la.'

'But everyone will ask where he is.'

'I'm just going to say he's... I don't know... late, picking up more drinks, getting ice – that's a good one, thank you – or my usual, working. I'm getting good at covering up for him. Except, missing the girls' communion... it was bad enough not coming to their party, but doing it again...?' For a moment, I thought her voice cracked.

'Are you okay?'

'Yes... of course I'm okay. I have to be okay. It's people like Ross who can just drop out of their lives, excuse themselves from all their responsibilities.' Her voice broke again and she cleared her throat. 'Look,' she said. 'You have to back me up, okay? If anyone asks about Ross, lie. Okay? He's working... he'll be back soon... the massive man-child is momentarily detained.'

'Who knows? Do his parents know? Anyone?'

'No one,' she said. 'Just me, obviously. And now you. Don't say anything.'

She rang off and I was left to poach a salmon, make the hollandaise sauce and rehearse what I would say to my brother-in-law if I ever saw his sorry face ever again.

15

A giant 'Have A Happy And Holy Communion!' banner was hung across the landing, fluttering in the breeze from the open front door, which was flanked by two bunches of silver helium balloons. I hauled the crates and cool boxes of food for the party into Shona's house from the taxi. In the living room, the long table was set with a white tablecloth, the plates stacked, the napkins and cutlery in neat piles, glasses glinting in the summer morning sunshine.

Shona stood in the kitchen doorway looking magnificent – full make-up, hair in loose waves, wearing a tight green dress and killer heels.

'Don't say anything.' She held up a hand. 'This is me performing as a woman in full control of her life, aided by a very small gin and tonic. Deep breathing doesn't work, deep drinking is what is required.' Her smile was that of a maniac's before she was distracted by the thundering of Daisy and Kitty as they ran into the kitchen, two cumulous clouds in their snow-white communion dresses, followed by Mum, carrying my cake.

'I found this on the front step. Your dad was about to eat it, saying finders keepers.'

We could hear Dad in the hall with the twins. 'Well, well, well,' he was saying. 'Who are these exceptionally clean young ladies? I've never seen them before, with such neat hair! No knots or tangles anywhere!'

'Where's Ross?' Mum asked Shona brightly. 'Is he still upstairs?'

'He's working,' Shona replied. 'Sadly. He's going to try and make it for the church.' Her eyes met mine briefly.

'I'm sure he'll make it,' said Mum. 'His clients won't mind when they know how important it is.' She turned to me. 'Will you be all right here, Cinders? While we go to the ball?'

'Maggie!' Dad called to Mum. 'Come and see these two, they claim to be our granddaughters but I've never seen them before in my life! They are immaculate!'

Mum laughed and went to join them. In the kitchen, like an actress going on stage, Shona steadied herself by holding on to the kitchen island. 'Wish me luck,' she muttered before walking briskly into the hall. 'Kitty, you're not wearing your old anorak. Daisy, is that nail polish on your dress? It's too late now. Dad, isn't that tie something out of the seventies? No, I didn't know Mum had kept your old ones. And Mum, I thought you were going to wear your high heels...'

And they were gone.

Meanwhile, I set to work. Cream whipped, mini pavlovas adorned with strawberries, herbs chopped and scattered over the potato salad and the hollandaise – my second attempt – spooned into a bowl. The cake was iced with white buttercream and on it I placed two little photographs of Daisy and Kitty when they were babies. I looked at the time. Nearly 12.30 p.m., they'd be back in an hour, just time to make the salads and slice the cucumbers to adorn the salmon.

And then I heard a key in the door.

Heart beating, I thought it was a burglar. One of those types who stalks communions, knowing people will be at church and that it's the perfect moment to denude the house of any valuables. He'd probably already fleeced all the houses in the area.

'Hello?' I called out, my voice wobbling.

And then a man's voice. 'It's me. Ross.'

'Ross?' He'd made it, I thought, he was back to make everything right. I went out to the hall to chivvy him to get his arse into gear and down to the church. Ross was wearing his green Ireland rugby top, a pair of cream chinos and deck shoes and was shining with good health, a golden glow, a kind of religious statue of well-being.

'Hi, Roisín, how's it going?'

'Grand,' I said, briskly. 'If you hurry, you'll be able to catch them...'

But the golden glow was mixed with something else, I realised. And then it struck me. Guilt. He hadn't thought I was going to be there, he'd only come when he knew everyone was going to be out. His eye twitched as he tried to work out how he should play this.

'Yeah...' He hesitated.

'I'm just preparing the buffet,' I said. 'Shona asked me...'

'I'm just... well, have you spoken to Shona?'

'About what?' I asked innocently, trying to keep the reins on my rage which was in danger of galloping off.

'About... well, us. I'm staying in town for a bit... just sorting through a few things.'

'No, she hasn't said anything.'

'I mean, I love my family,' he said, as though he'd prepared a script, 'more than anything. But sometimes things get too much. And... well, work is very challenging... I just need to take some time out for me,' he rambled on. 'Just find out who I am, you know? I've forgotten who the real Ross is over the years. And I want to reacquaint myself with him...'

He waited for me to speak, and when I didn't, on he went.

'I read an amazing book called *Finding The Man Within*...' He laughed awkwardly. 'But that's what I'm doing, finding the man within, because we are all so defined and confined by the exterior – the careers, the family, one's good looks...' He laughed nervously. 'And all that, and I need to... I just need to... it's imperative that I...'

'Find the man within?' My incredulity had reached stratospheric levels.

'Exactly. I'm just going to...' He motioned upstairs. '... you know, collect some things... my... you know...' He started to walk sideways, like a crab, towards the stairs.

'Absolutely,' I said, not able to even smile back at him. 'I've got to finish the food. For the communion.'

In a few minutes he was back again, carrying a sports bag, a suit carrier and his golf clubs.

'Bye, Roisín,' he said, hovering at the kitchen door. 'Good to see you again. Say hi to your mum.' I crept into the living room, like a spy, standing far enough away from the window not to be seen but close enough to see Ross walking briskly across the drive. He hurried, like a speed walker in the Olympics, towards a low black sports car parked on the road, the passenger door open. After throwing the golf clubs into the back, he ducked his head, pulling his sports bag and suit carrier in with him, and slid into the seat just as the car revved off. The person driving had blonde hair, sunglasses pushed on the top of her head, a pair of expensive leggings, and Ross was smiling. It struck me that I had never seen him smile either. He looked utterly unlike himself, the man within was obviously nothing like the man without.

* * *

An hour or so later, I heard cars pull into the gravel driveway. And then doors slamming, voices... and then there was the rush of seemingly hundreds of people, more cars arriving, more voices and children running through the kitchen. I was in the middle of making the ham and mustard mini rolls when Shona appeared.

'I can't believe you've done all this,' she marvelled. 'I really can't.'

It did look impressive. I wasn't quite sure how I'd managed it all but I'd been focused and organised and kept it all relatively simple – apart from the hollandaise.

Shona went straight to the fridge and yanked open the door.

'Careful, don't dislodge the pavlovas!'

'They look amazing.' She took out a small can of gin and tonic and swigged it down in one. 'Don't say anything.' She wiped her mouth with the back of her hand. 'I'm only having a drop to keep the edge off. Just to keep myself topped up.' She sat on one of the high stools. 'Like oil in the car. And I promise I won't get drunk. I've got the girls to look after. Just take the edge off the day.'

There were voices in the hall as more guests began arriving.

'I'm going to have to go out there. I've already done three hours of it, being nice, nodding along, shaking hands and remembering husbands' names.' She stood up. 'I'm going to have one more tiny sip, and then that's it.' She opened the fridge, hiding behind the door again. It wasn't so much a sip as someone quenching their thirst after being lost in a desert. 'Okay, here we go,' she said. 'Showtime.' She turned and went into the hall. 'Hello!' I heard her say. 'Yes, it was a lovely service, I know! And so nice of you to come! Yes, such a special day...'

Kitty and Daisy rushed in, both flinging their arms around me and pressing their heads against my body. 'Dad didn't come.'

'He said he would.'

'He said he would try,' said Daisy. 'Which isn't the same.'

'I am sure he did try.' I kissed their heads where their neat plaits were already coming loose. 'But he just couldn't.' What a selfish man Ross was – first missing their birthday and now their communion. What next? Missing the rest of their lives? I thought of Dad, leaving us for Maxine and how for literally years afterwards I would wake each morning and know something wasn't right with my life and realise what it was – my Dad didn't live with us any more.

'Did you do your meringues?'

'And cake?'

'Take two meringues from the fridge now,' I told them, 'and I will make sure there are two more left just for you later tonight, okay?'

They began scoffing the meringues as though food hadn't passed their lips in weeks before running straight into the garden and up onto the bouncy castle in one giant leap.

'Hello, darling!' Dad was followed by Hugh. 'We're on the hunt for Ross's secret bottle of whiskey.' He put his finger to his lips. 'Don't tell Shona, will you, but do you have a notion where it might be? Or...' He turned to Hugh. 'We could wait for Ross to come home and ask him?'

Hugh shrugged. 'The man is proving to be as elusive as the Scarlet Pimpernel,' he said, 'so I think we are well within our rights to go on a search for his whiskey. He might keep it in one of the high cabinets. I gave him a very nice single malt for Christmas... that has to be somewhere... I've tried calling him but his phone is always on the blink.' He came over and stole a slice of cucumber, which I'd arranged in intricate scales over the salmon. 'Aren't you marvellous doing all this? You really should be a professional. I'd come to your restaurant.'

'Shouldn't she just?' Dad was opening and shutting cupboard doors, like an Irish farce. 'She's a modern Escoffier.'

'There was a time,' went on Hugh, 'that you wouldn't get on a plane if you knew the pilot was a woman and I remember some fellas at the golf club not being happy when we voted to allow in the girls. Not that they'd ever go back nowadays, but things change.'

Dad winked at me as I tried to look impassively polite.

'And there was the time that they brought in a woman chef,' droned on Hugh. 'Some of the fellas thought that was a step too far. Thought a woman couldn't cook a steak. Well, she showed them. Either it's not that hard, or she's a very good chef. Perfectly cooked. Medium rare. Nice bit of blood... exactly right.'

'Dad, can you help me bring all the food to the living room and put it on the table?' I asked. 'Here, you take the salmon. Hugh, would you mind taking these two bowls of salad? I'll carry in the tray.'

In the living room, the women were all dressed for a royal wedding, only more glammed up.

'He's on his way,' I heard Shona say. 'He had to go to the office to work on this case he's doing. But he doesn't want to miss anything. I'm sure he'll be here soon.' She briefly caught my eye again. 'Why don't we eat?' Shona went on. 'My sister, Roisín, has done the honours.'

'Oh, it looks fabulous!' Fionnuala had already grabbed a plate and a napkin. 'I do hope you have done that asparagus quiche you did before... and I can see your meringues! Oh good lord! Veronica! Veronica!' she called to someone. 'You must save space for the meringues. To die for!'

One of the super-powered women sidled up to me. 'Are you a professional caterer?' she said. 'Only I can't find anyone to do my Sorcha's communion in two weeks. I did have someone but she now says she's double-booked. Which I don't believe at all. I think someone swooped in and gazumped me.' She was eating one of the breadsticks wrapped in Parma ham. 'These are delicious. Would you do me? Please?' She lowered her voice. 'If you don't, it will be supermarket sausage rolls and packets of crisps. And that can't happen. They'll think we don't have the money.'

'You know,' said another woman, positioning herself between us, 'I need you to do my Joshua's communion. Saturday, two weeks. A small, select crowd, just family and friends. A few neighbours... colleagues, pals from the golf club, the girls from Pilates...'

The first woman rolled her eyes. 'Roisín is mine,' she said. 'I just asked her. We just shook on it, didn't we, Roisín?'

'But you will love our kitchen,' insisted the second woman. 'We've just had it done, and it's great for prep and... I don't know, whatever else you might do. We've got a wonderful collection of knives. My husband keeps buying them from Japan. Doesn't use them, of course, but insists on showing them to everyone. And our fridge is huge. Ideal for...'

The first woman had elbowed her way in front of her. 'Sorry, Anne-Marie,' she said, smiling. 'You'll have to find someone else. Or I heard that McDonald's delivers these days. Wouldn't that be nice? The kids would love it...'

'My children have never gone to McDonald's!' Anne-Marie was almost tearful. 'And you know it!'

'Actually...' I felt it was time to finally speak up. 'I can't do any more communions. I only did this for Shona because she's my sister. I'm really sorry and I've actually got my own supper club next week...'

'But we'd be paying you...'

'I know... it's just. I can't.'

Fionnuala grabbed my arm, pulling me away from the women who were now eyeing each other evilly.

'The food is delicious,' Fionnuala said. 'Much better than at Ronan and Amanda's the other week...' She nodded over at Ross's brother and his wife who were standing at the fireplace talking to another couple, a tiny girl in a tutu and a faux-fur gilet sat at their feet, chocolate smeared over her face. 'Pity Ross wasn't there.' She paused. 'He is my golden child.' She lowered her voice inadequately. 'Such a good son and wonderful husband. Missing his children's communion is a sacrifice he obviously feels he has to make in order to provide for his family.'

'Everything okay, Mum?' Ronan called from the fireplace. 'She can't stop telling everyone how I'm her favourite child. It's sad, really. But don't worry, Mum, Ross can't even be bothered to turn up at his own daughters' communion! If you're going to prioritise work... then...'

I backed away, slipping in beside Shona. 'Are you okay?' I said, in a low voice.

'What do you think?' she whispered back. 'This party has me teetering on the edge of insanity.' She closed her eyes for a moment. 'I never thought he'd do this, you know? I didn't think he would ever be that kind of man, or that I would be that kind of woman. But, of course, it turns out I am exactly that kind of woman. Why does he choose now to have some kind of midlife crisis? I can tell you this, my sympathy levels are very low. Very low indeed.' She shook her head. 'Oh, hello, Mary.' Her voice changed as one of the guests came up and put their hand on her arm. 'You are looking lovely, such a beautiful dress...'

Back in the kitchen, Ronan, Ross's brother, cornered me.

'So what's going on?' he demanded.

'What do you mean?'

'With Ross. I know something's up, because when I last spoke to him he was really nice and my brother is not renowned for being nice unless he has something to hide. What is it?'

'You should ask Shona,' I replied.

'I can't ask Shona, I don't want to upset her... especially if Golden Bollocks hasn't been behaving himself.'

'It's not like that at all,' I said. 'He's trying to find himself...'

Ronan laughed. 'That's hilarious.'

'He called in while I was cooking, earlier, I don't think he knew I was going to be here. He thought the house would be empty and he needed his golf clubs...'

'What an absolute arse.'

'And he told me he was taking time off to find the inner Ross.'

Ronan covered his face with both hands. 'My God, what a joke of a man. I mean, I know he's my brother and everything, and apparently I have to love him however unlovable he is, but my God, he's got the emotional intelligence of a gnat. Or a gnu. Whichever is the least emotionally intelligent.'

I thought of the blonde woman and Ross's hop, skip and jump to join her in the sports car.

'There was a woman...'

'Ross?' Ronan looked sceptical.

I nodded. 'He went off in a sports car, she was driving.'

'But he's a man who has an arse for a face and a microscopic penis...'

I nearly laughed. 'Please, I don't want to know...'

'I know, I remember when we were growing up and I'd catch a glimpse of the tiny thing, and I'd be like, when is it going to grow?'

'Please don't, I'm going to have pay for counselling to deal with this knowledge and you'll be liable.'

He grinned. 'Look, if there's anything I can do, if Shona wants me to talk some sense into him. I always thought she was too good for him, I really did. And now he's just proved it.'

He looked up as Mum came in. 'I thought I might have a nice cup of tea in here,' she said.

'He needs those golden bollocks removed with a rusty scalpel,' whispered Ronan, meaningfully, as he left the kitchen. 'Hello, Maggie,' he said in passing, 'lovely party, isn't it?'

'It really is.' Mum beamed, and then, when he was gone, said, 'Who needs their golden bollocks removed?'

I tried to think. 'He was talking about himself,' I flapped, 'he often does that, talks about himself in the third person. It's a thing he does...'

Mum looked confused. 'Poor Ronan,' she said, as a maul of children rolled past us from the garden and straight into the hall.

'As he would say himself!' I thought of Shona's gin and tonics in the fridge and contemplated downing one very quickly.

'I was just looking at a photo in the hall, the one with the three of us on the boat...' Mum said. *Shining Light...* do you remember?'

I nodded. 'Of course, it's a great photo. Even Shona is smiling...'

'I remember your father taking the photo right at the end of the day. We had sailed down to Arklow and back... it's funny how you can remember a feeling, they never disappear, even if the events themselves get a bit hazy.'

The maul of children now appeared from the hall and ran through the kitchen, screaming and shouting, and back to the garden. Mum took a forkful of cake. 'Oh, my good lord, this is magnificent. Now, when are you going to start selling these? You are definitely doing the supper club, aren't you?'

'It's next Saturday,' I said, feeling sick. 'It's too late to back out now.'

'Look, Roisín,' she said, putting down her mug of tea, and looking straight at me. 'So Brody has his book, what do you have for you? What are you passionate about?'

'Cooking,' I admitted.

She nodded. 'Passion, the thing that makes your heart sing...'

The morning had been incredibly satisfying and enjoyable. The sight of everything I had made gave me a feeling deep inside which was hard to describe, like a low-down feeling of warmth, something that was just for me.

'Courage and confidence, remember?' Mum went on.

'I'm going to try,' I said.

Mum smiled. 'Good. Because I think you are extremely talented. And we're all behind you, okay? Every step of the way. Now, cut me another slice of that cake. It's just too good.'

16

I called in on Harry on Sunday morning bearing leftovers from the communion.

'Ah! Roisín!' he unbolted his door, evidently pleased to see me. 'I've been dying to show you how much I have managed to do today. You've really inspired me to keep going.'

'I've brought you some leftover salmon,' I said. 'And a few other things...'

'Ah!' He looked approvingly in the Tupperware container. 'Anchovies and black olives. First time I had those were in Brindisi.'

'And some recipe books.' I held up my heavy tote bag which I had filled with some of my favourites – Nigel, Nigella, Jamie and Gordon. 'I thought you might be inspired...' There was a 'cooking for one' book as well and another on stews. I was thinking he could borrow my slow cooker and the stews he could make would keep him warm when the weather started getting colder. 'And for later, I've brought you a slice of my mum's apple tart.' I handed him the foil-wrapped package I had hidden from Brody and kept for Harry. 'I thought you might like it.'

'Ah, what a treat,' he said. 'My Nora used to make a great apple tart. Lots of cinnamon was her trick.' He took the bag from me. 'And bedtime reading, thank you. And borrowed so won't add to the piles in the house.'

He led me inside. 'Cyril was here earlier and he's being very strict. He has organised a van from the St Vincent de Paul to come and take some of my boxes. I am allowed to keep only five per cent of everything, he says...' I followed Harry along the brown and gold passage to the kitchen. 'If I waver for a second, he puts it in the donate pile. We're becoming quite an efficient team. You should see Cyril's house, neat as a pin, his old engineering books categorised using the Dewey decimal system, only three ornaments – all belonging to his late wife. Newspapers straight into the recycling after reading, tins washed and recycled, he doesn't buy anything unless it's to replace something and he's warned me never, ever to frequent a charity shop. For someone like me, he says, it's like an alcoholic entering a pub.'

'I can help this morning,' I offered. 'I could help you do the kitchen, and get you back using it again.'

The kitchen was still piled high as Harry and Cyril hadn't got that far yet. We had to get on with it, I thought, at least make a route from the sink to the cooker.

'Why don't you eat the salmon now?' I suggested. 'And I will start. I think...' – I looked around, dust catching in my throat, feeling suddenly overwhelmed – '... I think we just do as much as we can for two hours, and we can add to Cyril's collection for St Vincent de Paul.'

It turned out Harry needed and liked practically everything. It was all useful or would be handy some day. Other things were like lost treasure and were greeted with exclamations of joy. 'Oh, I'd forgotten about that,' he would say or, 'I've been looking for that for ages.' And he would hold the object – a falling-apart book, a cup without a saucer, a tea towel with 'Beautiful Bundoran' printed on it – as though they were precious artefacts. I was already filling up some more boxes for the charity shop, holding things up and Harry would hold up a thumb for 'keep' or down for 'donate'.

'I feel like a Roman emperor,' he told me.

'Whatever it takes just to get a bit of breathing room,' I said.

We worked on. It was close to midday when I finally felt we had done enough for one morning. The area around the cooker was now clear and clean and I had filled three boxes with things to give away and four refuse bags for things to throw out. We had managed to uncover the stove, the sink and the fridge – all of which I had scrubbed and scoured – so there was one little shiny Bermuda Triangle of hygiene where he could cook. I had cleaned out one of the cupboards and replaced some of the pans. The fridge, which was now bacteria-free, contained just milk.

'What do you think?'

'You've done a marvellous job,' Harry said.

'You'll be able to cook now,' I told him. 'And I can still drop round some meals.' I had to go home and start on lunch for Brody's parents, who were joining us for the afternoon.

'Thank you,' Harry said. 'But only if you can spare it and they'd only go to waste. I don't want your writer chap to go unfed.'

'Don't worry about him, he's in no peril of fading away.'

* * *

'Would you like a glass of wine, Sandra?' I asked. 'Or just some sparkling water?'

'She'll have both,' Jim answered. 'And so will I. We don't stand on ceremony, if you don't. Open the bottle we brought, it cost a packet, but we reckon you get what you pay for when it comes to wine. Not that I am what you might call a bon viveur, eh, Brian?' He reached over and squeezed Brody's knee. 'I mean, Brody!'

Brody winced in pain. 'No, Pa,' he deadpanned, 'a bon viveur you most definitely are not. And I wasn't aware that you and Ma drank wine. I thought you were both shandy drinkers.' He began to laugh to himself.

'What's so funny?' Jim asked.

Brody wiped away a tear of mirth. 'I was just remembering the time when I was telling you about *Tristram Shandy* – the novel! – and you asked me if it was a drink!'

His parents glanced at each other, while I quickly went into the kitchen and brought out the corkscrew and glasses. I had witnessed others reverting to being sulky teenagers in the presence of their parents before but Brody really took it to another level.

'So!' I sat back down again and filled everyone's glasses. 'This is lovely. We don't get to see enough of you two.'

'It's Jim's shifts,' said Sandra. 'He's always up at the crack of dawn and then does doubles...'

'It's the only way we can get away to Palma de Majorca every summer, it's our special place, isn't it, Sandra?'

She nodded. 'It's heaven, it's where we've been discovering wine. We like a nice glass of Spanish.'

'Not that we know anything about it,' said Jim, with a hasty look at Brody. 'Or food. But we eat really well there.'

'Lots of fish,' Sandra went on.

'And seafood.'

'Crispy squid,' said Sandra, 'that's my favourite.'

'Squid?' Brody awoke from his bored semi-slumber. 'You eating squid! That's hilarious.'

'Brody doesn't like seafood,' I explained. 'I tried to make clams—'

'Oh, I love those!' exclaimed Sandra.

'Delicious,' agreed Jim.

There was silence from Brody. 'Really? The three of you, ganging up on me? Really? Has it come to this?'

'No, no!' I tried to backpedal. 'I was only saying—'

Brody's eyes were icy slits. 'The three of you were having a laugh at my expense, just because I don't happen to like clams...'

'But Brian, they are delicious,' said Sandra. 'And Roisín was only saying that she liked them and we agreed.'

'But the three of you deliberately agreed about something that you all know I don't like.'

'It doesn't matter,' I said. 'We were just making conversation.'

'Drink your wine, Brian, it's very fruity.'

'Drink my wine!' spluttered Brody. 'Drink my wine! You want me inebriated so I don't feel ganged up upon or ignored or deliberately left out. My own parents.' He glared at them. 'My own wife.' He turned that look on me, the glower I had once found Heathcliffian verged now on the unsettling. 'And I'm Brody. Not Brian.'

'Of course, Brody,' soothed his mother. 'And anyway, I was going to tell you an amusing story about Roger.'

'Roger.' Brody looked at her. 'What makes you think I might be remotely interested in the comings, and preferably goings, of my loser younger brother?'

'It's just that he... well, he rang and told us about this man that came into the pub...' She turned to me. 'He works in the Happy Leprechaun in Melbourne. He loves it there. He's been promoted to bar manager and is bringing in a new lunchtime menu. Says he's going to introduce Australia to an Irish classic – cheese and onion crisp sandwiches!' She laughed. 'He's going to call it the vegetarian option!'

Jim and I joined in with the joke, but Brody looked furious.

'And that's your amusing story?' he asked.

'No,' Sandra insisted, sobering up quickly. 'I was just saying about the sandwich. He doesn't take himself seriously at all,' she said to me. 'Roger's always been a very easy person, hasn't he, Jim?'

'Stupid, more like,' said Brody. 'Or as we must call it these days, dyslexic.'

I couldn't quite reconnect the two Brodys – the seemingly sophisticated writer I had married with this truculent person who was jealous of his brother.

Sandra held out her empty glass. 'Could I trouble you for a top-up?' she said to me. 'I don't know how it disappeared so quickly.'

Jim also held out his glass. 'I wouldn't mind a refill, and then we can't stay too long. Don't like leaving the dog all day.' He and Sandra exchanged a meaningful glance.

'No problem at all,' I said, rushing into the kitchen to retrieve the bottle from the fridge and wondering if anyone would notice if I just stayed there and didn't return.

17

Little Eden Supper Club
Tomato bruschetta
Lasagne and garlic bread
Green salad
Tiramisu

'Right,' said Richard, 'everyone here? Jools, Roisín, Sam? So, the Little Eden Supper Club is on, thanks to Roisín. Thank you for meeting on a Monday evening. We only have five days until our inaugural night. We now need to discuss menus, drinks, decor...' He turned to Sam. 'What else?'

'It's all on the agenda...' Sam pointed at Richard's iPad screen. 'There...'

'Of course.' Richard smiled at Sam. 'Thank you.'

'Good God, Richard,' said Jools, reading the spreadsheet on her phone. 'I thought this was meant to be a fun charity event. What exactly are we organising? A presidential inauguration?'

'It's the same principle,' said Richard smoothly, signalling to Mike behind the bar. 'It's a Monday, shall we just have one drink? Bramble Spritz? Any objections?'

Jools and I looked at each and shrugged. 'None at all.'

'Four of your specials,' he addressed the waiter. 'And some pistachios.'

'Now we know what you're like in work. Efficient and scary.'

'I'm worse in the office. This is me being friendly.'

Sam nodded his head in agreement. 'He never smiles at work. His secret nickname is Magnum. Because he's ice-cold.'

Jools and I laughed, and even Richard was smiling, as though he liked being teased by Sam.

'Well, if it isn't a dark, handsome stranger!' Richard looked up at someone just behind me. 'Sam,' he was saying, 'this is Paddy, Jools's big brother.'

Richard was standing, hugging Paddy. 'It's so great to see you,' he was saying. 'You're back just in time to help us with the supper club.'

'Jools was telling me...' Paddy's voice was the same, deep and low.

'Paddy is a dab hand at DIY if you remember,' said Richard. 'Those shelves you built for me... what, eight years ago? Well, they're still standing.'

'At your service,' Paddy responded. 'Whatever I can do.' He looked straight at me and, it seemed, everything that had ever happened between us was known and acknowledged in that split second. 'Roisín... how's it going?'

'Don't be so unfriendly, Pads.' Jools gave him a push. 'Give Roisín a hug.' She shook her head. 'Sometimes it's like he's fifteen again, all socially awkward and weird.'

Paddy came over and gave me a hug. 'Good to see you again, Roisín,' he said. I'd forgotten how long his eyelashes were, black like his hair and contrasting with the ice-blue of his eyes. 'Still cycling?' he asked. We used to go on long rides. We'd follow the coast for miles and miles and stop off at various places for tea and cake or pints or whatever took our fancy. And then back to mine. It was one of those easy, uncomplicated relationships which you imagined only worked simply because it wasn't a real relationship. There was no pressure, no expectation, just being nice to each other. And spending a great deal of time in bed.

'Of course,' I replied. 'Still don't have a car.'

He smiled. 'Nor me. But I'm getting old, bones are creaking... too much damp in the joints, so I wouldn't mind a car...'

'How could you?'

He laughed. 'Yeah, well...'

'Paddy's bike shop is amazing,' said Jools. 'You all should go down and buy a new bike. Roisín, you deserve a nice, new shiny one, and Richard, you just get off your arse and start moving!'

'I move enough, so the shop is going well?'

Paddy nodded. 'It's going grand, still getting in deliveries of different bikes. A few racing bikes, some really nice Danish cargo bikes for families.'

I'd forgotten how incredibly relaxed he always was as he slipped into the chair Richard pulled out for him. It was good to see him, I realised, and he seemed to feel the same as he looked across at me and smiled.

'So, you can help with the supper club, Paddy?' Richard was saying, as the waiter brought four more drinks. 'And eat some of the nuts, keep your strength up. You're the brawn of the operation.'

Paddy laughed, reaching across the table to take a handful of nuts, the hair on his arms glinting in the late evening sun. 'Didn't realise I was brawny.'

'Oh, you're an ideal combination of both brains and brawn,' said Richard. 'Just like myself. Although, I think I err on the side of brawn to brains.'

Sam laughed.

'I might get a friend of mine involved as well.' Paddy smiled. 'Erik. He's working in Dublin for a few months. Is that okay?'

Richard nodded. 'The more the merrier, but next to the food. Roisín? So, starters,' he went on. 'What have you decided?'

I had decided that I was going for an easy menu, one which no one would complain about and one which wouldn't expose my lack of professionalism or talent. I'd gone for simple crowd-pleasers, things that wouldn't be too taxing on me, but were always popular. Also, it had been our favourite when we were at college. Every now and then – normally at the beginning of term when we felt flush with cash after our holiday jobs, we would splash out and go to Casa Italia in town, the kind of Italian with pepper grinders the size of toddlers and Parmesan cheese which would be sprinkled over your plate like snow. Or foot dandruff, as Richard used to call it.

'Tomato bruschetta to start with.'

'Bruschetta?' Richard looked shocked. 'As in tomatoes on toast?'

'Everyone likes it,' I said. 'It's nice.'

'Yes, it's nice, but people are paying for it. It has to be really good.'

Jools backed me up. 'Roisín's bruschetta is amazing, she made it for my birthday last year. And you said it was the best meal you'd had in ages.'

'And that's because it was, but I'd just spent the previous six weeks in Brussels and was fed up of haute fecking cuisine... but don't you think we need to haute it up a bit?' He turned to Sam. 'What do you think?'

'I love bruschetta.' Sam shrugged.

'Who doesn't love bruschetta?' Paddy joined in.

Richard turned back to me, defeated. 'Okay, bruschetta for starters. Main course?'

'Lasagne.'

'Lasagne?' Richard looked as though he'd just sat on an electrified fence. 'Who eats lasagne these days?'

'I do, now I am free of Darren and back on the carbs.'

'Me too,' agreed Paddy. 'Could eat lasagne every day of my life.'

'I thought everyone liked lasagne.' I was rapidly losing faith in myself and my menu.

'But it's lasagne... it's not exactly special, does anyone actually like lasagne these days?' Richard wondered. 'When was the last time anyone ordered it?'

'I order it all the time, except it's never on menus any more.'

'I rest my case.'

'It definitely hasn't gone out of fashion,' said Paddy.

'Oh, it has, it definitely has.'

'Lasagne,' said Paddy, 'is a retro classic'.

'A retro classic,' repeated Richard, slowly. 'A retro classic is something like steak au poivre or crème caramel... not canteen slop.'

'Richard!' exclaimed Jools. 'Come on... I remember you when you thought Super Noodles were a balanced meal.'

'True, true,' he admitted. 'I still hanker for them from time to time, usually when I've had too much corporate wining and dining.' He sighed. 'It's just that I want us to do something really good and I know you can do it, Roisín. What about dessert? Although I think I know what's coming...'

'Tiramisu.' I knew what he was going to say.

'I knew it,' he said. 'Okay, so the meal is unambitious. But nice... enough. I get it, Roisín, I really do. I just want you to push yourself...'

'I thought this was about raising money for charity?'

'But Roisín,' he sighed. 'I know you are better than this.'

'It's really scary cooking for strangers,' I admitted. 'I feel under pressure and out there. Everyone will be judging me and... I'm terrified.'

'Oh Roisín!' Richard grabbed me, pulling me towards him and throwing his arm around me. 'Being scared is normal... you just have to get used to being scared. Sam knows to bring me my chamomile tea at 3 p.m. because that's when I start losing the confidence I have built up all day. It's like it all starts to leach out and I have to refocus and breathe deeply to keep it in.'

'It's scarier for me if I don't bring the tea,' Sam volunteered, making Richard smile.

'Sometimes I think I want to run back home to Dingle,' Richard sighed, 'I want to keep chickens and an apple orchard, and make my own cider to sell in the market every Saturday. But I am even more scared to do that.'

'I'm scared too,' said Jools. 'Of everything. My clients are terrifying, always asking me about how they can get rid of fat in places where they should have fat and wanting me to tell them off all the time, as though they want me to be this weird fat-busting dominatrix telling them if they've been bad or good. And then they all want 5.30 a.m. sessions or 10 p.m. sessions and I am too scared to say no. And I'm scared I will never meet a nice man, one who doesn't measure his food in macros or keeps looking at himself in mirrors. Just someone nice and normal. Is that too much to ask?'

We all shook our heads and I reached out and held Jools's hand.

'I'm terrified of losing my apartment and having to go home,' said Sam, 'back to my parents. I can barely afford the rent and the landlord keeps putting it up.'

Richard looked at him. 'Why didn't you tell me?'

Sam shrugged.

'Paddy, what about you?' Jools asked. 'He's probably scared that one day he will have to settle down and be sensible and stop his bachelor lifestyle.'

Paddy met my eye for a second. 'No, not that, but other things, like tarantulas...' He gave a laugh. 'And being stuck in a lift, that kind of thing.'

I wished I could tell them I was scared that they might be proved right and that I now realised I was married to a complete stranger.

Richard picked up his Bramble Spritz. 'Here's to facing our fears – from tarantulas to horrible clients and to the Little Eden Supper Club!'

* * *

Later, when we had all said goodbye, I went to the bike rack to unlock my bike. Paddy was just behind me.

'Congratulations, by the way, on your marriage,' he said. 'To Brody Brady. I used to read his column.'

'Thanks.'

'At least one of us managed it.' He gave me a look, one eyebrow raised.

'Getting married? It wasn't that difficult...'

'It's been done before...' He laughed. 'But seriously, congratulations. I hope you are deliriously happy and all that.'

'Oh, we are,' I said. 'We're the Beyoncé and Jay-Z of Sandycove. Crazy in love.'

He laughed again. 'I should hope so. And I just wanted to say that it's nice to see you.' He smiled, and for a moment we were back where we had been, that smile before we'd go home together.

'You too,' I said.

'I was hoping that we'd be friends...'

'We are!'

'You know what I mean... after everything... it doesn't always work.'

'Well, we can make sure it does.'

He crouched down beside me, unlocking his bike. That summer, when we couldn't keep our hands off each other, was like a long-ago mirage.

'So, what's cycling in Dublin like after Copenhagen?' I asked, needing to change the subject.

'Hair-raising, I had forgotten that you take your life in your hands every time you get on a bike here.' When Paddy had worked for a tech company in Dublin, he'd been miserable, living for the weekends. He used to talk to me about feeling depressed and how the only thing that kept him sane was cycling. He looked happier and healthier than I had ever seen him, tanned, his hair lightened. He'd been offered a chance to go to Copenhagen, and he'd taken it. For the first time, I saw he'd been right to go. I stood back, holding my bike, ready to leave.

'You'll have to come into my shop,' he said, 'upgrade your bike.'

'Upgrade?' I looked at my scratched, slightly bashed bicycle. The handlebars were as soft as buttery leather, the saddle like sitting on a cushion. It never felt like riding or work, even up the steepest of hills. 'Never. It's going to carry me into my dotage.'

'We'll have to get you one of those cargo bikes. Find someone who will cycle you around.'

Again, for the splittest-second, we looked at each other. Was he remembering that night I sat on his crossbar as he pedalled through the lamplit streets, his breath on my neck, his left hand holding mine?

'So, what's your husband writing?'

'A novel,' I hoped my voice was steady. 'He's going to finish it in a few weeks. Obviously changes and edits will have to be done but the deadline is so close.'

Paddy shook his head. 'Wow, impressive. What's it about?'

'Um...' I tried to remember. 'An old farmer called Seamus...'

He waited for me to say more. 'And...?'

'And that's it. Not much happens. There was a storm which brought down an old tree, I think, and there was the tractor part that required a trip into Cavan Town... and that's it, really.'

Paddy nodded. 'It sounds very deep and intellectual.'

'It is, I think,' I said. 'Brody says it's a meditation on existentialism.'

'I couldn't have put it better myself,' said Paddy. 'Which is why he's the writer.' He put his helmet on, strapping it under his chin. 'Looking forward to this supper club thing. See you soon, Roisín.'

* * *

Brody was in front of the television when I arrived home and I went to kiss him on the top of his balding head. He hadn't been exactly thickly thatched when we met but he'd lost hair at an alarming rate ever since, like a stop-motion film of a receding hairline. The stress of the novel was really taking its toll. His beard, however, was having the opposite issue and Brody was in danger of tipping over from hipster woodcutter to mad man of the forest.

'Everything all right?'

He looked up at me, puzzled. 'Yes, why? Am I not allowed to watch television?'

'Sorry... it's just that... you don't normally.'

'I am trying to write a novel and you think I am just watching television. God, you'd think my wife would understand what I was attempting.' He shook his head in total bewilderment. I sat down beside him on the sofa. It was just nice that he was downstairs instead of being in the spare room. 'It's research.'

Brody used to behave as though I was the perfect person for him. The morning after Richard's party, he rang me about the room and arranged to come and see it. When we went for a drink, which turned into a few, he told me that he'd never met someone like me before, someone who understood him. His feelings seemed to intensify over the following weeks and months: he told me he loved me within two weeks, he hated me going out without him, he would call me when I was in work saying how much he missed me and hated being away from me. It was like a thunderstorm of love, pelting down, and the only thing I could do was throw away my umbrella and embrace the cloudburst.

Except, sometimes I couldn't quite remember that Brody, the one who said he missed me so much while I was at work that he wrote my name over and over again in his notepad. Or the Brody who said I was the most intelligent person he'd ever met, and his equal. But now Brody didn't seem that into me, as though I was disappointing to him, as though I wasn't quite the perfect woman he thought I was.

'By the way,' said Brody. 'There's no food in the house any more. For my lunch. I get nibbly around midday and there always used to be left-overs, and now there's nothing. I'm starving all day.'

'I've been taking them to Harry.'

'Who?'

'Harry Daly. Our neighbour.'

'And why are you feeding him?'

'I've been helping him tidy up, that kind of thing, and just bringing him a plate of food every now and then. Not every night, but there's always cheese and crackers in the fridge for you.'

Brody was looking at me as though I'd gone mad. 'Cheese and crackers?' His face was almost pulsating, there was a throbbing in his temple. 'I tell you what's crackers, it's you! I can't exist on cheese and crackers! They are what children have for their packed lunches. You'll have to stop feeding random strangers and start feeding your husband!'

I was about to respond when I noticed something move under the cushion between his head and the arm of the sofa.

'Is that Fyodor?' I asked. 'Is Fyodor out of his cage?'

'He feels trapped in there. He likes to stretch his legs.'

'He stretches them on that hamster wheel of his.' I stood up, horrified. 'He stretches them for hours at a time, all night long!'

'It's Fyodor who likes to watch television,' he said, 'not me.' He reached behind him and pulled out Fyodor. 'There we go, little fella, you relax and enjoy some TV, while Roisín makes us a snack.'

For a moment I didn't know what to say. Was he expecting me to make dinner for the two of them, even though Fyodor was admittedly very low maintenance, just a handful of his special mix and the odd cardboard toilet roll thrown into the cage? But it was the entitlement. Being made food, being prepared a dinner was a privilege... Brody was like a king demanding his victuals. But as I didn't want an argument and we were only weeks away from the goal, I stood up. 'Coming right up!' I said, smiling.

Brody kept his eyes on the television, only Fyodor looked at me. And I wasn't quite sure if there was an apologetic look on his face as though he empathised.

18

It was Wednesday morning and I stared out of my office window across the sea remembering *Shining Light*, Dad's old boat. I could still feel the wet hair clinging to our faces, salt on our lips, hands numb with cold, and then the feeling of that moment before the wind filled the sail and *Shining Light* turned, cutting through the waves. Dad would stand at the prow, facing into the wind, like a colossus, shouting out instructions and, when Shona or I couldn't quite muster the strength, he'd bound towards us and pull on the rope effortlessly, and the boat would begin to turn, the snap as the sail filled and away we whooshed. I would feel invincible on those days, hands were raw and sore, my feet soaked through, but there was a sense that the three of us – Dad, Shona and I – could do anything.

Saoirse came up to me. 'Have you started on the planning yet?' she said. 'Because I would say not to waste your time, everyone says it's impossible. JP has only given it to you just to keep you busy and tick that box...'

'I know, I don't expect to complete it.'

'It's funny that he doesn't trust you with a proper planning application. Anyone would assume he didn't think you were up to it.'

Dermot looked up. 'Saoirse, the planning for the Hall needs to be completed one way or another. If Roisín wasn't doing it, either Frank or myself would have to give it one more go. And we're mentally deranged by the thing, so we can't.'

'I wouldn't bother, if I was you,' said Saoirse. 'Just throw the file in the bin.' She gave me a dead-eyed look and walked away.

I had to give it a go and I spent the rest of the morning reading the whole file, everything from the initial plan eight years earlier, to each architectural drawing, to every change made after every complaint from a local resident or concerned citizen. As JP often reminded us, our job was to facilitate the evolution of the area, to preserve the integrity of the area and also to look to the future. Whatever concerned citizens and environmental groups believed, sometimes buildings weren't fit for purpose.

The old half-timbered building stood on waste ground and behind it was a derelict, boarded-up amusement arcade. There was report after report from engineers and health and safety officers stating that the hall should be condemned and that it was beyond saving. After spending a century facing bravely into the storms whipping in from the Irish Sea, the walls had so much rising damp and brick rot that it was slowly crumbling like a forgotten wedding cake. The hall had fallen into the council's owner-ship and was in daily use by a group who made lunches for the commu-nity. Reading the report, the council were desperate to get it off their hands as the building was in breach of all health and safety rules and it would take too long and too much money to bring it up to modern-day standards.

I remembered from my Irish dancing days the water which dripped into carefully placed buckets, pigeons flapping against the rafters, mice squeaking and scurrying, the bones of the building creaking and swaying in the wind whipped up from the sea. In other words, it was an unheated, rat- and woodworm-infested pile, full of a hundred years of dust and permeated by the smell of damp and decay. I suspected Lady Immaculate Hall was now beyond restoration.

The initial developers had finally given up on trying to make any money on the site, and it had since been sold on to another company and then to another. The current developer – MoMo – had plans to demolish it and create a retail and mixed-use 'experience'. According to the proposal, there would be benches, picnic areas, a playground, shops and restaurants, all open to the sky. It looked very attractive.

In the file, I could see that Frank, to try and save the building, had worked out how much it would cost to bring Lady Immaculate Hall up to modern-day standards, and the sums were eye-watering. The bill would fall to the council because the developers weren't interested in paying it.

I read on. There was a Save The Hall group who had consistently written to the council, objecting to the Hall's proposed demolition. There were letters, emails and a petition with thousands of signatures. Many planning applications were difficult, but this looked like chaos.

'So, you've been reading the Lady Immaculate Hall application?' Dermot called over.

'Yes, it's impenetrable,' I said. 'I can see why it's reached this impasse.'

'You have nothing to lose.' He paused. 'Except your sanity. It's like a constantly renegotiated war. And just when you have got both sides to agree after months and months of minuscule changes and infinitesimal compromises and peace is finally declared, you realise someone else has started another bun fight somewhere else. And on it goes, the hamster wheel of planning.'

'Don't mention hamsters,' I said.

He laughed. 'Why?'

'We have somehow acquired one.' That morning, I had woken to find Fyodor was again on the loose and the door of his cage was wide open. For a moment, I was torn between being concerned for Fyodor's fate against the vicious cat two doors up and being relieved that he was finally gone. But then I heard a scratching sound from behind the fridge and I tempted him out with sunflower seeds. When his twitchy whiskers peeked out, I managed to scoop him up and imprisoned him once again. 'I'm sorry about this, Fyodor,' I had said. 'It's not much of a life being locked away like this. But at least you're safe from the cat at number thirteen.'

'I don't understand,' Dermot was saying, 'how a hamster can just be acquired. I can imagine acquiring a hedgehog or a stray cat, but hamsters aren't the type to just turn up.'

'This was premeditated, just not by me. Anyway, you were giving me the benefit of your wisdom regarding planning.'

He nodded. 'The most important thing to remember,' went on Dermot, 'is that it is just a game. Never get embroiled on any personal level because

that is where madness lies. Stay away from the developers and the objectors, don't meet them, don't talk to them. Don't listen to their sob stories
about money lost, about culture destroyed, whatever side they are on, don't
get involved. And the same goes for any objectors. If they sniff even a whiff
of weakness you will be destroyed by them. Communicate with everyone
only through email.' He turned to Frank. 'What do you think of my pearls
of professional wisdom, Frankie?'

Frank nodded. 'It's one of the reasons I have no friends,' he said. 'You
never know who might be looking for a favour to get their planning
through or their extension approved. Trust no one.'

'Exactly.' Dermot sat back, satisfied. 'You need to be an ice-blooded
assassin. Unemotional, get the job done and get out. Frank and I are relationship lepers. Working here has made us suspicious. I once went out
with a woman for three months. Turns out, she was only with me because
she wanted to build a house for her mother in her back garden.'

Saoirse was walking past my desk. 'The reason why you are still single,'
she said to Dermot, 'is because you have no discernible personality and a
face which looks like a plastic toy which has melted on a radiator.'

Dermot grinned. 'And that, Saoirse, is exactly the look I'm going for.
Melted toy. Success at last.'

* * *

It was only a few minutes' walk along the seafront, and in the park, in front
of the Hall, the farmer's market was in full flow. I stopped at the fruit and
veg stall, looking at the amazingly large strawberries.

'Wexford,' said the man behind the table, with hands that were rough
and weather-beaten like a pair of garden gloves. 'The best in the world...
take one.' His face reminded me of someone, I thought, in the way it
suddenly opened into a smile and crinkled around the eyes.

'They taste amazing,' I said. 'So sugary.'

'We grow Sweet Delight, you can't beat them. And we've got green
beans. The sweetcorn were only picked yesterday. We've also got the best
tomatoes.'

I thought of the supper club. Maybe he would supply us for the following three weeks? According to daily texts from Richard, ticket sales were going well. My hopes of no tickets being sold at all – and therefore not having to go ahead with the bloody thing – were fading fast.

Moving closer, my feet kicked a cardboard box under the cloth-covered table. I kneeled down and there in a wooden crate, in a nest made out of a fleece blanket, was a tiny chihuahua. She was blind in one eye, an ear was gone, her fur matted and her nose almost off-centre. She had a resigned look on her face, as though she knew she wasn't the kind of dog anyone would want. She looked like a wise little soul, a dog too good for this world.

'That's Foxy,' said the man. 'No one wants Foxy. She's an old dog, too small and... well, you might say she wouldn't win the Rose of Tralee. She's a little homely-looking.'

Foxy gazed back at me. 'You'll find someone soon,' I said. 'Someone who can look after you, okay?' I stroked her behind the ears, and she turned her head to give my hand a lick as though she understood. 'She's a sweetheart,' I said to the man.

'She is that indeed,' he said. 'You wouldn't be tempted? No?'

'I can't,' I said. 'I'm at work all day and my husband... well, he hates dogs.'

'Hates dogs?' The man tried to absorb this bombshell. 'As in... not like them? At all? Not even a little bit? Hate is a very strong word to use about dogs.'

'He lived next door to a Jack Russell,' I explained, 'when he was a child, and it used to growl at him every time he walked past.'

'Well, there you go then,' he said, as if that explained everything. 'That little Jack knew he was a foe rather than a friend and was just telling him that he had him sussed. I suppose not everyone is a dog person.'

'He's actually a hamster person.'

The man laughed. 'Well, that's a first. I didn't know there was such a thing.' He chuckled to himself. 'A hamster person... that's a good one.' He looked down at the box. 'Sorry, Foxy. It's not going to be today. Dogs are like children,' he said to me, 'they need looking after. Now, don't tell me your husband doesn't want one of those either?' He laughed again.

'A child? Well...' Having a baby was definitely part of my life plan but children, like everything else, were off the table until the book was done. And I had to convince Brody that he didn't hate babies after all. 'I'm hoping he might,' I said. 'Soon.'

'There's no soon, there's only now. The time we wait for is already here. My six children are all grown and flown. Two in the business. Rachel in the office, doing all the paperwork, Sarah in the polytunnels with me.' He held out a hand. 'Gerry,' he said.

'Roisín.' I smiled at him. 'I might order something for a pop-up restaurant I'm having.'

He nodded. 'Call Rachel, my daughter.' He handed me a card. 'She'll do it all and I can drop whatever you need to wherever you need it.'

'Thanks, Gerry.' I slipped the card into my bag and turned around to walk towards Lady Immaculate Hall.

* * *

The Hall was even shabbier than I remembered. Shrubbery grew out of the gutters, every window seemed to be broken or cracked and the brickwork was crumbling. One sudden gust of wind and the whole thing looked in danger of keeling over.

'Well, hello there, Roisín!'

I looked around to see Marian Yeats, my old Irish dancing teacher, walking up the driveway with another woman. 'Roisín has got married, she said, to... let me think? Is he a writer?'

I nodded.

'Brody Brady!' exclaimed Marian. 'I remember now. Sheila, he's the one who wrote those columns in the *Irish Times* about men...'

The other woman nodded. 'Ah...' She was unimpressed. 'I remember.'

'And he's writing a novel, isn't he?' went on Marian. 'He'll have to write one about Lady Immaculate Hall and everyone who works in her...'

'Maybe,' I said, thinking that an inanimate building might have more life in it than poor Seamus the farmer.

'So you saw the notice, yes?' Marian continued. 'Come on, we'll be late. Sheila and I were at a meeting... we don't normally scoot up at this time.'

'What notice?'

'In the *Sandycove Gazette* looking for volunteers,' said Marian, in that brisk way of hers. 'You can help us serve lunch.' Marian wasn't the kind of woman to whom it was easy to say no to and I recalled those Irish dancing classes where she'd have you leaping about for the full hour and then rope you into putting away all the chairs at the end. We'd all be exhausted.

I followed her and Sheila into the Hall, through the front entrance, with its heavy doors held open by old rusty weights. Large wisps of cobwebs hung from the porch roof beside the bare bulb of a light. Immediately, I was brought back to being eight again and the music from the old piano as we took our places in the line, ready to fling our legs in the air, our arms at our sides.

'You remember the Hall, don't you, Roisín?' Marian was asking, as she walked swiftly on. 'It's a community concern now, after the nuns handed it over when they gave up on it. And you know the religious orders don't give up on many things, except for women's rights... isn't that so, Sheila?'

'It certainly is,' Sheila agreed, with a determined nod. Ahead of us, through the next set of doors, I could hear the soaring sound of people's voices.

'They should have repaired the roof and fixed the floors and installed a new heating system. But they cut their losses. We inhabit it now,' Marian went on.

'Squatters' rights,' said Sheila, with a nod. 'We're here to stay, aren't we, Marian?'

'We certainly are.' They exchanged a purposeful look.

Marian pushed open the door and unleashed a tsunami of sound. People of all ages, from women in saris and whole families in African-print dresses, to old, white-haired ladies in hand-knitted cardigans, were all sitting on four long tables running the length of the room. At the far end, there was a large serving hatch leading to the kitchen and in the far corner an older man played the old piano, the one which Marian had once played during the dance lessons.

'Who are all these people?' I asked Marian. I should have left then. I should have declared my interest in the Hall but I didn't, I stayed.

'The community, of course,' she shouted over the voices, walking straight to the kitchen. 'Senior citizens, brand-new residents, mothers, grandfathers, babies... anyone is welcome. Come with a good heart, that's what we say, and stay for a good lunch. Somehow, we've been providing lunch every weekday for the last three years. Food, Roisín, is about love. Did you know that? If you cook for someone, then you must cook it with love, and that love will make its way to the person who eats your food.'

We slipped in through the side door and into the kitchen. 'Quick, pinnies on,' Marian shouted. 'Come on, we'll start serving.'

Before I knew it, Sheila was tying an apron around me and I was standing behind a counter with plates thrust in my direction as I served out dhal, rice and naan breads. Marian knew everyone by name and kept up a running commentary. 'How's the back, Johnny? Good, good... glad to hear the Pilates is working. Ah, Mr Ahmad, you look well... putting a little weight on at long last. Hello, Bashir, how is your wife? Is she feeling better?'

After twenty minutes everyone had been served and we began clearing away the serving trays. 'Dessert next,' said Marian. 'We do a proper old-fashioned Irish pudding, apple crumble always goes down well...'

'And a tray bake,' Sheila added. 'The tray bakes always go down well... with a cup of tea.'

'Or even a flapjack, it never fails to surprise me how well a flapjack goes down with everyone. No one ever says no.'

I looked up at the clock, realising it was time for me to go back to work. 'I've got to head off, I'll be back tomorrow,' I said without thinking, untying my apron, half in a daze.

'Glad you came?' Marian asked, walking me to the kitchen door.

I nodded. Except I knew that no one could find out about this back at the office. This must be the Save The Hall crowd, the other side to the developers. By even being here, and particularly returning, I was veering towards partiality, the one thing I knew I shouldn't do. But maybe there was no harm in it as long as I remained steely-eyed and clear of head.

'What is it you work at?' asked Sheila, coming over.

'I'm in the—'

'Your mother mentioned the council,' said Marian. 'That's handy for here. You can run along the seafront and you won't have missed much.'

'What department?' Sheila was obviously very much a details person.

'Just general departments, just very... you know... nothing specific... just general.'

Sheila fixed me for a moment with a gaze that was not only steely but all-seeing. 'Well, say hello to everyone at the council, I used to be in Parks once upon a time.'

'Will do,' I said, breaking into a jog across the dusty woodblock herringbone floor and again into the outside world, my heart beating hard and fast in my chest. My first day as a planner and I had already taken sides on the longest-running planning application in Sandycove history. But the feeling that I wanted to volunteer with the community lunch again was bigger than anything. I just had to make sure that I remained impartial. And anyway, no one was ever going to find out.

19

'Have you eaten?' I asked Harry, standing on his doorstep, holding up a plate covered in foil. 'I have quiche and potato salad.'

'I was just about to have something, all right,' he replied. 'Quiche sounds like a treat.'

I had been popping in to see Harry most evenings, helping him fill a box or two, and chatting about food. 'How's everything going?' I asked, following him into the house. 'How have you been getting on?'

'Cyril is going great guns,' he said. 'They filled a whole van today and my sitting room is looking very nice. Cyril is very handy with the hoover, gave it a going over and then we had a cup of tea in the front room admiring our work. And I've been reading those books you lent me, a few nice things in there. I'm not sure if I am quite up to them, but it's very interesting, anyway.'

'You could give one or two a try,' I suggested.

He nodded. 'I might, but it's very kind of you to lend them to me, nonetheless.'

He sat at the kitchen table, peeled off the tin foil and began to eat. 'Exquisite,' he said. 'Absolutely delicious. Melt in the mouth. What's in the potato salad? Capers? A little bit of horseradish? Scallions?'

'Exactly,' I smiled, 'and Dijon mustard.'

'Dijon! Of course!' He carried on eating, his eyes closed. 'Heavenly.'

The kitchen was looking very clean, I noticed, but there was still only the small saucepan drying on the draining board. I suspected he was still on the baked-bean diet and I was determined to either keep feeding him or help him rediscover his love of cooking.

'How are your two nieces?' he asked.

'They are fine,' I said. 'Full of life... I love them so much.' I had been thinking of them pretty much constantly since their communion. They must have suspected all was not well between Shona and Ross and it must have been such a confusing time for them. I'd texted Shona earlier to see how she was and she had just responded:

Still drinking gin. No change to report xxx

If things deteriorated, I worried, then Daisy and Kitty would be in the same position as Shona and I had been in all those years ago. I hoped Ross would come to his senses and come home before the marriage became irretrievable.

'We would have liked to have children,' Harry was saying. 'Nora was particularly sad about it, but we tried to be philosophical. Maybe God had other plans for us, we used to say. Not that I'm a believer. Never have been. But you do try and find a reason for everything. Nora was a librarian by then, and she used to organise lovely things for the children, book readings and colouring competitions and Christmas parties, that kind of thing. She would have made a lovely mother.' He stood to wash the plate at the sink. 'You don't always choose what happens to you in life, but you should always choose who you spend your time with. I chose well with Nora. And there was a time when I made a decision to leave an old life behind. It was hard, but it had to be done and if I hadn't, I would never have had the courage to join the navy or even to ask Nora to have dinner with me that first time.'

'You were very brave,' I said, wondering what he was referring to but not wanting to pry.

'Ah, well... sometimes it's sink or swim. I chose to swim. But I brought with me a photograph of my mother... she was a great cook... before she was unwell, obviously. But I remember being knee-high to a grasshopper and eating her brown bread with blackberry jam and she'd always give me the heel with extra butter because I was the youngest. But that was before she went into hospital.'

'What was wrong with her?'

'We weren't told anything. My father didn't think my brothers and I were important enough to tell the truth to. But it's only as a grown-up I was able to do a bit of research. Nora helped me and I went into the library in Sandycove and I asked the very nice woman behind the counter did she know anything about the Pigeon House hospital. Anyway, she tapped away at the big computer in front of her and said that she thought it might have been a place for those with tuberculosis. And then...' – he tapped his head – 'it all fell into place.'

'Had you not been told anything?'

'Not a word,' he said. 'But the revelation was like a final piece in the jigsaw. Before, you see, I couldn't understand why Mam stayed away for so long. My older brother told me once that she left when I was two but he didn't know why either. And my father...' Harry sat down at the table and looked up at me. 'He was a bully. I just thought that was how fathers were meant to be. Big voices, terrifying, could reduce you to the size of a flea with just a look. We had to be clean and tidy. We couldn't take up any space at all. Us three boys shared a bed, even though there was another bedroom. And during the day we fended for ourselves. Mam died and we weren't even told that she had, it was just something that the woman in the local shop said. "I'm sorry for your loss," she said. And I said what loss and she said, your mother. And then she said another strange thing, "You poor boys, living with him." And she gave us all currant buns. Which we ate, and enjoyed, but none of it made much sense at the time. By the time I was sixteen I'd given up on the world, or rather, I felt as though the world had given up on me. I had been... silly to say it now, but I really felt as though I had been abandoned. And even though I knew, deep down, my mother wouldn't have gone unless she had to, that feeling doesn't really leave you.'

And it was when my brothers had already left home, I saw a piece in the *Irish Press* about joining the Merchant Navy. My hands shook as I put the money in the slot on the old telephone on the village Main Street and asked what I had to do. And that was it. They said, yes, and I escaped. That's what I meant about choosing who and who not to spend one's life with. I left with just a small bag – I had nothing to pack anyway and nothing to leave behind – and I left while it was still dark. I will never forget that feeling, walking along the road from my father's house to get to the bus stop which would take me to the recruiting station. The birds were up already. First the blackbirds. Then I heard a robin. And then the wren. I'd been listening to these birds all my life, but this morning, they were different. They were sending me on my way, saying farewell. They gave me strength. I was so scared that my father would find me and pull me back, you see. He could do that. But on I went, legs along with my hands, shaking. And I walked to the next bus stop along – another four miles away – just to give myself even more distance, and waited for the bus.'

'I'm glad you got away,' I said.

He nodded. 'So am I, so am I. The navy gave me confidence to be true to myself, and then meeting Nora taught me about love. But...' He stopped.

'What?'

'I sometimes wonder why I have accumulated so much. Some people drink, some smoke... and I bring things home. I watched a programme on the television once and it said it can relate to things in one's past.'

'You'll have to ask that nice woman in the library. See if she can google something.'

'Google what?'

'It just means search on the internet,' I said. 'But why do you think you like to accumulate?'

He shrugged. 'I'm not good at letting go.' From the inner pocket of his brown suit jacket, he took out a wallet. His bony fingers pulled out two small, creased photographs. One was a side-profile of a woman looking away from the camera, her face serious.

'That's my mother,' he said. 'It was the only thing I took from the house. It was kept in a book and my brothers and I would look at it whenever we could. Anyway, when I left, I stole it.'

'She's beautiful.' I stared at her face, wishing her story had ended differently.

'She was my mam, I have no memory of her. Nothing. No hand-holding, or kissing or tucking me in bed. And that day I left the house, birds singing, all that, and I caught the bus, there was just me in the world. Until I met Nora.' He gave a tiny nod with his head. 'I was a lucky man that day.'

20

On Friday afternoon, Saoirse came over to my desk. It was the day before the first supper club and I had lists of everything, my timings worked out and all the food ordered. Gerry from the market stall was delivering most of it first thing in the morning.

'Where are you going for lunch lately?' she demanded. 'You never usually leave the office and you've been heading out every day.'

'It's the summer.' My cheeks felt hot. 'It's nice to get some fresh air.' I'd been to the Hall every day that week, rushing in, putting on my apron and serving food and helping with the clearing up, and then going back to work.

'Saoirse?' Dermot looked up. 'I thought you were snowed under? Weren't you complaining of having to redraft those applications?'

'I am having a conversation with Roisín,' she said, holding up her hand to silence him. 'Thanks for your input, I'll let you know if I need further advice from you. I know you think you're in charge with JP being away.' But Saoirse had spotted my menu sticking out under my notebook which she snatched up. 'What's this?'

'Just a menu.'

Saoirse was reading through it. 'I can see it's a menu but what's it for?

Why are you writing a menu? Who are you feeding now?' she asked. 'Didn't I tell you to stop it? It's so passive-aggressive...'

'Just some charity thing I'm doing with friends. It's nothing...'

'Saoirse?' Belinda cut in. 'What's going on? I thought you were meant to be digitising 1995? Or have you finished? Are you ready to start on '96?'

Saoirse spun around. 'But Belinda, I was only asking Roisín why she was being trained up...'

'I'm not being trained up.'

But Saoirse ignored me. '...and I have to do endless admin and the skivvying.'

Belinda blinked at her for a moment. 'Skivvying?' she said. 'I wouldn't describe what we do as skivvying. I, for one, am very proud of being an office administrator and if some of that work can be described as mundane, then so be it. I would imagine that even the most interesting job has its more prosaic moments. Even Buzz Aldrin was probably bored at times...'

Dermot nodded in agreement. 'They were sitting in a spaceship for weeks and then all they got to do was one small step.'

'A giant leap actually,' said Frank, 'although that was metaphorical.'

'Thank you, lads, without administrators the world wouldn't work. Saoirse, you're an excellent administrator. You are organised and efficient. And I know JP appreciates your work.'

'Yes, but...' – Saoirse was not going to be sweet-talked by Belinda – '...it's just not fairly done. She's now a planner.'

'Saoirse,' said Dermot, 'come on. Roisín's been asked to look at Lady Immaculate Hall. JP needs a fresh eye on something which has lingered like one of Frank's farts...'

Frank shot him a look.

'...for far too long in this office,' continued Dermot. 'Who knows? JP might ask you to take on one of the other impossible challenges in this department. Like, how can we stop Frank from eating all the biscuits on a Monday morning? Or, why won't the windows open to allow for ventilation from Frank's aforementioned broken wind? Or, most perplexing of all, why can't you just be nice to your colleagues?'

Saoirse shot him a withering look. 'Shut up, Dermot. It's just that it's not the right decision. Roisín is only good for making cakes and forcing them on us—'

'You really should renew your subscription to charm school,' remarked Dermot. 'You need a top-up.'

'Roisín's cakes are the highlight of my life,' said Frank. 'Roisín's lemon drizzle was probably the best thing to happen to me so far this year. Fact.'

'Oh, Roisín's chocolate cake was even better... to die for.' Belinda beamed at me. 'I'm going to have another go at your recipe because God knows what I did wrong when I tried, it wasn't the same. Dry as a bar the morning after Paddy's Day.'

Saoirse was still reading my menu. 'You've written down supper club. That's a bit pretentious, don't you think? Supper club? What if it's shite?'

'Um... it's for charity...'

'Put me down for one of the nights,' called Dermot.

'I'll come too,' said Belinda. 'I'll see if some of my salsa group would like to come.'

'And put me down as well. A night away from the Discovery Channel would be a novelty.'

'I'll come this Saturday,' said Saoirse. 'And I'll bring some friends. The lasagne had better be good.'

Dermot called over. 'Saoirse, did you receive the file about the report on Dutch elm? I need to know how extensive it is.' He glanced at me and then back to her. 'Quickly, Saoirse, I've got a deadline.'

'I'll check the internal post.' She gave a bored shrug and shuffled off.

'I'm definitely going to mention it to my salsa girls. I know they will love a night out. It can get a bit lonely of an evening on my own, the other girls are the same. I can't wait.'

Frank peered at her from over his computer and then looked away.

* * *

Later that evening, when I'd come upstairs to go to bed, I found Brody lying on the bedroom floor, his face pressed against Fyodor's cage. He was either dead, drunk or had succumbed to the madness of solitude. Or all three.

'Brody?' In one move, I slid to my knees towards him. 'Brody? Are you okay? Brody?'

His eyes flickered open. 'Just talking to Fyodor,' he said, dreamily.

'Why, Brody?' I kneeled beside him, using my nice gentle voice.

'Because he's lonely and doesn't want to be in a cage any more. He wants to be set free.' He started humming a tune.

'Brody,' I said. 'He's fine. He likes his cage. He has his wheel which he never...' – I tried to stop sounding hysterical – '...which he never gets off. It's constantly whirring and spinning... loudly. Very, very loudly. He's happy. He's a very happy hamster.'

Fyodor was eyeing us both warily, as though waiting to hear his fate.

'But he's not happy,' insisted Brody, poking a finger through the cage. 'He told me. He spoke to me.'

Oh God.

'Brody...' And then I smelled something, something that reminded me of student parties.

'Brody, have you... I don't know, have you smoked anything?'

He rolled onto his back, one hand on the cage, the other behind his head.

'Might have done.' He giggled. 'I am high on life. Just sharing good times with my very good friend Fyodor, the hamster, here.' He pressed his finger to his lips. 'Don't tell, Fyodor. Never tell!'

This was a nightmare. I had the supper club the following day and was hoping to at least get a good night's sleep. Brody and Fyodor would have to leave the bedroom so I could go to sleep.

'Brody, why don't you sleep on the sofa tonight?' I suggested, gently. 'You and Fyodor could have a lovely night chatting downstairs. I am sure Fyodor has lots more to say.'

Brody rolled his head in my direction. 'He does,' he agreed fervently. 'He does have a lot more to say.'

'Well, come on then.' I pulled at one of his arms. 'Let's get the two of you downstairs and all cosy on the sofa.'

He managed to get onto his knees but flopped forward into child's pose and then, like a sea monster rising from the depths, he staggered to his feet.

'Go on,' I said. 'I'll carry Fyodor down. And the two of you can chat away.'

He fell more than walked down the stairs but eventually we got to the living room where he slumped heavily on the sofa. I placed the cage beside him, set the lights to low, and went upstairs and got into bed. Downstairs, I could hear Brody's voice and the hamster wheel creating the kind of energy which would have powered the Industrial Revolution.

* * *

At dawn, Brody crawled into bed, his body cold, his eyes back to normal. 'I'm sorry,' he whispered.

'For what?'

'For smoking that spliff. Anna gave it to me. She said it would relax me.'

'Anna, our neighbour? I didn't know you were friends.'

He shrugged. 'There's a lot you don't know about me. She understands how stressed I've been about the book. I haven't actually...' He stopped.

'Haven't actually what?'

He lay on his back, staring into the gloom of the morning.

'Nothing. It's just that... I don't know. I need inspiration. And I thought maybe smoking something, taking drugs...'

'Brody, you can't though.'

'I don't blame you for being angry. You can shout at me if you like, I don't mind. I'll take my punishment. Go on, shout away.'

'But I don't want to shout. I just don't want you smoking spliffs in the house.'

'I know. I promise I won't do it again.'

'And why is Anna giving you them?'

'She smokes them as part of her yoga practice, says it connects her with a higher state of mind. She's in PR and she says trying to write a press release is the hardest form of writing known to mankind. Finding new superlatives is impossible, she says, and smoking something makes everything flow. I thought that would be the same for me. But it didn't work.'

'Of course it didn't work.' His hands on my body were freezing cold and

I flinched and pulled back. 'I need to sleep,' I said. 'My alarm is set to go off in one hour. I've got the supper club today.'

'Of course,' he said. 'Absolutely. And I'm sorry again. I love you, Ro. You are too good for me.'

He fell straight to sleep while I lay staring at the ceiling, wondering if any of this was normal and how I was going to get through the very first supper club.

21

In the morning, the cage door was wide open and Fyodor was nowhere to be seen. I had already scrubbed the kitchen twice over the night before and would now have to do it again once I had recaptured Fyodor. It had happened twice before when Brody brought his cage downstairs, I would come down in the morning to find the door open and then have to pull the fridge out and recapture him. Now, however, I was convinced Brody was deliberately letting him loose. How else did Fyodor keep getting out? He couldn't open his cage with his tiny paws or claws, or whatever hamsters had, and it was happening too often for it to be just an accident.

Only eighteen months earlier, I lived here in this house and it was calm and quiet and now everything in my life felt off-kilter.

There was a beep from outside. It was Gerry, the fruit-and-veg man.

'It's all here,' he said, 'everything on your list. Tomatoes, onions, the finest garlic grown on Irish soil... goat's cheese from the market. And...' – he winked at me – 'did you order an ancient chihuahua?'

'I wish I had, how is Foxy? Is she with you?'

'She's in the front of the van, don't like to leave her at home because my wife is in and out and we don't want Foxy to be lonely, not when she's in her dotage.'

'Why don't you keep her?' I asked him.

'I've got my own collie, Guinness,' he replied. 'And Foxy just wouldn't be able to keep up with him. She needs a nice quiet home.'

Through the window of the van, I could see Foxy in a box on the floor in front of the passenger seat and she looked up at me with her big brown eye. If I didn't have a husband on the brink of mental collapse and a hamster on the loose I would take her in a flash but my chaotic household wasn't remotely suitable for the poor little thing.

I waved Gerry and Foxy off, carried in the crates and went through all my lists for the millionth time. I could feel the nerves building.

At 9 a.m., Richard, Sam and Jools knocked on the front door.

'And where is the Great Author?' Richard used his deep actor voice, making Sam giggle.

'Still in bed,' I whispered, beckoning them in. 'He was up late last night.'

'Of course!' said Richard, too loudly, still doing the voice. 'He's been scribbling into the early hours, you can't let a second be wasted when you have great thoughts which must be recorded.' He looked at me, innocently. 'What? I'm just explaining how hard it is to be a writer, that's all!' He winked again at Sam.

In the kitchen, Sam handed out clipboards with the day's itinerary on it, phone numbers, copies of the menu and who was doing what and when.

'We don't want to disturb the Great Author's beauty sleep,' said Richard, 'so we'll make sure we keep the noise down.' His hand slipped, causing a teetering pile of baking trays to crash to the kitchen floor. 'Ooops,' he said, making Sam laugh again. There was the sound of the tiny scuffle of Fyodor's feet from under the fridge. And then his whiskery face appeared at the side.

'Fyodor!' I shouted, kneeling down and poking a long wooden spoon behind one side of the fridge, my hand forming a trap at the other. I had enough practice recapturing him over the last week to be good at it and I snatched him up and dashed into the living room and his cage.

'What,' asked Richard slowly, 'the hell. Was. That?'

'A rat, I think,' said Sam. 'If I am not mistaken.'

'No, it was just a hamster.' I returned and washed my hands at the sink. 'And he's super clean. And everything is FINE!' I sounded unhinged.

'You need to get rid of that thing,' said Richard. 'I mean, was it your idea to get a rat?'

'It's a hamster, and no, if you must know, it wasn't my idea.'

Jools was nodding in agreement with Richard. 'There are hamster rescue charities,' she said, kindly.

'Especially if you are preparing food,' said Sam. 'I'm pretty up on food hygiene for the supper club. I've read many, many documents this week.'

'I'll get rid of it,' Richard offered. 'Having been brought up on a farm, I have no qualms about pest control. In fact, one summer I held the record for the extermination of the most rats. I became quite the celebrity in Dingle.'

'It's fine.' I felt exhausted already. 'And don't worry, I will scrub down the kitchen before cooking. But Brody's under pressure with the book and I think Fyodor is some kind of stress release. It's all...' My face felt hot. 'It's all been a little intense.'

Everyone was listening carefully, as though they'd been waiting for this conversation. My face grew hotter under the glare of their collective stare.

'It's just...' I didn't know what I wanted to say exactly. I couldn't even begin to put into words how confusing everything was.

'It's just...?' prompted Richard.

'Nothing... honestly...' What I wanted to say was that this wasn't working. My home was no longer my home. I hated the book and sometimes I thought I hated Brody. Fyodor was perhaps the one thing I didn't hate. Nothing was rational or reasonable any more and it was as though normal life had been suspended. Where there had been calm was now chaos.

The doorbell rang. 'That's Paddy,' said Jools. 'I told him we'd be here. I think he's bringing his friend as well, remember?'

'So, you'll cook the lasagne here,' Richard was saying. 'We'll go to your mother's garden, from henceforth known as Supper Club HQ and...'

Jools returned to the kitchen. 'Paddy's here.' She stood to one side to allow Paddy in. 'And this is...' She looked as though she was in shock. 'Erik...'

Into my poky, cluttered kitchen entered a titan of a man, a face chiselled by glaciers, eyes the colour of a crystal-clear fjord, shoulders like ice-capped peaks, legs two giant fir trees.

For a moment there was silence and then Richard breathed, 'Good God. It's Thor.'

The Norse God laughed, his hand held out to shake Richard's, then mine, then Sam's. 'Not quite,' he said, in perfect English. 'More like Thor's uglier, runt cousin.'

'Hardly. That's some handshake, by the way.' Richard cradled a nearly broken, limp hand in the other, as mine throbbed from Erik's vice-like grip.

'All the men are like this in Copenhagen,' laughed Paddy. 'I felt like Gulliver in the land of the giants. I was confronted by my inadequacies on a daily basis. If I left Ireland with my ego intact, it's not any more.' He caught my eye for a moment, smiling.

'You're not so bad yourself, Paddy,' assured Richard. 'But none of us Celts can compete with the Vikings. No wonder we were so easily over-powered by their pillaging. Note to self, go back to the gym.' He turned to Sam. 'Book my personal trainer for Monday morning, 5.30 a.m. sharp. No, make it 4 a.m. I have a lot of work to do. And if you see me eating carbs, please take them away from me.'

'But carbs are good, no?' asked Erik. 'The best part of every meal?'

'We're having a lot of carbs tonight, it's basically a keto nightmare. Pasta, bread, more bread, sugar, more pasta...'

'It sounds like a perfect meal,' said Erik.

'It is my perfect meal.' Jools smiled at me.

'Erik's working here for three months and says he's happy to help with the...' Paddy turned to Richard. 'What is it now? Dinner club?'

'Supper,' said Richard. 'Or in Denmark, what might we be eating there?'

Erik shrugged his huge shoulders. 'Smørrebrød? And beer?'

'Sounds better than my menu,' I said.

'Roisín, please. Confidence, I thought we agreed that your menu is a retro classic. Just imagine you are running a little Italian restaurant in the hills of Tuscany. You are an ancient Italian grandmother and you are cooking for your family on a Saturday night from the kitchen of your farm-house... all will be well.'

'So, what do you need us to do?' Paddy asked.

'Now, we're heading over to Supper Club HQ, aka our Roisín's mother's garden. Sam, will you hand Paddy and Erik their itineraries? Jools, you're with Roisín all day. Sam and I are off to prep the garden, print menus, check the guest list. Paddy, what are you and Thor, I mean, Erik focusing on?'

'We're going to finish the new floor of the summer house,' said Paddy. 'And finish the bar. There's lighting to put up and the tables and chairs to collect from the hire place. We were at the garden yesterday evening.' He turned to me. 'Had a good chat with your mum. And your dad.' He raised an eyebrow slightly. He knew all about Dad and Maxine but I hadn't filled him in on the latest developments.

Richard turned to Erik. 'Will you be staying for the evening? You will be paid in lasagne in exchange for waiting on the tables and serving drinks.'

'What else would I be doing on a Saturday night in a strange country?' said Erik, smiling a straight-toothed smile at us, causing us to blink in the rays from his teeth.

'Aprons!' exclaimed Richard. 'We'll all be wearing aprons.' Sam handed him a pile of folded linens and Richard shook one out like a tore-ador. It was a flaxen-coloured linen apron with vertical blue stripes. *Little Eden Supper Club, Sandycove,* was stitched on it in red.

'It's lovely,' said Jools, studying hers. 'Thank you, Sam.'

'Right, everyone, synchronise watches, good luck and Godspeed! To our stations!'

'To our stations!' we shouted in unison, but then one by one, the words faded from our lips as we caught sight of Brody standing in the kitchen doorway, looking as though he had been dragged along by a runaway horse at a rodeo. His hair and beard were all over the place, he was wearing his old T-shirt and if his underpants had seen better days, they were so long ago, they probably couldn't remember them. Brody looked at us all one by one, stopping for a quick double take when his eyes fell upon Erik.

'Good morning, Brody!' Richard beamed. 'What a beautiful day it is too. Sun shining, birds singing!'

'What's going on?' Brody asked. 'What are all these people doing here?' He had a half smile on his face as though he was having a private joke with himself.

'It's the supper club tonight,' I said. 'Remember? We're just having a last-minute meeting.'

'Will you be here all day? Because the noise from the kitchen... I have to write.'

'I know.' I was contrite. 'I'm so sorry.'

'That was me, I dropped the pans. And I have been told that my voice carries very well. I would make a good opera singer, I think. If only I could sing.'

Brody gazed back at him. 'It's really hard to write in a noisy house. It's a huge pressure... to create, to be creative...'

Everyone seemed slightly stunned as Brody's eyes were darting around from one face to the other. He turned to me. 'You've told them, haven't you?'

'Told them what?'

'Told them about last night,' said Brody, glaring.

Everyone was looking at us. 'No, I haven't.'

'Are you sure?'

'I honestly haven't!'

'Told us what?' Richard asked. 'And whatever it is, Roisín hasn't said a word.'

'I smoked a spliff!' said Brody. 'Okay? Not a crime... it's just that I was sure you were all talking about me.'

The paranoia had obviously set in, I thought, as Richard and Jools exchanged a quick look.

'Brody,' soothed Richard. 'We have to go and get on with the supper club. We weren't talking about you smoking wacky tobaccy, or whatever the kids are calling it these days.'

'Definitely not that, anyway,' said Jools.

Oh God. What were they thinking? What was Paddy thinking? I hoped the smile on my face conveyed an air of unbothered nonchalance.

'We artists need space and quiet to allow the mind to reach a state where no thought, no action, no emotion is impossible to channel and to make indelible on the page.'

'You're a writer?' asked Erik. 'What have you written?'

'I was a columnist for the *Irish Times*,' Brody puffed his chest out, 'but I am on sabbatical in order to write my novel.'

'Ah,' said Erik. 'And what is your novel about?'

'It's too difficult to summarise.' Brody seemed to be perking up and had perched himself on the edge of the kitchen table, his hairy bare legs stretched out in front of him. 'It's like asking what *Ulysses* is about?'

'A man goes for a walk around Dublin?' suggested Erik.

'Well... I suppose everything can be summarised. But not its soul. My book is...' He looked heavenward as though he was in need of strength or inspiration.

'It's about a man called Seamus who lives on a farm.' I was trying to be helpful.

Brody rolled his eyes. 'Thank you, Roisín, Please do not attempt to speak on my behalf. I am more Jonathan Swift to your Jilly Cooper.' He winked at Erik, as though they were on the same wavelength. 'It's about masculinity, survival and resilience, and it's about looking into the dark abyss of one's soul.'

'That sounds... very... um, interesting.'

Brody stood up. 'Time for me to go back to my writing, books don't write themselves.' He smiled at everyone but didn't meet my eye.

'See you, Brody,' said Jools, as he left the kitchen and went back to bed. For a moment, no one said anything, and then Erik turned to me. 'Is that your flatmate?'

I shook my head. 'Not really, he's my husband.'

'Okay...' Erik nodded deeply but before anyone could say anything else, Richard was packing up.

'Come on, people,' he was saying. 'Let's get this show on the road.' He hugged me goodbye. 'I love you, Roisín,' he said, looking me straight in the eye. 'When I was just a skinny kid from West Kerry mainlining pure monosodium glutamate for dinner, you saved me. Just remember that. Your food changed my life.'

I laughed, feeling better. 'Thank you, Richard, I love you too.'

Paddy gave my arm a very quick pat. 'Good luck with the cooking,' he said. And they were all gone and it was just me and Jools and a day of lasagne-making ahead.

22

By 3 p.m., everything was all ready to go. The tiramisus were in the fridge, the garlic bread prepared, the salad ready to dress and eight huge lasagnes were ready to bake. We packed everything in Jools's car and began the short journey to Mum's.

'I feel sick at the thought of ever making a lasagne again,' I said, as Jools drove along my road. 'I should have listened to Richard.'

'It's just catering on such a large scale.' Jools had seemed preoccupied all day. 'Talking of which... what do you think of Erik? He's the man equivalent of catering for a crowd. He's like two men rolled into one.'

'It depends on which two men he is.'

'I don't think I care,' she said. 'Not that he would look twice at me. I only ever get the misfits and the oddballs, the ones with mother complexes, neuroses and out-of-control athlete's foot. The Darrens of this world.'

'Don't be ridiculous, if anything, you are out of Erik's league. You've just been unlucky with a few duds. And you need the duds to appreciate the gems.'

'Like Erik.' She shook her head in disbelief. 'My God, he's gorgeous.' She shrugged. 'But Erik actually looks comfortable in his skin so he's not going to be interested.'

'He should be so lucky, he's probably thinking the same thing.'

'He is such a ride, though,' she said. 'I am just going to enjoy looking at him while he's around. But I hope he doesn't get snaffled by someone else. Knowing my luck, he will be.'

'I thought you were settling in for the single life?'

'I am!' she exclaimed. 'That hasn't changed. It's not as though anything is going to happen. It's like being on a diet but having a look through the window of the cake shop. Look, tell me if I'm out of order but I couldn't help noticing that...' She stopped.

'What?'

'Well, Brody seemed very much on edge.'

'It's the book, it's going to be finished two weeks on Friday.'

'And smoking a spliff?'

'Lots of people do it.'

'But are you okay with it?'

I shrugged. 'He's apologised.'

'And the hamster?'

'I'm going to make sure the cage is more secure.'

'And are you okay?'

I nodded. 'Of course I am.'

Jools didn't say a word, just raised an eyebrow.

'It's not much fun living with a writer who is on a deadline,' I admitted, keeping my voice low. 'Poor Brody is locked away in the spare room and only appears for dinner. I feel like I'm his housekeeper.'

'And rodent catcher.'

'We're at a low ebb, that's all,' I said. 'But as soon as the book is done, things will be so much better. I know they will. We'll go back to being a happily married couple. The pressure will be off and we can start doing things together... and on the last night of the supper club, we'll have that little celebration for Brody and the book.'

'Great idea,' agreed Jools. 'We'll drink some fizz and raise a glass to Brody and his book.' She smiled at me. 'It will all be fine.'

* * *

When we stepped through the back gate of Mum's house, the garden looked absolutely beautiful. The lawn was mown, looking like a perfect carpet of green, lights had been strung through the trees, and beneath them were long tables and benches in rows. The summer house had been power-hosed and sparkled in the sunlight. Inside were more lights and jewel-coloured velvet cushions which I recognised from Richard's flat.

'It actually looks like a place you'd want to go to,' I said to Jools.

'It's fabulous,' she agreed.

On the wrought-iron bench beside the back door, Dad, Paddy and Erik were sitting in a row.

'These lads have been most industrious,' Dad announced as we walked over. 'They haven't stopped.'

We sat down beside them on the old lawn chairs.

'I wish I could say that I was any use,' Dad went on. 'But these two fellas had it all in hand. They did say that they would make me a cocktail later from the bar. I'm looking forward to it, Erik,' he said. 'I've never had a cocktail made with Akvavit before. It's Scandinavian Poitín, I like the sound of that.'

'There's always a first time for everything, Jack, you are never too old for a novel experience.'

I felt my body tense at the word 'novel'. I tried to concentrate on what we had to do next. Did I have everything? What if the food was awful? Maybe next week, I should do everything in Mum's house, which meant that I wouldn't disturb Brody and that would reduce some of the stress.

'Erik was telling me about his line of work.' Dad addressed me and Jools. 'These new developers are a breed apart from the old guard. It's all about the environmental and societal emphasis. Isn't that right, Erik? And Paddy here has a bike shop.'

The nerves were really settling in now and the butterflies were accumulating so quickly that I wasn't really listening.

'Hello, darling,' said Mum. 'Hello, Jools.'

Sam, Richard and Mum appeared from the house.

'Thank God the chef's arrived.' Richard clapped his hands. 'We can't have a supper club without supper! And good news, everyone, we're fully booked, everyone has paid their twenty-five euros and will be here from 7 p.m. Drinks on the lawn and then a sit-down meal, made by the wonderful Roisín and her glamorous assistant, Jools.

'Now, people! I don't mean to be a drag and make everyone get up off their arses and get to it but get off your arses and get to it! Except for lovely Maggie here...' He smiled at Mum. 'Who is to put her feet up and not do anything.'

'I will be taking Maggie out to the cinema,' said Dad. 'Isn't that right, Maggie?' Dad seemed almost possessive of Mum, as though a little jealous of Richard and their special relationship.

'Thank you, Jack.' Richard ignored any tension. 'So, if everyone has read Sam's meticulous spreadsheet, you will know that we are precisely six minutes behind schedule, so... chop-chop!' He clapped his hands again. 'Let's get going.'

23

It was clear the evening was going to take a disastrous turn the moment Saoirse turned up. Not that I could blame her for the burned garlic bread, the overdone lasagne and the under-set tiramisu but as soon as I looked out of the kitchen window and saw her arrive with some of her friends, a feeling of doom settled into my bones.

The guests began to arrive at 7 p.m. and Richard and Sam – dressed in their matching aprons – welcomed everyone before sending them over to the apple trees to sit on the benches. Sam's brother was in a jazz quartet and they had set up just outside the summer house, the sounds floating in the air. Inside the summer house and behind a bar made out of an old door balanced on two trestles, Erik and Paddy, also both in their aprons, were opening bottles of Prosecco and adding peach juice to make Bellinis.

I swallowed back my nerves.

'God, Erik looks good in an apron,' said Jools. 'There is something about a man in an apron, don't you think? And the tea towel on the shoulder? I am so fed up of seeing men in Lycra in my line of work. I've never appreciated the humble apron before.'

'Jools, just ask him out, you can't spend the next few weeks lusting after him!'

She drew back from the window. 'I am not lusting after him.' She went red. 'I only said he looked good in an apron. Anyway, I told you, he's out of my league. Now, if he's got hang-ups, or addictions or a personality disorder then I might be in with a chance. But Paddy has assured me he's sane and nice. He's even got a dog back in Copenhagen who he's really missing, apparently. His mum is looking after it, and Paddy said he Face-Times the dog every day.' Jools peered out of the window again. 'He's like something from an X-rated Hans Christian Andersen story, some wood-cutter or huntsman. And if Paddy likes him, he's got to be a good person.' She came towards me. 'If only Paddy would meet someone nice. He's told me he wants to be single forever...'

'Who, Paddy?' I looked across at her.

'He said he's not keen on being hurt.'

'Who has hurt him?' I asked.

'I don't know,' she replied. 'He doesn't really tell me much. But I just think anyone who is in a relationship has my respect. Maybe Paddy and I are cowards by not wanting to get back into one ever again. To make your-self vulnerable, to hang in there. Even at the low ebbs.' She smiled at me.

'I don't think it takes guts to hang in there,' I said. 'I think it takes guts to leave.' I was the coward, I thought. I was hanging in there because admitting my marriage wasn't working after only a year would be humili-ating. I couldn't end my marriage after one year, not after forcing everyone to celebrate with me and making Jools be my bridesmaid.

'And Paddy said he'd forgotten how much you made him laugh, you know, if you weren't married, I might fix the two of you up.'

I looked at her. 'You wouldn't mind?'

'Why would I mind? I'd be delighted.'

I stared out of the window, not wanting to say anything else, trying to get my thoughts in order. And then I spotted Saoirse. 'Oh my God... Saoirse's here. I didn't think she would actually come.'

'Who's Saoirse?' Jools came over and peered out.

'She's from work. Just one of those people who hates everyone.'

Saoirse was followed by three friends, and all of them were dressed as though going to a hen party in Ljubljana, all rainbow feather boas and novelty Elton John glasses. I heard her voice over the sound of the jazz quartet. 'Where's the chef?' she shouted. 'We're friends of the chef!'

'Let's get back to work,' I said to Jools. 'We need to get the bruschetta ready.'

Jools nodded and we stood at our stations, ready to griddle the bread and drizzle it with olive oil. 'Roisín?' Paddy stuck his head around the back door. 'There's a friend of yours outside, says she wants to say hello.'

'I'm a bit busy.'

But then we heard Saoirse call my name. 'Where is she?'

'I'd better go, before she shouts again.'

'I'll do the bruschetta,' said Jools.

In the garden, I saw Dad take a tray of Bellinis from Erik. 'I'll hand these around, young man, you stand there and look handsome.' He slapped Erik on the back.

'Oh, there she is!' called Saoirse, spotting me. 'Dressed in character! Enter the chef!'

This was my garden, the place I'd played in as a child, I knew every nook, every cranny, the glossy brown stone in the paving, the way the purple flowers sprouted over the top of the wall every spring. The apple trees which blossomed and greened over the seasons, the rickety path from the house to the summer house. But I wished none of this was happening and that none of these people were here and that I didn't have to spend the next three Saturdays cooking for people. It was as though my home had been invaded.

Saoirse and her friends were already rowdy. 'What is this place?' Saoirse called, as I walked towards her. 'I almost twisted my ankle on the lane.'

'It's just a charity event,' I said, trying to downplay everything. 'And this is my mum's garden...'

'Your mum's garden?' repeated Saoirse. She was drunk already, I realised, her eyes glazed, the edges of her speech rubbed away. 'This place? Could do with a tidy up, bit of weeding. We should send round some of the guys from Parks, right? They could throw some weedkiller around.'

'Yeah...' I tried to laugh. 'Would you like something to drink?' I asked Saoirse. 'We have various...'

'Coming up!' said Dad, looming behind us with the tray. 'Your wish is my command.' He beamed at Saoirse and her friends. 'Now, you are very welcome to the inaugural Little Eden Supper Club, in this beautiful garden...' He offered the tray around. 'Who would like a little appetite-whetter?'

'What are they?' asked Saoirse suspiciously, a half-drunk bottle of tequila poking out from her bag.

'Venetian Bellinis,' said Dad, grandly. 'Invented by the Medici in 1785. Probably. That sounds right enough. The greatest drink ever invented. And made by those charming gentlemen over there.' He nodded towards Erik and Paddy. 'One Irish, one Danish. Both devilishly handsome. But if the drinks can still strictly be called Venetian, I am not entirely sure.'

'Yes...' Saoirse rolled her eyes, making her friend next to her – in matching boa and glasses – giggle. 'But what are they?'

'Delicious, that's what they are,' said Dad, briskly, handing out the glasses.

'It's peach juice and Prosecco,' I explained.

'Avril,' said Saoirse, 'get out the tequila. These need to be spiked.'

Avril reached into Saoirse's bag and produced the bottle of tequila. 'Here.' She splashed some into Saoirse's glass. 'Who else wants some?'

The gang all leaned in to have their drinks tequila'd while Dad smiled benignly and moved on.

'I'll see you later,' I said. 'I hope you enjoy the meal.'

'We'd better!' cackled Saoirse. 'Or we'll be looking for refunds!' Her gang laughed and started to light up cigarettes.

'Who are those people?' hissed Richard, grabbing my arm, as I made my way back to the kitchen. 'They're friends of yours?'

I shook my head. 'One of them is a colleague and I don't know the others.'

'But they're drunk, I feel like we've borrowed our parents' house and we promised the party won't get out of hand and then a gang of kids have arrived and they are about to start ruining everything!'

'Richard, we have borrowed my parents' house... that's exactly the scenario.'

'But my nice vibe is already gone awry,' he insisted, his voice going squeaky. 'You can't hear the jazz band because they are laughing so loudly.' Richard's eyelid was twitching which it only did at moments of high stress.

The last time it had twitched like that was when he was revising for his finals.

Sam came over and put his hand on Richard's arm. 'Come on,' he soothed. 'It's all fine. It's not ruined.'

'Yet!' shouted Richard, making everyone look at him, as Sam led him away.

Back in the kitchen, Jools was just dressing the salad. From the window, I could see Saoirse's gang were throwing the almonds into the air and trying to catch them in their mouths. The bottle of tequila was in the middle of the table. And then our nostrils began twitching.

'What's that smell?' asked Jools.

'The garlic bread!' I screamed, racing for the oven. 'I've burned the garlic bread!'

'I'll shave the burnt bits off,' Jools said, taking a large knife and chipping away at the edges.

'The bloody Aga,' I said. 'I used to be able to cook in it, and now it's got a mind of its own.'

Dad came into the kitchen. 'Everything all right?' He beamed. 'Your mother and I are off to the cinema now. Leave you all to it.' He stopped suddenly, sniffing the air like a dog. 'Do I detect carbon?'

I nodded, near tears. 'It's all ruined,' I wailed. 'It's all gone wrong.'

'It's all right,' said Jools, 'we're going to just sort it out and it will all be fine.'

Dad came over and put one arm around me, pulling me into him. 'Feck them,' he said, nodding to the crowd outside. 'Feck the lot of them. Serve with a smile. If I know anything, it's do everything with a smile. Don't let them know how you're really feeling. Yes?'

'He's right,' agreed Jools, who had now amassed quite a pile of blackened bread, it looked like she was going to light a barbecue. 'It's not worth it.'

Dad looked up and saw Mum. 'Ready? Shall we leave these young entrepreneurs to it?'

She nodded. 'It's getting rowdy out there. I think it's best if we make ourselves scarce.' She slipped a hand through Dad's arm. 'Shall we go?'

'My pleasure.' They smiled at each other.

'Bye, you two!' called Mum, waving as they stepped outside the front door.

Richard and Sam entered the kitchen. 'Next course!' shouted Richard, back to his usual self. 'Chop-chop! Lasagne and garlic bread!' He stared at the charred chippings. 'Oh God. Did we have an accident?'

I nodded. 'It's the worst meal...'

'Too late for that,' he said briskly. 'We need utter confidence, total self-belief. How the hell do you think I survive the corporate environment? Fake it until you make it, okay? If we act like it's the world's most delicious meal, then they will believe it. Now, come on. Get it out and we'll slop it on the plates. Jools, hand over that garlic charcoal...' He winked at me. 'Come on, if the three of us haven't learned that you have got to make the best of things, then we've learned nothing. Now! Lasagnes, please!'

I lifted the dishes out of the Aga and out he and Sam went with one in each hand. 'You bring the other two out,' said Jools. 'I'll carry the salad.'

Outside, Saoirse's gang were already chewing on the garlic bread. 'We're starving,' she shouted at me. 'I don't consider olives to be an adequate starter. The bruschetta was just tomatoes on toast. And I can't eat salami... it sticks in my throat.'

'Here, have some lasagne...' I lifted a large slice and placed it on her plate, moving to her friend next to her, and the next.

Saoirse placed her nose close to the lasagne. 'Is this made with meat?'

'Of course!' I said.

'What kind of meat?'

'Beef,' I said.

'Beef as in cow?'

'Yes, beef as in cow.' You're the cow, I thought.

Saoirse poked at it with her fork and then took up the tiniest crumb, nibbling as though it was poisonous. Her friend sitting beside her, a tanned man in a white shirt open halfway down his chest, giggled. 'Saoirse! Saoirse! Saoirse!' He chanted.

'What's wrong?' I asked.

'It's like dog food,' she said, making her friends laugh. 'A discount supermarket dog food.'

I moved away from them, hating her, hating the food, hating cooking, hating this stupid night and even hating Richard for making me do it.

* * *

Finally, when it was all over and we were washed up and cleared away, we sat at the kitchen table, eating leftovers and spooning tiramisu into our mouths. The adrenaline and fear finally had dissipated and I realised everything tasted slightly better than I had feared. Nothing was exactly brilliant but the lasagne definitely didn't taste of dog food and there was a certain comforting claggy-ness to it all. But I knew I was better than this. I had aimed low and delivered a mediocre meal – which admittedly tasted better than it looked.

'Well, that was fun!' Erik didn't seem remotely fatigued. 'All those people... so many characters. It's true what they say about the Irish. They know how to have a good time.'

'Even with Italian food.'

'Next time,' he said. 'With Irish food.'

'Next time?' I quailed at the thought.

'What's Irish food anyway?' Jools asked.

'Crisps,' Paddy answered. 'And Cadbury's chocolate.'

'Chicken burger and chips.'

'And Guinness.' Sam looked up from his laptop. 'Guinness is a food.'

'And you all stop for tea,' said Erik. 'All the time. When I was at a meeting the other day, we had to have tea before and tea afterwards. Some drank tea during the meeting.'

'It's Irish rocket fuel. Without tea, we are nothing. Mere husks of humanity.'

Paddy laughed, nodding in agreement. 'It's our tap water, part mountain stream, part Connemara lamb urine. Best in the world, apparently.' He grinned across the table at me.

'Next Saturday, it's going to be even bigger and better.'

'And that Saoirse is banned.' Jools turned to me. 'If she wants to come again, tell her we're full.'

'I had to wake her up and tell her that it was time to leave,' said Sam.

'She became quite aggressive and tried to hit me and then she vomited in the back lane.'

'Oh God.'

'Don't worry, I hosed it all down, she staggered off, saying something about still being hungry and wanting to find a burger van.'

'Well, I think it was an amazing night.'

'So do I.'

'Me three.'

'Me four.'

'That lasagne was the best I've ever tasted,' said Erik. 'I love lasagne to be on the brink of indigestibility, yes? It's the kind of thing you need after a day cross-country skiing or ice climbing. I ate three portions.'

Richard caught my eye. 'As retro classics go,' he was smiling, 'it was a triumph.' He held up his mug. 'Here's to the Little Eden Supper Club. Long may it reign!'

'Can't we just call it a day?' I pleaded. 'That swim to Howth is looking more and more attractive.'

'No! We never give up!' shouted Richard. 'What don't we do?'

'Give up!' shouted everyone else. They all turned to me. 'Roisín?'

'Never give up,' I mumbled.

'To claggy lasagne!'

'To claggy lasagne!'

24

'So, how was it?' On Monday morning, Dermot wheeled himself over to my desk and put his chin in his hands as though ready to hear a bedtime story. Saoirse was yet to arrive and I dreaded what she might say about Saturday. She had somehow taken the shine off our lovely supper club. I hadn't realised how much I was going to enjoy it, and having paying guests wasn't much different to cooking for friends. People – excluding Saoirse – were lovely and several had come up to me and said how much they enjoyed it.

'Did Saoirse come to your gathering in the end, Roisín?' called Belinda from her desk.

'She did, yes,' I replied. 'I don't think she was particularly keen on the food. I shouldn't have made lasagne and garlic bread.'

'But what's wrong with lasagne and garlic bread?' Dermot asked.

'The bread was burned and the lasagne like a brick.'

'But that's exactly how people like it,' he said. 'If people wanted light-as-air pasta or bread that is not charred, then they wouldn't ask for lasagne and garlic bread. I would feel cheated if they didn't taste like the lasagne and garlic bread of my youth.'

He was making me feel better already.

'Frank,' he called. 'Which do you prefer? Lasagne which is just full of air, or a big slab of indigestible carb that you can really sink your teeth into?'

'The slab,' Frank replied, without looking up. 'No question.'

'And garlic bread? Underdone, or charred?'

'Charred, obviously.' He looked up and smiled at me.

Dermot turned to Belinda. 'Bel? Lasagne and garlic bread. Do you like?'

'I do, a good hearty lasagne... and I have been known to have a few chips on the side. But...' – she patted her stomach – 'I can't risk that these days. But I would say it would be one of my favourite meals. I make quite a good one myself. And I make chips in proper beef dripping. They come out so crispy...'

Frank was giving her a side-eye look again.

'You can't be telling us that, Belinda,' said Dermot. 'Not on Monday morning with our stomachs rumbling.'

'I'll have you all around for dinner sometime, for a feed of chips.'

'Now you're talking.' Dermot swung back to me. 'And Roisín here will make the lasagne.'

'Thanks, Dermot.'

'I'll be along one of these evenings to your supper club, maybe the week after next? Frank? You on?'

'And I have nearly heard from all the girls from salsa, I'm just waiting for one or two more confirmations and then we'll book in.'

'Me too,' said Frank.

'Oh my God!' Saoirse was walking through the door. 'I'm still not right, you know,' she shouted in our direction. 'Yesterday I felt like I'd been driven over by a tank...' She threw her handbag on her desk and collapsed on her chair. 'My stomach... oh sweet mother of divine Jesus... I must have eaten something rancid.' She looked across at me. 'I've been trying to think what I ate...'

I kept my head down, not wanting to look at her. Was she suggesting she had food poisoning from the lasagne? Richard, Sam, Eric, Paddy and Jools had all eaten it and were all fine. So was Brody and I'd even brought some round to Harry who had told me about the time he was in Naples in the early 1960s and discovered garlic for the first time – 'like bathing your insides with warmth' – and, thankfully, he was still alive (hopefully). But, of course, Saoirse would be the one who was ill.

'Why is everyone ignoring me?' Saoirse demanded. 'Belinda?'

'Yes, Saoirse?' Belinda looked up. 'Sorry, I just needed to respond to some of the objections to the Castlecourt development. They are coming in thick and fast this morning. The amount of people emailing saying our website keeps crashing...'

'Belinda,' said Saoirse, 'it's just that I am not feeling well and I still came into work.'

Belinda blinked at her. 'You mean, you don't think you should be here?'

'No, I don't. I'm not feeling well... but because I didn't want to let you down, I am here. Despite the fact that I feel like I am being stabbed by my own stomach.'

'Would you like to go home?'

Saoirse slunk further down into her chair. 'It's just that I went to Roisín's dinner and I think that it was there...' – she threw a poisonous glance in my direction – '...that I think that I ate something dodgy.'

'I didn't think you ate very much,' I said. Considering how much tequila you had drunk, I thought.

'Which just shows how toxic it was, it must have been swimming with parasites or whatever. Did you make it in the public toilets on the seafront or when was the last time you washed your hands? I just don't think these kind of pop-up places are legal. What about the health and safety of your customers? You work for the council. You should know this kind of thing.'

'I'm not sure...' I knew she hadn't been poisoned by my food. I could not have been more careful with cleaning everything and not a single other person had been ill.

'Don't expect me to come to the next one. I can't do that to my body. Couldn't keep anything down. And if I wasn't such a reasonable person, I would sue for damages.'

'On what grounds?' Frank asked.

'That my digestion has been destroyed. It will take my gut biome months to recover.'

'Saoirse, please, your bodily functions are as inappropriate to this office as Frank's are. By the way,' Dermot turned to Frank, 'did you sort out your wind issue? Remember? You were going to go and see that specialist?'

Frank just shook his head at him. 'Funny, ha ha. Thank you, Dermot.'

'I went along out of the goodness of my own heart, to support a charity and a colleague,' insisted Saoirse. 'And I brought my friends with me, and... well, let's just say that I saw the inside of my own bathroom more than I saw any of the rest of my house yesterday.'

Belinda stood up. 'Why not have a cup of peppermint tea to settle your stomach, Saoirse? And then see how you feel as the day goes on.'

I wished I could tell her that she was wrong and to leave me alone but I felt so wretched that I kept my head down, hoping she would just disappear. I had to get out of the office quickly. I picked up my bag and cardigan and left, down the back stairs where I wouldn't meet anyone, and into the sunshine, desperately trying not to cry.

* * *

The sea glittered like the Koh-i-noor as I walked briskly along the seafront, passing the dog walkers, the office escapees clutching their lunch boxes and looking for a free bench, the power-walkers. Lady Immaculate Hall gleamed in the summer sunshine. Two children hung from the trees by their hands, like chimpanzees. Three men were sitting on a bench, laughing and debating over a crossword.

At the Hall, things were getting busy with groups of people, all ages, all ethnicities, chatting and talking together, waiting for lunch. In the main hall, the tables and chairs were being set out by a group of white-haired women, the kind of people who get things done. I wondered if any of them were the writers of all those letters to the council. There was nothing unethical with me being here. All I was doing was helping to cook lunch. I wasn't asking about the redevelopment plans and no one had mentioned them to me. Yes, there was a poster on the noticeboard in the foyer with 'Save The Hall' on it but I hadn't stopped to read it.

'Ah! Roisín!' Marian called to me from under the food hatch. 'You're nice and early today. Come on, come on... they'll be letting everyone in shortly. Mary needs help with the onions. She's in charge today. Irish stew is on the menu.'

I'd always known there was something comforting in cooking, but at the Hall, this took it to another level. Serving great big bowls of comfort food and chatting to Gita or Mary who seemed to be the head chefs. It didn't matter if it wasn't perfect, it was the vibe, the context and the spirit of the lunch. If Saoirse hadn't been there on Saturday night, I wouldn't be feeling such a failure. I stood talking with Gita, asking her about the curry she had made the other day.

'Cardamon is the secret ingredient,' Gita was saying. 'You can make it with fifteen other spices and you will know it is missing.'

'It was delicious,' I said.

She nodded as though it was incontrovertibly good. Gita cooked with confidence and somehow it came through in the finished dish. It tasted as though there was no other way that this plate of food could taste, that this was the very essence of the dish. Standing with Gita at the stove, I felt happy, as though I was in the right place at the right time, as though ordained by the universe.

But it was a feeling I didn't have at home. I had married Brody too soon. I had married someone I barely knew. Once the honeymoon period ended, all that was left were two strangers wondering who the other person was and Brody was probably feeling exactly the same way I did.

But what to do now? Carry on and get to know each other properly once the book was done? Or face the embarrassment and humiliation and tell everyone that they were right and that we shouldn't have got married? There was still a chance that we would get through this, be that long-married couple who look back on their early days, laugh at the risk they took, how everyone said that they were crazy and yet they proved them wrong.

25

Richard called me on Tuesday morning. 'So, second menu? Sam wants the booking form to go live tonight. Latest tomorrow. We're already getting emails from people wanting to come again. News is afoot of a new supper club in Sandycove. A whole salsa club has enquired to see if we can fit in eight of them. Sam has told them they can come to the final night, the following week, the twenty-ninth.'

'That's Belinda, a colleague...'

'Oh no, not another of your reprobate colleagues. What's she going to do? Start a fist fight? Set fire to the summer house? Snort cocaine off the garlic bread?'

'She's nothing like Saoirse,' I assured him. 'Belinda's lovely and very well behaved. Office administrator by day. Salsa dancer by night.'

'Okay, she's sounding more acceptable by the second. But what about the menu this week?'

'Something using local vegetables... and cheese.' I thought of what Erik had said about an Irish menu. I thought I would pop by Gerry in the farmer's market and see what he and the other stallholders had. 'I'm not sure what, but I'll email you and Sam by tomorrow morning.'

Richard sounded pleased. 'Great. By the way, we've had three people wanting to know your lasagne recipe. Someone said... where is it, Sam?

Where's the feedback?' I heard Sam's voice in the background. 'Oh yes, here it is, a glorious trip down memory lane, a retro-fabulous piece of cooking. We'll be back! Now, isn't that nice?'

'Or deranged,' I said.

'By the way,' he went on, 'I meant to say that I saw your brother-in-law in town yesterday. Ross. Looking pleased with himself as usual. Except...'

'Except what?'

'Nothing... just... well, I don't know what to think, actually. But it was probably nothing.'

'What was it?'

'He was having lunch with a woman... and, I don't know... but he saw me and just as I was about to smile and go over for a quick chat he looked away. Odd, I thought, as though he was hiding something.'

'Was she blonde?'

'Yes. And they looked happy, and maybe that was it, because I knew he looked different because in all the times I've ever met Ross he's never even smiled. I thought he was incapable. But I was rushing to bring Sam's lunch back because the supper club booking form had a glitch in it and he spent his lunch break sorting it out.'

I didn't know what to say about Ross. He definitely wasn't on a search for inner peace and happiness. I changed the subject.

'I thought Sam was your assistant, I didn't know you bought him lunch.'

'Yeah, well... having a well-fed assistant is better than one who is hungry and cranky. Not that he's ever cranky. He couldn't be nicer.' He paused but didn't say any more.

'Yes?' I prompted.

'Nothing. Anyway, see you soon. Now, remember. Email me the menu.'

* * *

It wasn't my intention to cycle past Paddy's bike shop on my way to Mum's, but as I freewheeled past, I realised it was too late to turn around. The old launderette had been transformed into something quite beautiful. *Life-Cycle* was in pink neon, bulb lights were strung from a lamp post at the front of the shop to either corner. In the large glass windows on either side of the door were two bikes – one large, family-sized cargo bike, and in the other window, a tiny commuter folding e-bike. And standing in the doorway were Paddy and Erik. They both looked up, Paddy squinted for a moment and then waved.

'Roisín!' called Erik. 'Come over!'

I had no choice but to cycle over to them.

'The shop looks amazing,' I said, smiling.

Paddy looked up at the neon sign. 'That went up today. It's not a bit garish?'

'Garish is good, and whoever said disco and bikes don't mix?'

'You always need a bit of disco...' I remembered the night when he and I were out with friends and then we found ourselves in a club and stayed on the dance floor for hours.

'We need your advice,' said Erik. 'In Copenhagen, there's no such thing as just a bike shop. They've all got somewhere to get a coffee, a pastry...'

'Danish, obviously,' Paddy added.

'Obviously.' I grinned back at him. This was fine, I thought, we were back to where we were before... everything. Just Jools's brother and her best friend hanging out. Nothing weird, nothing awkward.

'We need your opinion, what do people in Dublin like to have?'

'Same as Danish people,' I replied. 'Coffee and Danish pastries.'

'Nothing different?'

'Fairy cakes?' I suggested. 'Little old-fashioned fairy cakes, the kind your mum used to make for parties. And chocolate crispies? Proper ones, in little paper cases.'

'I love it,' Paddy said. 'Cup of tea and a chocolate crispie. Heaven.'

'What is this chocolate crispie?' Erik asked. 'Some kind of Irish delicacy?'

Paddy and I looked at each other and laughed again. 'No, the opposite. But incredible. Cornflakes, melted chocolate. Stir. Done.'

'I look forward to sampling one, maybe you would accept a commission to make the treats for the café?'

'Really?' I looked back at Paddy. 'I don't know...'

'We'd be honoured if you would just do one or two days a week,' Paddy said. 'Whatever you can manage. Why don't you have a think about it?'

'Okay.' The cargo bike in the window caught my eye. 'Gorgeous bike,' I said. 'It's huge.'

'But incredibly light to cycle,' said Paddy. 'It's the future of commuting. You can fit four children on there.'

'And how many adults?'

'Two.' He looked at me, curiously. 'Why? Do you want to have a spin?'

'Maybe...' I was thinking of Harry, actually. Or maybe he'd be okay on his own electric bike? I wanted to get him mobile and independent again, cycling was one of my favourite things and it never failed to make me happy. Why not Harry?

'Well, you know where we are now. Erik's not here most of the time because he has his other, far more important, business going on.' Paddy smiled at Erik. 'But I'm around.'

I got back onto my bike. 'See you both Saturday, anyway.'

'Lasagne again?'

'That word is to be banned, I never want to hear it again.'

They laughed and waved me off, and for a moment I felt like myself again, the person I had been before, when I'd had a social life and a fizzing anticipation that life was a full of fun and love... a time when anything seemed possible.

* * *

'Aha! Well, if it isn't my beautiful daughter, Roisín!' said Dad, on the doorstep, catching me in a surprisingly meaningful hug. 'We were just talking about anchovies!' He ushered me through the hall and into the kitchen. 'We had them on our honeymoon. I didn't even know what they were! I thought they came in a tin...'

Mum was sitting at the kitchen table, a mug of tea in front of her, and stood up to hug me hello. Shona, standing against the Aga, gave me a wave. Through the window, I could see Kitty and Daisy playing on the swing. The only traces of Saturday night were the fairy lights strung through the trees and the chairs and tables neatly stacked in the summer house.

'Anchovies do come in a tin,' I said.

'But being just a boy from Dublin, for whom anchovies were a paste, I had no idea that they were fish. I thought they only came in a tin. Like shoe polish or pasta.'

'Pasta doesn't come in a tin.' I hugged Mum and sat beside her at the table.

'It did, there used to be only tinned macaroni. Pasta that you boil was all very newfangled when it arrived on these shores.' Dad took the other chair beside Mum. 'But it was on our honeymoon, wasn't it, Maggie?'

Mum nodded. 'London. Found this little Italian restaurant just beside our hotel.'

'Bloomsbury. The hotel was shabby, the woman at the front desk wore these little glasses which she peered through. "Oh, Ireland, is it?" She had a sneery voice, didn't she, Maggie? "Oh, Ireland, we've had a few of your lot recently."'

'We didn't care, we were so excited to be in London. And we had tickets to a play...'

'*As You Like It* at the National Theatre,' said Dad. 'But first, the anchovies.'

'Like nothing we'd ever had.'

'It turned out we'd never actually experienced flavour before, there was sweet, savoury and bland and not much else. And then we ordered pizzas thinking they were just bread and cheese but... oh, my word...'

'Our minds were blown.' Mum looked at him, smiling.

'Who knew a tiny fish on a big pizza could change your life? Or maybe it was the company...'

The two of them gazed at each other for a moment. I didn't dare to look at Shona.

'And then,' said Dad, 'afters. What is this, we said, poking at it with our spoons. Looks creamy and is that chocolate... coffee... all together... what is this marvellous alchemy?' He acted the ingénue trying his first posh dessert.

'You took the first bite.'

'Brave like that, I am.'

'His face was a picture, like a—'

'Man reborn,' Dad joined in. 'As though bathed in holy water or dunked in the Sea of Galilee itself.'

'You're talking about tiramisu?' Shona asked. 'God, I hate tiramisu. It's disgusting. Like vomit.'

'I made tiramisu on Saturday night for the supper club,' I told her.

'Maybe yours is nice,' Shona conceded. 'But make something nicer next time. Not something that brings back memories of shabby honeymoons in horrible boarding houses...'

'It was a nice little hotel actually. The woman at the desk was just a little unfriendly.'

'Where was your honeymoon?' Dad asked. 'Didn't you and Ross go somewhere a little more far-flung?'

'Maldives,' said Shona, biting her nails.

'I've been to paradise,' sang Dad. 'But I've never been to Meath...'

Mum laughed as though it was the funniest thing she'd ever heard, making Dad beam proudly.

'Tell Ross we need to see him soon,' went on Dad, after Mum had recovered. 'All work and no play makes Ross a dull boy. Same as Bridie...'

'Brody,' I said.

'Of course! Why do I keep calling him Bridie? And girls, I've booked a table at the yacht club for my birthday on Friday evening. I would be honoured if my family would join me. It wouldn't be a birthday without my daughters, and granddaughters and my sons-in-law. Will you come?'

I found myself nodding. 'Of course.'

'Wouldn't miss it for the world.' Shona glanced at me.

There were shouts from the garden from the twins. 'Come on, Maggie, let's see what the girls want. Probably pushing on the swing, or a wheelbarrow race.'

As soon as they were gone, Shona turned to me. 'It's like he owns the place! As though he is the doting grandfather and husband when only a few weeks ago he was living it up on the Côte de bloody Azur!'

'I know.'

'I heard the girls telling one of their friends' mothers that their grandparents were a couple again,' said Shona. 'The mother was most confused...'

'As am I.'

'Her face, trying to work it out. I had to step in and mumble something about him working away in France and then coming back... which is kind of true. But I left out the part of him abandoning her and running off with Maxine. And now returning to Mum, like a mongrel dog with his tail between his legs.' She smiled. 'So how is Bridie then?'

'Don't you start.'

She grinned at me. 'Still writing *War and Peace*, is he? Can't wait to read the masterpiece.'

For a moment, I thought I was going to tell her everything, that she had been right and that I married too soon, too hastily and how much of a fool I was. But embarrassment kept me quiet.

'At least you know where he is,' Shona was saying, 'tucked away in your spare room. My husband could be anywhere for all I know. I keep asking myself what I did wrong? Was I too pushy, not pushy enough? Should I have been working, taking the pressure off him? Was I nice enough, loving enough? And now I have nothing without him. No job, can't pay a mortgage, no skills. I have ridiculously little work experience... I was pregnant doing my law exams, for God's sake. I wouldn't count any of those months I spent in that solicitor's office sorting out people's boundary-wall issues as experience.' Shona shook her head. 'I have no idea what to do with my life. He just needs to come back.'

'Have you managed to speak to him yet?' I thought of what Richard told me about a happy-looking Ross having lunch with a woman.

She nodded and her eyes filled with tears. 'He told me... he said that... well... he's... not sure if he loves me any more. Or rather, he says he loves me... but not like he used to.' She twisted a tea towel in her hands. 'Quite a devastating thing to hear your husband say, actually.' Shona walked over and sat on the chair next to me. 'After all these years, I thought we were good, I mean, not amazing, but better than some and as good as most. I looked at all the other couples we know and there's bickering and niggling and needling.' A single tear rolled down her face. 'Pride comes before a fall? Well, I've bloody fallen. I was smug, one of those awful people who thinks they have it all.' Shona wiped away the tear with the back of her hand. 'I told him I was sorry for taking it all for granted, for not truly appreciating what I had but he just said he hadn't been happy for a while. Years, he said. Says he needs space and would I please respect that.'

Outside, the girls had picked a large pile of daisies and they were concentrating on threading them together to make chains. Mum and Dad were sitting together, chatting quietly. Peace and love is never guaranteed, I thought, it's only when you're older, when you have enough experience under your belt, when you're not so pushed and pulled by currents and eddies, do you finally find your calm seas.

* * *

Later, in bed, as Brody worked in the study next door, and Fyodor whirled furiously around on his wheel, I finalised this week's menu for the supper club. The bar was low, I figured. Nothing could be worse than the stodge I'd served, but if I concentrated on nice, fresh, summery ingredients, then I couldn't go far wrong. I wrote up a new menu and sent it off to Richard and Sam. Richard emailed back immediately:

I like v much xxx

26

Over dinner, on Wednesday evening, Brody updated me on Seamus's latest adventure. Apparently, he had decided to scythe the long grass in the field. 'I think it is important to make the reader feel like they are a blade of grass...' Brody said.

'A blade of grass?'

Brody nodded. 'It's about the elemental nature of the relationship between writer, reader and character...'

I stared back at him, trying to think of some response. 'So they need to be a blade of grass?'

'Exactly. Or a leaf, or a ladybird. Whatever. Just something that places them in the scene. They even could be the cancerous mole on Seamus's nose.'

'Seamus has cancer? The poor thing!' For the first time I thought the book actually could go somewhere. Poor Seamus – working outdoors all his life and then is struck down by a melanoma. It was good plot line, I thought, and it might alert people to the risks of not wearing sun cream.

'No, of course not,' said Brody. 'I was just saying it as an example. Seamus is perfectly healthy, just a touch of arthritis in his hands which flares up when he is oiling the scythe.'

I went back to my baked potato, wondering if this was how I was going to spend every evening for the rest of my life. Brody was probably thinking the same, I thought, from the exasperated look in his eyes. We didn't know each other, and whatever earthly plane we once connected on no longer existed. It was like that best friend you make on the first day of college and you spend three days together drinking, laughing hysterically and believing that you are mates for life, only to realise that you trauma bonded in the mêlée of fresher's week and in fact you have absolutely zero in common.

'How many words have you written?' I blurted out, needing to know that this era of hopelessness was nearly over.

'Words?' Brody put down his fork. 'Words! You can't ask about words. It's not about starting on page one and ending on page whatever. It's an organic process. A novel grows like a human being, from nothing. A tiny egg of an idea, meets the sperm of an artist, and so the creative process begins.'

Was I in the middle of some kind of art project? Was this a game show to see how long someone could string someone else along? I thought about what Gerry had said. Was Brody just a hamster person? Would he ever be a child person? I just had to know, it wouldn't change my mind but, depending how he answered it, might help in the decision-making process.

'Brody, do you think...'

He forked food into his mouth and glanced up at me.

'Do you think,' I tried again, 'when the book is finished, or completed or—'

'When I choose to pass the creative process on to the next artist, the reader?'

'Yes, then... how do you feel about... I don't know... a child?'

'A child?' Food flew out of his mouth, a meat-missile flying past my face. 'What do you mean?'

'A baby—'

'I know what a child is, thank you, Roisín,' he spluttered. 'I know that they are small and demanding and take up people's time. They destroy relationships, make everything dirty, and throw their food around and insist on Peppy Pig being shown twenty-four hours a day—'

'Peppa.'

'No thank you. But back to children. They can't talk properly for years. Not until they are really quite old, so you are forced to endure the witterings of an imbecile for so long that you are driven mad. They go on and on and on about the same thing.' He glared at me. 'I thought you understood this, that I already committed enough?'

'Committed to what?' Brody had no commitments that I was aware of. He didn't pay rent, bills or hold down a job. He didn't even commit to a daily shower or an appointment with his toothbrush. 'I was under the impression that you liked children.'

He shook his head. 'Not remotely,' he said. 'Babies are annoying. Everything was fine until Roger came along. God, he was so irritating. But in the meantime, I was thinking of adding to the family in another way... adopting—'

'Adoption? No, Brody, not adoption—' No right-minded social worker would allow us to adopt, I thought.

'Yes, adoption,' he said, happily. 'A baby hamster, a friend for Fyodor.'

Was all this some kind of game to keep me guessing and wondering and never quite in control of anything that went on in this house? Perhaps this was as good as life got, me working, cooking, cleaning and paying the bills, and him writing, the two of us in this endless circle, forever, with a house full of hamsters all whirring on their wheels. Where would it end? One of those houses you see in the newspapers which have had to be fumigated, the carpets burned, the floorboards torn up, because it was overrun with hamsters.

'I doubt any one asked Rembrandt if his paintings were finished,' Brody mumbled. 'You don't just decide to draw the creative process to a close.' He flung his cutlery down on the plate. 'I'm going back upstairs,' he announced. 'I'll do a spellcheck, maybe even the grammar check.'

'I hope Seamus cuts the grass okay.'

He stopped. 'Who?' For a moment, Brody looked utterly bewildered.

'Seamus,' I said. 'The scythe.' Brody was still utterly blank. 'The one he was sharpening,' I prompted. 'I was hoping he might have a happy ending.'

Brody's nostrils flared. 'You, of all people, Roisín, should realise there is no such thing.'

* * *

I called in to see Harry again, with a plate of food.

Lately, I'd noticed that the frying pan – scrubbed clean – was now on the drainer every evening, and I saw that there was more food in the fridge, a bit of cheese and some eggs.

'How's the cooking going, Harry?'

'I've been reading your cookery books,' he said. 'And I'm not sure I'm up to it.'

'Up to what?'

'I think you get to a certain age and there are so many things you can't do... you lose your nerve.'

'Your nerve? For cooking?'

He nodded. 'It's the lists of things, the instructions, the timings! Before, I used to just cook so confidently and it always turned out well. Last night I tried to fry an egg and it went wrong, shell in the egg, too overdone, under-done on the other side, yolk running everywhere. And I thought to myself, I can't even fry an egg. I used to fry fifty of them every morning for the lads on the ship. I've lost it,' he said. 'It's gone.'

'But you can get it back.'

He shook his head. 'They tried to get me to avail of meals on wheels, my doctor said I was looking peaky. I've resisted so far.'

'Have you ever thought about the lunches at Lady Immaculate Hall? Have you heard about them?'

'But I don't need feeding, I don't want charity—'

'No,' I said. 'I thought that you should do the feeding.'

'You mean an old person like me gets to feed the other old people? And you could meet people and chat.' Harry shook his head. 'I don't know if I still cán. I see you and Cyril, no one else. I'm a bit scared, Roisín, if I could be truthful.'

I knew exactly what he meant.

27

By now, as I rushed through the dining room of Lady Immaculate Hall, I knew faces and names as I waved at those gathering for the community lunch at the Hall. Harry would love it here, I thought. The food, the company, doing the crossword.

'Afternoon, Gita!' I called, tying my apron and rushing to take my place. 'Hi Mary, Marian! What's on the menu today?'

'Roast chicken and roast potatoes and all the trimmings today. And strawberries and cream for dessert.'

Outside it was a warm summer's day, the old fire escape doors were open to allow a cool breeze in, but no one was going to say no to a hot lunch – not when it was roast chicken.

Later, as I was helping to wash up, I overheard Marian and Sheila talking. 'It's no good,' Marian was saying. 'We've tried everything. They've given us a deadline of Sunday week.'

'That soon?' Sheila shook her head.

I knew immediately what they were referring to. That morning, I had received a letter from the developers saying that the negotiations with the Save Our Hall campaign group had ended and Save Our Hall had agreed to give up their fight. The Hall was going to be demolished and the development could continue unhindered. I had been extremely naive to think that my two roles – that of a would-be planner and a happy lunchtime volunteer – could co-exist. I would lose my job, but also, what if Marian and Sheila and all the others found out that I worked in planning? Would they hate me, knowing that I was on the other side? And what about the developers? What would they say if they discovered that someone from the planning department volunteered with the lunch group which was part of the Save Our Hall campaign? I felt sick as I dried the plates, stacking them in a pile ready to be put away until the following day.

'It's such a disappointment,' Sheila was saying.

'It's devastating.' Marian shook her head. 'I am so furious, so angry that the council did not step in and do something! Does it not want to protect the seafront, care for the heritage?'

I didn't know if I was imagining it was said for my benefit. I turned around. 'What's going on?' I tried to look innocent, but inside I felt awful.

'We'll have to close,' said Marian. 'We've been fighting it for the last five years, but it seems the developers have won. The council say we can go to another facility, over in Mounttown, but it's not on a bus route and it's got as much soul as my cat's litter tray. The building says something about this area, it's minded people for a hundred and fifty years, it's taken them in, music and voices have echoed around these walls... the stories it could tell. There used to be political meetings here, the Irish suffrage organisation had it as their headquarters, Count John McCormack, the great Irish tenor, once gave a performance in this very room for the workers on the old tramline... it's just not good enough to say it's too expensive.'

'This whole area is about to be redeveloped,' said Sheila. 'It's a crying disgrace. This building, gone. The amusement arcade, gone. Community spirit, thrown to the wolves!'

Marian nodded. 'Under building regulations, we can't continue with the lunches. There are no accessible toilets for one...'

'We all wheel people in,' said Sheila. 'No one minds. We open doors for everyone. Micheál is a great man for lifting wheelchairs and buggies and whatever else up the front steps.'

'And fire regulations, we don't have enough fire doors.'

'But we're so careful, we always check that every light switch is turned off. We don't deep-fry anything and at Christmas, when we had the party for the little ones, Micheál made sure that the tree lights weren't bought off his brother's stall, because they are known to be a little dodgy, but he went into town and bought them in Arnotts. And they were lovely and we didn't have so much as a spark from them.'

'And we can't afford to heat the building. As soon as one radiator goes on, the heat immediately is sucked out of the windows...'

'Or holes,' said Sheila. 'We've asked and begged for money and the council just say no. Too expensive. There are a hundred thousand other things that need paying for and we're not important.'

This building was damp, draughty and had no wheelchair access or toilets. There were buckets at the side of the dining room to catch the drips from the roof after any kind of rain, Marian had explained, and if there was a fire, then there was only one escape route. 'The council say they can't insure us for another year,' said Sheila. 'They've done their best, but it's time to give up.'

'They have given us use of another building at Mounttown... and it's compliant in all health and safety, accessibility and has the right energy system,' said Marian. 'It's all eco-something or other.'

'But it's on the other side of Sandycove, and it means this part of the village will become...' She paused. 'What's the word?'

'Soulless?' Finally, I found my voice.

Marian glanced up at the wonky clock on the wall. 'You should head back, it's gone two. Quick, you don't want to be late.'

I untied my apron, picked up my bag and began my dash back to the office. I had been utterly pathetic, assuming that the building was unsalvageable when it wasn't necessarily. I'd already wasted two weeks. But what could I do, when Frank, Dermot and everyone else had looked for ways to save it? Marian was right, the developers had won.

28

The last time I'd been at the Sandycove Yacht Club was years ago with Dad, after one of our Saturday sailing days. Shona and I would sit up on the high stools at the bar with our fizzy drinks and crisps. It still had the whiff of an old boys' club about it with the aroma of cigars and a scent of the sea. It was thickly carpeted in eye-dazzling blue and gold, furnished with large, heavy chairs and there was a blazing fire even on this summer's evening and men with handlebar moustaches and a glass of brandy behind copies of *Sailing* magazine. Mum and Dad were already in the bar, sitting on a sofa at the far end of the room, with a view straight out to sea. The following day was the second supper club and I was feeling nervous. Everything was ready to go at home, Gerry was arriving first thing the following morning, but I didn't want to produce another disaster like last time. How did professional chefs do it, night after night? This was agonising.

'Aha!' Dad stood up when I walked towards them, smooshing me into another one of his hugs. 'So good of you to come!'

'Of course I came,' I said when released. I handed over his present, kissed Mum and then sat down.

'Oh, Roisín.' He looked very touched, turning the present over in his hands. 'I didn't expect anything. It's bad enough me making you come out for dinner when you could be at home with Bridie, I mean, Brody... but thank you...'

I thought of Brody upstairs at home, writing away. Earlier, he had put his arms around me. 'I love you, Roisín,' he had said. 'Listen, I know you were asking about a child yesterday and I know women get broody. It's their nature. Women's hormones rage from time to time like a furnace. Look, I get it. But I'm a different kind of rooster to all the normal roosters out there. I just think hamsters are far less annoying, less expensive to run, and also far cuter. And don't worry about being hormonal. It's absolutely fine. I can take it.'

'Open it,' I said to Dad. 'It's just something I thought you would like.'

He carefully removed the paper. For a moment, he didn't speak and just stared at the present, then showed it to Mum who smiled at me. It was a copy of the framed photograph of him, Shona and me in *Shining Light*, his little boat.

'I don't know what to say.' His voice squeaked a little. 'It's... well, that was a long time ago. I'd hardly recognise that handsome young man with the black hair... and his two beautiful girls...' He looked at me, a strange expression on his face. 'I will cherish this,' he said. 'Like lost treasure buried at the bottom of the sea.'

I had agonised over what to buy the man who had everything, and then I thought of an old photograph I'd kept in a box. 'I just thought...' I didn't know why I had given it to him and I had worried that it was too personal... did Dad deserve to know how much those sailing days meant to me? Shouldn't I have given him something generic, like a pair of socks?

We heard Shona's voice behind us. 'There they are,' she was saying. 'Come on, we're late.' Shona was walking speedily towards us, flustered, the girls scurrying behind her.

And behind them was Ross. The last time I'd seen him was on the day of the communion.

'Happy birthday, Dad,' she said, hugging him briefly.

'Ross!' Mum stood up in surprise as Dad then hugged Ross. 'Good to see you,' Dad was saying. 'How nice of you all to come.' Daisy and Kitty hugged me and then both went to sit on the same armchair as Mum, on either arm.

'Welcome home,' Ross was saying. 'I'm so sorry that I haven't been around much lately, just up to my eyes.' He glanced at me. Shona's jaw was tight, her smile seemed fixed.

'You work so hard, Ross,' said Dad. 'A trojan, that's what you are. Maggie and I are just so pleased that you're able to be here tonight.'

Ross had always been perfectly pleasant company but I had seen another side to him, the Ross who sneaked into his own house so he could avoid his wife and children and then sped off in a sports car.

'Let's get some drinks,' Dad was saying. 'Ross, you'll have a whiskey, won't you?'

'I certainly will,' said Ross. 'I need one after all those nights in the office.' Again, he glanced at me.

'So,' Dad was saying, 'what are you working on?'

'A big case... you know lawyers, get caught up in our work, tend to prioritise it over everything. Which is not right, not right at all.' He looked over at Shona, smiling. 'Shona's been amazing, holding the fort, looking after the girls.' Shona was examining her nails, pushing down one of her cuticles. 'Do you know something?' he went on. 'There's no place like home, it's only when you go away you realise how much you miss it.' He turned to Mum and Dad. 'I've been telling Shona for years that she should go back to work,' went on Ross. 'Now the girls are old enough, it's time for Shona to shine. Maybe train as a Pilates teacher? Or get a job in a nice flower shop... something just for her?' He picked up his glass of whiskey and took a large sip, while Shona wouldn't make eye contact the entire time. When she went to the bathroom, I followed her in.

'So when did he come back?' I asked.

She sighed, and leaned against the basins. 'Last night, said he's sorry, says he's made a mistake and that he missed family life. And that he loves me.' She flicked the water off her hands and picked up a small towel from a pile. 'I am under no illusion he actually does.'

'Do you love him?'

'I have to. He's the father of my children. I don't want to be divorced. I have two girls, just like we were.' She looked at me. 'And... I can't face being alone. It's too terrifying. I mean, getting a job, being on my own, all that, I can't do it. It's the bare look of my life when I have spent so long filling it up. Even if he's never home, even if we sleep in the same bed and never touch, even if we barely speak, it's better than the alternative.'

I gazed at her for a second wondering what to say. It didn't matter that I thought she was making a mistake, that he hadn't been having an existential crisis and that he was, or at least, had been seeing someone else, Shona was willing to take him back and I had to support her.

'The girls are very happy about it,' she said. 'And frankly, that's all that matters.'

I nodded. 'Of course.'

'Come on, let's go and eat... I'm going to have something nice because I'm not drinking. Unlike Ross, who's had far too much already.'

* * *

Later, we all stood outside the yacht club saying our final goodbyes.

'Can I have a go on your bike?' Daisy asked. 'Just around the car park?'

'Of course,' I said. 'Just be careful... stay close to us. It's dark now.'

'I'll pull the car round,' said Ross.

'I'm driving,' Shona insisted. 'You've been drinking.'

'I know, but I'm not going to drive us home, what do you take me for?' He was slurring. 'One of those criminals we are forced to defend? I'll just reverse the car out and then you can take over.'

'No, Ross, don't... best not to. I'll do it in a moment.' She hugged Mum and Dad goodbye. 'We'll see you soon. I'll pop in tomorrow and help out at the supper club, okay, Roisín?'

'I'm on a trip all day with the gardening group,' said Mum. 'We're taking the early morning ferry to Wales, a day trip around some National Trust properties and then the late ferry home.' Daisy and Kitty were both on my bike, one on the seat, the other standing on the pedals.

'And I'll be at Philip's house,' said Dad. 'But if you need me to do anything, let me know.'

'Dad's driving!' shouted Daisy.

'Girls!' shouted Shona. 'Get off that thing! Quickly!'

The big black car, its lights on full beam, reversed out of the parking space and turned in an arc. Ross's face was behind the wheel of the Range

Rover as he revved towards us and then lurched forward as Daisy and Kitty jumped off the bike, letting it crash to the floor, as they raced to stand beside Shona.

I think I must have screamed when there was a crunch as Ross drove over my bike, dragging it under the wheels, and came to an abrupt stop beside us.

Shona turned to me, her face white.

'He could have killed us,' said Daisy.

'Both of us,' said Kitty.

'Which would have been better than just one of us.'

'If we go, we go together.'

'Oh my God.' Shona was shaking.

Ross was totally unperturbed, stepping out of the car as though nothing had happened. 'Your carriage awaits, madam,' he slurred, the collar of his rugby shirt now flattened rather than standing crisply to attention as it did when he arrived. He tossed over the keys which Shona dropped and fumbled for on the ground before climbing into the driver's seat, the girls seat-belted in the back, Ross in the passenger side. He hung out of the window, like a man who owned the world. 'Glorious evening!' he shouted, as the car pulled away, leaving the mangled mess of my lovely bike. 'See you all again soon!'

Mum and Dad helped me pick it up off the ground.

'Oh Roisín,' said Mum. 'It's gone.'

I nodded, a wheel in one hand, a pedal in another.

'What was wrong with him?' asked Dad. 'What an absolutely stupid thing to do.'

'He wasn't himself,' said Mum, near tears. 'Neither of them were. And then the whiskey drinking... he must have had four, plus the wine.'

I removed the bell from the bike, the basket and my lock, my hands shaking. The rest of the remains I left in a pathetic pile at the side of the yacht club.

It wasn't Daisy or Kitty, thankfully. A bike was only an ingenious clatter of metal and rubber... but it was my clatter of metal and rubber. I had loved that bike.

'He's a fecking idiot, that one,' said Dad, shaking his head. 'My God, how did we not notice?'

'You haven't been around?' said Mum, sweetly. 'While you have been in France, I have been noticing.'

Dad said nothing but just rebalanced one of the wheels against the wall. 'Come on.' He put his arm around me. 'Let's go home. The taxi can drop you off first, Roisín, and then us. I'll come down tomorrow and pick up the bike. There's not a lot that can be done for it, so I think I will have to take it straight to the recycling centre.'

* * *

I walked home in the early hours of the morning, through the dark and silent streets, aware of the giant, invisible weight that pressed down on my shoulders as though I was carrying something far too large and cumbersome. And it was getting heavier. Cycling was always joyful, and however I was feeling, a cycle ride was like an endorphin shot in the arm. I was failing and flailing in life and I had no one to blame but myself for the fact that I was unhappily married.

How could I admit I'd been so stupid? How could I confess that I, a grown woman, had made such an immature, impetuous mistake? Upstairs was all quiet when I carefully opened the front door and tiptoed in, the whirr of the hamster wheel the only sound. Thank God Fyodor hadn't escaped. Brody was in his study while I quickly got ready for bed. And then I heard another sound. Fyodor? It was a kind of whimper. A human whimper. And it was coming from Brody's study.

'Brody?' I knocked on the door. Maybe he'd had a stroke or had such bad repetitive strain injury from all that typing that his limbs had seized up. Or maybe this was the moment I would be confronted by his book-fuelled meltdown. I braced myself for the sight of him with his ear cut off or hallucinating on absinthe. Or another spliff.

Brody was sitting on the sofa bed, his feet up on the small table, headphones on, watching the large TV. The one he'd told me didn't even work. His eyes were closed, his head had fallen back. In one hand was a games console and on the screen was a computer image of a soldier, machine gun in hand.

'Brody?' I shook his leg. 'Brody?'

His eyes flickered open. 'You're back...?' He glanced at the screen, a guilty look spread across his face. 'I thought you were at that... you know...'

'It's one thirty in the morning.'

'I was... I am... I just took a break. And fell asleep.' He glanced at the screen again. 'After doing so much, I'm just very, very tired.'

'What are you doing?'

'Having a nap. Which is allowed, by the way. Sleeping is an essential bodily function.'

'I know that. I mean, what have you been doing?'

'Okay, okay!' He sighed heavily and rolled his eyes. 'You got me. Oh, so clever Roisín. Caught in the act. If you must know, I was playing *Code Of Honour*. Just a computer game. Somehow, despite being one of life's more sensitive types who can fill a fountain pen with ink, but not rewire a plug, I managed to get this TV working. Anyway, Anna—'

'Anna down the road, Anna?'

'Yes...' he said wearily. 'Yes, Anna down the road, Anna. Well, Anna just so happens to have a collection of computer games. And she lent them to me.'

'Right...' I tried to take this all in. Brody had never mentioned computer games before. I had no idea that he and Anna were exchanging games. And I was even sceptical that he would be able to re-ink a fountain pen. I had literally never seen him do anything remotely practical. He didn't even take the rubbish out because he said the smell was too bad and made him feel sick. He'd stopped shaving because he said his skin was too sensitive and he once tried to put staples into the stapler and ended up drawing blood. 'What's it about?'

'What's what about?'

'The computer game?'

'Oh... nothing... I don't know... I can't remember. It's not very good, anyway. I mean, I can't really use this twizzle-stick thing.'

'The console.'

'Exactly. Anna thought it might help with my stress... but I ended up being shot at and it was quite terrifying.'

'Okay...' I really didn't know what to do. Did other people find married life as confusing? I suddenly felt incredibly tired. 'I'm going to bed,' I said. 'I'll leave you to your games then. I have the supper club tomorrow.'

'Don't wake Fyodor,' he said. 'He needs his sleep.'

29

At dawn, grey light began to creep into the bedroom. I'd been awake for hours. My bike, I thought, my lovely bike. Many of the best moments in my life had been on that bike, the utter joy when you tip off the top of a hill after a long slog up, the wind whooshing in your face and you feel alive. There was that day when Paddy and I cycled to Wicklow and lay on our backs in the sun, nestled in the heather holding hands, staring at the blue sky and talking about what we wanted to do with our lives. Two tiny bodies on a mountain on a perfect summer's day. On the cycle home, I felt like my bike and I were going to take off with joy and happiness and... whatever else I was feeling. And now it was gone. All of it.

The only sound in the whole street – the whole world – was Fyodor furiously exercising, like a mini Davina McCall, forever working on his fitness. Beside me, Brody – a mass of beard and body – lay flat on his back, his mouth open, a low rumbling snore emanating from the recesses of his throat. He sprawled starfish-style, his belly rising and falling like the swelling of the sea.

I got married by mistake, I thought.

In a week's time, I told myself, there was a chance that we would be able to reclaim our relationship and be back where we started. We could just pretend that this whole year never happened and pick up as honeymooners. We could spend evenings together, weekends... Brody could become part of my life. Now, he was on a separate planet and until then, I just had to hang on. My phone beeped. Shona:

I'm so sorry about the bike. I will pay for a new one. Money being transferred now xxx

There was another beep as a notification popped up that €500 had gone into my account.

I went downstairs and called her.

'Did I wake you?' she asked. 'It's five in the morning.'

'No, I've been awake for ages.'

'I'm so sorry about last night,' she said. 'I can't believe that happened.'

'It's okay,' I replied, my voice flat. 'It's only a bike... and thanks for the money. I appreciate it.'

'It shouldn't have happened.'

'It was an accident...'

'He was drunk,' she said. 'And I just have to accept that marriages are difficult, people get drunk, and sometimes people leave for a time just to get their heads together... I met Ronan the other day and he says he felt obliged to tell me that Ross has been seeing another woman.'

I was silent.

'I mean, I didn't believe Ross when he said that Ronan was jealous of him. He used to say that Ronan hated the fact that his parents preferred him. But now I see that maybe Ross was right. I mean, I would know if Ross was seeing someone else, wouldn't I? I would know. Female intuition. Trusting your gut.'

'Why do you think Ronan told you?'

'I met him in Dunnes doing the shop and we were talking and he asked me how I was, and I started crying, right beside a massive pyramid of washing powder. And he just said he thought I should know...' Shona was crying again. 'He said that it wasn't fair that I didn't know. Apparently, he saw Ross jogging around Merrion Square one lunchtime and there was a woman with him. And when he flagged them down, Ross introduced her in such a way that Ronan put two and two together and made five.'

There was silence for a moment.

'He made four, though,' I said, eventually.

'What?'

'He didn't make five, he made four.'

'Are you saying that Ronan isn't lying?'

'Yes.'

There was no sound from Shona.

'Shona?'

'Roisín, you too?' There was a slight wobble in her voice which broke my heart. 'If you know something that I don't, then I think you should bloody well tell me.'

'I don't know anything,' I said. 'Except...'

'Except what?' Her voice was icy.

'Except that he came back during the communion when he didn't know I was cooking... remember? And I don't know, I just wondered if, you know, there was someone else.'

'Why?'

'I don't know, I really don't. But I wondered. And then there was the sports car.'

'The sports car?'

'A small black thing, two-seater. He drove off in it.'

'He drove?'

'No, he got in the passenger side.'

Silence again.

'Shona? Are you still there?'

'I'm still here,' she said, quietly.

'And Richard saw him in town, having lunch with a woman...'

'And what makes you suggest that she wasn't a colleague? He's always having lunch with colleagues...'

'Nothing, except Richard thought something was strange, that's all.'

'And Ronan is just jealous and you and Richard have jumped to this conclusion, like Mr and Mrs Marple...'

'Miss Marple was a Miss,' I said, 'she never married.'

'I wish I hadn't either,' she said.

Nor me, I thought.

'Look, Roisín,' she went on, 'before you start throwing around baseless and really very damaging claims about my husband, the father of your nieces, who I am really trying very hard to support, then I would suggest you look at your own marriage. We never see Brody. Sometimes I wonder if he really exists and it's some kind of elaborate plot. Did you borrow him on the day of your wedding? I can't even remember what he fucking well looks like, and you dare to suggest that I don't know my own husband! So what if Ross had lunch with someone? He's allowed. And so what if a friend gave him a lift? So what?'

'Sorry, Shona.'

'So you should be,' she said. 'So you bloody well should be! I can't talk about this any more. Go and minister to your non-existent, phantom husband, and I will get on with providing a stable home for my daughters.'

And the phone went dead.

30

Little Eden Supper Club
Selection of canapés
Rachel's goat's cheese, apple chutney, home-made sourdough bread
Castletownsend crab tart and dressed crisp green salad
Roisín's vanilla ice cream, chewy meringues and strawberries and lemon curd

Gerry's van arrived promptly at 7 a.m. and I heard him opening the back doors and hauling out the crates of vegetables and food.

'Not too early for you then?' Gerry shouted.

'Not at all,' I said, trying to keep my voice down.

'How's the pop-up restaurant?' he shouted, his voice echoing down the street. 'They're all the rage now, aren't they? There are two lads running one on Dollymount Strand out of an old horsebox. And two girls have taken over an old hay shed for the summer. Apparently, everything they make will be from a five-mile radius. We've all gone back to basics. The old ways are the best ways. Now, where do you want these?'

'On the doorstep,' I said, pointing in the direction of the house. 'I can carry them in. This way...'

I followed him as he stepped on to the pavement and across to my house. 'Just put them there... thanks, Gerry.'

He laid the crates neatly on the front step. 'You sure you don't want me carrying them in?'

'No, it's grand,' I said. 'My husband's still asleep and I don't want to wake him up.'

'Ah, the husband!' He grinned. 'The one who doesn't like dogs or children. How's the hamster?'

'Still up all night. On his wheel.'

He laughed. 'Like I said, some are hamster people and others like proper animals, like dogs or horses or goats. And talking of which, lovely bit of cheese, in there,' he said, gesturing to the crate. 'Rachel says we had perfect conditions for the grass this spring. The goat's milk is perfection, she says. My mam kept goats, years and years ago. We got rid of them when she died. I don't remember much, but when I eat some of Rachel's cheese it brings it all back.'

'And the herbs smell amazing,' I said, taking one of the crates from him, the scent of the still-warm-from-the-sun strawberries, the freshness of the vegetables was as though I had crawled into a polytunnel and laid on my back in the warmth.

I thought of Shona and hoped she would forgive me and of Brody playing computer games and the deadline which was only a week away but felt further than ever.

'Picked them late last night,' he said. 'Best time to pick herbs, at the end of the day, full of flavour.'

He walked back to his van and slammed the two doors shut. 'Good luck tonight,' he shouted again. 'I'll tell Rachel to call you about next week.'

'By the way...' I walked to the passenger side of the van. 'How's Foxy? Have you found a home for her yet?'

'Not yet,' he said. 'Still looking for someone. She's just down there if you want to say hello.'

Foxy was in her box, on the floor in front of the passenger seat, her big brown eye stared at me, her tail twitched in hope and optimism. Maybe, she looked like she was thinking, this person will take me home.

'I can't take you, Foxy, but someone will.'

'The right dog will always find you,' said Gerry. 'When you open your heart, the right dog always turns up.' He got back into the van and called over. 'Good luck with the pop-up thing tonight, hope it all goes well and you raise lots of money.'

'I'll let you know. Take care, Gerry.'

'Will do.' He gave me a nod. 'See you next week.' The van pulled away just as Harry walked up.

'Good morning, Roisín.' He was dressed immaculately in his brown suit. 'I've got St Vincent de Paul coming over today.'

'The actual St Vincent de Paul?'

He smiled. 'The charity people. They are going to take more of the boxes, the ones you've helped me fill. It feels good that they are going to a good home,' he said. 'I used to have a St Vincent de Paul medal in our house, growing up. When my mother died, I remember wearing the medal thinking it would keep me safe from anything happening to me. When someone dies it can be a little worrying. If it's unexplained, then maybe you're next.'

'Have you still got the medal? It's definitely kept you safe,' I said.

'I have, it's in a box under the stairs. I'll show it to you next time you're over. But just off to get my morning paper. And I promise, Roisín, I'll be passing it on. Cyril says he will be happy to take my papers when I've finished with them and then he passes them on to Mrs O'Donoghue in number three and she passes them on to Mrs Goodall in number eight. We're all very careful, no creasing, I make a start on the cryptic and we all add in little bits.' He gave me a wave. 'Recycling in action!'

* * *

Inside, Brody was already awake and consuming a rasher sandwich with extra rashers. 'Brain food,' he said, tapping his forehead. 'It really works. A combination of connective tissue and marrow and you're flying.' He masticated madly, meat and marrow were being tossed around in his mouth like clothes in a washing machine. I was too busy making the ice cream for later to go with the strawberries to really listen. 'Mmm... yes...' I murmured, boiling the cream and sugar with the vanilla and doing all the timings in my head of what I should do when and how.

'Do you ever read books, Roisín?'

'Of course...' Would the ice cream freeze in time? I'd learned a lot from the first week, and even though this menu was slightly less crowd-friendly and a little more sophisticated, I hoped it was still simple enough that if I just followed my menu plan step by step then I wouldn't mess it up.

'When I was a child,' Brody was saying, sinking his teeth into his rasher sandwich, 'Dad used to frisk me for books before dinner every evening. You're not sneaking one of those in here, he used to say. You concentrate more on your food and talking to your family.' Brody looked up at me. 'Can you imagine a child being encouraged not to read? Go and play football, he used to say. Go and get muddy.' Brody laughed. 'He used to tell everyone he had an intellectual on his hands.'

I was trying to listen to him, but I was also having an internal panic that the ice cream wouldn't freeze in time. I had to get it into the freezer as soon as possible. Brody had taken up too much of my mental energy. Today, I didn't have the time.

'And then I think I am going to paint my testicles green, white and orange for Paddy's Day,' Brody said.

'What?' I looked up.

'Just seeing if you were actually listening to me,' he said, leaning against the sink. 'You're the kind of person who can only do one thing at a time. People go on about men not being able to multitask, but with us, it's the other way round. You can only focus on one thing; I can do several things at the same time.'

Talking and eating, I thought. 'I'm just trying to plan this evening,' I said. 'The ice cream goes into the machine and then into the freezer and then I want to get going with the crab.'

'Crap?'

'Crab.'

'Oh, right.' Brody nodded and wiped his mouth with the back of his hand. 'I'll go up and start the next level...'

'The next level?' But I wasn't really listening again as I was much more interested in whisking the egg yolks with the sugar.

'I mean, the next chapter... Seamus is going to... he's going to...' Brody stopped. 'He's found a button in the milking shed.'

'A button?'

Brody nodded. 'He thinks it's one from his mother's old coat but it turns out to be just one from his old anorak.'

'Oh, right. It's so good that it's nearly the end, just another week to go and then his adventures will be over. And then he can go home or whatever... have a happy ending.'

The doorbell rang. 'Not them again.' Brody scowled. 'Why are they here? Don't they know I need a quiet house? Lee Child needs his house to be so completely quiet he makes everyone tie dusters to their feet. And Hemingway actually shot someone who coughed just as he was writing a particularly important scene.' He stomped up the stairs heavily, like a furious child.

'Are we allowed in?' whispered Richard, Jools and Sam standing just behind him, when I opened the door. 'Will the Great Author be annoyed at our presence?'

I shook my head. 'He'll be fine,' I said.

'He's like a mad man in the attic, isn't he?' commented Richard, making Sam laugh. 'Like something out of a Victorian novel.'

'Thanks for that, Richard,' I said. 'Very helpful.'

'Sorry!' But he winked at Sam. 'Okay, so let's get down to business. So, Jools, you know your role? Roisín's assistant, like last time. Erik and Paddy are with us again today. I think Erik has a business meeting this morning and then he and Paddy are in charge of chairs and tables and then cocktails as they did last week. Sam, you're in charge of decoration, laying tables, glassware, corralling the musicians... and I'm the maître d' again... managing everything.'

Sam grinned at Jools and me.

'He was always like this, Sam, bossy. Can't stand not being in control.'

'Richard is one of those people who has an emperor complex. Born to rule.'

'Emperor complex?' said Richard. 'Moi? Like Napoleon? Or Alexander? I could live with that.'

I quickly talked everyone through what we would be making and all the different additions and garnishes. I felt almost like a proper chef as everyone nodded and made appreciative facial expressions and then I saw Brody standing in the kitchen doorway.

'Doesn't look like much work is going on here,' he said, smiling. 'Thought you all were meant to be doing some kind of soup kitchen? Or something like that. I can't remember what Roisín was saying...' He made it sound like I was nothing, just someone rabbiting away and not worth listening to.

'Supper club.' Richard eyed him carefully. 'It's the second week. The first was a tremendous success... we had roast hamster...'

Jools laughed, as Brody looked horrified.

'Sorry, I mean, lasagne,' went on Richard. 'Talking of which, how is the precious creature?'

'Fyodor is very well,' said Brody. 'He's upstairs in the bedroom.'

'The bedroom?' Richard looked at me.

I wanted to say it wasn't my idea and that sweet as Fyodor undoubtedly was, the sound of his whirring wheel was giving me nightmares, but annoying Brody was time-consuming and exhausting.

'We would never leave him on his own,' Brody interrupted. 'That would be cruel. And anyway, he's part of the family. Who wouldn't want a hamster in the bedroom?' He smiled at everyone and gave me one of his brooding glowers before swishing out of the kitchen like some unromantic hero.

'Now, there's a man in need of a good kick up the arse,' said Richard, under his breath, and then looked at me with wide, innocent eyes. 'The words just fell out of my mouth, I didn't have any control over them!'

But he was right, I knew he was. Except I was stuck with him.

31

Jools and I cooked all day and brought everything over to Mum's in the late afternoon. By 5 p.m., the whole supper club team were lying in the sun, taking a breather. The ice cream was in the freezer – and actually frozen. Sam and Richard were going through the bookings on the laptop.

'Is your husband still writing his book?' Erik was lying back on the rug, his hands under his head.

'It has to be finished by Friday,' I said. 'Less than a week away. And I thought we could celebrate it next Saturday?'

'Finally,' said Richard. 'The book is dead, long live the book.' He turned to Paddy and Erik. 'What's that joke? How do you know someone is a writer? They tell you.' He gave me a look.

'Well, I think being a writer is interesting,' said Jools.

'So do I,' said Sam. 'You are an accountant... it's not exactly renowned for being fascinating.'

'No, but I don't go on about it. I don't expect other people to be tantalised and scintillated by my working life.'

'It's not Brody's fault he's a writer,' I said. 'And it's really hard writing a book, especially a good one.'

'Well, when he writes a good one, I'll take it all back.' Richard glanced at Sam, who smiled. 'Look,' he went on, taking my hand. 'I know I'm being mean. It's just that... we need you back. We need you talking and laughing and having the craic.'

'I am here, aren't I? Having the craic with all of you...'

'Are you though?' Richard looked sceptical.

'Shut up, Richard,' said Jools. 'Stop going on about Brody. You're just jealous because the last book you read was *The Celestine Prophecy* when you were nineteen. Do you remember? You bought a mandala bracelet and said you were going to wear it for the rest of your life. In the end I had to cut it off you because it was so dirty you were worried you were carrying the bubonic plague.'

'It was disgusting,' agreed Richard.

'I remember that book,' said Erik. 'I read it one summer when I was trying to find myself and find some way of dealing with my family, all of whom are super-successful. My father is an Olympic athlete. My mother is a surgeon and my sister was a piano prodigy and is now also a surgeon. It was kind of a super-competitive family with no room for failure.'

'Failure is essential,' said Paddy. 'Failure should be celebrated, not success. Failure is where you learn who you are.'

Erik was nodding. 'I know that now, but it takes a long time to shed yourself of the lessons you learned as a child.' He shrugged those huge shoulders. 'I'm trying to let go of a lot of... what's the word? Shit? I don't need to compete, there's no competition in life, not unless it's an actual competition, of course.' He grinned at us.

'I'm Dingle tiddlywinks champion, 1986,' said Richard. 'So you could say that I know all about success.'

Erik smiled. 'A couple of years ago, I would have had to be running the club, or off doing some kind of sport, mountain running...'

'He runs up them,' said Paddy, 'not just down.'

'That kind of thing.' Erik propped himself up on his elbows. 'I met Paddy here in a cycling club. I joined it because I realised that I wasn't a team player and in our bike club, it's not a race. We start and we end together. Like this supper club.' He turned towards Paddy and slapped him on the back. 'This man here has taught me a great deal. He moved to Copenhagen to find himself, and his own journey is pretty inspiring.'

Paddy reddened a little. 'Thank you, Erik,' he said.

'Did you?' I didn't mean to speak out loud.

'Did I what?' The look on his face was unutterably kind. His eyes were soft like butter, melting at the edges.

'Find yourself?'

He shook his head. 'No, but I did discover that you never do. No one does. And that's the point. Each day is hopefully an improvement on the one before.'

'But you're lonely.' Jools had crept forward and was sitting on the rug with us. 'You told me.' She turned to us. 'Can you believe Paddy is still single?'

'Inconceivable,' said Richard.

'Shocking,' agreed Sam.

'I'm not lonely, just sometimes. Like everyone is.'

'Yes,' said Sam, 'but you just need to be aware being alone tips over from being healthily lonely, to being unhealthily lonely.'

'All the more reason why the supper club was a genius idea,' Richard commented smugly.

'I'm going to find you someone, Paddy,' said Jools. 'We will find some nice woman for you, someone to make you happy...'

I glanced up at Paddy and for a second our eyes met.

'I keep remembering this poem, something like, Believe that further shore... Is reachable from here...'

'... Believe in miracle and cures and healing wells,' I finished. 'We did it as well.'

He looked at me again. 'It's about having faith in yourself... all will be well.'

'Is that an Irish poem?' Erik asked. 'Has to be with all that talk of wells. Tonight, I will try and remember some poems from old Norse legends... but I need to be well lubricated for that. I will have to open my Akvavit again!'

'We want to hear some of those Norse legends,' said Richard, 'stories of your ancestors and I will tell you some stories of mine, most of whom were convicts and criminals or hid in wardrobes during the Easter Rising. No legends or songs will ever be written about them. Or maybe I will commission the great Brody Brady to write something?'

I felt a flash of rebellion stir within me, maybe it was the poem that Paddy had reminded me of, that idea that all is never lost, you keep going, keep believing. Harry was determined to improve his life, even after losing Nora. Even Mum and Dad and whatever friendship they were reforging were determined to make the future happier. 'His real name isn't Brody,' I said, 'it's Brian.'

'Brian!' Richard looked delighted. 'Brian Brady!'

'What's wrong with Brian?' asked Paddy. 'It's a good Irish name, like Brian Boru, the great Irish chieftain. It's a good, sensible name.'

'I think he wanted something more memorable, I think Brian wasn't quite writerly enough.'

'Well, I prefer Brian to Brody,' said Richard. 'Brian sounds like an accountant you can trust. Brody sounds like he's trying too hard.'

'You don't have to try all the time, yes?' There's a saying in Danish, which goes like this, sometimes you just have to lie back and let life's hands run all over you? Maybe that's what you need to do? Stop trying and more lying back...'

'Erik, keep those hands to yourself,' said Richard.

Erik laughed. 'Sorry, maybe my translation wasn't quite correct. In Danish, it's quite poetical. Is that a word?'

'I wouldn't mind,' said Jools. Her throat sounded dry. 'I think that sounds like a good idea... you know... lying back...' She looked down at her hands, as though she suddenly didn't know what to do with them.

'Hello!' I heard Shona's voice from the kitchen.

'It's my sister,' I told everyone, just as Shona's head appeared from the back doorway. She glanced at me, looking apologetic and sad and everything you don't want your sister to look.

'I'm here to help,' she said. 'I was at a loose end and... I'm sorry.' She staggered towards me, her eyes full of tears, her arms outstretched. 'I'm sorry. You were right. And Ronan was right and...' She buried her face in my neck and started to cry while I patted her on the back and started to cry as well. Eventually she peeled herself off me. 'I'm fine,' she said, wiping her eyes. 'I'm fine.' She looked like Shona used to look at eleven years old, trying to be brave.

'I'm sorry,' I said.

'No, I'm sorry. I should have believed you. And why would Ronan be jealous of Ross? He's actually nicer and happier... but I didn't want to know.'

She looked around at everyone sitting on the grass. 'Yes,' she said. 'I do always make an entrance like that. I like to make an impression.' Everyone laughed.

'Shona, Erik, Erik, Shona,' I said. 'And you remember Paddy, don't you?'

'Of course!' Shona shook Erik's hand and then Paddy's. 'Didn't you come to Mum's rescue once, when she broke down and had to be towed?'

Years ago, Paddy had been staying over at mine when I had got the call from Mum. Shona was on holiday with Ross and the girls, and Paddy insisted on coming with me to help. There was a blizzard and we found Mum in the middle of the road with cars driving on either side of her. Paddy managed to push the car to the side of the road and then, as Mum and I managed miraculously to get a taxi, he waited for the tow truck to bring the car home. When he eventually got back, Mum made him a hot whiskey and made him sit by the Aga until he had warmed through.

'My twins are on a sleepover,' said Shona, 'so I thought I'd come and see how you were all getting on.' She smiled at us. 'And just FYI my husband has been having an affair. He told me he had to take some time to sort himself out but it turns out there was someone else.' She smiled at everyone, even though she was still holding my hand tightly.

'Have you booted him out?' Richard asked.

'Not yet,' Shona replied. 'Still trying to think what to do. At least I know now. Anyway, let's forget it for now, and you can tell me all about the supper club. And it doesn't look exactly laborious with all of you lying in the sun.'

'It was,' said Richard, 'and it will be again. But troops need tea. And we're trying to introduce Erik to the delights of a proper Irish brew.'

Erik shook his head. 'The delights still escape me. I prefer coffee. Tea, as far as I can tell, is basically a cup of hot water with little discernible flavour to which milk is added.' He shrugged. 'Nothing special.'

'But it's more than a drink, it's a way of life.'

'Yes, it's not meant to taste of anything,' I said. 'It's more a religious experience.'

Paddy nodded. 'The most religious experience you can get in Ireland these days.'

'I've stopped drinking tea,' Shona said. 'I drink coffee from dawn to dusk these days. It's the only way to make life excitingly edgy. Until it's time to open the wine.'

'Ah,' Erik said to her, with great solemnity. 'What is it, that rain falls but the sun will always shine? You need to remember that the sun is always there, waiting for you to notice again.'

'Profound words there from our Danish friend.'

'Actually,' said Erik, 'it was Paddy who helped me see the sun again. He made me join the cycling club. Obviously, I cycled, but this was serious cycling...'

'The kind you have to wear Lycra for.'

'The first weekend, eight of us cycled a hundred miles...'

'Just a little jaunt.'

'I thought cycling was meant to be a way of getting from place to place, but this was too strange,' said Erik. 'But I got home that night, and sunk into a bath... something I never do, but I thought if I don't then I may never use my legs again...'

'He was hobbling,' admitted Paddy. 'I was quite worried.'

'But I realised, as I lay in the bath, that I was smiling.'

'He'd been very serious before.'

'Life is serious, no?' said Erik. 'Have you read Kierkegaard?'

We shook our heads.

'Well, he's very serious and very depressing. Us Danes love him. But while I'm in Ireland, I find I am less serious and less depressed. Ireland is good for the soul.'

He looked over at Paddy. 'By the way, Freja was asking for you...'

Paddy's eyes flickered towards him. 'Oh yeah?'

Erik was smiling. 'She called me just for a chat but...' He raised his eyebrows. 'I think it was just to see how you were...'

'Who's this?' asked Jools, excitedly. 'Freja?' She nudged Paddy. 'You never mentioned a Freja!' She turned back to Erik. 'Is she tall with blonde swishy hair?'

'Kind of,' said Erik. 'She's very nice, that's what she is. And a little lonely it seems.'

Paddy was blushing. 'I'm sure she's fine,' he was saying. 'Freja was never short of suitors.'

'Ah, but there was only one of you,' Erik said. 'I promised I would get you to call her. She says she knows it's over... but she misses you.'

'I'll call her,' said Paddy. 'Okay?'

'But who is she?' Jools had rolled onto her stomach and had her chin in her hands. 'Tell us everything!'

'She's Paddy's... what's the word?' said Erik.

'Girlfriend?' suggested Jools, excitedly. 'And I thought you wanted to remain single forever!'

'She's...' Paddy opened his mouth to speak when Richard clapped his hands. 'Back to work, people! It's 5.45 p.m.... action stations, please!'

And we all stood and dispersed and all I could think about was I had a husband at home and he had Freja with the swishy blonde hair.

32

In the kitchen, Jools and Erik were talking to each other in low voices. Jools turned to me when Erik slipped back into the garden. 'Would you mind if we swapped around?' she said, not quite meeting my eye. 'Paddy says he wouldn't mind doing the kitchen and I could do the drinks and set up with Erik.' She blushed. 'And anyway, Paddy's a better cook than me. And I...' She shrugged, and suddenly smiled. 'I don't know, I just think...' She looked at me. 'If you don't mind...'

'I don't mind at all.' I smiled. 'So suddenly you're not content to just look at Erik...?'

'I'm just being friendly,' she replied. 'International relations, that's all.' She grabbed my arm for a second. 'He's the most handsome man I have ever seen. I can hardly look at him... have you seen his arms... and... oh my God... his...' She stopped, as though overcome.

'Go!' I waved her away. 'Go and objectify this man! Go!'

Jools didn't so much as run from the kitchen into the garden, as sprint a hundred metres final.

Meanwhile, Shona sat at the kitchen table ineffectively chopping onions, while Paddy and I stood between the Aga, the sink and the old wooden island.

'So what happened?' I asked Shona, quietly.

'I looked at his phone,' she said, 'after I spoke to you and it was all there...'

'What did you say to him?'

'Nothing, just said I was going out, and left him there. He didn't look bothered that I was going. He's probably already gone to phone Victoria.' Shona wiped her eyes. 'I have to try and be one of those women who knows but pretends not to know so as not to uproot the whole fecking tree for her children's sake.'

'But maybe you...'

She shook her head. 'I can't. The girls have their bedrooms, they have their trampoline, they can walk to school...' She shrugged. 'I just have to get over it. Ross is back and...'

'For now,' I said.

'What?'

'Ross is back for now.'

'You mean, you think he's going to do it again?'

I shrugged. 'I don't know, but nor do you. And you have to live under that not-knowing cloud.'

'Yes, but for my children I would do anything.' Her voice wobbled. 'Anything. Look, you go back to cooking, don't mind me, just give me jobs to do, okay?'

Paddy smiled at me as I walked back to where he was preparing the food.

'Jools likes Erik,' Paddy was saying. 'She thinks he's out of her league though...'

'Which he isn't...' I was staring at my notes, trying to focus on what still needed to be done for the evening. 'Canapés next,' I said. 'You cut the baguettes.' I handed him a bread knife. 'Thin slices, please.'

'Yes, chef!'

'Do you think anything will happen?' I asked.

'I hope so,' he said. 'I would like my sibling to be happy and to have a nice relationship with a friend of mine.' I could feel the weight of his stare and I looked up. He shrugged. 'I just think it's nice, that's all. Someone I like being happy with someone I love.' He gave me a look.

I nodded, pretending I didn't know what he was trying to say. All that time we were together, I was so insistent that it wasn't fair on Jools, but here was the same situation in reverse and Paddy was fine about it. But Jools was different. I had been her best friend since school, we were more like sisters.

'She just needs to believe in herself,' went on Paddy. 'We all should.'

I looked up again, and then realised that I couldn't focus on what he was saying and make sixty canapés for our guests who would – I looked at the clock – be here in exactly forty-seven minutes.

'What about some music?' he suggested. 'Do you mind?' He propped up his phone. 'A bit of Paul Simon?'

'Perfect...'

As the music started playing, we began singing along.

'I love this song,' I said. 'You used to play it all the time.'

'I did, yeah...' He looked at me. 'I remember how much you loved this album, I didn't just put on something random, for me.'

'Well, thanks.'

'I went to see Paul Simon,' Paddy told me when the song ended. 'In Copenhagen. I was going to call you to see if you wanted to come over.'

'Why didn't you?' I wanted to ask about Freja. Why would he want me to come to a Paul Simon concert when there were beauties like Freja available?

'Well... Jools told me about Brody. She said you'd met someone and was madly in love.'

I carried on slicing the tomatoes. 'You could have still asked me, it wasn't as if we were going out with each other. Hadn't we said we'd be friends?'

'Yeah...' He smiled to himself. 'But I didn't really want to be friends.'

'What do you mean?'

'I mean...' He stopped. 'Ah, it doesn't matter now. I'm glad you are madly in love.'

For a moment, I didn't say anything. 'Me too,' I managed.

'I'm going to have that wine now,' Shona called over. 'Anyone want to join me?'

Paddy shook his head. 'I'm grand, thanks, Shona.'

'I can't, I'm working.'

'Well, I'll only have a little glass,' she said, going over to the dresser where there were some bottles of wine. 'Just a small one. Or a large one... especially...' – she peered at the label – '...when it's one of Dad's. A Côtes du Rhône... which I presume is a good year... 2015... Dad, you see,' she told Paddy, 'only buys expensive wine. It's the sole reason he moved to France.' She expertly twisted off the cork, poured some wine into a tumbler and came and sat at the kitchen island. 'You know I just wanted to be different to Mum and Dad?' said Shona, speaking to me and Paddy. 'I really wanted to have a better marriage. And I thought I did. I was smug.' Tears filled her eyes and she drank deeply from her wine. 'So,' she continued, after she had resurfaced, 'I went through his phone and I found texts from a Victoria. Rather eye-opening texts, going back months and months... last Christmas, while I was making everything perfect, he was texting Victoria. Easter, when we were in Croatia and he had to go back to Dublin suddenly for work was because little Victoria was missing him. My birthday, when he didn't come home for dinner, was because he was with Victoria. I even saw messages from Ronan. They gave him a right bollocking. Told him to get back to his family and stop acting like a self-serving prick.' She refilled her glass. 'Last week I was feeling sad and abandoned, this man I loved, my husband, the father of my children – my world, my life! – was having a nervous breakdown. But he was fine! And having great sex, as it turns out. Explains the new wardrobe, the haircut and the endless sit-ups, his feet hooked under the bed, while I tried to concentrate on my book.' Shona's hand was shaking as she lifted up her glass. 'I gave up my life for him. My career. My individuality. And yes, I was only delighted to do it. After Dad, I wanted someone completely different, and I was so convinced I had. I never for a single second thought that Ross would... be just like Dad. I mean, what a loser!'

Paddy made a squeaking sound, his face turned to the door, frozen. Dad stood at the kitchen door, looking puzzled, as though he was trying to work out what was going on. And then there was a flash of something on his face which I had never seen before. Hurt. Sorrow. And then in a moment he was back to himself again.

'Aha!' he said, walking into the room. 'Is that red wine I see before me? Just what the doctor ordered. I need something to take the edge off the day.

I've been up to my oxters in Uncle Philip's papers... give me the Lord's strength and perseverance... but my nephew...' – Dad smiled at us – 'he's a trying lad... a very trying lad. It's like having a conversation with a tooth-brush... no, scrap that. Toothbrushes have too much personality. Well, this all looks wonderful, Roisín. Doesn't it, Paddy? Is my daughter not excep-tionally talented?'

Paddy nodded. 'Very. I've just tasted the ice cream... it's incredible.'

Dad took one of the glasses and filled it up. 'Anyone else? Top-up, Shona?'

'Go on, Dad,' said Shona. 'Carry on like everything's all right. Swan through life, and let everyone else pick up the pieces.'

'Shona, darling,' he said. 'What's wrong?'

'What's wrong?' Shona shouted so loudly Dad's wine swooshed in his glass like a wave. 'What's wrong is that I married your clone, a man who doesn't value his family and puts his own sexual needs before that of his wife and his children, that's what's wrong!'

Dad seemed slightly stunned.

'And you broke Mum's heart!' Shona was warming to her theme. 'And now you waltz back in and expect...'

'Roisín, everything ready?' Richard was walking into the kitchen. 'We need the nibbles to go with Erik's brand-new cocktail which tastes amazing.'

Dad had one arm around Shona and was edging her towards the table, while carrying both their glasses. I could see that look in his eyes again, hurt and sad.

Paddy was leaning over my notebook, trying to ready my hieroglyph-ics. 'So,' I asked Paddy, 'what stage are we at?'

'The crab tarts need to go in the oven,' he said. 'And then we need to make the salad. The cheese straws are done and the honey-roasted nuts are cooling over there.'

'Has anyone seen Sam?' shouted Richard.

'He went to get some more lemons.' Jools came in behind him. 'He said he'd be five minutes...'

Richard checked his phone. 'He hasn't rung... but quick, we've got to get the food out...'

From across the room, I could hear Dad's voice. 'You're tired,' he was saying. 'You work so hard with the girls...'

'Tired!' shouted Shona. 'Yes, I am tired of you acting like you are the only important person in the world.' And she began to cry again.

Sam edged in through the door of the kitchen, walking as though he'd lost the power to turn. Robotically, he shifted his whole body to face us. 'My car... went into the back of another... and we had to swap details. The cars are both fine, it's me, though. I think I've got whiplash.'

'Oh my God!' Richard went to touch him, his fingers reached for his neck. 'You poor thing.'

'I'm so sorry,' said Sam. 'I had to leave the car on the side of the road and walk here... I tried to get back as soon as I could.'

'Don't worry,' said Richard. 'You can't do anything now, for the rest of the evening. I'll be your assistant. What's best? Lying down? Sitting up? Maybe you should go home?'

'Lying down.' Dad immediately stood up. 'Flat on your back on the floor. Go on, down you go. Keep the spine totally straight, don't move your head, stare at the ceiling.'

Sam was gingerly lowering himself to the ground, Dad knelt down to help him. 'No cushion, until you feel better. Keep everything straight and don't move a muscle.'

Sam was now lying down on the cold terracotta tiles. 'I'll be all right,' he was saying to Richard, who was also kneeling beside him. 'You go where you're needed...'

'But...' Richard was conflicted.

'I'll be fine,' said Sam. 'Go on, go.'

'I'll look after him, son,' said Dad. 'You do what you need to do.'

'Richard,' I said. 'The starters.'

'Yes, yes, of course.' He half stood up. 'You stay there.' He turned to Dad. 'You mind him, right?'

Sam had his eyes closed. 'Don't worry,' said Dad. 'We'll look after him.'

I tried to focus on getting the food out, Richard was barking orders, Jools and Erik were front of house and Paddy and I were garnishing, olive oil drizzling, black pepper twisting...

'Go, go!' Paddy was shouting as we finished another run of plates just as Jools rushed in to take more.

'Family isn't something you can put down and pick up...' I heard Shona say, finishing another glass of wine. 'You don't get to play with it every now and then... when it suits you.'

Stressed and sweaty, Dad was on the floor holding Sam's hand, as well as trying to make sure he was looking at Shona, probably too afraid not to maintain eye contact with her.

As soon as the starters' plates were being returned, Paddy and I began on the main course, the two of us working together. This was totally different to the first week where we had sliced the lasagne and sent it out, like an extra-large dinner party. This was like an actual restaurant with Paddy and I in total synchronisation, both instinctively knowing what our next move was.

Out of the corner of my eye, I could see Shona laying her head down on the table. 'I'm just done,' she was saying. 'Done with trying to be perfect. Done trying to be good, done with the men in my life. You're all such disappointments!'

Dad patted her arm and nodded. 'Yes, yes we are,' he agreed.

By 9 p.m., we were scooping out the ice cream and strawberries and crumbling meringue on top.

'These look pretty good.' Paddy was adorning each one with a mint leaf. Jools came into the kitchen and took the last four plates.

'I'm so sorry,' Sam called from the floor. 'I've been so useless this evening.'

'It's going really well out there,' Jools said, coming in. 'They are loving everything.'

Shona was now sitting in the armchair beside the Aga, with Mum's old picnic rug pulled over her, fast asleep. Dad had collapsed in the chair beside her.

* * *

After I had put Shona into her old bed, and Dad had gone up to his, I looked out of the window where Richard and Erik were piling up the plates. Sam was still lying on the floor, out of earshot.

Paddy turned to me. 'We did it,' he said. 'Well, you did it, I just helped a little.'

'No, we did it.' I smiled at him.

I was pouring a glass of wine for us both from Shona's third bottle. 'One of these?' I passed it to him.

He sat on the edge of the table, next to me. 'It's good to spend time with you again,' he said. 'I was so worried that we wouldn't be friends... I would have hated not being friends with you.' He touched his glass to mine. 'Here's to old friends...'

We sat in silence for a moment. Poor Brody, going slowly mad with writing but by next Friday the book would be finished and hopefully we would have a chance to make things work. So far, married life was like being in space, where no one can hear you scream.

'I've always thought you were amazing,' Paddy was saying.

'That's going a bit far.'

'Well, I did.'

'You never said.'

'I didn't think you wanted me to. You were always so afraid Jools would find out... it was all very clandestine, very Cold War.'

'I didn't want to hurt her,' I said. 'Her best friend and her brother...' I shrugged. 'It seemed the right thing to do at the time.' Now, it seemed ridiculous, tying myself up in knots over a fear of what my friend might or might not have said.

Paddy shrugged. 'Ah well... it's all in the past now. And I'm glad we're still hanging out.'

'Me too.'

'And I'm glad I went to Copenhagen,' he went on. 'It was an amazing opportunity. It's such a great city. And I would never have had the confidence to come back and open up the bike shop if I hadn't met the people I did. Cycling is on a whole different level there...'

'It was really brave of you to go,' I said, the red wine already having an effect. 'I really admired you.' I missed you, I wanted to say. I didn't want you to go.

He nodded. 'I needed to change things, and running away sometimes works.' He laughed. 'It mostly doesn't but for me it did. Helped me focus on myself...' He looked at me for a moment. 'But... oh, I don't know... you sometimes wonder if you did the right thing but at the end of the day you just have to get on with it.'

'You mean be at peace with your life decisions?' I was finding it hard to find peace around that decision I had made.

'Yeah,' Paddy went on. 'You could tie yourself up in knots thinking of the paths not taken... but all you have is the road you did take.'

'Suck it up, then?'

He laughed. 'That's exactly what I mean.'

Outside, Jools was laughing at something Erik was saying.

'Jools looks happy,' he said. 'She and Erik seem to be getting on well.'

'He's a great guy and an amazing developer,' Paddy was saying. 'One of the best... the seafront in Sandycove is going to look incredible.'

I stopped and turned to him. 'The seafront?'

Paddy nodded. 'The one at the old amusement arcade? I assumed you knew? But I suppose you're dealing with so many applications all the time.'

Erik was the developer and far from being impartial, I had been spending time with both parties. Not only was I friends with the developer, I had also been volunteering with the protestors. Maybe there would even be an enquiry and my name in the papers. The office would refer to me in aghast, hushed tones. After all the planning problems of the previous decades where a hefty 'contribution' would get you the planning approval you wanted, I was going to bring the office into disrepute again and take poor JP down with me.

I finished my wine, just as everyone else came in from the garden, all in high spirits and Paddy got swept up in the noise. And all I could think about was that I had made a mess of my life.

33

For the rest of the weekend, I felt sick with anxiety. I left Brody in bed on Monday morning, flaked out, and opened the door to the study and looked in. His laptop was on the desk with five mugs of cold, old tea like modern megaliths. There was no sign of the console, I thought, relieved. And, guiltily, feeling like a spy, I crept downstairs, left the house and walked to work.

At my desk, I went straight to the planning application and the name of the new developers. MoMo. The name meant nothing and I had no idea of the names of the company directors. I typed in MoMo. A photo of Erik, looking handsome, smiling for the camera, appeared on screen. I read on. 'Erik Larsen runs MoMo, an environmentally sensitive, aesthetic design practice.'

I was going to be sacked, I thought. I looked up at Frank and Dermot who were quietly getting on with their work, the voices from Frank's transistor radio on his desk the only sound in the office.

Oh God. These were my friends and they always had my back and now they would find out what a spectacular mess I had made of everything. What had possessed me to keep returning to the Hall? Why hadn't I asked Erik exactly what he was doing in Dublin?

From the window of my office you could just make out the top of the

Hall. I stood for a moment, looking out, seeing the tiny figures of people walking along the seafront, and trying to ignore the Hall which had been such a big part of Sandycove's skyline for the last 150 years.

Dermot came up behind me. 'Feeling defeated?'

I nearly jumped, and tried to arrange my face into that of someone who was totally innocent. 'Yes, it's a shame I won't be able to see it through.'

The two of us looked across at the Hall. 'It's a beautiful building, but it's just not appreciated by the majority of people. The campaign to save it was too small. It's in a prime position and we can't afford to buy it off the developers and do it up. It's all about money.'

I nodded. 'Everything always is, isn't it?' I thought of our ex-colleague who had ingratiated himself with planners and signed off on any development just so he could receive a brown envelope stuffed with cash. And then there was me who'd become emotionally involved with the Hall and had also become friends with the developer. Either way, any decision I made could be accused of being partial. The Hall was doomed now and had no chance of survival.

'Look,' Dermot was saying, 'if you fail, then there's no shame. Frank did, and he has been a planner for an embarrassingly long time. I did, and I'm what is known as the planner's planner...' He called across the office. 'Aren't I right, Frank?'

'Sorry Dermot,' said Frank. 'I missed that pearl of wisdom.'

'I'm the planner's planner, aren't I? A talisman, a wizard for our planning brethren.'

'Oh Jesus Christ,' said Frank, 'you really couldn't make this man up, could you?'

Dermot turned back to me. 'That's a yes in Frank language, so, anyway, no shame in not getting this one over the line. I'm sure when JP makes his triumphant return to the office, he will give you something a little less intransigent.'

'What's this?' Saoirse walked up to us. 'What am I missing?'

'We're just talking about what a lovely day it is,' said Dermot, 'and how after the rain you can often see a rainbow. My favourite cloud formation is cumulous... what's yours?'

'Clouds?' Saoirse narrowed her eyes. 'You weren't talking about clouds and rainbows... you were talking about the planning application.' She turned to me. 'Ready to give up yet?'

'Yes,' I replied, 'I don't think I'll be able to do anything with it.'

Saoirse smiled, delighted. 'I knew it,' she said. 'What exactly was the point of all that? Why bother giving you a planning application if nothing happens?'

'Saoirse, Saoirse,' said Dermot, 'I have a suggestion. When you wake up in the morning and you get out of bed... which way do you turn?'

'Turn?' Saoirse scrunched her face up in confusion. 'I go right. My bed's against a wall, and so I get out on the right. But what's that got to do with planning?'

'That's where you are going wrong. Move your bed, and try getting out on the left. You just keep getting out of bed on the wrong side.'

'By the way, Roisín,' called Belinda. 'We're booked in for your supper club thingy on Saturday. The lovely man who rung back to confirm my booking said it was the last night...'

'Oh, thank God,' said Saoirse. 'The stomachs of South County Dublin might remain E. coli free.'

Belinda ignored her. 'There will be eight of us salsa girls. We might even have a little dance.'

'Book me in,' said Frank loudly. 'I'm coming. And Dermot will come too.'

'Yeah... I'd love to.' Dermot seemed amused.

It was all suddenly too much – work, Brody, worrying about Shona, the memory of Dad's face when he came back, all hurt, having to do another bloody supper club... and Paddy. I was stuck with a husband on the verge of a creatively induced nervous breakdown, I was about to be sacked or dismissed from work, and I wished I had told Paddy all those years ago that I loved him. I hadn't realised until this moment that I had never just liked Paddy, I loved him.

I stayed by the window, staring out, blinking back the tears. What a fool I was. My life had gone wrong.

'Everything all right, Roisín?' Belinda asked, coming over. 'What are you thinking about?'

'Nothing...' I said, smiling. 'Everything's grand.'

'I know not grand when I see it.' She stood next to me.

'No, I'm fine, honestly, just wondering if there's life beyond the office.'

'It depends on what you might call life,' said Belinda. 'Some people have awful lives and being at work is a pleasure. Other people have wonderful lives and can't wait to get back to them.' She looked across at Frank who was eating a cheese sandwich out of a lunch box. 'Which are you, Frank? Live to work or work to live?'

'Live to work,' he said. 'I like being here. It's better than being at home staring at the four walls.'

'Oh, Frank!' Belinda exclaimed. 'That's not right, that's not right at all. That's a terrible thing to say... a fine man like you!'

Frank shrugged, still chewing on his crusts. 'Not everyone can have an exciting social whirl, like you, Belinda,' he said. 'Or a satisfying hinterland. This is as good as it gets. Coming to work means I interact with others, and am exposed to their thoughts and opinions. Even Dermot's are better than nothing. I find work interesting, satisfying and the best thing about my day.'

Belinda was speechless for a moment. 'Well, Frank,' she said finally, 'I see it as a great honour to be one of the people with whom you work. We can take each other for granted, can't we? And from now on, I will remember your words every time I pick up my bag and coat and get ready to come here. Thank you for the reminder of how lucky we all are. And Dermot,' she went on, 'I just want to say how much I enjoy working with you. I like your wit and your determination to make our working days a little lighter and more jovial.' She turned to me. 'And Roisín, you're a ray of sunshine, a beautiful girl and lovely all-round person. You are a pleasure to work with...'

And then I began to cry, long, deep sobs of shame and embarrassment. Belinda reached up and put her arms around me, patting and shushing me as I tried to speak through the tears.

'I can't stand anything about my life,' I said. 'I used to love my home but now it's horrible. Brody's taken over the whole house and I just cook and clean and there is nothing for me any more. And... and... and... Brody just goes on and on about his book, and I've completely messed up the planning for the Hall, and JP is going to be back this week... and... my Dad... his face. He looked so sad and hurt and... well... everything...'

Frank, Dermot and Belinda were staring at me, all with a look of concern mixed with total befuddlement. But I couldn't stop.

'And all he goes on about is Seamus, this farmer... and all he does is contemplate blades of grass and tractor parts. And I come to work, and I don't know what I'm doing or why I'm here. I fell into admin, and I know JP is being kind and trying to be encouraging by giving me the Lady Immaculate Hall planning but the building is doomed, just like me. I love them all down there... but I couldn't stay any longer because it is unethical...' I tried to breathe and to calm down but I was like a runaway train, the only thing that could stop me was crashing into a wall. 'And my dad has come back and it's really nice but it's not right... and Shona... her husband has been having an affair... and...' I realised that as well as Belinda's arms around me, Dermot was holding a hand and Frank was patting my shoulder awkwardly. 'I've done everything wrong. I've ruined my whole life!'

'Frank,' ordered Belinda, 'you go and get Roisín a glass of water. Dermot, angle the fan on her face. Roisín, you try and lean back a bit and take in some deep breaths... that's it... nice big one... lovely... and another... go on, that's great... you're doing so well... another big one... gorgeous... and another... fabulous... that's it... and another huge one, get all that oxygen filling up your lungs... feel it zooming around all your blood cells... lovely... there you go... one more... thank you, Frank... now, Roisín, try and take a sip of water... Frank, did you use the cold side, because the cold side of the water fountain can be too cold... oh, okay... that's it, take a sip... excellent, now, aren't you a great girl...'

Shame and mortification filled my very soul. In all the years I'd worked in this office, I'd never so much as complained about anything, and now I had just spread my guts out for their delectation or probable disgust. It was one thing crying in front of Belinda, but Frank and Dermot? They must be as embarrassed as me.

But they were both hovering, looking intently at me.

'How are you feeling?' asked Frank.

'Better, I think,' said Dermot, peering at me like a doctor.

'She needs a bit of space,' said Belinda, swatting that back. 'Come on, let her breathe.'

'I'm fine,' I said. 'I'm so sorry, I don't know what came over me... I didn't mean to let that all come out.'

'Don't mind us,' said Belinda. 'Better out than in.'

'Unlike Frank's farts.' Dermot ignored Frank's glare.

'You're finding life a challenge,' went on Belinda. 'Ah, I know that feeling...'

'Me too,' said Frank.

'Me three, when I was getting divorced, I felt like such a failure...' Dermot paused. 'Not that you're getting divorced, of course, maybe you and your husband will be able to work through whatever it is. But marriage can be challenging. My wife didn't love me, it turned out. I mean, can you imagine someone not loving me? I know, it's a shock. But it took me years and years to feel like myself again. Longer to stop feeling like a failure. I quite like myself again now. Only took a decade.'

Frank was next to speak. 'My father wasn't the nicest of men, when I graduated from college, he went off to the Galway Races instead. My mam came with me to the ceremony, but I remember being there in the O'Reilly Hall and thinking that there was something wrong with me that my own father didn't want to be there for me. That was the day I realised I didn't have to like him. But it lingers... I think if he'd loved me, then I would have loved myself enough to find someone to love.'

Dermot and Belinda were listening to him. 'Frank, your father didn't deserve you,' said Dermot.

'He sounds like a complete waste of space.' Belinda patted Frank's hand. 'As does that ex-wife of yours, Dermot.'

'Ah well... it's long past now.'

'And my father is long gone,' said Frank. 'But I didn't have what you have, Roisín. I'm a miserable old git, and you're the bright spark of the office. You're always so good to all of us, bringing in those cakes, making sure we all have a happier office.'

Dermot and Belinda were nodding. I had no idea that Frank thought anything of me, never mind being so nice.

'Thank you, Frank.' I was in danger of blubbing again.

'Let's all have a cup of tea and take a break.' Belinda disappeared to the kitchen.

'I'm really sorry to have cried like that,' I said. 'I didn't mean to, I must be tired or fed up... or haven't eaten enough...'

Dermot and Frank nodded understandingly.

'Frank gets like that if he hasn't had his Weetabix.'

'And you're like it all the time, whether you've had your Weetabix or not. You're permanently on the verge of something.'

'On the verge of genius, maybe.'

Belinda came back carrying a tray with four mugs of tea on it. 'When my Johnny passed on,' she said, 'I found the only thing that helped was my salsa classes and the salsa girls. They rallied around and let me talk about him as much or as little as I wanted.' She wiped away a tear. 'It took time, but over the months things got easier.' She began to sing. 'Into life some rain must fall...'

'But too much is falling in mine,' joined in Frank. He gave her a shy smile. 'Ella Fitzgerald. One of my favourites.'

'Mine too!' Belinda beamed at him. 'Into each heart some tears must fall...' she sang.

'But someday the sun will shine,' sang Frank.

They turned to me. 'The sun always comes out again,' said Frank.

'It always does,' said Dermot. 'Guaranteed.'

But they didn't know about me volunteering at the Hall or about Erik. When they discovered these things, they wouldn't be nice to me.

'What's going on in here then?' Saoirse was standing just behind us. We hadn't heard her come in. 'Have you been crying?'

I shook my head. 'Allergies.'

'Maybe she's allergic to you?' said Dermot, sweetly. 'Just a thought.'

'But Roisín is just attention-seeking,' she said. 'Don't you see it? Little Miss Drama, Me! Me! Me! It's like she's fallen off the stage of the Abbey Theatre... God, we're here to do work, not look for sympathy from colleagues. Hardly professional, is it?'

I went back to my desk, wiping my eyes, feeling like a total fool. And Saoirse was right. I wasn't professional. I wasn't anything.

34

It was Tuesday and I was mentally counting down time until D-Day – manuscript handing-in day. I called in to see Harry on my way home.

'Ah, Roisín,' he said. 'Come in for a cup of tea.' He beamed at me. 'You'll be glad to know that the kitchen is completely finished. Do you know something, it looks just like it did when Nora had done one of her spring cleans. Cyril is a dab hand with a scrubbing cloth.'

I followed him into the kitchen. It gleamed. The red Formica table was shiny, the dresser was tidy, no piles of papers anywhere. The sink and draining board were free of any crockery and pans and the cooker was pristine. 'I've already had a few neighbours in to have a look,' said Harry, standing to one side, like the proud owner of a brand-new kitchen. 'We've had them trooping in all afternoon, once Cyril got the word out. He says I have to keep it "visitor ready", that's what he says.'

'Harry, it's gorgeous,' I said.

'So, would you like a cup of tea? And maybe I could invite you and your husband around for dinner sometime. Nothing too fancy, but perhaps a few spuds and a nice chop.'

'We'd love that,' I said, knowing that it would just be me. 'Maybe you would be my guest at the supper club, the one I've been doing with my friends. It's the last one on Saturday. Would you like to come?' There was a feeling of foreboding, that it was the last days of innocence, soon I would be unmasked as a fraud, my naivety and stupidity on show for everyone to see. Brody's book didn't seem as important any more, I was perfectly capable of ruining my life all on my own.

He looked decidedly pleased. 'I would be honoured,' he said. 'I'll see if I can find my good jacket. Give the buttons a bit of a polish, so I will.'

'I'll ask a friend to collect you. What about half past six?'

'That will suit me very well,' he said.

* * *

Richard called when I was making dinner that evening.

'How is our Michelin star?' he asked.

'Fine... how's Sam?' I tried to sound normal and functional, not someone on the brink of personal disaster.

'He's totally fine,' said Richard. 'He's here now. Wearing his extremely fetching neck brace.'

I could hear Sam in the background saying something and Richard laughed. 'No, it doesn't look like an Elizabethan ruff and no, you do not look like Sir Walter Raleigh... so, Roisín,' he went on, 'the final week... the big finale... what are you thinking, menu-wise? Sam wants to put it up on social media... we're all sold out anyway, but it would be nice to know...'

'You're just worried that I will do another lasagne, aren't you?' I tried to laugh, but really, I had no idea how I was going to get through this week. I was about to be sacked if anyone found out that I had been fraternising with both sides of the planning problem, and my husband's mental health was on a knife-edge. And worse, I would have to stay married to this eccentric stranger for the rest of my days. My future was bleak.

'And by the way, Roisín,' he went on, 'the dinner was fabulous. You really upped your game. More of that, please.'

'It's like being spoken to by a teacher.'

'An encouraging one, I hope,' he said. 'A mentor. One which you will remember fondly in your autobiography, that one teacher who changed your life. Anyway, we made more than two thousand euros on Saturday,' Richard was saying. 'We're already nearly sold out... your colleague's salsa club are all booked in, a few others from your work... who else?' He called again to Sam. 'Ah, yes, a Frank, a Dermot... and...'

Please don't say Saoirse, I thought.

'No, that's it. Some of Jools's friends from the gym...'

'What about a Mexican evening?' I asked. 'For the salsa club. Margaritas? Proper Mexican, not Tex-Mex, but authentic...'

'A Mexican feast,' said Richard. 'Sam? A Mexican-themed evening? He loves the idea,' reported back Richard. 'Double thumbs-up... what's that? If we need more lemons, can someone else go this time?' Richard laughed.

I started scribbling down some menu ideas to send to Sam, and then to Gerry's daughter, Rachel. I just had to get this week over with, hand in my notice at work, try and fix my miserable marriage and... what? Survive the rest of my life? I quickly thought of a menu. Chilli rellenos were something I had had years ago in Mexico on a trip with Jools. Main course? A chicken mole, rice, beans and charred corn with lime and paprika? Dessert...? What about a coconut ice cream and chocolate tarts with a candied lime zest? Too ambitious? Maybe I should just focus on surviving this week, and never, ever cook again. On Friday the book would be finished. Friday, my marriage might be saved.

35

My week was one of survival, bleakly counting down until Friday, when it was deadline day. Brody was barely talking to me, Shona wasn't answering any of my texts and in work, anytime anyone called my name, I jumped out of my skin.

Shona eventually called me back on Thursday evening while I was making dinner.

'Ross has gone...' she was saying on the phone, just as Brody came into the kitchen. 'I told him this morning... said I knew about Victoria...'

'What's for dinner?' Brody asked.

'Baked potatoes,' I mouthed to him. 'Go on,' I said to Shona.

'He went pale,' she said, her voice sounding strained, 'and then shouted at me for accusing him, denied everything...'

'What's for dinner?' Brody asked again.

'Baked potatoes,' I mouthed again, trying to smile and nod at Brody to keep him happy.

'What?' he said. 'Just speak to me.'

'Sorry, Shona. Just one minute.' I looked up at Brody. 'It's baked potatoes, cheese and beans...' I went back to Shona. 'Go on...'

'Well...' she began.

'Baked potatoes, cheese and beans?' said Brody, who had come right up to me and was inches away from me. 'What do you think I am? A student? I can't eat that. Where's the protein?'

'In the cheese and beans,' I said. 'Sorry, Shona, one moment, I'll call you back.' I couldn't stand up to him, I realised. I had to let down my own sister just to keep him happy. I turned back to Brody. 'I just haven't had it for ages and it's one of my favourites. Also, it takes minimal cooking and I am tired of feeding people.'

But Brody wasn't listening. 'Beans...' He shook his head as though trying to make it compute. 'Beans?'

'Nutritious, tasty, cheap...' I said.

'Cheap being the operative word. Cheap and nasty. I'm just not a beans kind of person.'

So I now had to discuss his nutritional needs and what kind of person he was? 'I just thought, with the deadline this week, that you might just want something nice and tasty...'

'My what?'

'Your deadline. Handing the book in? It's tomorrow.' I wasn't sure what it meant for us that the book would be done and dusted tomorrow but I was taking each day as it came. I had stayed away from the Hall, I had typed up my response to JP that the Hall could not be saved and that the developers were moving on with Phase II. I felt guilty about all of it.

But Brody was looking furious. 'I feel under immense pressure, I mean, what's it to do with you if I have a deadline or not? I don't ask if you have a deadline at work, a project to finish... that's none of my business.'

'Well, you could ask, I would be happy to tell you but my work isn't—'

'Interesting,' he said. 'We know that. It's just that my work is interesting, and every cat on the street wants to be involved. You're stressing me out. If I didn't have Fyodor...' And he put his hand in the pocket of his tracksuit bottoms and pulled out Fyodor, cradling him to his chest. 'This little guy doesn't stress me out,' he said in a baby voice. 'This little guy is always nice to me. This little guy is my best friend. He doesn't hassle me, he's always pleased to see me and he's a very intelligent person.' He put Fyodor back into his pocket. 'Come on,' he said. 'We're going out.'

'What? The potatoes are in the oven.'

'Not you!' Brody snarled. 'Fyodor and I,' he said, 'are going to get some fresh air. Let's go, Fyodor...'

The front door closed behind them.

* * *

I took a deep breath and I called Shona back, trying to hold it all together. 'Sorry, I couldn't talk earlier... you were saying about Ross...'

'I've chucked him out,' she said. 'Packed his horrible clothes, including his red trousers that make him look like his dad and that awful shawl-jumper thing he loves, and he's gone. The girls are at Guides and I just couldn't look at his face for a second longer.'

'What happened?'

'He is still in contact with Victoria. I actually thought I was going to stab him with the butter knife which would cause minimal harm but probably have me in court for attempted murder. I summoned up any shred of dignity I had left and asked him to leave. I think I may have sworn a bit. A lot.'

'And he left?'

'I think he was relieved, actually.'

'But what about the girls?'

'I've just told them,' Shona went on, starting to cry. 'I felt like Mum must have all those years ago. I wanted to protect them but sometimes you don't have a choice. You can't control things.'

'And what did they say?'

'Daisy said she was pleased but I think she was just saying that to be nice to me and Kitty said that it would be good because they would have two lots of presents at Christmas. They seem remarkably well adjusted, actually. I've just been up to kiss them goodnight and they were both asleep.'

'In the same bed?' I thought my heart might break if she told me they were in the same bed.

'No, they were in their own beds...'

Thank God.

'Now, what about you? What's going on with you and Brody? Everything all right? It's just that you sounded distracted...'

'Well...' Where to begin? You were right? I married a man I didn't know and now he's left me? 'We're sort of in the same boat.'

'Who is?'

'You and me. He's gone.'

'Brody? Gone where? For good?'

'I don't know but... I don't think I care as much as I should do.'

'Okay...'

'It's actually Fyodor I am most concerned about. What if he falls out? What if he is squashed in Brody's pocket?'

'Who the hell is Fyodor?'

'He's Brody's hamster and Brody has taken him with him.'

'Okay, so it's now official. Your life has taken a turn for the farcical. It's time to turn it around now. Do you want to come over?'

'He might come back.' I was still thinking of poor little Fyodor.

'Will you text me when he does?'

'Yes...'

'Will you be okay?'

'I think so.'

'I am calling you first thing tomorrow. Okay?'

'Okay.'

I stayed up late, missing Fyodor whizzing around on his wheel. By 11 p.m., they still hadn't returned and Brody's phone was still switched off. Eventually, close to midnight, I heard Brody's key in the door.

'Brody? Where have you been?' I followed him back into the living room where he flung himself on the sofa.

'For a walk,' he said.

'I just wanted to say sorry for putting so much pressure on you. It wasn't fair... and I shouldn't have asked all those questions... I promise I won't again.'

'Good.' He pouted. 'I don't like questions.'

'Okay... except I do have one...'

'You promised!' He picked up the remote control and began flicking through the channels.

'Fyodor. Is he okay?'

He shook his head. 'He disappeared. God knows where he is. He must have jumped out of my pocket.'

'Oh my God. He'll have been killed.'

'He'll be back,' he said. 'He always is.'

I would have done anything to hear him chewing loudly on sunflower seeds or scratching away at his cage.

36

I didn't sleep at all that night, listening out for signs of Fyodor's return, hoping to hear the scrabble of tiny feet behind the fridge. The next morning, I went straight to Fyodor's cage hoping he'd somehow found his way home but it was still empty. I checked the pocket of Brody's tracksuit bottoms, dreading the discovery of his tiny, squashed body, but it was thankfully Fyodor-free. But if he wasn't mangled in the pocket, then where was he? I pulled out the fridge, hoping to find him there eating some stray crumbs, and the washing machine, but there was no sign of him.

In the morning, I walked straight to Paddy's shop. Through the large plate glass windows, I could see him unpacking a delivery of bikes. The bell rang as I stepped inside, my heart beating. I wasn't sure what had brought me here, but... I wanted to see him.

'Roisín!' Paddy turned around. 'What are you doing here so early? Everything all right?' He was standing, moving towards me, his face a mixture of surprise and concern.

'Everything's fine, just passing... you know how it is...'

He was nodding, listening.

'I need a new bike, actually... mine was run over... last Friday evening...'

'Your bike was run over?'

'My brother-in-law.'

'Ah, Ross...' He acted as though that was entirely expected behaviour from Ross. I'd forgotten how much Paddy knew about my life, even down to the fact that my brother-in-law was the kind of man who would drive over a bike. 'You loved that bike... why didn't you tell me?'

For a moment I thought I was going to cry again, over the bike, over the fact that my whole life had gone wrong, and perhaps because Paddy was the kind of person who would entirely understand why losing my bike was the last straw.

'My bike was stolen in Copenhagen two years ago,' he was saying. 'I was bereft for days, checking every bike rack, staring at people's bikes as they cycled past... it was like my dog had gone missing...'

'There's a little dog I've fallen in love with, Foxy. She's an ancient chihuahua who needs a home.'

'Well, we've got to rescue her, then, what do you want to do first, new bike or old dog?'

'New bike.'

'I'll do you a deal,' he said. 'Mates' rates.'

Mates. Better than nothing. He showed me some of the new bikes but there was one which stood out, a bright ruby-red one. 'I'll take it.'

'And what about that dog? Foxy?'

'I can't get a dog, but we could just visit her...'

'Why can't you have a dog...?'

Because, I wanted to say, I don't have exactly a stable life at the moment, I have no idea if I will have a job this day next week... or a marriage... or friends?

'How long until you've got to be in work?' Paddy went on.

'About forty-five minutes.'

'Plenty of time. Enough for a coffee as well.'

After he had locked up the shop and hung a 'Back soon!' sign on the door, we cycled down to the seafront, just beside the council building, and towards Lady Immaculate Hall and to the farmer's market. And after locking our bikes together, we walked in through the gates, along the path and towards the stalls. My mind had been so full of all that chaos, all those thoughts, and now, being back on a bike in the warm, summer morning sun, I felt a little better. The Hall looked beautiful, its red brickwork had held up amazingly well, considering how little had been done to preserve it. I looked away, feeling guilty.

Gerry had a queue of customers at his stall. 'Well, if it isn't Roisín, the restaurateur!' he shouted across. 'She's got a supper club, you know,' he said to his customers. 'Ever heard of one of them yokes?'

A few faces looked up. 'Is that the one in Sandycove?' asked one woman. 'I heard about it from a friend. She was at it on Saturday. Had a very nice time.'

Paddy elbowed me. 'That's good to hear.' He gave me a very pointed look.

'I'll have to come down some evening,' she said.

'It's our last one this Saturday.'

'Well then, I'd better get my skates on. See you, Gerry.'

'We're only here to see Foxy,' I said to Gerry. 'I was telling Paddy about her.' I kneeled down. 'I'll just pick her up for a second.' Foxy was light and soft as a feather and she pressed her head into my chest.

'Hello, Foxy,' I said, 'you lovely girl.' It was the closest I had got to comfort in weeks. I kissed her head and nuzzled her ear.

'Wouldya ever just take her?' said Gerry. 'Ah, but the husband...' He winked at Paddy. 'He's not a dog person. Have you ever heard the like?'

Paddy laughed. 'Outrageous.'

'Isn't it just? But good news,' he smiled, 'we've found a home for her. They are coming to collect her tomorrow. Lovely family, they need a dog so the two-year-old doesn't feel left out with the arrival of the new baby.'

'That's brilliant...' Disappointment washed over me. Obviously, going to a new home was exactly what Foxy needed... except, don't toddlers manhandle dogs?

'How's that fella of yours?' asked Gerry. 'And how's the hamster?' He threw Paddy another wink.

'Lost, both of them. One physically and the other mentally.'

Gerry laughed. 'And who do you miss the most?'

'Definitely the hamster.' They laughed again and I reluctantly placed Foxy back in her box. 'Good luck in your new home, hope the toddler is gentle with you.' I was delaying going to work and facing the reality of my professional car crash.

'So you're back on Saturday, yes? The last whatever it is you're doing? Have you sent the list to Rachel?'

I nodded as I stood up. 'Why don't you come on Saturday?' I said to Gerry. 'Bring the family... we'll make room for you, won't we, Paddy?'

Paddy nodded. 'Of course. We need to look after our suppliers.'

Gerry looked pleased. 'Well, we just might do that, it's my seventy-third birthday and we were wondering how to celebrate. I'll bring my wife, Bernadette, and maybe Rachel, if that would suit you? Rachel needs to get out there and find someone nice. She spends too many Saturday nights in watching the telly with us.'

We said our goodbyes and Paddy and I bought two teas and two croissants and sat on a bench together.

'I wonder if you would do me a favour?' I asked. 'Would you mind collecting a friend of mine on Saturday night. He's called Harry, he's my next-door neighbour and doesn't have a car.'

Paddy nodded. 'Of course. It's a good opportunity to try out the cargo bike. Leave it to me.' He was still looking at me. 'Now, tell me if I am being intrusive...' he began.

I looked at Paddy. 'What do you mean?'

'Brody,' he said. 'I just have to ask... I don't know... as your friend, I was wondering...'

I said nothing.

'It's just that you made that joke about the hamster... and...' His voice faded out. 'Well... I thought that... I don't know what I thought, I just wanted to make sure you were all right... that you were happy.'

'Happy?'

He nodded. 'Happy.'

For the last year I had been in survival mode. Happiness didn't come into it. My determination to stick at my marriage had overridden everything. Getting married was a foolish, misguided attempt to create a feeling of safety and security, without any real basis. Happiness was something else, something which I felt very deeply. It was how I felt when I picked up Foxy or cooked a great meal or laughed with my friends. It wasn't what I felt with Brody. Sometimes when you are firefighting in your life, you make bad decisions everywhere else. It might explain why everything was imploding.

Paddy was waiting for me to speak.

'I'm not really, it's been... challenging. I think...' I stopped. 'I've made a mistake. Lots of them. Work is stressful and... God, that's going to be a mess when it all blows up but...' I looked at him, wondering what would happen if I finally told someone about Brody. The easier way was just to hang in there, take my punishment for my reckless decision to get married, to not let anyone know what a mistake it had been. The harder decision was to be honest. 'I want to leave,' I said, 'but I can't.'

And that was it, the words were out. Someone knew. It felt both terrifying and immediately incredibly liberating. I needed Paddy to tell me it was going to be all right, that people survived worse marriages. Who knew? We might even be happy... Brody would be at home right now probably doing his spellcheck or writing *The End*.

Paddy looked at me. 'Why can't you leave?'

'Because I can't!' I nearly laughed. 'We've only been married for a year. People don't get divorced after a year! And...' I stopped.

'And what?'

'And I married someone I had only known for six months and I can't admit I was wrong...' I tried to smile at the ridiculousness of what I was saying, hoping Paddy would smile too and agree with me. Of course I couldn't leave. I had to see this thing through. Getting out would be giving up and mature adults stuck things out. Marriage wasn't like a pottery evening class which you tried out and gave up on when you realised you weren't much good at it. But Paddy was looking at me with a serious look on his face, his eyes concerned. I didn't need sympathy, I needed a hard-headed talking-to.

'Of course you can,' he said.

'I can't.'

'People make mistakes every day.'

'I know. But not this kind of monumental mistake. Not marrying someone. And anyway, maybe it will all be all right. The book is due to be finished by today... and...' I stopped.

'And?'

'And maybe things will improve. I've been waiting for this day for a whole year. I can't give up now, not when we are so close.'

Paddy took a sip of his tea and sat back on the bench, his long legs stretched out. 'Okay then,' he said, as though giving up on me. 'Sorry for asking. I just wanted to make sure you were okay.' He stood up. 'Come on, I'll walk you to your bike.' And then I heard him say, 'Erik, *hej*!'

I looked up. It was Erik, in that tight suit, his long hair smoothed back. '*Hej*!' Erik enveloped Paddy in a bear hug and then turned to me. 'Roisín, great to see you!' And then it was my turn to be subsumed into his body, like I was a Connemara sheep being enveloped by a mountain.

And then I saw someone standing at the gates to the park staring across at us. Saoirse, a look of pure delight on her face.

37

'Looking forward to tomorrow,' said Frank to me in the office. 'I'm trying to decide what to wear.'

I was avoiding Saoirse's eye, even though I could feel her staring at me. She'd been looking across at me all day while I sweated at my desk, oscillating between drafting resignation letters and trying to work out what to say to save myself. Who would ever believe that I just happened to volunteer and also accidentally became friends with the developer?

'The brown jumper is it, Frank?' Dermot asked. 'Or the brown jumper?'

'You leave him alone,' said Belinda. 'A brown jumper is a perfectly good thing to wear. I know some women who wouldn't trust a man in a bright jumper. This new fashion for every colour under the rainbow doesn't suit everyone.' She gave Frank a big smile.

For once, Frank didn't rise to Dermot's jibes. 'The brown jumper,' he said.

'Excellent choice,' Dermot returned to his screen. 'Exactly what I would have gone for myself.'

Saoirse's shadow fell over my desk. 'I knew I knew him from somewhere? The man you were with this morning. He hugged you. And he was at your dinner thing, the one I got food poisoning at. I knew I knew him! You've been fraternising!'

There was a gasp from Belinda. 'Saoirse, please! Don't use that word. Not after He Who Shall Not Be Named! Our Roisín would not do such a thing, so keep your accusations to yourself!'

Saoirse ignored her. Her eyes were blazing, her face full of utter delight and contempt. 'The tall, good-looking fella... he's the developer of the seafront. I knew I'd seen him before. But JP asked me to deliver the latest decision, remember? About a month ago? I was going into town and it needed to be sent by 5 p.m. on a Friday? The office is in town and I was going out. It was a real hassle but JP promised me I could come in late on Monday morning as a thank you... it was him! You're friends with the developer...'

'But I didn't know,' I protested lamely.

'And I followed you at lunchtime on Friday and guess where you were? At the Hall, with those women who do the lunches! They are the protestors. That Marian Kingston is the one who's been writing to us for the last five years!' She looked delighted, as though it was Christmas morning and Santa had left a bottle of Tia Maria in her stocking. 'Just what the hell have you been playing at?'

'I know nothing,' I said, lamely.

'Really? Really? Well, explain that to JP... and anyway, I don't believe you... it's written on your face. You've been playing some kind of game. Who's paying you? What's going on?'

'Nothing's going on,' I said. 'Nothing...' I looked at Frank and Dermot. 'I didn't know Erik was the developer and I just started volunteering at the lunches...'

Dermot looked at Saoirse and me. 'What are these accusations?' he said.

'She's been hanging out with the developer and the protestors. She's been friends with them. I think we need to hear exactly why she's been doing it, don't you? You and Frank don't fraternise, do you?'

'Can we not use inflammatory language, please, Saoirse?' said Frank. 'I find it very upsetting.' But he and Dermot were looking at each other.

'It's true,' I said. 'All of it. I am friends with the protestors and I have been hanging out with Erik the developer. And it's a mess, I know that.'

'So what have you been doing?'

'Cooking, mainly,' I said. 'At the community lunches with the protestors, and then for the Saturday night dinners with the developer.'

'Look,' said Dermot. 'It's Friday afternoon. Why don't you go home and take the weekend to think about it? We can sort all this out on Monday morning, which we will.' He looked at Frank again.

Saoirse looked triumphant. 'See!' she said. 'Even your cronies aren't sticking up for you.'

'We are, Saoirse,' said Dermot. 'We most certainly are.'

Frank stood up, crumbs from his lunch falling like snow from his shirt. 'I'm not a fan of bullies, I had a few in school. They used to call me Princess, only because my mother used to make sure I was neat and tidy and my shirt ironed. My hair was smoothed down with brilliantine as well. And I had no dad, no one to intimidate the boys. And... well, suffice to say, I'm not a fan of bullies.'

'Nor am I, I feel the same as my friend, Frank...' Dermot gave him a quick smile. 'You think when you get to a certain age, you put all that behind you. You really don't expect to find it at work.'

'But she's done something wrong, that should be called out. I'm the whistle-blower.'

'The only thing you're blowing is out of your arse,' said Dermot.

'But JP said we had to be squeaky clean, don't you remember?' Saoirse was going red in the face. 'He said we had to be whiter than white... whiter than Widow Twankey's laundry...'

'She's right,' I said, stepping forward. 'All of it. It's my fault. I went along to the lunches every day... I knew it was wrong. I was just hoping I wouldn't get found out...' I glanced at Saoirse who had the look of a Bond villain about her, a sly smile on her face as she looked just beyond me.

'You'll have to declare it all,' said Saoirse. 'All of it. If you're going down, you're not bringing down the whole department.'

'Bringing down what department?' We all looked up to see JP standing in the office. 'I've only been away for two weeks and I come back to discover that the department is being brought down. What's going on?' He looked at us in turn.

'Ask her.' Saoirse pointed at me. 'She's only going to bring down the entire department. You'll lose your job, JP, we'll all lose our jobs!'

JP shook his head, incredulously. 'Roisín, so let me get this straight. You've been volunteering at the community lunches with Marian and her crew?'

I nodded.

'And Erik Larsen is a friend of yours?'

'Well, he's a friend of a friend,' I said. 'And we've been...'

He held up his hand. 'I've heard enough.' His voice was quiet. 'I don't know what to say... except...surely you knew it was wrong?'

I nodded miserably. 'I know, which is why I am going to resign to save you the bother or the hassle of sacking me. Thank you, everyone, for being such great colleagues. I've had a really good ten years...' My voice started to wobble as I began trying to fit my mug and other bits from my desk into my handbag.

'Roisín,' said JP, 'hold on a moment, we need to talk about this first... what in the Holy God's name is going on?'

'I started volunteering at Lady Immaculate Hall...' I admitted.

'At those lunches?'

I nodded, feeling utterly wretched. I had been so stupid. 'I didn't mean to...' I sounded like a pathetic child. 'It just happened.'

JP looked as though he couldn't quite believe it. 'But why?' he managed. 'It's not as though I didn't warn you?'

'And she's been friends with the developer,' said Saoirse gleefully, stepping forward. 'I saw him at the dinner the other week... you can't miss him. I thought I recognised him then but I didn't for the life of me think it was the developer... he was wearing a T-shirt and an apron... but then this morning she hugged him!'

'How in Holy Christ did you allow any of this to happen?' JP was still shaking his head as though he couldn't quite believe it.

'It just happened...'

'And they have both spoken to you about the development, yes?'

I nodded, not saying any more because there was nothing more to say.

'Roisín, look,' went on JP, 'I think what's best is if we all think about this over the weekend... I just can't get my head around why you'd be so reckless... all I asked you to do was take a look at the proposal... not get into bed with either of them.'

'Aha!' Saoirse stepped forward again. 'She's been sleeping with that blonde guy? And I thought you were married to that... eejit who wrote those awful columns!'

'You go home.' JP looked grave. 'I'll think what to do.'

'Now? But it's only 2 p.m.'

He nodded. 'We'll meet back here at 9.30 a.m. on Monday.'

I walked through the office, all the way down the stairs and out into the fresh air, trying not to cry.

* * *

At home, I called up the stairs. 'Brody?' He would have sent his book off by now, I thought. 'Brody?' I called again. But the house was entirely empty. The door of the study was wide open, Brody's jacket had gone from the hooks downstairs, the wheel in Fyodor's cage was poignantly still. I tried Brody's phone but it was switched off.

It wasn't until after 9 p.m. that Brody's key scraped at the lock. When I opened the front door, he had fallen to his knees, his forehead touching the front step.

'Brody?'

He looked up, not able to focus, his eyes gazing somewhere just beyond me. He reached out, grabbed on to me and pulled himself up.

'Jussst been having a few drinnnks with...' he began to laugh. He was having difficulty hanging his jacket on the rack and let it fall to the ground in a crumpled heap. 'Annnna. Such a lovvely lady.'

I was in no mood for games. 'Did you send it in?'

'Ssssend what in?' He looked at me.

'The book.'

'Book?'

'The book. Your book! The one you've been writing for this last year! The one you finished today.'

He looked blankly back at me.

'You know, Seamus?' I reminded him.

'Ah...' he laughed again. 'Seamus! Oh, him...'

'Well? Did you send it in? Today was your deadline, remember? So, did you?' I felt total panic. Nothing was going to plan. 'So, did you?' I felt like his mother asking if he'd done his homework.

'No,' he said.

'No?' Suddenly everything went silent. The one thing I was sure was going to happen, the one thing around which I had planned my whole life – my entire existence – this last year hadn't happened. 'What do you mean no?' I stared at him.

'I haven't done it.' He shrugged. 'So...'

'You haven't sent it in or...?' I had to focus on getting the words out. 'Or you haven't written it?'

'The latttter. I haven't written a book. I mean, I have it written in my head. I have the story up here...' He tapped his temple. 'But not on paper as such.'

'Do you mean it's in your laptop, on your hard drive? Do you mean, it's just not printed or sent yet? Because we can do it now... I'll do it for you... It must be hard to let go of something you've worked so hard on... I can email it for you...'

He shook his head, still smiling. 'No, not even that.'

'Are you joking?'

He shook his head.

'How much have you done?' I asked.

'I don't know...' He leaned his head back, thinking. 'Something like a thousand...'

'Pages?'

'Words.'

I stopped. 'A thousand words?'

'Something like that. I've done a lot of deleting.'

'Oh my God.'

'Oh my God, what?' He pushed past me and was taking off his coat. 'Why are you being so dramatic?' He had suddenly sobered up and was looking at me furiously. 'What's it to do with you anyway?'

'But...'

'I may not have written a novel,' he said, 'but I have become extremely proficient in a certain computer game. I am now on Expert Level.' Brody looked delighted with himself. 'Not bad for a bookworm like me.'

'But the book, you have a contract... what are you going to do?'

'I am going to ask for an extension, writers do it all the time. I'll ask for another year. We'll just carry on as we have done. So, it's no skin off your nose, I don't know why you are looking so appalled...'

I crept up the stairs and into the bedroom. I lay in bed thinking about the last year. I had thought the end was in sight, but this was so much worse. There was no beginning, or middle, or end. It was a nightmare.

38

Little Eden Supper Club

Margaritas
Stuffed chilli 'rellenos', served with crispy, spicy home-made tortilla chips and
Rathcoole polytunnel avocado guacamole
Mexican-Irish chicken mole, served with spicy rice, beans, charred corn with
lime and paprika
Coconut ice cream, chocolate tart and candied lime zest

Sleep again remained elusive. I lay in the dark, wishing we were even a few weeks back, when I still had hope and Fyodor was alive and I had optimism about my life and my marriage. Everything was now all gone. I would be sacked on Monday and stuck forever waiting for Brody to finish his book.

Just before 6 a.m., I found Brody asleep on the sofa and I shook him awake. His eyes unpeeled slowly and he stared as though he wasn't quite sure who I was. Maybe I was as much a stranger to him as he was to me? Maybe he hated being married to me and the reason he hadn't been able to write was that he had realised he too had made a massive mistake?

'I have to get everything ready for the supper club,' I said.

Wordlessly, he managed to stand up, his body creaking to upright, and made his slow way upstairs. He farted loudly as he flung himself onto the bed, just as I heard the rumble of Gerry's van outside.

'Morning!' he shouted, when I opened the front door, as he began lifting the crates from the back of the van. 'How are you today? Grand day, isn't it?'

'It is,' I agreed, taking a crate from him.

'We'll see you tonight? My wife and Rachel will be coming. They say they are really looking forward to eating our food cooked properly!' His weather-beaten face beamed at me. 'None of us are very good in the kitchen. We're basic cookers. My mother was a very good cook, and my two brothers inherited that gene but unfortunately I was missed out.'

'No pressure then, Gerry!' I tried to smile. My only plan was to get through this evening and then... I couldn't think any further ahead. I didn't even have to turn up at the office on Monday for the final humiliation. I could leave the country, perhaps?

'By the way,' he said. 'I dropped Foxy off yesterday at her new family. She didn't look too happy about it. I could see it in her eyes. She kind of had this imploring look about her...'

Just when I thought I couldn't feel much worse.

'But she'll be grand, though, so she will.' Gerry gave me a cheery wave from the front seat and his van disappeared around the corner. I heard Harry right behind me.

'Morning, Roisín, it's the supper thing tonight, isn't it?'

'It's the last one, you are going to come, aren't you?'

And then I saw Anna behind Harry. 'Roisín?' she said, hovering. 'May I have a word, please?'

Harry moved on. 'Looking forward to tonight, Roisín,' he said. 'Morning, Anna.'

Anna stepped closer to me. 'Brody texted me late last night. He told me that you know he hasn't done any writing.'

'Well, I was hoping—'

'It's called writer's block, you know?' she pressed on. 'It's a very serious issue for creatives. And it's important that the rest of you understand how much pressure is put on writers. I mean, would you like to write a book?'

'No, but—'

'Exactly,' she went on. 'Poor Brody. No wonder he's been playing computer games. It soothes his anxiety. I have been talking to him about it for months. It was lonely being in his study all day. He said he felt like he was locked up in a cage, being made to perform. He said it was like being a prima ballerina, on the stage of the Bolshoi...'

I nearly laughed. 'He what?'

'And everyone standing around asking when he was going to do it, over and over again...' Her voice broke. 'Poor Brody. He said it was why he connected to the hamster.'

'Fyodor?'

She nodded. 'I think he saw himself and his struggle reflected in Fyodor. He used to say he wanted to set him free...'

'Well, at least he succeeded in one thing.' I needed to focus on the supper club. 'Sorry, Anna, I've got to get on...' I walked away and then turned around. 'By the way, was he playing games at yours?'

She nodded. 'Every day, and he'd leave mine to go back to yours. I think he did really want to write the book and he was always saying that he was really trying but staring at the white page was terrifying. Gaming was like therapy. And then it took over. And you've never played a computer game... have you?'

'Never.'

'Well, then you won't understand how cathartic, how transporting they are... I mean, one of the games—' She was suddenly animated and excited.

'Anna, I don't have time. I'm sorry.' And I left her standing on the street. The thought of being in the house while Brody slept off his hangover upstairs, in my bedroom, was unbearable. I called Mum. 'Will you come and pick me up?' I asked. 'Could I use your kitchen today? Something's happened.'

As soon as I saw her little red car, I began to cry. There is something about seeing your mother when you are on the brink of tears that brings them to the surface. I hurried out with my boxes and bags, my special knives and all my equipment.

Mum took one look at my face and asked, 'What's wrong?'

I shook my head, not wanting to speak.

'What's wrong?' she asked again, as soon as I got in beside her.

'Oh Mum...' And the tears fell, great, ratchety sobs catching in my throat, making it impossible to get the words out. 'I've made a massive mistake... huge...'

'What?' She hadn't moved the car and I wanted to get away from the house before Brody came out. Seeing his face – and his foul beard permanently encrusted with food – might have pushed me over the edge.

'He didn't write it, he was playing a computer game.' I looked anxiously out of the car window, as though we were being chased. 'Can we leave? Now?'

Mum made the getaway, zooming down the street. 'Do you mean Brody?' she said, as we sped round the corner. 'Are you talking about the book?'

'Yes!' I shouted. 'Who else? That stupid, bloody, crappy book! It doesn't even exist. He hasn't written it!'

'So, it's not finished?'

'He's barely started!'

She shook her head. 'So, he hasn't written it?'

'NO!'

'Jesus, Mary and Joseph.' She looked stunned.

'Exactly!' And I started to cry again. 'I can't believe it.'

Mum's lips were pursed and she shook her head a couple of times as though she was having a whole conversation in her head.

'What shall I do? Tell me, just what shall I do?'

'You already know the answer,' said Mum, parking the car outside her house.

'I don't, I really don't. I just need to know what to do. Tell me.' I needed someone to tell me exactly what to do, and I would do it, whatever it was.

'But you know,' insisted Mum. 'You're just not listening to yourself.'

'So you tell me then.'

She smiled. 'Trust yourself, and then you'll hear yourself. And once you start listening, you can't go wrong.'

I doubted I would ever get to that point, and anyway, I was the last person I should listen to. Just look at what I'd managed to get myself tangled up in. 'I just have to get through today.'

'Well, I'll help you,' she said. 'All of us will. Shona's here for a few days' rest. Ross is gone and she says she just wanted to come home for a bit. She's in her old room, back in her single bed. The girls are in the spare room and Dad is sleeping on the pull-out couch in the living room. Kitty and Daisy are at ballet this morning and a birthday party this afternoon and then they can watch TV later. So Shona and I are at your command. It will do her good to have something to concentrate on.' She reached over and took my hand. 'You're my courageous, wonderful girl. Feck Brody, feck that book, and you listen to that voice which tells you that you are brave. Because you are and the more you listen to that voice, the braver you will be.' We stopped at a red light and she looked across at me. 'That night when Jack left...'

'I remember...'

'It took me a while to listen to my voice... I spent a long time wondering what I had done wrong, trying to work out how I was going to do all this... and then... I don't know... I stopped all the internal chatter, all the noise, and I felt unbelievably calm... and actually excited about this new life I was on. And then I felt invincible.'

'I wish I did.'

'You already are,' she went on. 'And once you know it, there's no going back.'

* * *

Shona hugged me when I lumbered into the kitchen, with my boxes of equipment, my crates of food. 'Are you okay?' she asked.

'Are you?'

She nearly laughed. 'Oh God, we're a pair, aren't we?' She wiped away a tear. 'I can't believe I'm still crying over Ross. You'd think I'd have stopped by now.'

Mum put an arm around her. 'Heartbreak is like a storm. You have to wait for it to blow through. Give yourself time.' She pulled me into the hug. 'Both of you.'

But I wasn't heartbroken, I realised. Not about Brody, not really. I was just embarrassed that I had done something stupid, and made everyone celebrate my stupidity – and most of them even gave me presents for my stupidity.

'We've got to made a start,' I said. 'Supper clubs don't just happen, you know.' Jools was busy with clients all day so it was just Mum, Shona and I in the kitchen.

Mum scrubbed everything down, disinfected the work surfaces and insisted that we all tie our hair back. 'If we are a professional kitchen for the day,' she said, 'then we are going to act like one. We're not going to be shut down by the hygiene crew.'

We stood in a line at the kitchen table, my notes spread in front of us, preparing, chopping and talking.

And for the first time, I told them about Brody.

'He's been lying to me the whole time,' I said, as I sliced the onions. 'I still can't get my head around it. Why would he do that?'

'Fear of failure?' suggested Shona, who was on the celery.

'I feel like the last year has been a complete joke, he's been lying to me. And he lost Fyodor.'

'Who's Fyodor?'

'His hamster.'

'Oh God,' said Shona. 'The hamster? I mean, they are just rats in Afghan coats.'

'But in the end,' I went on, taking the finely chopped carrots from Mum, 'I grew quite fond of Fyodor. I can't bear to think of him, out there, on the mean streets of Sandycove.'

'I think the only thing you can really rely on is a dog,' said Mum. 'Remember Snuff? He was always there for us.'

'Always,' agreed Shona.

'He was the best,' I said. And I thought of Foxy. Everything – happiness, success, children, dog – seemed further away than ever.

The line Paddy had quoted came back to me. Believe that further shore... Is reachable from here. Believe in miracles... And cures and healing wells. Marriage to Brody had meant being totally at sea... it was strange how someone can bring chaos into your life. It was time to stand on my own two feet and find the courageous heart of me. If it existed at all.

I tried to listen to my inner voice, the one Mum said was in there, but at the moment all I knew was that I was going to have to relive the last year, like Groundhog Day.

I looked across at Shona. 'What about you?'

'I am recalibrating,' she said carefully. 'I am going to find a job and we're moving back to Sandycove. I want to be back beside the sea. I think I need to come home. I thought I had made a good decision by marrying someone very different to Dad.'

'Oh, your dad wasn't the worst, I've grown rather fond of him after all this time.'

'So you have forgiven him?' I asked.

'For what?' Mum looked surprised. 'What's he done now?'

'Left you!' exclaimed Shona. 'Abandoned you.'

'Has he? His toothbrush is still in the bathroom. All his clothes are in his room. Suitcase is still there.'

'No, not now, then, when I was ten and Roisín was nine... remember?'

'Oh, that,' said Mum. 'I can barely remember any of that.'

'But...' Shona looked at me.

'It was kind of seminal for us.'

'Why don't you decide to forgive him? The past is the past, and he loves you, and I love you... and in our own weird way, the six of us, and Daisy and Kitty, are still a family.'

Shona and I looked at each other. 'I will if you will,' she said.

'I suppose we could.' We smiled at each other.

'Shona, will you pass the other knife, please? this one is terrible.' She took the knife from Shona. 'I am thinking of selling the house and moving somewhere smaller.'

'No!' Shona and I said together.

But Mum nodded. 'I've decided to go, find somewhere close by, not so big, cheaper bills, a smaller garden. Still room for the two of you since you both refuse to entirely flee the nest.' She smiled at us. 'But somewhere to start again. I should have done it years ago.'

The three of us worked in silence for a moment or two and then Shona said, 'I think you're doing the right thing. You're never too old to start again, are you?'

'Never, and you can start again as many times as you like. This may not be my last restart. Who knows what's in store for me?'

'I'm really proud of you, Mum,' said Shona. 'You did all of this for us.'

'You two made it easy for me, you were the two nicest people I'd ever met. Still are.'

Shona wiped away another tear. 'We need to crack on,' she said, stridently, 'because I need to pick up the girls from the party shortly and I haven't started on the guacamole.'

39

By early afternoon, Jools, Richard, Sam, Paddy and Erik had arrived.

Erik sat next to Jools. '*Hej*,' he said to her, smiling.

'*Hej*.' She smiled back.

'Shall we do the bar again, like last week?' he asked.

'If Roisín can spare me,' she said.

'I can. I've got reinforcements here in the kitchen. We'll be fine.'

'Right, people!' Richard clapped his hands. 'Let's get this show on the proverbial boreen...' He slung his arms around my and Jools's shoulders. 'I presume Brody is happy that the infernal book is finally done?'

'He didn't write the bloody thing.'

'What bloody thing?'

'His book. He's going to take another year.'

Jools's jaw dropped open. 'Oh my God...'

'See,' said Richard. 'Should have listened to your wise uncle, Richie.'

'He was lying the whole time,' I said. 'He claims he's had writer's block.'

Richard rolled his eyes. 'What a cocklodger.'

'And the worst thing is, he lost Fyodor. He took him outside in his pocket and he lost him.'

'For that he should be arrested. For everything else he should be divorced.' He looked at me. 'Will you?'

'I don't know, I don't know what to do. I haven't made up my mind.' I had the instability and worry of work, getting divorced was a seismic move too far.

'Where's your—'

'My courage?' I replied. 'I don't have any, it turns out.'

'No, you do,' he said. 'But what I was going to say is where is your self-esteem? You deserve better! So much better! Not some lazy layabout!'

'Hello?' Dad was standing in the doorway. 'Anyone here? I've finally finished sorting through all of Philip's papers.'

'You look happy,' said Mum, who was standing at the sink doing the eighth wash-up of the day.

'Well, I am... but I have a couple of things to say. I've been doing some thinking. First to my daughters, I'm sorry. Richard, Jools, I hope you don't mind witnessing this lesson in humility. A heartfelt and sincere apology. Sorry for not being there, sorry for not being a better dad. Sorry for letting you down.'

'Dad...' I began but he held up a hand.

'I am here for you,' he said, 'for anything. I have been thinking and thinking about what Shona said to me, and anytime you want to berate me, let off steam, express your anger, please do so. I am ready to soak it up like a sponge, ready to be your dad again.'

Shona glanced at me. 'I shouldn't have said what I said last week,' she mumbled. 'I had drunk too much of your Côtes du Rhône ...'

'Nice, isn't it? Very good value...'

'Delicious,' she agreed.

'But you were right. I was an immature father and I let you down, all of you. I hope I have grown up a little but what I also want to say is that the last three weeks have been some of the happiest of my life. I love you, Shona, Roisín and Maggie. And Daisy and Kitty, of course. I love you all more and more every day. And I'm sorry.'

'Life is complicated,' said Shona. 'You try and simplify it, come up with a formula to make it work and make everything add up, but it is too unpredictable.' She began to cry again.

Dad walked straight up to her, arms outstretched. 'Come here, darling,' he said, 'it's all right, it's all right...' Shona laid her head on his shoulder while he patted her and smoothed her hair back, making soothing and shushing sounds.

'It's just that I thought I knew what the future looked like,' she said. 'But it's all so scary. I've got to do it all on my own.'

Dad's eyes were full of tears. 'I'm so sorry, I'm so sorry he's done this.' He looked across at me, smiling. 'I'm so proud of the two of you, and I know I don't deserve to feel such pride, but I do anyway.'

'We love you too,' I said, meaning it. I put my arms around him and Shona.

'We do,' said Shona, muffled, from inside the group hug. 'We both really love you.' Dad gave a sob as he clung on to us.

'Room for one more?' Richard had his arms out. 'Come on, you can fit me in there. I need a hug too, you know!' He wrapped his arms around us all. 'I'm a member of this family as well, you know.'

We laughed and pulled apart. Dad's eyes were red as he looked straight at Mum. 'And I love you, Maggie. I love you more than words can say. I love you more than the first time I saw you at that bus stop when I jumped off because I had to know the name of the girl with those blue eyes. You are more beautiful now than at any time in your life. I've made mistakes and I've let you – all of you – down. Badly. But I am asking for a second chance.' He looked desperately, pleadingly, at Mum, as Shona, Jools, Richard and I turned to look her at her too.

Mum cleared her throat. 'Let's focus on the evening,' she said. 'Someone needs to pick up Daisy and Kitty. Jack, maybe you will?'

Dad nodded. 'I will go and get my keys.'

I looked at the clock on the wall. 5 p.m. Richard clapped his hands. 'Come on, chop-chop! Let's get this party started!'

40

While Dad, Daisy and Kitty watched a film in the front room, Paddy, Erik and Jools transformed the garden back into the Sandycove Supper Club and Sam and Richard were busy doing what Richard referred to as 'marketing and sales'.

Shona and Mum were quite happy to take instruction from me, Shona dutifully following my notes, Mum even cutting the cucumbers to the exact width I requested.

'Yes, chef,' Mum kept saying.

'Whatever you want, chef,' said Shona.

Jools stuck her head around the door. 'Do you have the limes for the margaritas? Or do you think I need to buy some more?'

'Definitely buy some more,' said Shona. 'You can't have enough margaritas.'

'Okay,' said Jools. 'I'll go. Roisín, will you bring the ones in here out to Erik? See you in ten!'

I went back to where my notebook and my lists were and began scanning through to see what we may have forgotten and what needed to be ticked off.

Outside, Erik was setting up a large metal contraption. 'A lime press,' he explained. 'Bought one in Guadalajara a few years ago but found this in a shop in town.' He started placing the sliced limes in the press and squeezing them, the pale green juice trickling out.

I needed to say something. After all, he had no idea I was about to lose my job over his development.

'Erik,' I said, 'you know Lady Immaculate Hall? The old building beside your development?'

'Ah, that thing...' He looked at me curiously.

Courage, I thought. Confidence. It was about time I stood up for something I believed in. And that was the Hall. And it was also me. 'You can't knock it down,' I said. 'I know it's going to take a lot of money to do up, but it's worth it. I want you to take it on as part of the development. I've been working with the team who run the community lunches... and I'm also a planner at the council. Well, I am in admin, but my boss... never mind... But what I'm trying to say is that we need to save it. It's a beautiful building and it's important.'

Erik's blonde eyebrows raised a few millimetres. 'My company buys projects that have hit problems. Rock-bottom prices, things other developers want off their hands. We call them "ball-aches", you understand? That building wasn't looked after by any of you. The council was in charge of it for twenty years and no one thought to fix the roof, insulate it, heat it or deal with the damp. You guys ruined it.' He shrugged. 'It's not my problem. I'm sorry.'

'I just thought that...'

'I am paid to finish it,' he said. 'We're going to get planning. We've ensured that the people inhabiting the building are well taken care of, yes? Another nice, new building for them? Job done. They're on the edge of giving in. Listen, we're not bad guys. We make sure everyone is looked after. And at the end of it, everyone shakes hands and is happy.'

'I know, but...'

'Now, let me tell you a story,' he went on. 'Just so you understand my psychology and where I'm coming from. I tell this story when asked to give motivational talks. So, it goes like this, when I was nineteen, I was obsessed with cross-country skiing. Have you ever been cross-country skiing?'

'Never...'

'It's the closest you can get to being an animal in the forest, a part of nature, at one with the elements, slipping through the trees, past the deer, the silence fills up your brain and your body, you are bathed in cold air and you feel more alive than you will ever be doing anything else. My own father represented Denmark in cross-country skiing at the Olympics. He was a man of... what would you say? A man of iron. He never gave up. Hard as nails... yes?'

I nodded. Erik had an intensity to him which was pretty powerful, his Viking genes undiluted by time.

'Well, so we watched him at the Winter Olympics. We were at home, myself and my sister. We didn't go to school that day, and we watched as our father, like a magnificent machine of a man, these black goggles, in a skintight snowsuit, represented our country. I could barely breathe,' he went on. 'And it started. My mother was in the kitchen, refusing to watch. My sister and I didn't say a word. He was the strongest man in the world, we knew he was going to do it. We'd seen him train, we'd been there when he had returned drenched in sweat. We knew how much he wanted it.'

'And...?'

Erik shook his head. 'He got silver. He lost. And he lost to a Norwegian! I could barely look at him when he came home, I was so disappointed. And so I went on to try and win that medal for him. I trained every day, before school, after school, into the night. I built a gym in my bedroom, I ate properly, I did everything I could. And do you know what happened?'

'You won a gold medal?'

He shook his head again. 'I wasn't even selected.' He smiled. 'I wasn't even a contender, just a very ordinary person. I wasn't an Olympian. But my father was. And I learned the lesson that silver is good enough. Silver is better than most people ever achieve, so I believe in trying for gold, but knowing perfection does not exist. And that's how I feel about every development. None of us will get perfection, but we will get good enough. You get silver. Sorry, it's the way the world works. Be happy with silver. It's life. We move on. We get over it.'

'Yes, but it matters to people because it is part of the community.' My voice broke for a moment but I carried on. 'Do you know about the lunches?'

He nodded. 'I am aware of them, yes. I have met... is it Marian?'

'And Sheila, yes. Well, it's a group that provides free lunches every day for older members of the community. Eating together is so important, right?'

He shrugged. 'Depends on who you are eating with. I know people I would rather never eat with again.'

'But these are nice people, and the Hall is falling down, I know that...'

'It's been condemned...'

'I know that,' I said, quickly. 'But a new roof would save it. And you can do that. You just need to allocate the money. I want you to change the plan, take on the Hall, save it. You would be going for gold, not just accepting silver. It's harder, more expensive, but the feeling when it's all finished will be incredible.' Erik didn't say anything so I pressed on. 'Too often developers and clients don't compromise. You go on about having to accept something which is less than ideal, but you are not compromising. You haven't changed your vision at all, but you expect everyone else to. All you need to do is agree to keep the building and I, as a member of the planning department, could approve the development first thing on Monday and we take it from there...?'

He was looking at me. 'Normally, planners don't get involved. Do you know you are the first planner I have met face to face? It's not seen as—'

'Ethical, I know, we all want the area developed but if you want the planning, you have to keep the Hall. End of.' I felt something surge inside me. It felt like courage. 'You're nearly at gold but it's a team effort, you'll be part of a team... you and Marian and Sheila and all the others.'

'But financially—'

'Financially you will have to take the hit, yes,' I said. 'I'm sorry. But the Hall will not be knocked down.' I stared back at him. 'I can't let it go. I have spent weeks in the Hall and it's beautiful. There are the most wonderful wooden carved doors, there is a terrazzo floor which is to die for, there is a feeling when you go in there that this has been a place of activity all its life. You can sense the spirits of all those who came before. We cannot be the generation who knocks it down.'

'We'd have to bring it up to current environmental standards.'

'Yes, we would.'

'Heat pumps, solar power, insulation...'

'Yes, exactly. And proper wheelchair access, nice toilets... all doable.'

He looked at me for what seemed like a very long time. 'Okay.'

'Okay? Okay what?'

'Okay, you have a deal. We will keep the Hall, we will bring it up to modern standards and we will integrate it into the scheme.' He held out his hand and shook mine, nearly breaking my fingers in the process.

'Thank you, Erik.'

'Okay, then,' he said, smiling and I flung my arms around him, just as Jools walked back in. 'He said yes, Jools!' I shouted. 'He said yes!'

41

Richard came into the kitchen clapping his hands. 'How are we doing in here? The guests are arriving.'

Through the kitchen window I could see people streaming in through the back gate and into the summer house where Erik and Jools were serving the drinks and Sam and Richard were serving the canapés. Gerry, his wife, Bernadette, and daughter, Rachel, were drinking margaritas. Belinda arrived with her salsa troupe, Frank and Dermot were standing together, margaritas in their hands. Even JP was there. Maybe he could just sack me now and save me from the humiliation on Monday?

'I'd better go and say a quick hello to everyone,' I said. 'I'll carry out some of the canapés.'

As Richard and I walked out, into the noise of chatter and the sound of the jazz band, the twinkling lights strung up ahead, he slipped his arm through mine. 'You've been magnificent,' he said, quietly. 'I just wanted to say it.'

Harry was talking to some of the salsa women under the apple tree.

'Thanks,' I said. 'I didn't know how much I needed to get out... and have fun.'

'I did.' He looked smug. 'My plan has worked. And...' He stopped. 'I'm... in love with Sam. We made our declarations. Well, he did and then I did. It all happened in the hospital last week? Who would have known the most romantic place in Ireland is St Vincent's A & E. I went and bought us a tea from the machine and two KitKats and when I came back, he told me he was going to resign. And I had this desperate feeling, like I was going to lose him. And I asked had he got another job or what was it. And he said he was in love with me and he had to go.' Richard had tears in his eyes. 'And... I told him I felt the same. And well... we may have kissed. But his neck was still bad... but we held hands and... oh my God. I'm properly, completely and happily in love.'

I turned and hugged him. 'I'm so delighted for you,' I said. 'You and Sam are perfect for each other.'

He smiled at me. 'You go and say hello to your colleagues and I will check on the bar.'

I swallowed before I turned to face them. They were all holding one of Erik's margaritas and Belinda was the first to hug me hello and then I shook hands with Frank and Dermot.

'I managed to get Frank out of his brown jumper into a brown blouse,' said Dermot. 'I consider that a triumph.'

'It's a shirt, Dermot, not a blouse.'

'It looks like a blouse,' Dermot shrugged. 'But if you insist...'

JP nodded at me. 'I hope you don't mind me coming but I thought it was an office night out...'

I nodded. 'I want to say sorry but also that I didn't mean to behave unethically...' I thought of everything about trusting yourself and that Mum was right about once you do, you can't go wrong. When you are clear about your intentions and your desires, you can't go wrong. 'That man over there...' I was aware that Belinda, Frank and Dermot were all listening in.

'The blonde Hercules?' said JP.

'He's Erik Larsen...'

'I thought it was,' said JP. 'He's unmissable.'

'He's agreed to keep the Hall, to develop it. I talked to him today.'

JP looked at me. 'Really? How did you manage that?'

'I tried a different approach,' I explained. 'I became friendly with both sides. The protestors and the developer.'

JP raised his eyebrows. 'And the number one rule of planning is no friends, no being nice, no fraternising. Ever.'

'I know... but... it just happened.'

'It just happened that you fraternised with both sides. By accident?'

'Kind of... yes.'

'Maybe fraternising with both sides means you cancel them out?' suggested Belinda.

'Like it never happened,' agreed Frank.

Everyone looked across at Erik, who was now sitting at the bar with Jools beside him, laughing about something.

'And did Erik Larsen have drink taken?' said JP.

I shook my head. 'Not then... he was sober. I promise.'

'But why would he agree?'

'Sometimes you have to know someone to do business with them,' said Dermot.

'But that's exactly what we are trying to stay away from.'

'Each case is different,' said Frank. 'We know Roisín doesn't have an unethical bone in her body...'

'Well...' I thought about all those times I'd gone into the Hall to volunteer, knowing I was breaking all the office rules.

'So, you've done it?' said JP.

'I hope so.'

'Well, I'd better go and introduce myself,' said JP, walking over.

'He's going to swoop in and take the credit, which is why they pay him the big money.'

'He deserves a little success, he doesn't get much of it.'

'He caught a fifteen-pound salmon, apparently, when he was on his holidays,' said Dermot. 'Released it unharmed though. Said he had a crisis of conscience, which is a first for a member of the planning department.'

'The last time you had a crisis of conscience was when you stole money from the collection when you were an altar boy,' said Frank.

'And I thought I could trust you with stories of my criminal past, it was twenty pence and I went and bought some sweets but I felt so guilty eating them that I gave them to a girl who lived on our road. And the lesson I learned that day was not to steal, but that to win the love of the fairer sex was to ply them with toffee bonbons.'

42

I dashed back into the kitchen and immediately started barking out orders to Mum and Shona. Dad had wandered in and found himself trussed into an apron and tasked with deep-frying the chilli rellenos.

'Mum, warm the plates, Shona, the guacamole, Dad, be careful!'

And in a blur of movement, the four of us working as though we had been cooking together all our lives, we began passing plates to Richard and Sam, who rushed back and forth while Erik and Jools were moving through the crowd, topping up the margaritas.

No sooner were the starters out, than we began on the main course. Again, the whir and blur of our hands as we plated up and shipped them out. Dad was on washing-up, wearing yellow gloves, and was soon lost in a steam of bubbles, and then drying everything and putting all the plates in piles on the kitchen table.

'How is Harry?' I shouted to Paddy, as he came in again for another six plates.

'Laughing and talking,' he shouted back. 'He looks really happy.'

Which was exactly the way I felt.

'Right,' said Dad, 'what's next?'

'Dessert. Chocolate tart, ice cream.'

Finally, it was all over. 'I don't know what just happened,' said Mum, 'but I think we just fed thirty people.'

Outside, everyone was finishing their dessert, the music from the band in the background and the voices of our guests swirled in the air with the lights and the glow of love. Dermot, I spotted, was in deep conversation with Rachel, Gerry's daughter. Frank and Belinda were laughing hysterically at something, Jools and Erik were sitting at the bar, both with a drink in their hands, Jools swinging her long legs.

Richard scooted up to me and whispered urgently in my ear. 'Dead writer walking... over at the gate.'

Brody, with Anna just behind him, was walking into the garden.

'It's decision time.' Shona peered out at Brody and Anna.

'Courage,' said Mum. 'Just listen to your voice, the one you know is right.'

I nodded, and headed out, with Richard bobbing at my side. And there, in my mother's garden, with the lights above, surrounded by people and love and music, I tuned in and heard myself loud and clear. Don't go back. Never go back. I wasn't going to do last year all over again. It hadn't been worth it.

Brody stood, blocking my path. 'She made me come,' he said sulkily, thumbing towards Anna. 'Just to reiterate, I haven't done anything wrong. Just missed a deadline. What writer doesn't do that?'

Anna looked apologetic. 'I was trying to help Brody, I knew he was struggling with writer's block. I am sorry for lying to you. I thought I was helping Brody by giving him a way to relax and switch off...'

'Which is also completely normal,' said Brody. 'Scott Fitzgerald used gin to relax, Oscar Wilde used opium, I just played a few computer games.'

'It's just that we are addicted,' Anna went on, 'the two of us. We are just a pair of hopeless addicts. We found each other, and we spiralled. We've tried to get off them, tried everything. Cold turkey, distraction, the whole thing, but we were too far gone. You become immersed in these worlds that are so much better than real life.'

'Was *Code of Honour* better than your real life?' I asked Brody.

He didn't hesitate. 'Much,' he said. 'Much, much better.'

I knew what I wanted, I knew what I was going to do.

I was done, I realised, done being a muse to a writer, done supporting him emotionally and financially. Done cleaning his clothes and cooking his meals. Done staying in, done listening to the stories of Seamus...

'I don't care what you do,' I said to Brody, 'but by the time I get back to the house, I want you gone. Take your books and anything else that belongs to you.'

'I think Roisín has wasted enough energy on you, Brian,' said Richard.

'Typical,' he said. 'I miss one deadline, you tell me our marriage is over...'

'You heard her,' said Richard.

'Well, Brody,' said Anna. 'You can come and stay with me. But we'll have to go cold turkey again. We'll send the games, the console, everything, to the charity shop. You can write in my spare room.'

Finally, Brody looked devastated, the loss of *Code of Honour* had hit him harder than the loss of his marriage.

'Sorry, Brian, sorry, Anna,' Richard began to usher them back to the gate, 'but we don't have room for you. This is a private gathering. Good luck with the withdrawal symptoms. Come along now...' He made swishing movements with his hands, as though herding cattle.

And that was it. My marriage was finally over. And it felt amazing.

* * *

I looked over at Harry, who was standing with Paddy, and waved. But he wasn't looking at me, he was staring at someone just beyond me. And then he made a noise, a cry which was almost anguished, something from deep inside, like a wounded animal. The band stopped playing and everyone in the garden turned to look at him. I looked behind me to see what he was staring at and it was Gerry.

Gerry had gone pale, as though he'd seen a ghost.

'Is it you?' said Harry, his voice shaking.

'Is it you?' said Gerry. 'Mother of Holy God, saints, angels, the whole fecking lot of them!'

'It is you!'

''Tis me all right! HARRY!'

'GERRY!'

Somehow they found strength in their legs of men half their age as they ran into each other's arms, crying. Gerry's face was in Harry's shoulder, Harry's eyes were squeezed shut, the two of them sobbing. 'I thought you were lost forever,' said Harry.

'I hadn't given up,' Gerry was saying. 'I was never going to give up...'

'Nor was I...'

'I said a prayer every morning...'

'I lit a candle every night...'

'I had the phone book fall apart from looking...'

'I checked the newspapers every day...'

'I missed you...'

'I missed you...'

They had their hands around each other's heads, holding each other and themselves up, their eyes full of tears. Everyone in the garden was wiping away their tears. Even Dermot looked as though he had something in his eye.

'What's going on?' Richard asked.

'I think... I think they've finally found each other.'

Paddy ran to the band's microphone. 'Gerry and Harry, everyone!' he said. 'They haven't seen each other in fifty years! Two brothers reunited!' And the band launched into a very jazzy version of 'Congratulations'.

* * *

Dad placed a glass of champagne in my hand. 'Come inside,' he said. 'I have a few things to say.'

Mum and Shona were in the kitchen, holding their full champagne glasses, their aprons still on, looking utterly exhausted.

'Can we just drink this now?' said Shona. 'I think I deserve it.'

'In a moment.' Dad stood in front of us. 'I want to make a toast. To you three,' he said. 'I love the three of you and the last three weeks, spending time with you all, getting to know you better, collecting Daisy and Kitty from school, all that... seeing you and the wonderful lives you live... the dramas, the love you have for each other, well... it's been...' His voice broke. 'It's been amazing.'

'Dad,' said Shona. 'You're not going to cry. Just drink your champagne.'

'Here's to you,' and his words went all squeaky at the end.

Even Mum had tears in her eyes.

'Here's to us,' Shona and I said to each other, and touched glasses.

'And just to let you know that Brody and I are now completely over,' I announced. 'I don't want to do another year of uncertainty. And I made my decision.' I looked over at Mum who nodded approvingly.

'Thank God for that,' said Shona.

'And I'm fine about it, so no sympathy. I just need my life back.'

Mum raised her glass. 'Here's to you getting your life back. And to Shona. And to all of us.'

Dad went and leaned against the kitchen cupboard with her. 'I want my life back too.' He suddenly dropped to one knee. 'Maggie, will you marry me all over again? Because I love you and I love my girls and I want to spend the rest of my life loving you all.'

'I love you, Jack...' began Mum.

Shona signalled for me to leave the kitchen with her.

'Oh my God, it's like a bad film,' she whispered as we walked out. 'You know, when the children try to get their parents back together again.' She slipped her arm through mine. 'I can't bear it!' She nudged me and I nudged her back.

'Thanks for today,' I said. 'You were amazing. What with everything going on...'

'You did me a favour, took my mind off Ross. And it's nice for the girls to be in Mum's house.'

'So you're definitely moving back to Sandycove?'

She nodded. 'As soon as we sell that monstrous pile. I want to come home.'

Frank and Belinda were sitting on the bench under the apple tree, talking, and Frank had an expression on his face that reminded me of a puppy who had found his forever home. Dermot and Rachel were sitting on the lawn chairs and over in the summer house I could see Jools and Erik were staring into each other's eyes. At the long table Gerry and Harry were in deep conversation. Harry looked up and waved me over.

'Can you believe it, Roisín?' he said. 'My brother, Gerry!'

'It's incredible.'

'Roisín,' said Bernadette, 'would you have any water? We have a dog in the car, who must be thirsty.'

'A dog?'

'Ah, she knows all about Foxy. Had her eye on her for a while. But her husband doesn't like dogs. I told her to get rid of him.' Gerry laughed. 'The husband, that is.'

'But that's exactly what I did.' I didn't dare hope. 'I thought Foxy was going to a home with a toddler...'

'They decided against it. Said they wanted a younger dog,' said Bernadette. 'Apparently Foxy is too old for them.'

'I'll have her,' I said, quickly. 'I'll take her now, if you like?'

'You sure?' she asked.

'I've never been surer of anything.'

'Well, then!' Bernadette stood up. 'I'll go and get her.'

* * *

In a few minutes, I had Foxy in my arms. She was warm and small and she looked up at me with her big brown eye.

'It's you and me, little Foxy,' I kissed the top of her head. 'It's us together.'

Over at the summer house, Paddy was standing on his own.

'I thought I'd introduce you to Foxy,' I said. 'Paddy, meet Foxy, my new dog. Foxy, meet Paddy, my best friend's brother.'

He took Foxy from me. 'I love her, ah, she's gorgeous.' He held her close and kissed her gently. And then he looked back at me and I remembered what it used to be like with Paddy, and how I once felt when I was with him, the secret hand-holds, the looks from across the room, the way we were when it was just the two of us. It was another life, now. I think I'd been in love with him but I'd never allowed myself to say it, even to myself. If we'd taken a different turn years ago, none of this would have happened. The last year with Brody had been transformative. I had been so desperate for love and a happy ending, I hadn't given enough thought to what was right for me. I had learned a big lesson and now the only thing I wanted was to enjoy being single.

We looked over at Jools, who was sitting in the summer house drinking something out of tiny shot glasses. 'What are they drinking?'

'Erik's Akvavit,' said Paddy. 'It's delicious. And lethal.'

Jools looked transformed, glowing not only with Scandinavian Poitín but with life. And if it was Erik or even the alcohol, it didn't matter, she looked happy.

'He's a good guy, she deserves someone nice.' He passed Foxy to me. 'I am so glad you have someone to love,' he said.

'You mean Foxy?'

He laughed. 'Of course Foxy.' His eyes met mine. 'I saw you talking to Brody earlier... everything all right?'

I nodded. 'Yes, completely.' I kissed Foxy on the top of her head. It was so nice to have something to love, something uncomplicated and easy. Even if it was just a dog. I was ready to be single, I was ready to own the decisions I had made – no regrets, nothing. Brody would be a footnote in the book of my life but I doubted if I would even get a mention in his. And as for Paddy, I knew I still had a good friend. And I'd let something good slip away but it didn't matter any more. I wouldn't be here, feeling this good, if I had made a single, different decision. It was what it was.

'He had writer's block, all this time. He hadn't written the book. And I thought that I would stick around while he did write it but I've decided to call it a day. And he'll be fine.' And then I began to laugh. 'He's been playing computer games... he's on Expert Level! I have wasted a whole year waiting for him, and all the time he was playing *Code of Honour*.'

'No!'

I nodded, still laughing, in danger of becoming hysterical. 'I wasted an entire year of my life waiting for something that was never going to come!'

Paddy shook his head, not finding it quite as funny as I did. 'I think you need a drink, I'll get two of Erik's specials. Or do you just want a beer?'

'A beer, anything stronger might tip me over edge.'

We sat together at a bench on the steps of the summer house.

'You know, you're one of the bravest people in my life... shouldering the whole of the supper club and standing up to Brody. Even marrying Brody in the first place, sometimes you have to take a leap of faith... whether it works out or not. I admire you. And the way you love your family and your friends, the way you're never judgemental and how you always want the best for everyone.'

'Isn't everyone like that?'

He laughed, and shook his head. 'No, no they certainly are not. But you live your life – what's the word? – wholeheartedly, and that's brave. And ending your marriage, getting out... that's courage.'

'Thank you,' I said, embarrassed, but we clinked our bottles together and for the first time in years, I felt really happy, that kind of contentment which comes from being at peace with the world.

* * *

By 10.30 p.m., the band was packing up and guests began to disperse. Frank was walking Belinda home and stood holding her bag while she hugged me. 'The best night I've had in years,' she said.

Frank was nodding. 'Magic, magic. The whole thing.'

Dermot hugged me next. 'You've got a talent, a real talent.'

Beside him Rachel was smiling. 'Start a restaurant,' she said. 'And we'll supply you. After all, you did reunite Dad with his brother. He has never stopped talking about him. Every year, in April, he'd light a candle for him on his birthday. And we looked and looked everywhere... but then we turn up tonight, and there he is!'

I hugged her, trying not to squash Foxy who was still in my arms.

JP came up to me. 'I've had a long talk with Erik Larsen,' he said. 'And yes, he's going to sign. We're meeting him at 9 a.m. on Monday morning in my office. Okay? I want you to be there.'

I nodded, just as I heard Shona calling my name. 'Roisín,' she called. 'Quickly. Dad's leaving.'

Dad was standing in the hall, his suitcase at his feet.

'Where are you going?' I asked.

'Uncle Philip's,' he said. 'Until I can find somewhere of my own.'

'But why? I thought you liked being here.'

'You just said you did,' said Shona. 'We were just getting used to you. Again.'

Dad nodded. 'I meant what I said, I love you all... it's just that...'

Mum stepped forward. 'I asked him to leave, I don't want to marry him and I've explained that I love him. But not enough to marry... and I thought it was best if he stays somewhere else.'

'Which I fully accept,' said Dad.

'You're abandoning him?' I turned to Mum.

'He'll be fine,' said Mum confidently. 'He always is.'

'I'm like a cat,' agreed Dad. 'Always land on my feet. And I'm not going to be far away. I will still collect the girls from school and be at your beck and call. All of you.' He looked at Mum. 'All of you, forever.'

She smiled back at him. 'Come here and give me a hug, you fool.'

Dad put his arms around her, squeezing her tightly. 'I love you all,' he said. 'My five wonderful girls.'

'Will you be okay? Shona asked. 'Like, are you able to actually cook and clean?'

'You saw me tonight,' said Dad. 'I think I'll manage.'

Mum, Shona and I stood at the door as he swung his case into the taxi and off he went, waving from the back of the car.

'It's time for a new chapter,' said Mum. 'For all of us.'

'Well, I'm proud of you, Mum,' said Shona. 'Knowing what you want. Knowing your worth. I think it's a good lesson for us all.'

Knowing your worth, that was the key to happiness. Knowing your worth and, more importantly, knowing the worth of the people you love. It might keep out those who weren't right for you and keep in the ones who were.

Shona and I slept in our old single beds, in our old bedroom, and talked late into the night. 'Do you remember the night Dad left, the first time?' she asked.

'Of course.'

'Do you feel still sad about it?'

'No...' And I didn't. 'Because we wouldn't be us if he hadn't,' I said. 'And I like us and who we are. And I like my life. And I'm excited.' I could feel Foxy's warm body at the end of my bed. 'I wouldn't change a thing.'

43

The following morning, Ross was standing on the doorstep, dressed in his red trousers and his awful shawl-collared jumper.

'I'm here to see my wife,' he said to me. 'I'm here to get my wife back.' I could see Ronan standing anxiously beside his car, as though he'd put Ross up to this. The twins were in the garden, well out of earshot.

'Are you referring to me, Ross?' Shona said, pushing past me. 'I think you must mean your former wife?'

'Technically,' he began, 'you are my wife...'

Ronan, his brother, stepped forward.

'Sorry, Shona,' he said. 'I'm so sorry to bother you but he came round to Mum and Dad's house last night after a skinful of single malt... he asked me to give him moral support.' He glared at Ross. 'Come on, pull yourself together!'

And then Ross started to cry. 'I've lost everything,' he began to blub. 'My children... my house... all I was trying to do was find myself...' Snot had begun to trail down from his nose as though a slug had slithered over his face. 'I was just trying to be happy. What's the harm in that?'

'He's really sorry,' said Ronan. 'He told me earlier...'

Ross nodded. 'Sorry, Shona.' Ross hung his head low, waiting for his punishment. 'Sorry...'

'Sorry for what exactly?' Shona asked.

'For...' Ross never looked overburdened with brain cells but right now he looked utterly clueless.

'Go on,' urged Ronan, giving him a shove. 'Go on, you total fool... this is your chance to save your marriage.'

'I... well, I'm sorry for all the times I let you down,' said Ross. 'I don't want to lose you or the girls.'

A large car had pulled in across the road and out scrambled Fionnuala, closely followed by Hugh. They clutched at each other, panic on their faces, looking up at Shona.

'Yes, go on,' said Shona to Ross. 'What exactly are you sorry for?'

'You've stood by me for all these years,' said Ross. 'That time I left to go back to work when you were in labour, the time we were in Majorca and I drank so much I vomited in the villa and you had to clean it up...'

Ronan looked at Ross in horror. 'You did what?' He wrinkled his nose. 'You utter, utter filthbag.'

Ross pressed on. 'The time when I couldn't pick you up when you broke down on the M50...' He stopped, and looked up at Shona, pleadingly. 'Do you want me to go on?'

She nodded. 'Please do.'

Fionnuala had her hands to her mouth, looking utterly devastated as she listened to Ross pleading for his marriage.

'And the time I pretended to be ill,' Ross went on, 'so I didn't have to go to the school play, or the time we went to Paris and I refused to go and see the *Mona Lisa* and I made us go and see the Paris Saint-Germain stadium instead...'

'Go on.' Shona's voice was like ice.

'And the time when we met Daisy and Kitty's hockey coach and I shouted at her for not putting them on the A-team...'

'And?' said Shona.

'And... I'm sorry about Victoria. I've lied, I've been selfish, and I have—'

'You have what, Ross?'

'I have betrayed you.'

She gave a nod. 'You have, Ross, you really have.'

'So will you?' He clasped his hands together like a child's first prayer meeting. 'Please?'

Even Ronan was looking up pleadingly. Fionnuala looked as though she was about to burst into tears. Hugh had his arm around her.

'Please, Shona!' shouted up Fionnuala. 'You're the best thing that's ever happened to him!'

'Please, Shona,' said Hugh. 'He came round last night and Ronan made him tell us everything and we're appalled. But everyone deserves a second chance.'

Shona surveyed them, like Cleopatra on the prow of her barge. 'No,' she said. 'No, it's over. All I know is that I want a fresh start and a new life. You're free to pursue whatever you want with Victoria because I know my worth, I really do. And we're going to be amicable and nice to each other, starting from now.' She stood back for a moment. 'Would you all like to come in for a cup of tea and see the girls?' She stood to one side as Fionnuala and Hugh walked up the steps, Fionnuala clutching at Shona as she went past. 'I'm so sorry,' she said, and behind them Ross, who still had snot running down his nose, and Ronan walked into the house.

'Morning, Shona, morning, Roisín,' said Ronan. 'Lovely day.'

'It really is, Ronan,' said Shona. 'It really is. And Ross, you really should wipe your nose before you see the girls.'

* * *

A little later, back at my house, Brody had taken his books, his laptop and most of his clothes except for a pair of holey, faded underpants that had been left in the middle of the bathroom floor and his yellow crocs which were beside the sofa bed in the study. The old TV in the study was gone, his toothbrush and, thankfully, there was no sign of his mug emblazoned with the unforgettable slogan:

Writing books is the closest men ever come to childbearing.

Pity Brody hadn't even written a book, he hadn't turned out to be a very good hamster parent either.

I placed Foxy on the bed while I cleaned the bathroom before showering and dressing, wondering what the whole of the last year had been for. But it was as though everything was happily in the past, the year, my marriage, the old me were all done and dusted. In its place was someone who was going to be nice to herself, to forgive mistakes. I thought of the Maya Angelou quote – if I'd known better, I would have done better. 'Well, Foxy,' I said, 'now I know a little better than I did last year.'

And what about Harry?

He answered the door dressed even more immaculately. As soon as he saw it was me, he drew me into a hug, his eyes filled with tears.

'Thank you, Roisín,' he said. 'Thank you. I don't know how you did it but thank you.'

'I didn't do anything, it was all a coincidence.'

He clasped my hand in his. 'It's a miracle, that's what it is. A miracle. I wish Nora was here to see this. I really do.'

'She's with you in spirit,' I said.

He nodded. 'I feel she is, maybe she has something to do with it as well. Before she died, she mentioned Gerry and Dan, she said if she had one wish that would be to find Gerry and Dan. Dan is with our mother but to find Gerry and Bernadette... it's more than I could ever have imagined. He and Bernadette came back here for a cup of tea last night and the three of us talked until gone midnight. And do you know what he said? He said every day he'd said a prayer that he would find me again, he knew I was somewhere, he said he just knew it. Do you know, I did exactly the same thing. When I woke up, they were the first people I thought of. I used to say to myself, I hope they are safe. But to find Gerry... well...' He was lost for words, his eyes full of tears. 'It's like finding lost treasure.'

'It's wonderful.'

'I am going to spend the day with him and Bernadette today, go for Sunday lunch and really get to know the family. Gerry wants to show me the whole holding. And they have goats, did you know that? Just like Mam.' He shook his head, as though he couldn't believe it. 'I feel as though you were brought into my life for a purpose, as though you are some kind of angel.'

'That's a bit strong,' I said. 'I wish I was able to carry out miracles. Wouldn't mind a few in my own life.'

'Just believe,' he said, 'that's all you need to do. Believe in yourself.'

The back door was open, sunlight was streaming in, it was a day for new beginnings. 'Harry, I've had an idea,' I said, 'how would you like to volunteer at Lady Immaculate Hall? They are always looking for volunteers.'

'Me, cooking?'

I nodded. 'I thought it might get you back in the kitchen again, you used to cook for all the lads on the ship, don't let that experience go to waste. How are your onion-chopping skills?'

He held up a hand. 'Not as quick as they used to be. But then, I haven't had to cook for thirty starving men in a long time. You had to get very quick, very quickly. Cooking for one is a slower pursuit. But the Hall...?'

'Do you think you might be ready? You said before that it was all gone. Perhaps, you might give it a go? And I thought I might ask one of my friends to arrange transport...' I wondered if I could borrow one of Paddy's cargo bikes and cycle Harry to the Hall and back.

Harry was looking at me, taking it all in. 'Maybe,' he said. 'I am learning that anything is possible. And there was a recipe in your book by a Nigel Slater which looked delicious. Chicken thighs in buttermilk. Mam used to cook with buttermilk and I thought I might give it a try. And when I do, will you be my guest? And I'll invite Cyril as well.'

'I would love to,' I said.

'And the hamster seems to have settled down... he's been a little agitated for the last couple of days but loved the nuts I gave him.'

'The hamster?'

'He arrived a couple of days ago. I'd been hearing some scraping sounds under the fridge...'

'The fridge?' Now, this was an actual miracle.

'And then, on Thursday morning, he poked his whiskers out. I think he was getting hungry. And I managed to get him into an old shoebox and he's been in that ever since. I've called him Seamus.'

I smiled to myself. 'So that's what happened to Seamus, then.'

'What?'

'Nothing, it's a great name. I have a cage that you can have... might be better than the shoebox.'

At home, after delivering the cage to Harry and seeing the hamster formerly known as Fyodor scamper into it happily – home at last – I went back into my house and began turning Brody's study back into a spare room. I swept out the crisp packets and drinks cans which were lurking under the sofa. I hoovered and wiped everything down with the window open, letting the fresh air stream in and remove the smell of stale male. Outside, I heard a bicycle bell. It rang again, and I put my head out of the window.

Paddy was standing in the street, looking up.

'Hello,' I said.

'Hello.' He smiled, his hand shading his eyes. 'Look,' he called, 'I don't know if I am out of line or what... but I just thought that I should say something.' He paused. 'If you don't mind?'

'I don't mind.' I felt my heart race. 'But I don't care if you say anything or not, it's okay.'

'I'm going to,' he said. 'Seize the day!' He had to raise his voice to be heard. 'Okay, Roisín Kelly, I missed you when I was in Copenhagen... and now I miss you every single moment I'm in Dublin. I think of you all the time. I think you are wonderful...'

I was smiling at him, he was smiling at me. 'I think you are wonderful too!'

'Thank God for that. What about a cycle? Up the mountains? With a picnic?'

I ran downstairs and let him in and for a moment the two of us just stood staring at each other, grinning.

'Shall we go?' he asked. 'I've got everything, sandwiches, biscuits, water...'

I nodded and grabbed my bag, put Foxy in the basket on the front of my bike, and off we went.

* * *

By bike, the route to the mountains was a long, slow climb of about two hours. Once you leave the city behind, and are subsumed by the countryside, at first fields and hedges in the lowlands, but as you rise, each stroke of your pedal pushing you further and further heavenward, the land around you is boggier, the colours the browns and yellows of the gorse, the purple of the heather in bloom. I kept close to Paddy's wheel, thinking how unfit I was, but how fabulous to be back. We used to cycle this road most Sundays, the two of us heading out for hours and hours, then returning to Dublin and to bed.

Finally, we arrived at the top of the Sally Gap, a crossing point of the mountains, and from there, after tying our bikes to a fence, we walked to the top of the climb. Foxy was too small to walk so I carried her in my arms.

The three of us sat in the heather. 'The last time I was here was with you.'

'Me too,' I said. 'Seems like a long time ago.'

'It's exactly the way I remember it, nothing's changed.' He looked at me. 'I mean it. Nothing's changed. Nothing.'

'What do you mean?' Foxy rested her head on my leg, closed her good eye and went to sleep.

'I mean, all the things I felt then, I still feel now. All the time in Copenhagen I was kicking myself for not telling you.'

'I didn't want to take you away from Jools, you were both so close.'

'Yeah, I know... And then when she told me that you were getting married...' He shook his head. 'I remember thinking that I had to move on, find someone else. Forget you. And I did. Kind of. I saw Freja for a while but my heart wasn't in it and she deserved someone who's was. And then I came home... and you didn't seem happy.'

'When?'

'The first night we were all in The Island. You didn't laugh like you used to. And then...' He stopped.

'And then what?'

'Well, I met Brody.' He shook his head. 'He seemed so up himself. I couldn't reconcile you with him and you looked almost panicked. I thought the least I could do is make sure you knew I was your friend.'

He smiled at me. 'You know, I liked you from the first moment I met you all those years ago. I should have told you how amazing and funny and beautiful I thought you were... and how utterly gorgeous in every way...' His eyes lingered on me. 'But I didn't think you felt the same. But I thought that if you did like me, you would have said something.'

'I did like you.' His face spread into a smile. 'I still like you.'

His hand was close to mine, and I felt his fingers wrap themselves around mine, and we sat there on the mountain, looking down into the valley as the clouds scudded overhead, and it felt good.

He kissed me. 'I love you,' Paddy said. 'And this time I'm telling everyone.'

EPILOGUE

A YEAR LATER...

'Come on, all of you.' Dad looked happier than I ever could remember him. His eyes shone, his skin was tanned and glowing. He was renting a small house in Sandycove, down by the harbour, and had rescued a small, shaggy dog called Mabel, who he walked along the seafront every morning, often calling in on Mum, on the other side of the village for mid-morning tea and toast.

'Come on,' he went on, 'get your coats, we're going out. Maggie, Shona, Roisín, chop-chop.' He paused in the kitchen of Mum's new house – beside the ancient dresser, which although Mum had only been living there for six weeks, already was as laden as it was in the old house. 'Where are the twins? I need them to see this.'

Shona had called in after her first week working. Mary Magahy, the village solicitor, was only too delighted when Shona rang looking for a job, after moving the girls back to Sandycove and enrolling them in a new school. 'Oh, thank God,' she said. 'I just can't cope with the amount of work I've got on. All these divorces. It may keep us in business but they play havoc with my ulcer.'

Shona's divorce was, as she told us, being fast-tracked. 'Ross and I are being extremely civilised to each other,' said Shona. 'As long as he gets to see the girls every other weekend, then he's happy... with Victoria.'

Richard had spotted Ross jogging around Merrion Square, looking exhausted and trailing a very fit and athletic blonde woman. None of us knew if he'd found the inner Ross, but the outer Ross looked as though he needed a nice sit-down and a cup of tea. Shona, meanwhile, had joined the sailing club in Dún Laoghaire and was spending her child-free Saturdays hanging out with a very nice-sounding gang of outdoorsy types, who all repaired to the bar afterwards for something a little bit more grown-up than a fizzy drink and a packet of crisps.

'Ross has taken them to see his parents,' said Shona. 'It's Fionnuala's birthday and Ross and Ronan have taken everyone out for dinner.' She smiled. 'That's the best thing about divorce, you can ditch your in-laws as well.'

'Where are we going?' I asked Dad. 'I said I'd meet Paddy at the bike shop. He finishes in twenty minutes.'

'Tell him to meet us down in the boatyard,' said Dad. 'Come on, quick-quick. Let's go.'

We followed him out to the car, Mum sat in the front and Shona and I in the back. We could have been us, twenty years earlier.

The last year had been one of the best of my life. That weekend, when I cycled with Paddy to the Dublin mountains, I made a promise to myself. 'Never be scared. The worst that can happen is failure.' And it had stuck. I had stepped off a cliff into the unknown and with every step, I had found a footing, from my catering company, to allowing myself to fall properly and deeply in love with Paddy. As well as being a good pet parent to Foxy, who was spending a happy retirement sleeping at the end of our bed.

Paddy and I had spent the weekend together, talking most of the time while lying in bed. We caught up with each other, while entwined in each other and the duvet. We only got up to make tea and toast and bring it back to bed, where we picked up our conversation exactly where we'd stopped moments before, and we plotted out my next few life moves. One of which was engaging a divorce lawyer – come in, Mary Magahy! – and the next was resigning from my job. The third was setting up my own catering company – the Little Eden Supper Club – as well as baking for the bike café which was proving to be very successful. And yes, chocolate crispies were our bestsellers. Even Erik had written down the recipe – if that's what you can call it – determined to introduce this delicacy to the sophisticated denizens of Copenhagen.

I had resigned from the planning department on the Monday after the last Little Eden Supper Club. JP and Erik met up that morning and they agreed a plan to develop both the Hall and the area around it. Deals were made, money was talked and the most important thing is that the Hall will be saved for a new generation. It wasn't until JP had shaken Erik's hand and walked him back down to reception, did he start to relax. To celebrate he made everyone a cup of tea – all far too strong and with far too little milk but we appreciated this was his way of telling us he was happy.

'The office well-being went up massively just by me being away,' he had said. 'That's obviously what I'm doing wrong all this time. You all look really happy. I didn't even know Frank could smile. And Dermot... you've been singing Celine Dion to yourself since you walked in.'

'We can blame Roisín and her supper club,' said Dermot.

'We drank margaritas, we danced some salsa...' said Frank.

'I showed them the steps,' said Belinda.

'And... it was life-changing.' Frank was smiling shyly across his desk to Belinda.

'Holy Mother of Divine Jesus!' said JP. 'So, all this time when I was trying to work on improving your well-being Roisín just holds a supper club – whatever one of those yokes is – and you all look like you have been bathed in holy water.'

'Love was in the air.' Dermot cut a heart out of a Post-it and stuck it to his chest.

'Et tu, Dermot?'

'Me too, JP, her name is Rachel. It means Oh Beautiful Farmer in Latin, which indeed she is.'

'Good God,' JP said. 'Anyone else? Frank, Belinda?'

'Us too,' they said together, smiling again at each other.

'Not me,' said Saoirse. 'I wasn't invited.' She glared across at me but I couldn't have cared less.

I was trying to work out how to resign from my job without becoming emotional. I really didn't want Frank, Dermot and Belinda to have to comfort me again.

'Right,' said JP. 'Anything else I need to be told?'

'Frank's bodily functions have improved, he hasn't farted all morning.'

'It's only 10 a.m.,' said JP.

'It's definitely an improvement,' said Dermot. 'Belinda, you are already working miracles. Next, you can work on the brown jumpers.'

I took a deep breath. 'I am handing in my resignation, I've decided to set up my own catering company. I already have a commission to make cakes...'

There was a loud, 'Of course she is!' from Saoirse. But I ignored it.

'I'm going to cater parties, communions, dinner parties...' I went on.

'Don't poison anyone, will you?' sneered Saoirse, and she laughed as though she'd said something witty.

'The only thing that's poison is you, Saoirse,' I said, sweetly. 'And, by the way, I hope your gut biome is destroyed forever.' Exhilaration rippled through my body. So this is what it felt to say what was on your mind. No wonder Saoirse always looked so pleased with herself.

'It's like a gypsy's curse,' breathed Dermot, impressed.

'Like a witch's spell,' said Belinda. 'My mother's great-aunt was one. You wouldn't want to cross her!'

'We're going to miss you,' Frank told me.

'I'm going to miss you too,' I responded, my back to Saoirse.

'It won't be the same without our Roisín,' said Belinda.

'It really won't,' said Dermot. 'And no cakes for our Friday elevenses. Belinda, what will we do?'

'We can buy them from Roisín's catering company.' She stepped forward, her arms open. 'Come here, you don't think you're getting to go away without hugging me.'

Dermot was next. 'Take me with you, please!' He whispered loudly in my ear. 'Don't leave me on my own with these eejits!'

Frank hugged me next and it wasn't half as awkward as either of us feared.

JP stood forward and his handshake turned into another hug. 'I thought I was going to make a planner out of you, seems like there's a life for you outside this office.'

'I hope so,' I said. 'Thanks for trying.'

Into my eyeline stepped Saoirse. 'Sorry, Roisín,' she said. 'I did overstep the mark a little. Apologies. And my gut biome is fine, by the way, it recovered very quickly so I don't think it was food poisoning, maybe alcohol poisoning. I drank too much tequila that night... and well... it's vicious stuff. I would have been better off drinking Jeyes Fluid.'

'We used to do exactly that,' I heard Dermot say to JP. 'Remember?'

'Thank you for admitting it,' I said to Saoirse.

'I wish you well in your new endeavour,' she went on. 'And congratulations on your planning success. Maybe one day JP will give me a chance as well?' She looked over at JP. 'Maybe?'

He nodded. 'We'll have a chat later.'

At lunchtime that day, I walked up the path towards the Hall to say my goodbyes, when I heard the ring of a bicycle bell behind me.

'Coming through!' It was Harry, sitting on the front of a cargo bike ridden by Paddy.

'Morning, morning!' Harry was dressed in a suit and tie, a small handkerchief poked out of the top pocket, his white hair was combed neatly over his head. 'I feel like the Queen of Sheba.'

'I can bring Harry to the lunches every day,' Paddy was saying, 'it's no bother to collect him. Harry, you've got my number, haven't you? And I've nearly finished working on that e-tricycle. It's perfect for him.' Paddy smiled at me. 'Oh, Harry,' he said, 'you've forgotten your notebook. The one with all your recipes in.' He handed over an old book, held together with an elastic band, stuffed with newspaper cuttings.

Inside Lady Immaculate Hall, I introduced Harry to the team and Gita put him on custard-making.

'You can make custard, can't you, Harry?' she asked.

'I used to make vats of it,' he replied, winking at me.

Paddy and I walked out of the Hall, his hand in mine. 'Did you do it?' he asked.

'What? Resign or call Mary Magahy?'

'Both.'

'Then I've done both, my resignation has been accepted and Mary said it should be simple and she would start the proceedings today, I just need to get some papers together. Though I think it was much, much easier to get married than it might be to get divorced. But...' I shrugged. 'It's not a bad way of fixing a mistake.'

Paddy laughed. 'It's not a mistake. It's a life experience.' He kissed me. 'Fancy a tea from the market?'

We sat on a bench looking out to sea and resumed our life-plotting.

'And maybe we could find a place for the two of us,' he said. 'Somewhere with a garden and a shed for my bikes.'

'Foxy would love some grass.' I was thinking that I didn't really fancy living close to Anna and Brody for much longer. I would miss Harry, but I would always visit him and, anyway, I wasn't going to go far. Sandycove was my home.

* * *

A couple of weeks later, Richard called. 'Sam and I have taken a big step,' he said. 'Huge. Massive.'

'You're getting married?' Oh, the delicious irony, I thought, after all his smug I-told-you-so looks.

'Of course not!' he shouted, appalled. 'Do you think I have taken leave of my senses? No! Nothing so ridiculous! We've bought a holiday cottage just outside Dingle. A tumbledown little house which I used to cycle past on my way to school every day. And anyway, Dad was talking to Johnny Fitz, the farmer who owns the field, and he said that he wouldn't mind selling it, as long as it was to me. And so, I bought it! Johnny Fitz has gone into the town today to get the papers all drawn up and Sam and I are heading down this weekend. Sam's already designing the garden. We're thinking of a few apple trees, a summer house. The mood board is very much Maggie's garden!'

'It sounds wonderful,' I said.

'And you and Paddy, and Jools and Erik, have to come with us,' he went on. 'We need you involved, every step of the way.'

That evening, I met Jools in The Island. I needed to tell her about Paddy but first she couldn't stop talking about Erik. 'I've decided to move to Copenhagen,' she said. 'I may as well. And it means I won't be bumping into creepy Darren and Ms Rippling Body UK and Ireland.'

'Can I come and stay?' I asked.

'You have to!' she said, looking me dead in the eye. 'I am only going if you promise to come and stay at least once a month.'

'Well, can I bring someone?'

'Who?'

'Someone who knows Copenhagen really well.' I felt nervous, what would she say?

'Who?' Jools looked confused.

'Someone who has been friends with me for years... someone who you know extremely well...'

'Who?' And then the truth dawned on her. 'Paddy?'

I nodded. 'I love him. Always have. And he loves me.'

'About time too!' she said. 'I always thought you two would be perfect. You should have got together years ago.'

* * *

Dad drove to the seafront and then pulled into the slip road towards the harbour and parked his car. The sky was a deep blue, there were walkers and joggers out running along the pier. I hadn't been down this far in years. 'Out you get... come on.'

Paddy was cycling towards us, a small figure pedalling along the bike path. He looked up and waved when he saw us. 'Ah,' said Mum. 'There he is. My lovely son-in-law.'

'We're not married,' I said. 'Remember? I've kind of gone off the idea.'

'A year ago, you had two sons-in-law,' said Shona. 'Now, you don't even have one. Some might say that was careless of you.'

Mum laughed. 'I haven't lost much sleep over my carelessness, come on, we'd better catch up with your dad. He's on a mission.'

'So what are we doing here?' asked Shona again, before hurrying up to Mum and slipping her arm through hers.

Dad had nipped into the boatyard, through the open gate where several yachts were balanced, their large keels propping them skyward. 'Now, where is she?' he was saying. 'Where has he put her? Aha!' His walk quickened. 'I came down earlier and Mick was just taking delivery.' And then he stopped in front of the smallest boat in the yard which had been hidden by a much larger one.

'Isn't she beautiful?' he breathed.

'Who?' I asked. 'Who's beautiful?'

'Dad, you do realise that we can't see anyone.'

And then Mum walked forward and reached up to put her hand on the side of the boat. '*Shining Light.*' She was smiling at Dad. 'Wherever did you find her?'

'Mick's been looking for me,' he said. 'He's had the call out trying to find out who owned her. We got there in the end.'

'Wait,' Shona asked. 'Is this *Shining Light*, as in our *Shining Light*?'

Dad was nodding. 'The very same.'

'Our boat? You found her?'

'The owners were ready to sell and it turns out *Shining Light* was ready to come home.' He was still smiling. 'I've missed her... like I've missed all of you.'

'And we can sail her?'

He nodded. 'That's the whole thing about *Shining Light*, she's only happy when the wind is blowing and the water is lashing against her bow and she's heading straight out to sea. A bit like me. I've bought some life jackets for Kitty and Daisy too. You let me know when it suits you and we'll do it. This week? Thursday evening?'

'Okay.' Shona stepped forward towards Dad and he stepped towards her and squeezed her tightly. 'I love you, my beautiful girls,' he said. 'I am so sorry for not being there for all those years.' He flapped his arm for me to join the hug. 'I love you both so much,' he said. 'Not a day goes by do I not think about the three of us on *Shining Light*. I loved those days.'

'Well, we can bring them back,' said Shona, 'can't we, Roisín?'

And then Mum joined in and by the time Paddy found us, we were a sprawling, blubbery mess.

'Don't mind us, Paddy,' Dad said. 'We're just making up for lost time.'

We stood back – Paddy's arm around me, Dad's two arms around Mum and Shona, and we all admired *Shining Light*.

'Looking good, girl.' Dad patted the side of the boat. 'Welcome back to port, welcome home.'

ACKNOWLEDGMENTS

Thank you...

To my kind, generous and fabulous agent, Ger Nichol. To the award-winning Boldwood team – Caroline, Amanda, Nia, Claire and Megan, thank you for looking after me. And to Ross Dickinson and his meticulous editing skills. To my friends, as always, who make me laugh and make me happy, especially to Merlo and Steve – the Kelly-Parkers! – have a wonderful life together! And most of all, to my daughter Ruby, my very own shining light.

MORE FROM SIÂN O'GORMAN

We hope you enjoyed reading *The Sandycove Supper Club*. If you did, please leave a review.

If you'd like to gift a copy, this book is also available as an ebook, digital audio download and audiobook CD.

Sign up to Siân O'Gorman's mailing list for news, competitions and updates on future books.

https://bit.ly/SianOGormannewsletter

ABOUT THE AUTHOR

Sian O'Gorman was born in Galway on the West Coast of Ireland, grew up in the lovely city of Cardiff, and has found her way back to Ireland and now lives on the east of the country, in the village of Dalkey, just along the coast from Dublin. She works as a radio producer for RTE.

Follow Sian on social media:

facebook.com/sian.ogorman.7
twitter.com/msogorman
instagram.com/msogorman
bookbub.com/authors/sian-o-gorman

Lightning Source UK Ltd.
Milton Keynes UK
UKHW041152031122
411542UK00001B/12

9 781804 267981